TOO RICH TO LIVE

Her name, typewritten on the folded paper, arrested her. She frowned. Who on earth . . .?

Opening the sheet, she quickly read the short typed message. "A beautiful gown, Mrs Whitney – but you will not wear it to the Little wedding. You will not attend the wedding. You will be dead."

She gasped and read it again, her mind blurring, disbelieving what she was seeing. She looked up, stunned. Who could have written such a dreadful thing? And *why*?

She saw him then, a distant figure standing in the shade of a tall bougainvillia bush on the far side of the car park – a startling, sinister apparition in black leather motorcycle clothing, his face obscured by the black plastic visor of his skull-like helmet.

Although she could not see his face, she knew he was staring at her . . .

TOO RICH
TO LIVE

Stanley Morgan

Hamlyn Paperbacks

TOO RICH TO LIVE
ISBN 0 600 20138 4

First published in Great Britain 1980
by Hamlyn Books
Hamlyn Paperback edition 1981
Copyright © 1980 by Stanley Morgan

Hamlyn Paperbacks are published by
The Hamlyn Publishing Group Ltd,
Astronaut House,
Feltham, Middlesex, England

(Paperback Division: Hamlyn Paperbacks,
Banda House, Cambridge Grove,
Hammersmith, London W6 OLE)

Printed and bound in Great Britain by
Cox & Wyman Ltd, Reading

For my wife, Linda
With Love and Gratitude

Through the Jungle very softly flits
A shadow and a sigh —
He is Fear, O Little Hunter, he is Fear!

Kipling

Part One

THE BEGINNING OF THE END

1

That Friday in mid-December was a rare golden day for Margaret Whitney. A little before five o'clock in the afternoon, she emerged through the northern exit of the prestigious Neiman Marcus department store in the Bal Harbor shopping mall in Miami Beach and strode ebulliently towards her Mercedes sports car, which was in a pool of shade beneath a cluster of royal palms.

It had been a perfect day, the temperature and humidity in the low seventies, the cobalt sky peppered with lazy puffballs of white cloud. But although the weather may have contributed to Margaret's sense of well-being, the prime cause was contained in a large cardboard box tucked protectively beneath her arm. At last she had it—the final and most important item of her new Christmas wardrobe—a full-length evening gown in jade-green silk, created for her, at astronomical cost, by Lejeune himself.

At this final fitting she had been staggered by its opulence, the breathtaking sensuality of its material raising goosepimples as it caressed her near-naked body. Never had a gown—or any other item of her substantial wardrobe, past or present—thrilled her so much. And now, impatient as a child, she couldn't wait to get it home and try it on again in the privacy of her bedroom.

In her fiftieth year, Margaret was of slender build and medium height, with blue eyes and pale auburn hair. At first glance she was an attractive woman; closer inspection revealed that her attractiveness stemmed from her clothes, quality and style, rather than from any physical attributes. Time, alcohol, and the Florida sun had done her no favours. A well-shaped mouth was undoubtedly her best feature in an otherwise unremarkable and frequently gloomy face.

3

Margaret possessed a nervous disposition, was constantly unsure of herself. Money had come late in life and she lacked the experience and innate confidence to cope with the level of society into which wealth had thrust her. Secretly she was afraid of the Park, but had never dared voice her fears to Arthur, to whom the Park represented the epitome of achievement.

At this moment, though, her thoughts were a long way from such problems. Smiling with good humour (while half-heartedly castigating herself for giving way to a giddiness she considered juvenile) she made her way across the landscaped parking area and reached her car.

Unlocking it, she placed her precious package on the rear seat, smoothed the skirt of her cream linen suit about her legs and slid in behind the wheel. Then she noticed the folded sheet of paper tucked behind the windshield wiper.

With a tut of annoyance at the Bel Harbor authorities for allowing the distribution of handbills, she got out of the car and removed the paper, preparing to crumple it and dispose of it in a nearby bin.

Her name, typewritten on the folded face, arrested her. She frowned. Who on earth . . .?

Opening the sheet, she quickly read the short typed message. "A beautiful gown, Mrs Whitney—but you will not wear it to the Little wedding. You will not attend the wedding. You will be dead."

She gasped and read it again, her mind blurring, disbelieving what she was seeing. She looked up, stunned. Who could have written such a dreadful thing? And *why*?

She saw him then, a distant figure standing in the shade of a tall bougainvillia bush on the far side of the car park—a startling, sinister apparition in black leather motorcycle clothing, his face obscured by the black plastic visor of his skull-like helmet.

Although she could not see his face, she knew he was staring at her. He stood in belligerent pose, arms folded, gazing eyelessly. And now, confirming her fears, he began to nod at her.

Margaret disintegrated, seized by fear. She unwittingly dropped the note to the ground as she threw herself into the car,

4

fired the engine, reversed screechingly out of the bay and whirled away to the nearest exit. Pummelling the wheel in exasperation as she waited for an opening in the heavy evening traffic, she shot out and almost collided with an oncoming bus. Then she found consolation in the embrace of the southbound bumper-to-bumper parade.

The threat of the creature's presence removed, she shed the paralysis of initial fright and turned her mind to the note. The note! Panic struck again as she hastily searched the car. She must have dropped the note in the car park, she decided. Stupid! She should have kept it for the police.

Nevertheless, its wording was all too clear in her mind. And with the realisation of the full significance of the words came renewed terror.

How did he know she was having a gown made at Neiman Marcus?

How did he know she would be collecting it that afternoon?

How did he know she was going to Elizabeth Little's wedding?

How did he *know* such intimate, secret details of her life—details she'd kept hidden from even her closest friends in the Park?

Her vulnerability staggered her.

Who was he? This was no ordinary "anti-rich" prank, such as the frequent finger-daubs on her dusty car—"Rich bitch", "You're gonna get yours, lady", "The poor shall inherit the earth", and the like. The note had been addressed to her by name and ...

Her eyes flicked to her rear-view mirror, the automatic glance of an experienced driver, then returned to the road but in the next instant flew back again to the mirror in a horrified double-take.

He was there, immediately behind her! Crouched over the handlebars of his motorcycle like a menacing black spider, his faceless gaze directed through her window into the mirror reflection of her eyes.

A scream choked in her throat.

Instinct drove her foot to the floor, but common sense

immediately eased the pressure off the accelerator. There was nowhere to escape to. The traffic was too dense. There were too many traffic lights along this stretch of Collins Avenue. And besides, his machine looked powerful enough to overtake the Mercedes and had the advantage of manoeuvrability.

She shuddered with fear.

The traffic ahead halted at a red light. She braved a glance into her mirror, dreading what she would find there—and found it, his terrifying faceless face filling her rear window.

Suddenly her anger erupted, momentarily subjugating her fear. She whirled in her seat and glared at him, for a long moment engaging him in a desperate confrontation. Then with a whimper of fright and frustration she turned away, defeated by the one-sidedness of the contest. She was staring at nothing but her own eyes, reflected in the polished convex surface of his black visor.

The lights turned to green. The cars ahead of her moved off. She remained stationary, stuck out her arm and waved on the traffic behind her, attempting to force him past her. But he didn't move. He stayed there, mockery and insolence radiating from his hunched posture.

With a gasped curse she accelerated across the junction, the dread rasping roar of his machine taking up the challenge. Down through the eighties and the seventies cross-streets he clung to her rear bumper as though attached to it by tow-rope.

In the mid-sixties, where the peninsular of Miami Beach is split by Indian Creek and cross-streets become impractical, a two-mile stretch of uninterrupted highway confronted Margaret. She took advantage of it. Thrusting the lever on the floor into third gear, she rocketed away, passed the car ahead, another, a dozen more, desperate to put as many vehicles between herself and that . . . madman as possible before Collins Avenue again joined the cross-street system.

Her heart was thudding brutally; she felt dizzy, sick. Her body trembled with tension as she hurled the Mercedes along the open road in a ferocious slalom, weaving into gaps between vehicles and out again as the road ahead cleared, constantly flinging glances into her mirror, praying she'd lost him. But always he was there! An expert, riding her wake with contemptuous ease.

Again a traffic light brought the stream of vehicles to a crawl.

She glanced up. Damn him, he was there!

Now, at this enforced slower speed, with less concentration needed for driving, she directed her baffled mind to questions and thoughts of counteraction.

Why was she suffering this torment? Why didn't she pull over to the curb and force him to pass her? Why didn't she stop and telephone the police and report him?

For doing what? She could visualise the conversation with the police.

"What exactly was he doing to you, Mrs Whitney?"

"He was following me."

"Yes? And?"

"And nothing—he was just following me. But it was the *way* he was doing it."

"How was that?"

"Threateningly. He kept staring at me."

"How could you tell he was staring at you when you couldn't see his face?"

With an exasperated expletive she abandoned the idea of calling the police. Besides, he would guess what she was doing and be miles away by the time they arrived.

No, she told herself, keep going, you're safe while the car is in motion. *Safe*? Safe from what? What could he possibly do to her on a busy road in broad daylight?

She wasn't prepared to stop and find out.

The cross-streets came and went. The peninsular broadened to its maximum width of one mile, and from here she was no longer dependent upon Collins Avenue for a southbound route.

At the next junction she suddenly accelerated into a right turn, shot over to Washington Avenue, went left screeching into Washington and continued south.

She glanced up hopefully . . . and groaned.

Fury engulfed her. Ramming her foot down, she hurtled along Washington at suicidal speed. At Fifth Street she was brought to a halt by crossing traffic. This was her turning point.

Fifth Street ran on to the Douglas MacArthur Causeway, the narrow, three-mile-long road bridge that linked South Miami Beach with the city of Miami.

Less than a mile away a service road led off the causeway to the right, into Little Park, her island refuge. Only a few more moments and she would shake this maniac off her tail for good.

The car was suddenly filled with the deafening roar of his motorcycle as he drew alongside, close, and nodded at her.

She drew away in terror and yelled at him, "Leave me alone! Why are you following me?"

He simply stared and nodded.

"I shall report you to the police!" She peered out of the window searching for his licence plate. It was concealed by black tape.

She gasped at him, "who *are* YOU?"

A horn honked imperatively behind her. She accelerated hard, screamed into a right turn and hurtled along Fifth Street and on to the causeway, the creature still, impossibly, glued to her tail.

Up ahead now was her turn-off into the Park. She veered towards the right lane of the causeway for the turn. The raucous blaring of his horn, his insolent farewell, sent her careening across the path of following traffic and into the narrow service road, her own horn blaring, demanding that the steel security barrier be raised.

The two guards inside the booth gaped in astonishment at the speed of her approach, one reacted instantly and activated the control button but not quickly enough. Spurred by panic, by her desperate need to get beyond the protective boom, Margaret misjudged the speed and angle of its ascent and accelerated a beat too soon.

Grimacing at the sickening metallic collision of car roof and boom, she sped on through, round the one-way circuiting road and into the macadamed driveway of number seventeen. Skidding to a halt, she grabbed her package from the rear seat, ran up the wide stone steps on to the verandah of the neo-colonial house, burst through the front door into the reception hall and continued into the drawing room, collapsing breathless and trembling on to a sofa.

Immediately, a pretty, dark-complexioned maid appeared in the doorway, her hands clasped with concern. "Señora! What has happened? Have you had an accident?" She ventured into the room.

Margaret shook her head irritably and waved her hand in the direction of a Sheraton corner cupboard. "Get me a brandy, quickly. A large one." She shut her eyes, attempted to calm her ragged breathing, reached for the telephone and tremblingly stabbed a number.

A man's voice answered immediately. "Security booth."

"Security, this is Mrs Whitney."

"Ma'am, are you all right? You hit the boom."

"I *know* I hit the boom. Who is this?"

"Sam Webb, ma'am."

"Webb, listen to me . . . have you seen any sign of a motor-cyclist near the entrance? He's dressed in black leather, black helmet, black *every* damned thing . . ."

"No, ma'am, I haven't."

"Well, keep your eyes open for him—and if you see him lurking around, call the police immediately, do you understand? He's dangerous. He's just followed me, threatened me, all the way from Bal Harbor."

"Yes, ma'am, will do."

Severing the connection, Margaret prodded another number, running a fluttery hand across her forehead as the number rang out.

A pompous male voice, archly English, drawled, "The Little residence."

"Storey, this is Mrs Whitney. Is Mrs Little at home?"

"I really couldn't say, madam. I shall enquire."

Margaret stifled a reaction. Cut the butler crap! she wanted to yell. Of course you know if she's there, you sanctimonious . . .

"Lucia!" She turned on her maid, anger and frustration and fear evoking stupid spite. "Where's my . . .?" She broke off. The brandy was on the coffee table at her knee.

With a shaking hand she brought the glass to her lips,

9

gagging on the swallow as Belle Little came on the line, her matron's voice low-pitched, almost masculine, and ripe with ill-concealed annoyance. "Margaret, what an unfortunate moment, I was . . ."

"Belle," Margaret interrupted pleadingly, "I *have* to speak to you. I have just had the most terrifying experience. Not half an hour ago I was shopping at Neiman's. I've had my gown made for the wedding there—by Lejeuna." Shocked though she was, Margaret found the presence of mind to drop this tidbit. "And I went to pick it up this afternoon. When I came out of the store at five o'clock I found a note stuck under the windshield wiper, addressed to me personally. Belle, it was awful!" Her voice broke, became a whimper. "It said something like . . . 'A beautiful gown, Mrs Whitney, but you won't wear it to the Little wedding. You won't attend the wedding . . . because you'll be dead!' Belle, I . . ."

Margaret heard a sharp intake of breath.

"Belle . . .?"

"Yes—go on, Margaret. What do you mean by 'the note said something like'. Don't you have it?"

Margaret sighed miserably. "No, I must have dropped it. Belle, I was so scared! The note was only the beginning of it. Suddenly I looked up and saw this . . . man . . . standing in the bushes, staring at me. He was dressed in black leather and wearing one of those fearful motorcycle helmets with an opaque visor that completely hides the face—you must have seen them . . ."

Belle tutted irritably. "Yes, yes, go on."

"Well, when I looked at him he began nodding at me and I *knew* he'd put the note on my car. Belle—the way he *stared* at me! He looked so hostile. I was terrified! I got in my car and fled, but the damn traffic on Collins . . . Then suddenly I looked into my rear-view mirror and there he was on his motorcycle, right behind me." Her voice quavered with reawakened hysteria. "And he stayed there all the way home. I couldn't shake him. And at Fifth Street, while I was waiting to turn, he drew up alongside and *glared* at me and nodded. Belle, I'm so frightened. How could he have known about the gown? I haven't told

10

*any*one I was having it made at Neiman's. And how could he have known I was going to pick it up this afternoon? I didn't even tell Lily or Ruth ..."

"Margaret—calm down!" Belle's voice cracked imperiously, silencing Margaret. "Think about it lucidly. Every one in Miami—my God, in Florida!—knows about Elizabeth's wedding. It's been in all the papers and glossies for weeks. And they've made a huge thing about all the clothes we Parkites will be buying ..."

"Yes, but how could he know ...?"

"Supposition! A lucky guess. He obviously knows you by sight—heavens, you and Arthur are in the papers often enough—and he followed you to Bal Harbor, saw you go into Neiman's, and put two and two together. It's a sick joke. You know how we rile people. It's a game the have-nots play, called 'Let's scare the hell out of the rich'. Margaret, forget it!"

Margaret shut her eyes, cursed herself, wondering how she could have been so stupid as to call Belle Little, whose overwhelming self-assurance always made her feel so gauche. "Then you don't think I ought to tell the police?" she offered weakly.

"No! I most certainly do not! Christ, Margaret, do you want to panic everyone? One *whisper* that something threatening or dangerous is lurking around here and the Miami Symphony will be playing to a congregation of *two* instead of two thousand next Thursday—that'll be Elizabeth and me! Now—*please*—not a word to anyone about this. Besides, what could you tell the police? That a man in black followed you home and kept staring and nodding at you?"

"But, Belle, the *note* ..."

"*What* note? You don't *have* the damned note. Now, Margaret, you listen to me ..." Belle's voice dropped half a tone and took on a furious, incisive edge. "This wedding is the biggest ... thing ... of ... my ... life!" She ground it out determinedly, emphasising each word. "And I will not allow anything to spoil it—not *anything*! Do you understand? You will treat this thing for what it is—a stupid practical joke. You will not say a word to anyone about it—not even to Ruth or Lily

. . . *especially* not to Ruth or Lily. Do I have your solemn word on that?"

"Y–yes, of course," stammered Margaret, shaken by Belle's unexpected vehemence.

"All right. Now I must go. I was about to step into the tub when you rang."

"Yes, I'm sorry . . ."

The dead phone hummed in Margaret's ear. Seething from the rebuff, she threw down the receiver, cursing herself again for having made the call and furious at Belle's peremptory dismissal of her fears.

But then, why should it surprise her? Had she ever known Belle Little to take a genuine interest in anybody's problems but her own?

The wedding. The goddamned wedding. That's all that mattered to her. The entire Park could be striken with leprosy, but so long as it didn't interfere with the wedding—get lost!

She realised she was being ridiculous—for heaven's sake, Elizabeth *was* marrying the son of the Governor—but she didn't care. She *wanted* to be ridiculous.

Suddenly she felt sick to death of the Park and its blue-chip residents and Belle Little and Elizabeth Little and the wedding and every other rotten thing.

Sensing Lucia's hovering presence, she turned. "What is it, Lucia?"

"Señora, cook would like to know if Señor Whitney will be home for dinner this evening."

Margaret sighed heavily, the reminder of her husband's continued absence and her own loneliness compounding her feeling of desolation. "No, Señor Whitney won't be home until Sunday night. Tell cook I'm not hungry—a slice of melon and some scrambled eggs will do."

"Yes, señora. Shall I run your bath now?"

Margaret nodded disinterestedly. "And put out my green silk lounging pyjamas."

"Yes, señora."

Margaret quickly drained her glass and held it out. "And get me another drink before you go."

Getting up from the sofa, Margaret crossed to the wide bay window and looked out across the Park to the huge neo-colonial mansion set back off the road to her right. Number fifteen—the largest and grandest house in the Park. Belle Little's, of course. She'd sited it perfectly, at the end of the elliptical island and on slightly higher ground, so that it looked down on the other twenty-nine houses. Like a school marm, perched on a raised platform, keeping an eagle eye on her class, thought Margaret.

No, she could think of a much more apt analogy than that—like an enthroned queen, gazing imperiously down upon her toadying subjects. Much more apt.

Suffused by depression—a dark, brooding emptiness—she gazed aimlessly around the Park, pausing momentarily at each of the magnificent homes that were visible through the foliage of their own trees and those of the central landscaped oasis—an extravagant arrangement of palm trees and flowering tropical shrubs surrounding an ornamental lake in which ancient Italian statuary and live flamingoes vied for immobility.

Beautiful, Margaret acknowledged—and meaningless. What did it all count for, living in a million-dollar home in one of the country's most elegant and prestigious private parks, when one couldn't rely upon the sympathy and understanding of one's friend in time of trouble?

Friend? She snorted derisively. Belle Little was nobody's friend. She was an island, a proud, unreachable entity—arrogant, ruthless, selfish and impossibly ambitious. This was *her* park, no one else's. She had built it. She owned it. She *was* the queen.

And what of the others in the Park? Was there anyone she could readily turn to for help and sympathy? Lily Parker, her neighbour in number sixteen, and Ruth Howard, across the Park in fourteen, were supposedly her closest friends, yet what did they have in common? Lily Parker, once extremely attractive, now waged war against advancing age with a succession of demanding love affairs, condoned by her philandering husband, Sam. A silly, aimless woman.

Ruth Howard was her antithesis—hard-bitten, ambitious, a

sycophantic disciple of Belle Little whose position she envied and whose style she attempted to emulate.

Truly, all they had in common was a dependence upon Belle Little, for whom all three husbands worked and to whom they owed their wealth and position. Sam Parker, the real estate manipulator; Bernard Howard, the legal mind; and Arthur, the builder. An unholy alliance jumping and jerking to their puppeteer—the queen. Machines in human guise.

"Señora. . .?"

Margaret turned and accepted the recharged glass from her maid, who then quietly left the room. Taking a generous swallow of the fiery liquid, she returned to the sofa and slumped down heavily. The prospect of getting drunk was suddenly enormously appealing.

Christ, what was the matter with her? She'd been feeling so down lately—nervy, depressed. Was it her age? Menopause, perhaps? Could it really be happening to her?

Arthur didn't help at all, being away so much. She needed him so badly at times. No, that was a lie. She didn't need Arthur at all. She needed company, someone to talk to. Arthur's conversation had consisted of little but Belle's next project—the building of a bridge, a dock, a factory, a shopping centre—for as long as she could remember.

She took another swallow of brandy, her thoughts drifting again to the incident at Bal Harbor. Could Belle be right? Had it just been a well-planned practical joke? She couldn't make herself believe it. That man, standing there in the bushes nodding at her, hadn't been joking. He'd meant it! Dammit, you *know* when you're being hated—and he had *hated* her. There'd been a radiation of charged aggression about him, an indefinable something.

But who could hate her so much? Who could he be? Except for her small circle of friends in Miami and Palm Beach she had practically no contact with people outside the Park—and she was certain she'd given no one cause to write death threats to her. The whole thing was preposterous! She wished she'd kept the note—because now she was beginning to wonder if there'd really *been* a note.

14

The brandy was reaching her, warming her body, gentling her fears. Here came that good old floaty glow. To hell with notes and kids on motorbikes and Belle Little and every other goddamned thing.

Yes—she would get drunk. Why the hell not?

2

Among her many accomplishments Belle Little was a consummate liar.

From earliest childhood she had learned that the truth, like potter's clay, was to be manipulated, teased, rearranged, shaped into any form which promised the greatest degree of personal expediency. It was, therefore, a matter of absolute indifference to her that she had just lied comprehensively to Margaret Whitney.

Belle had taken the phone call in her bedroom, a palatial boudoir more apartment than mere bedroom, which occupied a substantial corner of the first-floor. Its double-aspect windows offered a splendid front view of the Park, and, to the rear, the breathtaking vista of Biscayne Bay.

When the phone rang, Belle was not, as she'd informed Margaret, about to step into the bath—that was a ploy to get Margaret off the line. Belle had long since bathed and dressed for the evening in a suit of pearl grey silk. She had been sitting at her desk—a magnificent Queen Anne bureau, one of the many superb pieces she had brought back from Europe over the years—giving thought to the disturbing note she had received in the mail that afternoon, a typewritten threat. She was deciding to ignore it when Margaret's phone call prompted her to change her mind.

Now she was shaken and angry. She glared at the note, her mouth compressed into a furious, lipless line. She had never been blessed with facial beauty—her florid, Irish red-head's complexion always required the softening influence of cosmetics. The flush of anger that now rouged her cheeks negated the make-up she had so carefully applied.

In the aftermath of Margaret's shocking revelation, she read the note again. "You stand on the threshold of advantageous political achievement—but you will not cross it. Your daughter will not marry Robert Collier. Your reign is about to end, Queen Little. Watch for the signs."

When she had first read it she had contemptuously tossed it aside for later disposal with the junk mail she'd received that day. It hadn't troubled her in the slightest. It was by no means the first threatening letter she'd received, nor would it be the last. The world was in a state of rebellion. The have-nots waged war on the haves, and against the super-rich it was always open season. It was a condition of life one learned to accept.

No, the note itself had not disturbed her but Margaret Whitney's news had. The man on the motorcycle disturbed her. The element of human threat had been introduced, boldly, taking the written threat a stage further. The first "sign".

Who was the man? Why was he doing this? In her lifetime she had made many enemies ... was this retribution for some old wrong? Or for something Elizabeth had done in her brief but turbulent past?

Getting up from the desk, she crossed to the window that overlooked the rear gardens. Her eyes travelled across the spacious immaculate lawns to a distant tennis court on which a slender, dark-haired girl, dressed in tennis whites, was engaged in earnest competition with the daughter of a Park neighbour.

Belle's thin lips twisted in an amused smile. She had no illusions about her adopted daughter's nature, nor did she for a moment reject the possibility that this "thing" could be an act of revenge directed at Elizabeth. If so, she herself was to blame, and she accepted the responsibility readily. She had moulded Elizabeth in her own image, raised her to be a fit heir to the Little throne and, threat or no threat, she wouldn't have it any other way.

Again she glanced at the note in her hand and in an attack of sudden fury crumpled it. Turning from the window, she strode across the room towards the distant door but, catching sight of her reflection in the gilt-framed mirror above the fireplace, changed direction and stood before it, regarding her image intently with a sardonic smile.

The face that stared back at her pleased her. Ugly, perhaps ... its eyes no longer bright apple-green, more grey-green now ... but a strong, determined face, the eyes still piercingly alive, and—when she willed it—still intimidating.

"Does he realise who he's taken on?" she asked her image, her voice a low mocking murmur. "How can he know? Who but Belle Little knows Belle Little?" She grinned diabolically, the smile not reaching her eyes. "Belle Little is the *queen*, little man, indefatigable ... indestructible!"

Her grin faded. The note plagued her. Straightening it out, she read it again, whispering rhetorically, "Who the hell *are* you? What have I done to you to deserve this? Are you out of my present ... or my past?"

A twist of smile touched her lips. Her past? Was she really required to pluck a single cause of retribution from *her* past? She laughed aloud, challengingly, turned from the mirror and moved to the window that overlooked the Park, *her* park ... her ... beautiful ... park.

A single cause of retribution in ... how many years? Thirty?

She frowned, arrested by the thought. Could it really be thirty years since she and Harry first set foot on this island, on what had then been nothing more than a mound of snake-infested palmetto scrub?

She shook her head in wonderment, recalling in her mind's eye how the island had looked on that first day. Poor Harry ... he had never seen it finished, not the whole thing, not *her* park. He would have been very proud.

Her brow clouded with a frown. Good God ... what had Harry looked like? Quickly she shut her eyes, struggling for recall, couldn't picture his face at all. Go back ... to the first time ... as you walked into his hotel room. There he is ... standing by the window ... short ... paunchy ... almost bald ... smiling his shy, tired smile ...

She smiled with him. She had him now ... Harry Orville Little.

The beginning of it all.

"Harry ..." she whispered, angry again now, "... someone is threatening to take it away from me. Someone is threatening *me*! Tell him how it's going to be, Harry ..." The whisper swelled into a triumphant, challenging bellow. "Tell the poor bastard how it's going to be!"

Mashing the note into a ball, she hurled it across the room, pulled open the door and strode out along the landing towards the staircase.

Part Two

THE BEGINNING

1

BELLE

The Florida land boom of the early 1920s attracted into the state a flood of get-rich-quick opportunists, carpetbaggers, confidence tricksters and general villains.

With them came Earl St John, a tall, dashing, darkly handsome Englishman possessing magnetic charm, a ready wit, an impeccable aristocratic bloodline, empty pockets and a larcenous—not to say criminal—inclination.

Among St John's dubious talents reposed an unfailing eye for feminine beauty. This gift, coupled with a resolute determination that no available pretty girl should depart from his company unbedded, resulted in the birth of a baby girl to Kate Moran, an Irish-born speakeasy barmaid and occasional prostitute.

At the news of Kate's pregnancy, Earl St John, true to his nature, promptly embarked for less encumbered pastures and was not heard of again.

Kate, a kindly, easy-going girl from Protestant Belfast, the eldest of ten children, accepted her pregnancy with cheerful fatalism. She delighted in her baby girl's eventual birth, gave up her job, installed herself and her child (whom she christened Belle, after her own late mother) in a suite of rooms above the speakeasy on Miami's waterfront, and thereafter devoted her life to the more lucrative profession of a full-time prostitute.

As Belle grew to young childhood and was unavoidably drawn into the rough-and-tumble world of the tavern downstairs, she became a favourite among its male patrons. In their company she developed a keen, precocious interest in the wheeling and dealing of land and property, sensing it was the route to the fortune she avidly desired.

She was not a beautiful child, a quirk of heredity having denied her both her mother's prettiness and her father's lithe grace. And yet by the way of compensation it appeared she had inherited Earl St John's quickness of mind and aptitude for gainful larceny.

Belle listened assiduously to all that went on around her and stored away the knowledge for future use. When she was sixteen, her mother died suddenly of pneumonia. Belle moved out of the city into a one-room apartment in South Miami Beach and there dreamed her dreams and planned her future.

Finishing school the following year, she by now knew how she would set about attracting her fortune.

In that year of 1944 Florida lay becalmed, a giant pausing for breath after the collapse of the land boom in 1925, the devastation wrought by the hurricane in 1926 and the years of the Great Depression that followed. Now, due to the austerity imposed by America's entry into the Second World War, money was scarce and land ludicrously cheap.

Soon, everyone was saying, the boom would come again—and the time to buy was right now.

On the day she left school Belle stood naked before her bedroom mirror and studied her body, simultaneously assessing her prospects in the profession she had chosen to follow. Prostitution.

Clinically, she appraised her strengths and weaknesses. Though she was by no means tall and willowy, neither was she dumpy. Her skin was faintly freckled but perfectly clear. Her breasts were excellent, full and firm with large pink nipples. She considered her hair and eyes her most outstanding features. Thank God she'd inherited her mother's colouring—luminous green Irish eyes and hair the shade of bright new copper, which fell in gentle natural waves to her shoulders.

Her eyes descended to her pubic hair, a thick, lustrous growth but paler even than her hair. She would dye it dark brown, she decided. Men, she had heard, were excited by a dark, luxuriant pussy.

All in all, she decided, she had quite a lot to offer her future customers. But a sound, clean body was only the beginning.

Men were attracted to other qualities in a woman. In her mother's case they had been drawn to Kate Moran's gaiety and good humour—characteristics, Belle was only too aware, notably absent in her own personality.

So be it. She wouldn't attempt to emulate her mother, wouldn't try to be something she could never be. But she possessed qualities of her own that men were attracted to, traits undoubtedly inherited from her aristocratic father—a sense of style, a flair for fashion and colour, plus an innate toughness and a head for business that amused and intrigued men.

These qualities she would exploit to the full.

From the study of herself she turned her attention to her clothes. As generous as her mother had tried to be, Kate had never been able to provide more than a modest wardrobe for her, the best item of which was a pale green linen suit which she wore with a deeper green silk blouse and matching shoes and handbag.

This outfit she now put on, then skilfully applied her make-up and added a little gilt costume jewellery. When finished, she studied the result in the mirror. A maturity of feature —her toughness showing through—added a couple of years to her age. She looked a confident, well-dressed, desirable, twenty-year-old woman.

The prospect of a life of prostitution neither pleased nor daunted her; she was indifferent to it. She had seen her mother cheerfully endure it, even enjoy it, and didn't doubt that she would be able to do likewise.

But her approach to the profession would be very different from her mother's. There'd be no quick five-dollar tricks for her. She intended selling her favours much more expensively and in an environment that harboured the prospect not only of greater immediate financial return but of other gainful opportunities also. Belle Moran had no intention of earning her living on her back for a moment longer than was necessary.

Smiling conspiratorially at her mirror image, she picked up her handbag and gloves, descended to the street, and took a taxi to the Whispering Palms Hotel—the newest five-star hotel on Miami Beach.

2

Though essentially a girl of bedrock practicality, given to dreaming dreams but sceptical of their quick-and-easy realisation, Belle nevertheless, with hindsight, was obliged to attribute her choice of the Whispering Palms Hotel as the nudging of divine guidance. For it transpired that her very first client was in need of a service other than the temporary use of her body. Its gratification initiated Belle into the world of real estate dealing and drastically—and so fortuitously—changed the course of her life.

A man of late middle years on the brink of retirement, he had come south to look for a piece of land on which to build a retirement home. As a stranger to Florida, he didn't quite know where to begin looking. But Belle knew. She drove him around, introduced him to a builder acquaintance who owned property in Fort Lauderdale, and the outcome was satisfactory for all parties—a home for her client, a contract for the builder and a double commission cheque for her.

Belle Moran was in the real estate business.

Other moneyed men flowed through her life, though not all in the market for land or property. Many were businessmen who had travelled south looking for new territories to conquer. Belle used her contacts, knowledge and influence to help them.

Some of her clients were not from out of state. There were hotel conventions attended by local businessmen and politicians every bit as prone to an evening of illicit dalliance as their out-of-town brethren. While Belle accommodated their needs she encouraged them to talk, asked questions, added their answers to her considerable store of local knowledge, then used that knowledge to further her personal cause.

It was in the fall of her second year that her big break

came—the opportunity to use a specific piece of information she had been nursing for some time, sensing it could be worth big money to her when the right buyer came along. But in her wildest fantasies she could never have imagined just how big that money was destined to be.

In September of 1945 Harry Orville Little entered her life.

The war at last was over. Little was a small, balding, unremarkable-looking New Yorker, a quiet widower in his late fifties whose outward appearance camouflaged the astute business acumen with which he had amassed a fortune manufacturing clothing for the civilian and armed forces markets. Now, like so many of his contemporaries, he wanted to take life easy, find a piece of land and build himself a luxury retirement home in the sun.

Advised by a business associate to contact a certain Belle Moran on his arrival, he installed himself in a suite in the newly-constructed Flamingo Hotel in Miami Beach but debated for a day and night whether or not to call her number. Finally, urged by feelings of loneliness and disorientation in the unfamiliar city, yet still plagued by certain misgivings, he telephoned her.

He introduced himself, mentioned his business associate's name, briefly outlined his plans. Over the telephone he liked her voice, her interested, business-like response, and invited her to dinner at the hotel.

With a thoroughness goaded by ambition, she called their mutual acquaintance in New York and asked about Harry Little.

"He's a real nice guy, Belle," he told her. "Lonely since his wife died. You'll find him a bit shy, but don't let it fool you. He's one heck of a smart businessman ... made a *nawful* lotta money. Take good care of him and you won't regret it. He's got nobody else to spend his money on!"

Belle's heart had quickened. "No kids?"

"No relatives at all."

"Thanks, Frank. I owe you."

"Are you kidding?" he chuckled.

That evening, as she walked through the open door of the

hotel suite and saw him standing, forlorn-looking, at the window, she knew that Harry Little was the big fish she'd been trawling for more than a year.

Belle played her fish expertly. Acknowledging his shyness, she lowered her sexual heat and adopted the role of helpful companion, talked to him, encouraged him to talk, put him at ease.

"Frank was very pleased with the job you did for him," he told her. "He made me promise to contact you before anyone else."

"That was nice of him. I'll certainly do all I can for you, Harry. What specifically do you have in mind?"

"I'm not sure. This is my first visit down here, I don't know Miami at all."

She nodded. "OK . . . so what d'you say we start with a good look around? You hire the car, I'll do the driving."

"That sounds fine."

After dinner, sensing he wasn't interested in sex, she left him, returning the following morning. For several days she drove him all over Dade County and Miami Beach, as far south as the Florida Keys, north to Palm Beach, back through Fort Lauderdale. During this time their relationship remained platonic, Belle returning to her apartment each evening and rejoining him the next morning, allowing him to set the pace.

Gradually, as the days passed, a change came over Harry Little. He responded to Belle's pleasant, undemanding company, to her youth and vitality and flattering attentiveness. He also responded to the warm Florida sun and the fresh ocean air, began to relax, to shed the burden of widowhood and experience the stirrings of sexual attraction towards his amiable companion.

Sensing his change of feelings towards her, Belle at last took the initiative, seizing the opportunity to consolidate their relationship one evening in his hotel room when Harry lightheartedly commented on a stiff back from so much driving.

"I'll soon fix that," she declared authoritatively, flexing her

28

fingers. "Lie on the bed and Doctor Moran will operate. No, take your shirt off, I have to get *at* you."

Grinning, he did as he was told. Soon her gentle caress was stirring him to ecstasy.

"Hey—you're pretty good at this," he murmured languidly.

His heart pounded to the intimacy of her touch, and other parts of his body ached for her fingers.

"Turn over," she commanded.

He hesitated. "Belle . . . I . . ."

"Turn *over*."

He did so, grinning self-consciously as her eyes encountered the bulge of his erection. "It's all your fault, I didn't have anything to do with it."

She smiled impishly. "Close your eyes."

"What are you going to do?"

"Let's make it a surprise."

His heart thudded as her fingers removed the barrier of clothing and made the first tentative contact with his flesh. "Belle . . ." he whispered.

"You like that, Harry? Perhaps you'll like this better."

She took him into her warm, velvet mouth.

"My God . . . Belle . . . I can't hold on!"

"Then don't," she murmured.

She did not return to her apartment that night, nor any other night—except to collect her belongings. Thereafter she was Harry Little's constant companion.

The next day, as they drove south on Collins Avenue, she turned to look at him and asked, "Harry, mind if I ask you a personal question? It has a purpose."

"Go ahead."

"How much money have you got to spend?"

He smiled, cautiously. "Enough. Why?"

"How much is 'enough'? One million? Five million?"

He gave an uncertain laugh. "Why?"

"I know an island you could probably buy. It's in *the* perfect position—in Biscayne Bay, off the south end of the Beach."

He frowned. "An island? Why would I need an island?"

"To build your house on. You're a quiet man, you enjoy privacy. You'd get it on an island."

He demurred with a shrug. "You said 'probably buy'. Is it for sale?"

She smiled. "Not yet. But I know that the man who owns it is in financial trouble and is going to have to do something about his problem pretty soon. I think he'd take a reasonable offer for the island right now."

He digested the idea for a moment. "No harm in looking, I suppose. How far is it?"

She compressed a grin. "We're practically there."

Near the southern tip of the peninsular she stopped the car at the water's edge, cut the engine, and pointed out into the bay to one of several small islands, all covered with dense palmetto scrub, that formed a chain between the Beach and the city of Miami, three miles distant. "That's the one," she said.

Harry responded with the gamut of reactions from blank amazement to wincing disbelief. "I'd want to live on *that*? It's probably infested with snakes and crocodiles."

"Alligators," she corrected. "At the moment—yes."

He looked at her, his bewilderment profound. "You're kidding me. How could I possibly live out there? If I ran out of cigarettes I'd have to shop by cabin cruiser!"

Her eyes danced with secret amusement. "At the moment—yes."

He looked at her suspiciously. "What does that mean?"

"It *means* . . ." she smiled teasingly, ". . . that I know something that you and a lot of other people don't know yet. That's why I can probably get it for you cheap."

"Uh huh," he nodded. "And what exactly do you call cheap?"

"Two million dollars. It'd cost you four."

He threw back his head and roared with laughter. "Two million dollars! For what—maybe a hundred acres of floating jungle? That's cheap?"

"Yes," she insisted quietly.

He sighed with mock resignation. "OK, let's have it. What is it that you know and I don't?"

30

"It'll cost you, Harry."

His smile faltered. Disappointment lanced through him. Of course, theirs was a business arrangement, but he hadn't expected her to be so blatant. "Oh? How much, Belle?"

She shook her head. "Not 'how much', Harry—'what'. A job."

He frowned. "A job? What kind of job?"

"Your personal assistant. I want in on the development—the planning and design."

His good humour returned, expressed in a puzzled grin. "The development of what, f'Pete's sake?"

She gazed out across the half-mile wide stretch of water to the island. "Of Little Park."

"Hm?" His frown deepened.

She looked at him, her green eyes bright with contained excitement. "All you can see out there is a big mound of jungle. I don't. I see an exquisite residential park, an island paradise, perhaps thirty houses, no more, with two acres of land each, the rest of the island magnificently landscaped with palm trees and an ornamental lake and great explosions of colour—bougainvillia, magnolia, oleander, flame vine. The houses would be built with your design approval—and you'd lease the plots, retain the freehold. That way you'd retain firm control of *your* island. The homes would be superb, costing half-a-million dollars each, minimum—and each would have an unobstructed rear view of the bay, plus either Miami Beach or the city, depending on where it was situated. *Your* house would be built at the far end of the island—there, on the right—so that you'd have the whole of the bay, plus the Beach *and* the city to look at.

"Every house would have a large rear garden with a pool and tennis court—and an inlet wharf for a boat. Oh, Harry, it could be *the* place to live in Miami—maybe even in Florida. Look at its position . . . only half-a-mile from the Beach, less than two miles from the city—and yet offering all the privacy anyone could ever want."

Deeply thoughtful, stirred by her enthusiasm, Harry nodded, yet voiced a doubt. "Yes . . . but that's its drawback,

Belle—it's too private. There's no way of getting on or off the island except by boat, and the wealthy people you're hoping to attract wouldn't go for that, it's too messy."

The secret smile came again. "I agree ... but then I know something you don't know, don't I? Do we have a deal about that job?"

He laughed at her persistence and shrugged. "OK—*if* you can convince me it's worth buying and developing, you've got yourself a job."

"At what salary?"

Again he laughed, shaking his head. "No doubt you've got a figure in mind?"

"Yes. Two hundred dollars a week until the first tree is felled—then three hundred a week until the estate is finished."

He inclined his head thoughtfully, then nodded. "All right."

"Plus ..." she went on, "... one per cent of the purchase price as agent's fee for negotiating the deal."

He nodded again, smiling at her decisiveness. "Fair enough. Any more pluses?"

"Nope."

"All right—now tell me what it is you know that I don't."

Beaming demoniacally, she started the car engine and turned towards the north, delivering the revelation with playful off-handedness. "The city's going to build a new causeway, Harry, which will run from here, straight across to Thirteenth Street in Miami ... and pass within a coconut throw of Little Park. How about that—a four-lane highway right up to your front door?"

Belle Moran successfully negotiated the purchase of the island for one and a half million dollars, the agreement being finally consummated in the owner's bedroom after many hours of exhausting deliberation.

In addition to her one per cent commission as purchaser's agent, she also secretly received, as seller's agent, a two per cent commission from the grateful, and very relieved, owner.

32

3

Belle took charge of the project from the start. And Harry Little, more exhausted than he'd realised from a lifetime of hard work and three years of gruelling war production, was content to hover in the background and leave her to it, marvelling at her natural flair for business, her ability to control and manipulate men, and to squeeze the maximum value out of every dollar spent.

Returning briefly to New York to sell his garment business, he then settled with Belle in a temporary home in Miami Beach. When the house plans were drawn up, the initial clearance of the island got under way. And so, simultaneously, did the city begin construction of the new causeway. By the time the causeway was built, his island house was completed.

His house? he smilingly mused. No, it was Belle's house—the manifestation of her aspirations, the realisation of her dreams, grandiose in scope and beautiful in concept.

From what hereditary source this diminutive, modestly-educated, firebrand of a girl derived her innate sense of beauty, her flair for design, proportion and colour, he had no idea. But out it poured, naturally and effortlessly, to his continuing delight.

And as the months went by he became aware of another quality in her—the magical, uncontrived gift to entrance and amuse him, making these closing years of his life so very worthwhile.

Eventually, having lived as close companions for almost three years, and now that his island home was completed, Harry felt a compulsive need to formalise their relationship. In the spring of 1949 Belle Moran became Mrs Belle Little.

The following year Harry Little died in his sleep in the

garden of his home, leaving to his wife, his only living relative, an estate of forty-three million dollars.

The widow Little was just twenty-three years old.

The sudden acquisition of enormous fortune effected swift change in Belle Little. Far from being daunted or overwhelmed by it, she adjusted to her new position of power and influence with the natural alacrity of one born into land-owning aristocracy. She attacked the development of *her* island with precocious and intimidating authority, swiftly vanquishing the argument of any architect or contractor with whose opinion she disagreed, and frequently—and peremptorily—dismissing any individual who had the temerity to persist. "Bitch" typified the mutterings of many she had dealings with.

As an alcoholic or drug addict must wallow in his habit, so Belle embraced the heady addiction of power. Sex played no part in her life now. Not only had she endured too great a saturation of the wrong kind, but she had suddenly discovered a pleasure eminently more satisfying—sensually, spiritually, and physically—than mere copulation.

She played the power game to the limit, revelling in the proffered friendship of her intrigued fellow-rich, and in the fawning attentions of the milling would-be-rich. And yet, as her social connections grew, so—abruptly—did awareness of her shortcomings in matters other than land values and the weaknesses of men.

Her Waterloo occurred on the occasion of a charity dinner held in the Palm Beach mansion of Emily Van Doran, a matriarch renowned for her formidable wealth founded upon very old European money, for her art collection and sponsorship of art exhibitions, and for her almost pathological suspicion of new money.

Aware of this aversion, aware also of the importance to her ambitions of the acceptance by Emily Van Doran, Belle prepared assiduously for the occasion, determined to be seen as a woman of impeccable taste and breeding.

Arriving at the house, her first encounter with the middle-aged harridan passed satisfactorily enough, though while pleasantries tripped from Emily's prissily-pursed lips Belle knew she was being dissected by the wolf-grey eyes.

"I've heard so much about you," Emily assured her. "After dinner we must talk."

The dinner was a glittering affair. Seated amongst one hundred of Miami's wealthiest and most prestigious residents, Belle revelled in the glamour of the moment, pulsed with excitement that she was accepted by them, counted as one of their number. How far she had come in so short a time. It was a fantastic dream . . . no, not a dream from which one had eventually to waken, but a glorious reality.

Glowing with exuberance she mingled and chatted, thrilling to the friendliness of everyone she encountered.

Afterwards, after the dinner and the speeches and the appeal for financial support for Emily Van Doran's current endeavour—the establishment of scholarships for Florida's worthy artists—the guests retired from the table and engaged one another in informal discussion of the project and of art in general. Belle found herself, not too comfortably, in the presence of Emily Van Doran and several obvious art experts.

"You collect, of course," smiled Emily, directing her attention to Belle with the apparent intention of drawing her into the conversation. "I've heard so much about your lovely island home, I feel sure you must have spent a lot of time choosing some fine paintings."

Belle's heart missed a beat. All eyes were on her—Emily's in particular, half-smiling, cold as stone. "I . . ." Belle's voice choked in a dry, constricted throat. "I haven't completed the furnishing yet . . . it takes time . . ."

"Of course." Emily smiled sympathetically. "But you must surely have given your art requirements some thought? What are your preferences in paintings, Belle? The old school? Renaissance? Impressionist? Modern?"

Belle fought to contain the flush she felt creeping into her cheeks. You *bitch*, she seethed, recognising now the glow of victory in Emily's eyes. Emily was putting her on trial before her peers and she was about to fail hideously.

35

"My tastes are ... fairly catholic," she stammered, covering her nervousness with a quick smile.

"Good for you," countered Emily, luring her into a false sense of security with a pat on the arm. "But surely you have some favourites? What about those exciting French painters ... Pissarro, for instance? What do you think of his work, Belle?"

Belle's tongue sped across slate-dry lips. "I ..." They were waiting, silent, expectant. She prayed for an interruption, a catastrophe, that a hole would open in the floor and swallow her up. "I prefer ... his later work to his earlier ... I don't much care for his cube paintings ... those peculiar ... one-eyed women ..."

The silence of bewilderment encompassed her.

A pinch of frown appeared between Emily Van Doran's eyes. "Pissarro?"

A muted titter brought Belle around to face a tall, aesthetic-looking man whose face was contorted with suppressed humour. "Of course Mrs Little meant Picasso," he offered gallantly. "The names are very similar."

Belle countered reflexively, "Oh ... *Pissarro*! Sorry, I wasn't thinking ..."

Emily smiled, satisfied that she had revealed an imposter. "No matter. I'm sure you will have an enviable collection in due time. Now, if you'll excuse me, I must speak to the Duchess before she leaves."

That same week, in a state of ungovernable fury, Belle embarked for Europe and projected herself into a concentrated programme of education in the art galleries, concert halls and opera houses of London, Paris and Rome. For several years she commuted between Miami and Europe, cocooning herself in a protective veneer of knowledge in the subjects of art, music, wine, food, couture and antiques.

The butterfly that emerged was learned, chic and sophisticated, though endowed still with her basic characteristics of street cunning and passion for success—a combination of attributes which rendered her fascinating, attractive—and utterly lethal.

36

Thus equipped, she set about the consolidation of her tiny island empire. Offers for the purchase of the twenty-nine superb, individually-designed houses she had built on this unique site flooded in, and with the craft and diligence of a US president selecting his cabinet, she interviewed, considered, rejected and accepted her neighbours-to-be.

Two Superior Court judges, a leading surgeon, prominent attorneys, a former Miami mayor and a dozen assorted, highly-successful businessmen in varied fields. She chose from a social spectrum which, though broad, embodied one essential common factor—power.

Through these and other tributaries Belle Little widened her connections. The super-rich of Palm Beach, Houston, Los Angeles and New York became her intimate friends, and among them she came to be known, not always with affection, as the Queen of the Park—egocentric, eccentric, ruthless, but always interesting.

Her empire founded, her court assembled, it was on the occasion of a summer garden party, attended by most of the residents of the Park, that Belle was jolted into the realisation that, despite her wealth, position and achievement, there was still a fundamental and necessary element missing in her life.

As with every project she undertook, the party had been planned with taste and attention to detail. Tables with gaily-coloured umbrellas were set out on the lawn; a splendid buffet table, attended by uniformed chefs, offered an impressive array of delicacies; there was swimming and croquet and tennis for the amusement of the guests; and the weather, as though not daring to be otherwise, was perfect.

Belle, dressed in a pale-blue linen suit, strolled about the gardens, exchanging a word with her guests and basking in the unceasing compliments and tributes paid to her generosity, to the splendour of her home, her gardens, and the occasion.

Eventually she found herself in the company of three women with whose husbands she had recently formed close business ties, and who were now her adjoining neighbours. Of the three, she preferred Lily Parker, a beautiful, vivacious, dark-haired woman, a rebellious spirit not given, as were so many of her neighbours, to overt sycophancy. Lily had style, dressed well, exuded devilment. Belle felt a promise of amusing friendship there.

About Margaret Whitney she was struck with complete indifference. Though she dressed well enough, Margaret was spiritually dowdy, a nervous mouse, out of her depth in the Park. She would use her.

She liked Ruth Howard, wife of her legal advisor least of the three. Already she had noticed a change in Ruth since her arrival in the Park. Ruth had undoubtedly always been a closet snob, a biggot, and the Park had given her the opportunity to unharness her pretensions. Gaining confidence, Ruth saw herself as another Belle Little and indeed showed signs of emulating Belle in manner, speech and ambition. Belle decided to suffer the woman's obsequious imitation until it pleased her to squash it.

At her approach, the three women turned and greeted her according to their nature—Margaret Whitney with a nervous smile, Lily Parker with a casual but friendly "Hello", Ruth Howard with a gushing, "Belle, what a perfectly marvellous party. I do so admire your gift of perfection. I was just saying to Margaret and Lily how fortunate we all are to be living here in your park . . . really, it's heaven on earth."

"Just so long as you don't expect to run into any angels, Ruth," smiled Lily Parker.

Ruth's thin mouth primped with annoyance, her eyes searching Belle's for reciprocal censure of Lily's irreverence, but finding none. "I certainly won't expect to run into any around number sixteen," she countered peevishly, but was flattened by Lily's lewd wink.

"Damn right. I'll have an eternity of flying around with a halo and a harp after I'm dead, I don't intend practising down here . . . hmm, Margaret?"

Margaret offered a fluttery smile.

Interrupting the encounter, an attractive, dark-haired young girl, dressed in tennis whites, approached from the direction of

38

the tennis court, arriving breathless and flushed, with a warm smile of greeting for Ruth Howard, a nod of acquaintance for Margaret and Lily.

"Hi, Mom! Phew, it's hot. I'm absolutely baked."

Ruth returned a smile of maternal pride and turned to introduce the child. "Amy ... this is Mrs Little, your hostess. My daughter, Belle. She came home from school yesterday."

Belle held out her hand, stirred by an instant liking for the girl. "Hello, Amy."

"Thank you for inviting me, Mrs Little, I'm having a super time."

"You're most welcome. Why don't you go over to the buffet table and get some iced lemonade?"

"I think I will. See you later, Mom."

Belle watched the slender, coltish figure skip away across the lawn, radiant with life. How on earth could a woman like Ruth Howard spawn such a lovely creature?

"Delightful," she murmured, voicing her thoughts.

"Thank you," answered Ruth. "We're very proud of her. She's doing awfully well at school. We have the highest hopes for her."

"In what direction?" asked Lily Parker.

"Oh, nothing specific. We'd just like to see her marry well."

Belle, her attention still on the child, missed the exchange. In her mind was a picture of her own childhood and in her heart the remembrance of the warm relationship she had enjoyed with her mother.

Her eyes shifted from Amy to the house ... the big, beautiful house she shared with no one she cared for, only with servants. How good it would be to share her home and her wealth with a daughter, a child she could watch grow to womanhood, could mould in her own image—a future Queen of the Park.

The excited pounding of her heart provoked by the idea quite startled her. And as the day wore on the prospect not only persisted but blossomed, expanded, occupied her thoughts to a degree of obsession.

By the time the last guest had departed she had made up her mind. She was going to have a daughter.

The acquisition of a child by natural means was out of the question. Unable even to contemplate sharing her wealth and her absolute authority with any man, marriage was unthinkable. And as much as her eccentricity was tolerated, even applauded, by her friends, an illegitimate child would be going too far. Besides, the prospect of an ugly, distended body was anathema to her.

Adoption was the answer.

With typical incisiveness, Belle swept aside irritating conventional procedure and, through friends in the right places, struck at the heart of the matter, stating her exact requirements as no ordinary intending adoptor would have been allowed to do. *Her* daughter had to be "special" from the start, her lineage a blue-chip certainly, material from which a natural queen would grow.

A suitable child was found—the illegitimate issue of a New York débutante, the daughter of one of the nation's oldest families, and the teenage son of a former vice-president.

Elizabeth was, of course, a beautiful baby, possessing huge brown eyes, an abundance of dark brown hair and a quiet disposition.

For several weeks after her arrival in the Park she was the focus of Belle's attention, was loved and cuddled and nursed and played with. With customary verve, Belle devoted herself to the planning of the child's life up until her majority, selecting the very best private tutors, prep school, college and European finishing school.

And when that was accomplished and all that remained was to wait until the child grew into a communicative human being, Belle lost interest in the infant and continued her life as though Elizabeth did not exist.

Lavished with every conceivable luxury and amenity—with the notable exception of maternal love—cosseted by servants instructed to satisfy her slightest whim, it surprised no one that Elizabeth Little grew to be a spoiled, precocious, sinister child,

40

wilful and attention-seeking. Her acts of spite and wickedness, but for her mother's influence, would have resulted in dismissal from school on more than one occasion.

At the age of ten, her behaviour provoked her headmistress to request Belle's attendance at the school. Forewarned of trouble, Belle arrived in style, swathed in furs and jewellery, the daunting trappings of her wealth, prepared to do battle.

Ensconced in the headmistress's study, seated facing the severe, grey-haired autocrat, Belle unbalanced her opponent with an unexpected opening thrust.

"I was most interested to read about your plans for a new chapel ... such a worthwhile project. Expensive, of course. Understandably you're having to appeal to parents for financial help. I would be most happy to contribute. Say ... ten thousand dollars?"

The headmistress's dilemma was manifest in the compression of her lips. "That is exceedingly generous of you, Mrs Little. I ..."

"Now—about Elizabeth. You sounded so concerned on the telephone. Is it her studies?"

The headmistress glanced down at her hands, searching for an avenue of approach. "Unfortunately, no. Academically Elizabeth has given no cause for reproach ... she's a very bright child. It is in other matters ..."

"Such as?"

The teacher's eyes met Belle's uncertainly, clouded with concern. "Her behaviour, Mrs Little. We find her ... unruly."

Belle displayed a suppressed smile. "She is somewhat spirited, I know. Character in the making, I'm sure ... to be guided rather than subjugated."

The headmistress contained a troubled sigh. "If that were all, I wouldn't have asked you here, Mrs Little. But there are other, more worrying matters—incidents of lying, cheating, even cruelty."

Belle frowned. "Cruelty?"

"Yes. To give you an instance. We have a child here who is paranoically afraid of spiders. She sleeps in Elizabeth's dormitory. Three nights ago Elizabeth approached the child, wakened

41

her and emptied a jar containing several large house-spiders over her. The child went into screaming hysterics. She was so bad we had to summon the doctor."

"How awful," Belle commiserated. "A very stupid prank. I trust Elizabeth was suitably reprimanded."

"We tend to regard Elizabeth's behaviour in this matter as more than a mere 'prank', Mrs Little. Elizabeth was fully aware of her victim's dread of spiders. This was an act of the most callous cruelty, and, indeed, is not the first instance we have encountered. There was the matter of the dead hedgehog that Elizabeth placed in a pupil's bed. The poor animal was mutilated and bloody, and although we have no definite proof, there is the gravest suspicion that Elizabeth killed the creature herself."

Belle digested the report in silence for a moment. "Elizabeth, as you know, is an adopted child. I believe her, at heart, to be a good child, and regard this naughtiness as little more than an expression of unsureness, a means of seeking attention. I'm certain that with attentive care and guidance—and this is why I chose your school, knowing it to be the best possible one for her—she will soon grow out of it. I will, of course, personally reprimand her for this behaviour. Thank you for bringing it to my attention. Now, before I go, may I write a cheque for my donation to the chapel fund?"

During the next vacation, Belle remonstrated with Elizabeth regarding her behaviour at school, yet did so with reserve. Secretly she relished her daughter's "spirit", acknowledging it as a projection of her own character and regarding it as a necessary quality for a future queen.

Sensing her mother's covert approval, Elizabeth steered a canny course around her, realising that provided she refrained from treading on Belle's toes she was free to indulge in almost any havoc that sprang to mind.

Unable to tolerate the child's rudeness, arrogance and pernicious wickedness, many servants left the Little employ, occasionally during the night without notice.

Others were hired.

Thus, shortly after Elizabeth's fifteenth birthday, a Mexican couple, Fidel and Luisa Cesar, joined the domestic staff of the Little household as living-in gardener and cook, a couple who, though quiet, hard-working and respectful, were destined to be instrumental in bringing about the eventual downfall of the Queen of the Park.

4

From the moment of their arrival at number fifteen Fidel and Luisa Cesar detected tension in the house. Their interview with its mistress was gruelling. In return for top wages and luxurious accommodation, Belle informed them, she would insist on unswerving devotion to duty and scrupulous honesty. The slightest deviation—be it so little as a pound of filched sugar—would result not only in instant dismissal but also prosecution.

The residents in the Park, she explained, employed a great many Mexican and Cuban people from the Spanish barrio in Miami, and unless a rigid code of honesty was maintained in all the homes, anarchy would ensue.

Fidel and Luisa, a childless couple in their late twenties, were anxious to embrace the opportunity of high wages and a comfortable life. Although inwardly angered by her blatant presumption of their dishonesty, they accepted the terms of employment and were hired.

The accommodation offered was a suite of two rooms and bathroom in a staff bungalow situated in the grounds to the rear of the house, the bungalow also accommodated, in separate rooms, two Mexican maids whose names were Juanita and Constanza.

Delighted to remove from their poor barrio apartment to the splendour of the Park, Fidel and Luisa settled into the bungalow. At their first encounter with Juanita and Constanza they were warned of the difficulties of working for Señora Little.

"She is a hard woman, Luisa . . . *de caracter duro*," claimed Juanita, a pretty, buttoned-nosed girl in her late teens. "She will carve her pound of flesh from your bodies and then come back for a second helping. But as bad as she is, the daughter is the one to watch out for."

"Aye, aye—the daughter," nodded Constanza, a gentle woman of Luisa's age. "That Elizabeth . . ."

"The devil's own brat," scowled Juanita. "Never in my life have I hated any child, but—God forgive me—each night I pray that *that* one falls off her horse or tumbles into the pool and drowns."

Luisa exchanged a worried glance with her husband. "But how could she affect us?" she asked the woman. "What could she do to harm us?"

Juanita laughed scathingly. "Anything she puts her evil little mind to. She's a born troublemaker. She may lie to her mother about you . . . accuse you of doing something you didn't do. Stealing, perhaps. It's happened before."

"But why?" frowned Luisa.

Constanza shrugged. "Who knows. We think maybe she's not quite right up here." She tapped her temple. "Then again, maybe she just does it to get attention. She's an adopted child—Señora Little isn't her real mother. And their relationship is a strange one, they speak to one another more like two adults than mother and child. Very strange. Señora Little treats her . . . I don't know, like a 'possession' instead of a daughter, hey, Juanita?"

Juanita nodded. "Elizabeth is away most of the time at boarding school, but even when she is at home she's alone mostly—unless she brings friends in. Her mother is a very busy woman, she's always out at business meetings or charity things. She doesn't seem to have much time for her daughter."

"Hey, hey," sighed Luisa, "their ways are different from ours. Well, thanks for the warning, we'll keep an eye open for trouble."

In the weeks that followed, Fidel and Luisa saw almost nothing of Elizabeth. For the greater time she was away at school. Even when she was at home she was invariably accompanied by friends and didn't enter the kitchens or in any way interfere with Fidel's duties in the grounds.

45

No doubt, the Cesars began to assume, Juanita and Constanza had exaggerated the danger.

For many months, life continued happily and uneventful for the Cesars, their relationship with their mistress formal but not unpleasant. They enjoyed the benefits of their two worlds—the luxury of the Park during working hours, the comforting friendship of the barrio, a mere three miles away across the causeway, on their free days.

And so the pleasant life continued—until the summer's afternoon when the telegram arrived so unexpectedly for Luisa.

"For me?" She stared incredulously at the security guard, standing at the open kitchen door.

"It obviously went to your old address in Miami," he told her, glancing at the envelope. "A kid brought it to the booth."

Luisa, staring in trepidation at the cable, wiped her flour-covered hands on her apron and gingerly accepted the envelope, the first telegram she'd ever received.

"*Gracias*."

As the guard turned to leave, Fidel arrived at the door and frowned at his wife's obviously shocked expression. "*Que pasa, querida?*"

She proffered the envelope, her eyes wide. "A telegram . . . for me!"

"Oh? Well, open it."

She shook her head. "I don't want to."

He laughed. "It could be *good* news, you know. Go ahead—open it. Maybe an uncle has died and left you a fortune."

"Ha! Any uncle of mine would be asking for money, not leaving it."

Reluctantly, she tore open the envelope and extracted the cable form, her expression changing to one of delight as she read its message. "It's from Ana . . ."

"Ana?"

"My sister. My older sister . . . the one married to that . . . pig of a man, Patillas. I told you about him . . ."

46

"Ah—the monster who owns the cantina."

Luisa's eyes swept again over the cable. "Fidel, she's coming here. She and the three children ... they're on their way! They'll be here Friday evening!"

"*Here*?"

"Well, no—not here in the Park. In Miami. This went to our old address—Ana doesn't know we've moved. Oh ..." she sighed contritely, "... I've been meaning to write to her, I should have written weeks ago. She obviously thinks we can put them up. What are we going to do?"

Fidel shrugged. "Find them somewhere to stay ... the Leandros's, maybe, they have plenty of room. Does she say how long she intends to stay?"

"No. Just that they're arriving by bus Friday evening." She smiled happily. "How wonderful, I haven't seen Ana in almost five years. Poor thing ... I wonder how she's getting on with that terrible man."

"Maybe he has improved ... sent them on a vacation?"

Luisa snorted scornfully. "Oh, sure, like the Devil improves." She became pensive, re-read the telegram, her expression dark with concern.

"What's the matter?" asked Fidel.

She shook her head. "A feeling. I don't think this is a happy visit. I think something bad may have happened."

He smiled. "Oh, come now ..."

"No, I mean it, Fidel." She slipped the telegram into her apron pocket and returned to her baking, her thoughts a thousand miles and more away from where she stood. "Matamoros ..." she murmured apprehensively. "Something bad has happened there to Ana."

"How can you be so sure?" he chided her.

"Because nothing *good* ever happened to that poor woman, that's how."

He shook his head, smiling with gentle reproach. "Mother of Sorrows."

"Matamoros," she repeated, kneading the pastry dough. "How could any good news ever come from that dreadful place?"

5

ANA

Matamoros is a border town, situated in the extreme north-eastern corner of Mexico on the bank of the Rio Grande, close to the river's confluence with the Gulf of Mexico.

The area surrounding Matamoros is agricultural, the land varying in quality from rich to poor depending upon its proximity to the river, the source of irrigation.

During the governmental expropriation of privately-owned hacienda lands in the north, Tomas Ortega, with the ill-fortune that was to dog him all his life, received as his *ejido* fifty hectares of worn-out, non-irrigable land five miles east of Matamoros, and on it—assisted by his young bride, Carlota—he settled down to scrape a living growing crops of Indian corn, chick peas, lentils, beans and other vegetables.

During the first years of their marriage a daughter was born. They called her Ana. From earliest childhood Ana endured a life of brutal poverty, of unremitting labour in the stony sun-bleached fields. Each passing year brought increased hardship for the family as with mindless regularity Carlota produced child after child.

At the age of six, Ana took on the role of second mother, washing, feeding, and caring for the burgeoning brood of brothers and sisters while her mother worked in the fields.

Later, when she was old enough to appreciate the squalor of her surroundings, Ana determined she could not live in the adobe slum any longer. And yet escape seemed impossible. She had no money and nowhere to go. Directly across the Rio Grande the thriving, boisterous Texas town of Brownsville beckoned, yet without money, a passport and some decent clothes it was as unreachable as the moon.

At night she lay on her straw-filled *colchon* in the dark, stifling room, sickened by the odour of her myriad brothers and sisters and the pervading stench of the farm animals, and prayed tearfully to Mary, Mother of Jesus, for escape from this miserable existence.

But no immediate release came.

She suffered the drudgery and labour of the farm until, in the summer of her fourteenth year, a miracle happened. Or so it seemed.

That year, from early spring on, the rain fell and the sun shone in perfect agrarian harmony, producing a harvest of good quality vegetables that Tomas Ortega knew he could sell for a good price in Matamoros.

One evening in September, as Tomas absently watched his oldest daughter preparing a baby sister for bed, he was suddenly struck by Ana's beauty, by the sheen of her long raven hair and the blossoming maturity of her young body. With excitement the idea came to him.

"Ana," he remarked casually, "I've been thinking . . . you work so hard, never get away from the farm . . . how would you like to come into Matamoros with me tomorrow?"

Ana's lovely dark eyes lit up. "Papa!"

"I'll need some help to sell the vegetables. Wear your best dress and come with me."

Ana rushed across the room and kissed her father's bristled cheek. "Oh, Papa, I'd love to come!"

The next day they started off early, the mule-drawn cart filled with vegetables, and a small basket, containing a prime selection for showing, at Ana's feet.

Tomas made his first call at a run-down cantina, two miles out of Matamoros, an establishment called the Bar Las Vegas, the haunt of farm workers and fishermen.

Drawing to a halt in the dusty forecourt, Tomas turned to his daughter with a conspiratorial wink. "The owner's name is Ramon Patillas, I know him well. Go flutter your eyes at him and sell him lots of vegetables."

Nervous, yet excited by her new-found freedom, Ana climbed down from the cart and approached the open doorway of the dark, foul-smelling cantina, for a moment believing the place to be deserted. But as her eyes adjusted to the gloom, she saw the giant standing in a doorway at the rear of the room, his immense bulk all but filling the aperture.

"Well, well, well!" His deep, booming voice seemed to shake the cantina walls. He started towards her, looming ever larger, gross, dirty, terrifying. Now he towered above her, his evil-smelling presence overwhelming her. And the way his eyes looked at her! She felt naked under his gaze . . . wanted to turn and run, but couldn't move. She felt paralysed, rivetted by his size and those staring eyes.

"And who might you be?" he chuckled, the laughter bubbling in his gargantuan chest. "An angel from heaven, without a doubt."

She lowered her eyes, scarcely able to speak. "I . . . have vegetables to sell . . ." She gestured towards the door. "My father . . ."

Patillas inclined his head and peered through the doorway. "Tomas Ortega! *He* is your *father*? The sly old fox never mentioned he had a pretty thing like you at home." He raised a hand in greeting, called out, "Tomas! You should have brought her to sell your vegetables long ago—you'd be a millionaire by now!"

Tomas smiled and waved in response.

Patillas returned his attention to Ana, caught her by the arm and directed her towards the wooden counter of the bar. "Now, let Patillas see what you've got to offer."

She flinched at his touch. His hands and finger nails were filthy. Suddenly her new-found joy was gone. If this was the kind of man she would have to sell to, she preferred to stay at home.

She put her basket on the counter and retreated out of his reach and away from the stench of his body. Patillas regarded her with amusement, his eyes working over her face, her hair, and coming to rest on the swell of her ample breasts.

50

"What is your name?" he asked, his voice a broken growl.

"Ana," she whispered.

"Come closer, child, I'm not going to eat you."

She shook her head, provoking a rumbling chuckle.

"How old are you?"

"I'm . . . fourteen."

"Fourteen," he repeated with wonderment. "And so beautiful." He turned his attention to the vegetables, sorted through them, nodding approval. "They're good. I'll take a basket of each. Go get your first basket and I'll show you where to put them."

Relieved to escape from Ramon Patillas and the hateful cantina, she hurried out to the cart and told her father what she had sold. Tomas beamed delightedly. Why indeed hadn't he used his beautiful daughter before?

Returning to the cantina with a basket of corn, Ana found Patillas again standing in the doorway at the back of the room. "In here, Ana. There's a storeroom."

She followed him through a putrid-smelling kitchen to a small, dark, windowless alcove fitted with metal bins.

"The corn goes in that one," he told her.

As she lifted the lid, something scuttled in the dark depths of the bin, startling her and causing her to drop the lid with a loud clang.

Patillas's explosion of laughter shook the room. "Nothing to harm you—only a mouse or two."

Ana shuddered, quickly disposed of the corn and hurried out, her skin crawling.

When she reached the cart her father asked, "What's the matter, you look quite pale?"

She shook her head, grimacing. "The place is filthy. *He's* filthy. I don't like him."

"Now, now, that's no way to speak about a good customer, Ana."

She filled the basket with beans and returned to the cantina. The job seemed endless. On her final trip, having emptied her basket of peas, she turned to find Patillas blocking the doorway. Trapped in the awful room, she panicked.

"Please . . . let me pass."

"Aw," he tutted. "Can't you even pass the time of day?"

"No . . . I must go . . . my father is waiting!"

"Tell me, Ana—you have a boyfriend? A fiancé, perhaps?"

She shook her head, close to tears.

Patillas tutted disapprovingly. "Fourteen years old and no boyfriend? A beautiful girl like you should be married by now, don't you agree?"

She didn't answer.

He regarded her in silence, staring intently at her for a small, terrible eternity, then moved aside, beckoning her to pass, leaving so narrow a gap she was forced to rub against his protruding belly as she squeezed through.

His crackling laughter followed her as she ran through the cantina. Climbing up on to the cart, she sat with lowered eyes, trembling, as Patillas came out to pay her father.

"My compliments, Tomas, your vegetables are exquisite . . . as is your daughter." His eyes shifted to her breasts. "She will make your fortune. Consider me a regular customer . . . drop by next week and replenish my bins. *Adios.*"

On the journey into Matamoros Ana sat silent and dispirited, reflecting on the aptness of the vile man's surname—Patillas, the Spanish name for the Devil.

"He likes you," her father smiled, nodding with satisfaction.

"Well, I don't like him," she muttered angrily. "He has dirty eyes."

Tomas chuckled. "You'll get used to that—it's the way all men look at a beautiful woman."

To her dismay she found this to be true. At their subsequent stops at cantinas and cafés along the road she encountered numerous other Ramon Patillases, though none so completely loathsome as the original.

Compounding her misery, the town was also a big disappointment to her, not at all as she had imagined it. It's noise and congestion unnerved her, and she was glad when all the vegetables were sold and her father turned for home.

On the return journey she was morose. What had begun as an exciting adventure, the realisation of her dreams, had turned into a nightmare. Escape from the farm now seemed more impossible than ever.

"You did very well, Ana," Tomas told her. "For as long as the vegetables last, we will make this trip every Friday."

"Yes, Papa," she whispered miserably.

For the remainder of the year Ana accompanied her father on the weekly sorties into Matamoros, and gradually, with custom, her confidence grew. She learned to ignore the lecherous eyes of her customers and to enjoy the bustle of the town. Here, she came to realise, lay her only source of salvation from the farm, and she determined that soon, with or without her parents' permission, she would leave it and lose herself in the town's busy streets, find a job, live a new and exciting life.

During that winter and the growing months of the following spring, she day-dreamed of escape, of eventual love and marriage to someone she would meet in Matamoros, hopefully a handsome young businessman who would provide her with a life of greater comfort and happiness than she had so far known.

But this dream, like all her dreams, was destined to fade unfulfilled in the light of harsh reality.

In September, her father once again began his weekly journeys into Matamoros. Dreading the prospect of another confrontation with Ramon Patillas, yet appreciative of her family's dependence upon her success with him, she steeled herself for the encounter.

Nevertheless, her heart quailed as she climbed down from the cart, entered the dreadful cantina, and faced once again the obnoxious giant.

"Ana!" His dark eyes flared with renewed excitement. "Last year a child . . . this year a woman! Let me look at you."

"Look at my vegetables, Señor Patillas . . . this is all I've come to sell."

He erupted with laughter. "And how did your garden grow?" He cast an eye over her sample basket, pulling a disdainful face. "Yes, as poorly as all the others . . . perhaps not as

53

good as some I could have bought. A bad drought. But let me tell you—I refused to buy from anyone else, only from you. All right, my usual order. You know where to put them."

To her surprise and immense relief he did not follow her into the storeroom, but instead strolled out across the forecourt to speak with her father. Each time she returned to the cart she discovered them in earnest conversation, a discussion which faltered and died as she approached, resumed as she moved away.

The delivery completed, she rejoined her father and they continued into Matamoros, her father appearing unusually quiet and thoughtful on the way.

Entering the bustling town, her excitement and hopes were reawakened, and with sudden certainty she knew she would now be able to leave the farm and make her own way in the world. On the return journey, her heart pounding, she wrestled with the problem of how to tell her parents of her decision, only vaguely aware of her father's continuing pensiveness.

Nearing home, he suddenly surprised her by drawing off the road into the forecourt of the Bar Las Vegas, his manner now noticeably nervous.

"Ana . . . I . . ." He spoke falteringly, cleared his constricted throat. "You know . . . how bad things are at home . . . how badly we need money . . ."

Ana frowned, chilling with apprehension. Something was wrong. "Yes, Papa?"

Tomas looked down at his feet, his demeanour furtive, ashamed. "Señor Patillas has made me a very generous offer that would mean so much to your brothers and sisters."

Remembering her father's earlier conversation with Patillas, its nature, she sensed awful news. Her heart began to pound. In a whisper she asked, "What is the offer?"

"He . . . wishes to employ you . . . to do the cooking . . . help serve in the bar. He believes you will attract a lot of custom . . ."

"Papa, no!"

"Ana, he will pay us a lot of money! He . . ."

She cried out, "No! I'll take a job in Matamoros! *I* will give you money . . ."

54

"Child, you couldn't earn enough—not one quarter of what Patillas is willing to pay! And besides . . . I've already given my hand on the . . . arrangement."

Ana opened her mouth to speak, to continue the protest, but Patillas's voice boomed from the lighted doorway of the cantina. "That's right! It's all settled!"

Ana clutched at her father's arm. "Papa!"

He wrenched his arm away. "Go, child! He needs you to start right away."

He urged her down from the cart. Ana, dazed, looked up at him imploringly. "Papa, *please*! Take me home!"

Tomas brought the whip down hard on the mule's rump, goading it into startled flight. In moments the cart had disappeared into the darkness.

Patillas came up to her and placed his hand on her shoulder. "Ana . . ."

She shook herself away. "Don't touch me!"

The hand persisted, squeezed her flesh. "There's no need to be afraid of me. I'm going to look after you . . . provided you keep your part of the arrangement. If you don't, I shall beat you. It's a husband's right."

It took a moment for his words to penetrate. With an incredulous gasp she turned to face him. "*Husband*?"

Patillas frowned with genuine puzzlement, then came a twisted smile. "Ah . . . so the old crook didn't tell you. I've bought his permission to marry you—paid handsomely for it, too. No matter, I'll get my money's worth. Come—there's food to cook for hungry men . . . and afterwards you will serve in the bar. What you've been doing for your family, you will now do for me . . ." laughter bubbled in his throat. "And a little bit more."

Something inside Ana Ortega died that night.

Her strict Catholic upbringing denying her the temerity to believe God had deserted her, she sought refuge in the belief that this new and even more hideous role had been ordained *by* Him as a sacrifice necessary for her family's welfare. That being the case, she prepared herself to accept anything that came her way; but in order to achieve this preparation, she found it necessary to subjugate all hope, the essential spark of life.

She performed her duties in the kitchen and the bar with silent obedience, in almost trance-like state, seemingly oblivious of her surroundings, of the coarse humour of the cantina and the slavering attentions of its owner.

Patillas, desperate to get his hands on her but fearing repercussions from any pre-marital advance, hastened the wedding. Within a month of her arrival at the cantina they were married in a local church by a young priest who viewed with silent misgivings the great disparity of their ages and the obvious spiritlessness of the bride.

On their wedding night Ana submitted passively as the drunken Patillas tore off her dress and pushed her naked on to the bed. And she made no sound, either in pain or protest, as he crushed her with his malodorous weight and ruptured her hymen with a vicious thrust.

After he had ejaculated into her and rolled away to sleep, she got up from the bed, washed herself and went into the kitchen to prepare the meat and vegetables for the next day's cooking—knowing with uncaring certainty that the numbness that pervaded her mind and body was the prelude to eventual madness.

That she would have soon become deranged, but for the intervention of her pregnancy, she didn't doubt. The conditions of her life immediately after the marriage became so appalling that even her religion-inspired determination to accept her lot passively could not have prevailed against Patillas's brutality towards her.

Incensed by her silence and sexual coldness, he flew into towering rages which, in public, took the form of verbal onslaughts, and in private frequently resulted in beatings and sexual assaults.

"Bitch! Slut! Whore!" he would thunder. "You're not human! Cry, goddam you, cry!"

And so the nightmare continued until the advent of her pregnancy, the awareness of it bringing new life to her dying

56

heart and stemming the disease of her mind with joyous hope.

"I'm pregnant," she announced to Patillas, anticipating no reaction other than the bitter scowl he gave her, but knowing that at least the news of her condition would curb his physical violence.

"And what will it be—a pup?" he snorted. "That's what stupid bitches have, isn't it?"

It will be *my* child, she answered silently. My child and my reason to live.

A son was born that winter. She christened him Francisco.

6

Two years later Ana gave birth to twins, a boy and a girl. She called them Carlo and Maria. They, like their brother, grew to dread Ramon Patillas's violence.

In infancy, a precocious anger took root within Francisco, gathering, compressing into a core of venemous hatred for his father, a deadly weapon, primed and cocked, waiting for the one blow, the one degradation too many that would trigger its lethal charge.

That moment came in Francisco's fourteenth year during a night of storms. Sounds of human fury mingling with the crash of thunder and the drum of tropical rain on the cantina's iron roof awoke Francisco with a start, his anger soaring to the pitch of madness at the evidence of yet another beating.

Seized by whimpering fury he ran from his room into the kitchen to discover his mother bent backwards over a table, her face covered in blood from a battered nose, his father's fist drawn back for another blow. He hurled himself at Patillas, pummelled the giant's back with puny fists, yelling, "Leave her alone! Leave her alone!" But a thrust sent him flying across the room.

Sick with impotence, goaded by his mother's cries, he searched desperately for a weapon . . . anything with which to stop the beating.

On the floor near the stove lay a small axe, used for splitting kindling.

Francisco bellowed his warning. "Don't hit her again! Don't . . ."

His cry became a grieving wail and Patillas's knuckles smashed into Ana's face. Demented, Francisco snatched up the axe and brought it down with all his strength on the back of his father's head.

Ramon Patillas stiffened, fell forward on to his wife, rolled sideways and crashed to the floor, dead before he reached it.

Slowly, through the veil of shock and disbelief that clouded Ana's mind seeped the realisation that she and the children must escape. Instinctively she thought of her sister, Luisa, who lived in Miami. Of all her sisters, Luisa had always been the closest and often wrote to her, urging her to leave Patillas. Luisa would be glad to help.

But how could she possibly get to Miami, so far away, without a passport . . . money?

Huddled in the living room with her children, she voiced her thoughts and fears to them. "But who will help us? We can't do it by ourselves."

With a maturity, a calmness that amazed her, Francisco answered, "Robert Salar will help us. I'll go and ask him to take us to Brownsville in his boat. He'll do it, Momma, he likes you."

Among the regular patrons of the cantina were one or two men who had sympathised with Ana's position, had even openly objected to Ramon's treatment of her. Robert Salar, a young fisherman who worked the river and the gulf in his own small boat, had often offered her a word of encouragement as she served him at his table. Sensing Francisco was right, she allowed him to go. He returned half an hour later in Salar's truck.

A handsome man in his late twenties, Salar immediately took charge, his cool confidence an enormous comfort to the bewildered Ana.

"You're right, you must get away," he agreed. "Patillas wasn't a man, he was an animal, and no one should suffer because of his death. Don't worry, everything will be all right. I have a brother who lives across the border in Port Isabel, near the mouth of the river. I'll telephone Raoul now and ask him to meet us at the harbour with his truck later tonight.

59

First thing tomorrow, he'll put you on a bus. Once you're in Texas you'll be safe, there are more Mexicans there than Texans.''

Worriedly, Ana asked, "But what about this place? The customers will get suspicious if the cantina doesn't open . . . and the police are bound to be suspicious of a family that suddenly disappears. And what about . . . Ramon?"

"I'll take care of him. I'll put him where no one will find him—at the bottom of the gulf. As for your disappearance . . . I'll spread the word that you've all gone on a vacation to Baja California. Later on you can write me a letter, using a false address, telling me that Ramon has decided to abandon this pig-sty and settle on the West Coast. Who is going to dispute it? Now, we'd better get moving—collect a few things and be ready to leave in half an hour. Francisco—see what money you can find.''

An hour before dawn the little boat puttered into a deserted wharf on the north side of Port Isabel harbour and the family was transferred into the care of Raoul Salar, Roberto's older brother.

On the wharf, Ana clutched Roberto's arm, her eyes filled with tears of gratitude. "How can we ever thank you?"

"De nada, Ana . . . one of us should have killed that pig long ago and saved you all a lot of suffering. God go with you. I'll keep in touch through your sister, let you know what happens here."

Later that day, carrying their few belongings and what little money remained after buying the tickets, Ana and the children boarded a bus in Brownsville on the first leg of their 1,500-mile journey to Miami.

As the bus pulled away, Ana, suddenly overwhelmed by despair, by pity for her children and the life they had so far had to endure, by a feeling of helplessness to improve their lives, and by fear of the future, buried her face in her hands and wept uncontrollably.

Francisco slipped his arm around her shoulder. "Momma, don't cry, it's going to be all right, you'll see. I'm going to look after us all now. I'm the man of the family now . . . and nobody's ever going to hurt you again, I promise."

Ana smiled tearfully, touched by his manliness, but as her eyes met his her smiled faded, erased by the tortured anger she saw burning deep inside her fourteen-year-old son.

Brownsville, Corpus Christi, Houston, Beaumont . . . travelling almost non-stop, sleeping in the bus or on bus station benches to conserve their meagre funds, they covered the vastness of Texas, then traversed the seemingly endless flatlands of Louisiana, Mississippi and Alabama, and on the morning of their fifth day crossed the border into Florida. By nightfall, distressed with fatigue, they entered the city of Miami.

Fidel and Luisa Cesar were at the bus station to meet them, and the moment her sister stepped down from the bus, Luisa knew her fears of bad news were about to be realised.

The greetings over, Ana confided to Luisa and Fidel the reason for their arrival.

The Cesars' offer of help was instantaneous.

"But I'm afraid we can't put you up," Luisa told Ana. "Fidel and I gave up our apartment months ago. We're now working as cook and gardener for a wealthy woman in Little Park and live in the staff bungalow. But don't worry, we've fixed you up with Fidel's cousin and her husband—Isabel and Jose Leandros—who have a house in the barrio. Come, they have a meal waiting for you . . ." she smiled at the exhausted children, ". . . *and* nice soft beds."

The house on Eighteenth Street was a narrow three-storey clapboard frame owned by Jose Leandros, a short, stocky, fifty-year-old railway worker, and his matronly wife, Isabel.

They greeted Ana and her children warmly, listening to their story with grave sympathy, but deferring further discussion until the children had eaten and were asleep in bed.

Later, seated around the kitchen table, the adults talked about the past and the future, and Ana expressed her fears for Francisco's safety.

Jose smiled and shook his head. "I don't think there's

61

anything to worry about. Here in the barrio confusion runs riot. Since Fidel Castro took over Cuba more than *half a million* refugees have poured into Miami—imagine what chaos they've caused. There are a lot of Mexicans here, too. It will be easy for you and the children to lose yourselves in the crowd. But—for your peace of mind—we'll invent a past for you.

"Twenty-five years ago Isabel and I left Tijuana and emigrated to Los Angeles and we lived there for eighteen years before coming to Miami. We have many good friends and a few relatives in California. So—for the benefit of anyone who needs to know—Ana Patillas, following the death of her husband, has arrived here with her children from Los Angeles to be near her sister. Bien?"

Ana smiled gratefully. "Bien."

"We must get the children into school," Jose continued. "That should be no problem, there are lots of schools in Miami. Do the children speak English?"

"Yes, quite well, they were taught at mission school." Ana smiled. "They have even taught me a little."

Jose nodded. "Good, then they'll have no trouble settling in. As for yourself, I'm sure we'll be able to find you a job . . . as a waitress, perhaps, or maybe in a factory."

"Anything . . . I'll do anything. I'm just so grateful to be here. I don't know how to thank you for your kindness."

Jose gestured dismissively. "It is nothing. It's good to have children in the house again. Since ours married and left the nest I was beginning to feel old. You're more than welcome. What is important now is that you forget the past and build yourself a new life, knowing you're among family and friends. You'll find the people of the barrio very loyal. Nobody here cries for help without being heard."

Later, in the darkness of her room, aching with exhaustion, Ana lay in her bed and wept with relief that she and her children had at last escaped the tyranny of Matamoros and were safe in the care of loving people.

"Thank you, God," she whispered earnestly. "Now, *please* don't take this happiness away . . . please let everything be all right."

62

Drained, now, of all care and emotion, as though the poison of the past years had suddenly been purged from her mind and body, she fell into deep and dreamless sleep.

Within a week the children had been enrolled in school and Ana had started work as a machinist in a garment factory.

Their new life had begun.

7

Ana Patillas had barely begun to enjoy the security and friendship of the barrio when three disparate events occurred which were to alter tragically the course of her life and bring about her eventual destruction.

Less than a month after their arrival in Miami, a petty grievance between management and labour at the clothing factory at which she worked brought the work force out on unofficial strike. Ana was suddenly and bewilderingly unemployed.

In that same week, Juanita, Mrs Belle Little's young Mexican maid, discovered she was pregnant and gave notice in order to marry her fiancé, a Cuban taxi driver.

Belle, furious at losing a servant in whom she had invested so much training time, dismissed Juanita instantly in a fit of pique, then immediately regretted the hastiness of her action. In a few days time she was giving an important dinner party, and the prospect of doing so with new and untrained staff "appalled her"—as she told her cook during a discussion of the menu.

Luisa, aware that Ana had been laid off work, seized the chance to help her.

"Señora, I have a sister who is an excellent worker and has had experience of waiting at table. She'd be happy to help out until you can make other arrangements."

"Well at least, no doubt, she'll be honest," Belle conceded. "Bring her to see me."

That evening, Fidel and Luisa drove to the Leandrose's house to discuss the matter. With her children securely settled in their new home, Ana felt no qualms about being away from them during the week, and the prospect of working close to her sister, especially in such beautiful surroundings, delighted her.

"Of course you must go," Isabel insisted. "It will do you

64

good—and I'll be glad to look after the children for a few days."

At the interview the following day, Belle Little ran a critical eye over the quiet, deferential woman standing before her, and judged her, at least in appearance and manner, to be acceptable.

"No doubt your sister has warned you that I insist on strict discipline and *absolute* honesty," she warned Ana.

"Yes, señora," Ana whispered, her heart pounding, overwhelmed by the opulence of the house and the regal severity of its mistress.

"All right, you will begin a week's trial. If I find you satisfactory perhaps there will be a permanent position for you. You may move into the staff quarters today."

That evening, as Ana undressed for bed, her sister knocked and entered the room. "I came to say goodnight. How are you feeling? A bit strange, hmm?"

Ana smiled. "Yes, but very happy." She shook her head. "I can't believe this is happening to me . . . that I'm here, living in such a beautiful home. It's like a dream."

Luisa hugged her. "It's no more than you deserve. All the unhappiness is behind you now. Nothing can harm you and the children now."

Ana nodded, momentarily reflective. "My God, I hope so, Luisa. I couldn't bear to go through anything like that again."

"You won't have to. You have Fidel and me here, and good friends in the barrio who wouldn't let it happen." Luisa kissed her sister's cheek. "Goodnight, Ana, sleep well."

Ana did not sleep well. Her dreams awakened the horror of Ramon's death. He loomed above her, choking her, while behind him Francisco struck blow after blow with the axe. Yet Ramon would not die. Once, twice he fell to the ground but each time rose up and seized her by the throat, the blood from his shattered head splashing down into her face.

She awoke in the early hours of the morning, sick with depression.

Three days later she had cause to remember the dream and wonder at its prophetic nature. A letter arrived from Roberto Salar, the man who had helped her escape, telling her that

Ramon's body had been trawled to the surface of the gulf in the nets of local fishermen, and that the police were investigating the suspected murder and the disappearance of the Patillas family. On no account, Salar advised her, should she and the children return to Mexico.

Alone that night in her room in the staff bungalow, Ana sat on the bed and rocked with despair, Salar's letter clutched in her hand. There could be no peace for her—ever. She was cursed—a burden to her children and everyone around her. She had brought her children nothing but trouble. They would be better off if she were dead.

As the days passed, the shock wrought by Salar's news gradually subsided. Yet the question of self-worth remained, hovered on the perimeter of her subconscious like a spectre—a permanent attendant, biding its time until the next onslaught of misfortune signalled its moment to return.

Several uneventful weeks passed. Ana's life took on a pleasing, gentling rhythm of domestic routine and weekend visits to her children, unmarred by any discord that might threaten to wake the sleeping ogre of despair.

And so the tranquillity continued—until Elizabeth Little arrived home from school for the Christmas vacation.

8

Christmas in the Little household was an occasion of special social significance, as indeed it was in most well-to-do homes, many of which were occupied for only these few weeks of "the season" when their owners migrated south, fleeing the rigours of the northern winter for the Florida sun.

During these weeks house parties were *de rigeur*. A spirit of keen competition prevailed, each society czarina determining to outdo her rivals with an occasion of incomparable splendour.

Belle Little needed to excel over all.

This year her theme was to be an Arabian Night. A huge steel frame, secured to the house over by the rear terrace, would be festooned with swathes of multi-coloured silks, the tent furnished luxuriously with Oriental carpets, antique furniture and objets d'art from the house, adorned with crystal chandeliers and hanging baskets of flowers, and perfumed by the scent of ten thousand trellised roses.

Incorporating the garden's illuminated flamingo lake, the terrace fountains, and the spectacular night view of Biscayne Bay, the setting would undoubtedly surpass anything offered in competition.

By the first week in December one thousand invitations had been sent out.

The Queen expected everyone to attend.

Elizabeth arrived home from school on the afternoon of December 14th, and within moments of her arrival utterly destroyed Ana Patillas's growing confidence.

Ordered by Belle to help unload and bring in Elizabeth's luggage from the station-wagon, Ana descended the steps at the front of the house and approached the slender, dark-haired

67

girl dressed in blue jeans and red sweater who stood waiting with obvious impatience at the rear door of the vehicle.

Ana smiled nervously. "Miss . . ."

Elizabeth's dark eyes snapped testily. "Who are you?"

Having heard all there was to hear about this hateful girl from Luisa and Constanza, and now suddenly confronted by the verification of their opinion, Ana went to pieces. "I am Ana P-patillas, miss . . ." she stammered.

Elizabeth's eyes flared with secret amusement. "Oh, yes . . . I heard Juanita got herself knocked up. All right, get these cases out—and be careful with this valise, there's something breakable in it."

Ana frowned with incomprehension. "Miss . . .?"

Elizabeth sighed heavily. "Christ, don't you understand English? This . . . *valise* . . . be *careful* with it . . . there is *glass* inside it . . . a bottle . . . *botella*. *Comprende*?"

"Si . . . si, señorita."

"Jesus wept." Elizabeth turned away and ran up the steps. Ana, a suitcase in each hand and the canvas hold-all tucked under her right arm, hurried in Elizabeth's wake. At the top of the steps the unthinkable happened. Ana tripped, teetered forward, thrust out her hands to protect herself, releasing the valise which tumbled down the six stone steps and struck the asphalt drive with a muted crack of breaking glass.

Elizabeth whirled, face contorted with disbelief and erupting fury. "You . . . stupid . . . *bitch*!"

Ana froze, speechless.

Elizabeth's dark eyes bore into her, gleaming demoniacally. "You stupid Spic bitch," she hissed venomously. With a toss of her head she turned and strode into the house.

Aching with dismay, Ana returned down the steps to pick up the valise that was now stained with spilled liquid and redolent with the powerful smell of perfume. In tears she climbed the steps again, collected the two suitcases and entered the house, quaking at the sound of Elizabeth's tirade coming through partly-open doors from the drawing-room on the right of the hall.

". . . a *pint* of Joy, mother! Your Christmas present! Christ Almighty, *why* do we have to employ these bovine wet-backs?"

"Because they're *available*, Elizabeth," Belle answered shortly. "You've no idea how impossible it is to find domestic staff these days. And at least this one appears to be honest."

"Meaning you haven't actually caught her stealing yet? Well, she'd better keep out of my way. My *God*, do you smell that? The stupid woman's trailing it through the house!"

The drawing-room jerked open. Elizabeth stopped short, gaped at the miserable, indecisive figure standing there.

"*Don't* bring it through here, you're stinking up the house! Look—it's dripping on the floor! Get it out of here! Haven't you got *any* sense?"

Ana fled out of the front door and down the steps, her heart bursting, knowing with certainty that her days, perhaps hours, in the house were numbered.

That evening she complained tearfully to Constanza, "I'm trying so hard . . . and everything was going so well before this happened."

Constanza patted her hand. "I know. And is it surprising she makes you drop things? *I'm* a bundle of nerves when she's around. Never mind, she'll be back at school in three weeks— just try and stay out of her way as much as possible."

But avoidance was impossible. In addition to waiting at table, Ana was required to make beds and clean bathrooms, and frequently encountered Elizabeth, who liked to sleep late and lanquish in her bath tub. At these times Ana could sense Elizabeth's eye on her, watching her, as a cat watches a mouse, knowing it controls the situation and can kill at will.

Within a few days Ana's presentiment was realised. Elizabeth's attitude towards her changed from passive hostility to active cruelty. She relished, rather than resented, Ana's presence, revelling in her own power to command.

"Ana . . . draw my bath."

"Yes, miss."

"And put out my grey slacks and black cashmere sweater."

"Miss?"

"F'Crissake . . . *grey* slacks . . . *black* . . . cashmere . . . sweater."

"Yes, miss."

And later. "Ana—what is this?"

"Miss?"

"What is *this*? I told you to put out my red cashmere sweater."

"But surely . . . you said your black sweater, miss?"

"Don't tell me what I said! I distinctly said *red* sweater!"

"I'm s-sorry, miss . . ."

"You must learn to speak better English! You're a very incompetent servant. And, Ana, you do *have* a bath tub in the staff quarters, don't you?"

"Bath tub? Yes, miss."

"Then use it, I can't *stand* body odour."

"She hates me!" Ana sobbingly told Luisa and Constanza. "She insults me . . . tells me to do one thing then swears she told me something else. She's trying to drive me out of the house."

Constanza shook her head. "And spoil her fun? No, that's the last thing she wants, Ana, you're too good a punch bag."

Tears coursed down Ana's cheeks. "I can't take any more of it, Luisa . . . I'll have to leave."

"Then she'll have won," said Luisa.

"Let her. How can I possibly win against her?"

"By showing her your strength, Ana—by facing up to her. She's a bully—and all bullies back down against a show of strength. If it leads to your dismissal . . ." Luisa shrugged, ". . . well, far better to leave with your head held high than your tail tucked between your legs."

Ana nodded uncertainly, miserably. "You're right. After all—what is she? She's only a fifteen-year-old child."

"Wrong," sighed Constanza. "She's a fifteen-year-old monster."

Ana's stand against Elizabeth occurred quite unexpectedly two days later.

Mid-morning, as she passed the partly-open door of Belle's bedroom, Ana heard a sound in the room that puzzled her.

70

Believing Elizabeth—whom she'd earlier seen leaving the house, wearing a beach wrap—to be down at the pool, and knowing that her mistress was attending a charity function in Coral Gables, Ana gingerly pushed the door wider and peered in.

Elizabeth was standing before an open wall-safe, a bundle of bank notes in her hands. As Ana watched, Elizabeth peeled off a quantity of notes and stuffed them into the pocket of her wrap, replaced the bundle in the safe, locked the door, then turned to pick up from the desk the oil painting which hung over the safe.

Spotting Ana in the doorway, she gave a start and flushed crimson with guilt, but quickly recovered her composure and turned it into an affronted bluster. "What the hell are you staring at? What are you standing there for?"

Trembling, wanting to turn and run but realising the moment to make her stand had come, Ana stood her ground and met Elizabeth's belligerent glare with a calm, defensive gaze. "What are you doing in your mother's room?" she asked with quiet insistance.

The child gaped in astonishment. "My God ... who d'you think you're talking to?" She gave an appalled laugh. "Jesus! I'll report you to my mother for insolence ... you'll be out of this house by lunchtime!"

Ana fought to keep her voice steady. "And I ... shall report to your mother what I have seen."

Eyes wild with rage, Elizabeth advanced towards Ana. "Now, you listen to me! What I do in any *part* of this house is *my* business—because the house and everything in it, including *you*, is mine to do with as I please! Do you understand that? *Comprende?*"

Ana's tongue touched her trembling lips.

Elizabeth had almost reached her, and now the child's expression changed from glaring anger to an evil leer. "And how would it be, Señora Nosey, if I were to report to my mother that *I* had caught *you* rifling her safe ... hmm? What do you suppose would happen to you if I told her that? I'll tell you what would happen ... you'd be in Miami jail before you could say *'Caramba!'*, that's what would happen—and you'd stay there

71

till your teeth dropped out! Now get out of my sight and keep your goddamned mouth shut!"

With an explosive sob Ana turned and ran along the landing and down the stairs to the kitchen.

"It's no good," she told her sister. "I will have to leave . . . right now."

Luisa, alarmed by Ana's nervous state, her trembling, put an arm round her shoulder and held her close. "Sssh, calm down, now, calm down. Don't let her do this to you. Yes, I know she's a wicked minx, but, Ana, think of your children. It's nearly Christmas . . . you need money for them. Besides, Señora Little would be furious if you left before the big party. Look . . ." she took Ana's tear-streaked face in her hands, ". . . Elizabeth will get tired of this game soon. The round of parties will be starting and she'll have other things to think about. Try and hold out till Christmas is over and she's back at school, hmm?"

Ana nodded, wiping at her tears. "She really hates me, Luisa . . . you should have seen her face. I'm afraid of her . . . afraid of what she might do. What if she *does* tell Señora Little that she found me at the safe?"

Luisa shook her head. "She won't. She's a spoiled child, very immature. It makes her feel big to threaten you, to think she has power over you, but it's all talk. Ana, there's nothing she can do to harm you—not while Fidel and I are here to protect you. She wouldn't dare go that far."

9

The remainder of the week passed without incident.

Tormented at first by the expectation of imminent reaction to Elizabeth's threat to report her to Belle for insolence, Ana gradually relaxed, believing what Luisa had said about the emptiness of Elizabeth's threats.

On the occasions that she ran into Elizabeth, the girl seemed to have forgotten the incident. Her manner, though brusque, was no longer taunting or particularly impolite. Indeed, she seemed preoccupied with other matters. As Luisa had predicted, it appeared Elizabeth had tired of the baiting game and transferred her attention elsewhere.

Ana enjoyed a feeling of enormous relief. Suddenly life was good again, and this time, she felt, it would stay good. What other problems could there be?

By eight o'clock on the evening of December 22nd, the Arabian tent, the house, and the gardens were filled with guests, one thousand subjects who had come to pay annual homage to the Queen.

For the occasion, a score of extra servants had been hired or borrowed. Ana was among those attending to cloakroom duty, relieving the guests of their coats on arrival, retrieving them when the guests departed.

The party was an enormous success, the house resounding to music and animated conversation (everyone agreed it was *the* party of the season) until three o'clock in the morning, when the guests began to take their leave.

Belle, regal in a full-length gown of turquoise and gold velvet, her throat, wrists, and fingers glittering with diamonds and emeralds, took up a position in the drawing-room entrance to the Arabian tent and basked in the effusive compliments of her departing friends.

Mrs Emily Van Doran, the doyen of Palm Beach society who, so many years before, had put Belle to flight for Europe, was the first to shatter Belle's regal composure.

"Belle, darling, a *won*derful, wonderful party . . . so clever." Touching Belle's arm, she moved close, murmured confidentially, "A small matter, dear . . . but I do appear to have mislaid my diamond brooch . . . obviously it must have shaken loose from my coat in the crush. For heaven's sake don't bother about it now, I'm sure it'll turn up when the smoke clears."

Belle flushed with annoyance. For this to have happened to Emily Van Doran, of all people. "Emily, I'm so sorry. It will be returned to you first thing in the morning, I'll have the servants look for it right away. You can be sure it's here somewhere . . ."

"But of course!" Emily protested. "Darling, I'm not for a *moment* suggesting . . . well, anyone knows you have the most trustworthy servants in Florida. Goodnight, Belle . . . and thank you so very much . . ."

Emily moved away. Inwardly seething, Belle fought to contain her anger and fixed a smile for her next departing guest.

Within moments the unbelievable was happening again.

Doctor Frank Soper, head of Miami General Hospital and a Park neighbour, approached Belle with a pained, embarrassed expression that signalled instinctive alarm in Belle and turned her blood to ice.

"Frank—what's wrong?"

His smile was an apologetic grimace. "Belle . . . a most delicate matter . . . but I feel I have to expose it for your sake. I . . . went to get a business card from my wallet . . ." surreptitiously he opened the flap of his dark-blue barathea overcoat to reveal the wallet in an inside pocket, ". . . and . . . I'm dreadfully afraid some money is missing. I can't be mistaken. Before I came out this evening I put just two one hundred dollar bills in it . . ." he flashed a bleak smile, ". . . mad money, you know. And now one of the bills is missing . . ."

Belle paled, gasped in a hoarse whisper, "My God, Frank . . ."

"Belle, you *know* the money itself is of no importance, but in view of what we residents have agreed . . ."

"Yes," she said quickly, continued imploringly, "Frank, it has got to be one of the temporaries . . . my own staff wouldn't *dare* . . ."

Soper nodded gravely. "That's why I've mentioned it. Belle, I'm so sorry . . . it's been a wonderful party . . ."

"Yes . . . thank you . . . you were absolutely right to tell me . . ."

Belle Little was destroyed. Only by exercising superhuman control did she remain there, bidding her guests goodnight, instead of succumbing to the fury that boiled inside her and launching open war against the culprit.

But her torment was not yet over. Before the last of her guests departed two further cases of "mislaid" jewellery were confided to her—a compact studded with diamonds and pearls, and a diamond-and-ruby cigarette lighter.

When at last all the guests were gone, she released her anger in a bellow of outrage, startling the servants who were clearing away party debris, and bringing Elizabeth hurrying through the open french windows from the Arabian tent.

"Mother! What on earth's the matter?"

"God in *heaven*! We've got a thief here!" Crimson with fury, she strode to the telephone, waving her arms and shouting, "Frank Soper's had money stolen . . . Emily Van Doran, Joan Sellers and Maggie Agnew have jewellery missing! My God, I'll have the bastard garrotted!" She snatched up the receiver.

Elizabeth cut in, hesitantly, "Mother . . . just a moment . . . who are you calling?"

Belle shot an astonished glance at her. "Security, of course! I'm going to have them all searched!"

Elizabeth made an arresting motion with her hand, frowning pensively. "Just . . . hold on for a second. I wonder . . ."

"What?" barked Belle.

Elizabeth gave a small, reluctant sigh. "Look . . . it may be nothing, but I think it's worth mentioning now, it might save a lot of unnecessary embarrassment. A few days ago . . . the day you were in Coral Gables . . . I was down at the pool but came back into the house to get a book from my room . . . and as I passed your bedroom door I heard a sound and popped my head in to see who it was. I . . . found Ana at your wall-safe. She'd taken the painting down and . . . well, quite frankly, she seemed extremely interested in the safe . . ."

Belle gaped. "Why in God's name didn't you tell me?"

Elizabeth shrugged. "Well, I didn't want to throw unjust suspicion on her. I mean, she *may* have just been dusting the painting, though it did seem strange that she'd moved the painting on to your desk . . . and now that this awful thing has happened, I do remember her shocked expression when she turned and saw me standing there. I put it down to natural surprise at the time . . . you know, her thinking I was still down at the pool . . . but now . . . well, it *could* have been guilt, I suppose." She sighed again, torn between fairness and painful duty, her eyes straying into the tent to the distant figure of Ana Patillas, who was clearing dishes. "Mother . . . I think before we embarass all the servants, we ought to check her room, don't you?"

Following the direction of her gaze, Belle nodded stiffly. "Yes, I certainly do."

"You keep an eye on her, I'll take a look."

Elizabeth quickly left the room, returning a few minutes later, her face blank with horror as she approached her mother, opening her hand to reveal Emily Van Doran's scarab brooch. "It was in a shoe box at the bottom of her clothes closet. There's a compact and a lighter there, too—and a hundred-dollar bill."

Belle shut her eyes, snatched up the phone and stabbed out a number. "Carl! This is Mrs Little. We have a thief in the house—one of the servants. Call the police immediately, then come here, I want you as a witness when we search her room."

Slamming down the receiver, Belle strode to the french windows and shouted, "Ana!"

Ana looked up, startled, put down a pile of dishes and came forward, bewildered by her mistress's obvious anger. "Yes, señora?"

Belle pointed to an upright chair. "Sit down there."

Ana hesitated, glanced at Elizabeth and back to Belle. "Señora . . . is anything wrong?"

"Sit down there and shut up!"

Filled with rage, unable to share the same room with the creature who had caused her so much anguish by disgracing her before her friends, Belle turned and stormed out to the hall to await the arrival of her chief security officer.

10

Carl Krantz severed the connection after Belle Little's phone call, murmured with a deep-throated chuckle, "Well, now . . . looks as though things are gettin' interestin' around here at last," and prodded out a number.

His partner, Rudy Belgar, judging Krantz's comment worthy of his attention—a rare event—interrupted his reading and raised weary, heavily-pouched eyes to the red-haired giant. "Hmm?"

Krantz waved him wait. "This is Carl Krantz—chief security officer of Little Park. I've apprehended a thief at the Little house, number fifteen. Get a squad car here pronto. I'll be up at the house. See my partner in the security booth, he'll tell you where—OK?"

Belgar, a heavy, balding man of middle age and gentle mien, waited with a quizzical expression for Krantz to finish.

Krantz replaced the receiver and turned to him with a twisted grimace, the closest he could get to a smile, and clapped his huge hands together with a deafening report. "It's fun time! Belle Little's caught her a thief!"

"Who?"

"Dunno . . . one of the servants . . . a female." The lips curled into a malevolent smirk. "Pity I didn't catch her myself . . . could have bin interesting."

Belgar's eyes softened with a sardonic smile. "Could have sworn you just told the cops you did catch her."

"Fuck off, Belgar."

Krantz removed a brown peaked cap from a corner stand and quickly left the booth, ducking his head to clear the doorframe and slamming the door behind him.

Belgar winced and drew a heavy sigh, wondering how he

could continue to share the death watch shift with a man he despised so much, even for the extra money.

Belgar knew all there was to know about Krantz, had made a point of finding out about him; he had an enquiring mind.

Krantz fascinated him. At their first encounter—in the very first moment of that meeting—Belgar had detected in the huge, raw-boned man an emanation of intrinsic evil that was at once hypnotic and frightening.

After their first night of duty together, unable to draw Krantz into even a semblance of serious conversation, Belgar had amused himself with a project of discreet investigation. From a friend in Four Square records, from guards who had shared shifts with Krantz and, gradually, from Krantz himself, he had compiled a mental dossier to support his initial opinion that Carl Krantz was a natural-born, thorough-going, perverted, homicidal psycho.

Born in Iowa of German farming stock and poorly educated, Krantz had hit the road at sixteen, taking any job that turned a buck, the rougher the better. Circus boxer, rodeo rider, oil rigger, Las Vegas casino bouncer—he'd wound up on the Los Angeles police force. He was dismissed for excessive brutality while apprehending a young Chinese boy, a store-breaker with no previous record, whose neck he had broken, condemning the kid to a life of wheelchair paralysis.

Removed from the protection of his uniform and fearing reprisal from the Chinese community, Krantz had moved to Miami and joined Four Square as a guard.

In the booth of Little Park, his size and brutal appearance had caught the attention of Belle Little. A private interview followed, resulting in Krantz's promotion to chief security officer, with substantially extra money, on the understanding that he would always be on duty during the most vulnerable hours of ten at night to six in the morning.

Krantz had responded to this special attention with a swagger that added further burden to the crudeness and ignorance imposed upon any death watch partner.

Rudy Belgar, a studious man, himself an ex-policeman from the Miami force who had served most of his term in Juvenile

Division, found Krantz's personality unnerving, his habits and predilections sickening.

Violence radiated from the man, shone with manic brilliance in the pale blue, almost colourless eyes that lay deeply in the sun-pink, pock-marked skull of a face. What shocking acts of cruelty he had perpetrated during his roustabout years Belgar could only guess at, though a fair indication had been offered by Krantz in lurid yarns about his term with LAPD's vice squad, an environment of unqualified sordidness in which Krantz had obviously been as happy as the proverbial pig in filth.

But even without this evidence, Krantz's mentality—in Belgar's opinion—was adequately reflected in his reading habits. His desk drawer was filled with pornographic magazines, hard stuff, in true-life colour and glorious close-up.

So OK, Belgar conceded, there was room in every man's life for the occasional elbow nudge, man-to-man wink and dirty chuckle; but these illustrations constituted Krantz's *only* reading matter, ever. The man's mind was a sewer.

Belgar's thoughts and sympathy went out to the female thief whom Belle Little had caught. Whatever she was guilty of, she didn't deserve what was about to happen to her. One situation he would not wish his worst enemy was to be trapped between Belle Little and Carl Krantz.

With a shake of his head he returned to his Ira Levin novel. The kid, whoever she was, was in for a very rough time.

From her position in the drawing-room, the bewildered Ana could see her mistress pacing back and forth across the hall, twisting a green tulle kerchief in furious hands. Suddenly Belle changed direction, moved to open the front door though no chimes had sounded and admitted the awesome figure of Carl Krantz.

There was a brief consultation, during which Krantz glanced into the drawing-room at Ana, the ice-blue opalescence of his eyes filling her with dread.

What was happening to her? What terrible thing was happening now? Some kind of disaster had occurred, but how could it possibly concern her?

Belle Little and the guard moved across the hall, out of her sight. She glanced at Elizabeth, who was standing near as though guarding her, her heart erupting with new anguish as she encountered the girl's piercing, triumphant smile.

"What has happened?" Ana begged.

Elizabeth's smile became a mocking grin. "As if you didn't know. Well, I did warn you what would happen if you were caught stealing. You've had it."

Ana gaped. "Stealing!"

"Oh, come off it," scoffed Elizabeth. "The stuff's right there in your room! Pretty stupid to hide it in your closet, wasn't it? It's the first place anyone would look."

Ana stared incredulously, sensing rather than understanding the charge. "Stuff? What ...?"

Elizabeth sighed indignantly. "Oh, come *on* ... the jewellery! ... the things you stole from my mother's guests! The things I've just seen hidden in your room! The brooch and the lighter and the compact ... and the hundred-dollar bill!"

Ana mouthed unintelligibly, dumbstricken. This wasn't happening to her ... it was a dream ... a nightmare. She'd gone mad! What was she doing in this house, this evil house? She had to get away! Her children ... she had to get home to them. They needed her. Why had she abandoned them? She ought to be with them in the barrio ... among her friends ...

She got to her feet, took a faltering step, like a blind woman.

Elizabeth moved in front of her. "Sit down!"

Ana shook her head. "No ..."

"I said sit ... down!"

Elizabeth reached out to grab Ana's arms. Seized by panic, Ana lashed out, the blow sending Elizabeth toppling over the chair, screaming shrilly as she went down.

Ana ran from the room into the hall, pulled open the door and ran out across the verandah and down the steps. Approaching headlights flared to high beam, blinding her. Now Elizabeth burst through the door, her shouted warning echoing out over the Park.

"Stop that woman! STOP HER!"

Car doors slammed and bulky silhouettes came at her against

the lights, seizing her arms and urging her back towards the steps.

"OK, lady, take it easy . . . let's go back inside and sort this out."

During the brief investigation, Ana sat huddled in the chair, hands welded together in her lap, her eyes fixed on the floor, her mind occupied with the vision of her children—and beyond that incapable of thought.

Later, as they led her from the drawing-room into the hall, she was vaguely aware of Luisa's tormented face, her hysterical protest, but that was soon gone, and her next awareness was of riding in the rear seat of an automobile and of its soothing, lurching rhythm.

They were taking her home . . . to her children. She would never leave them again. They needed her. And how she needed them!

Belle Little closed the front door on the departing police and Carl Krantz, and hurriedly entered the drawing-room to make a phone call, her fury now damped-down to a seething simmer.

"Who are you calling?" asked Elizabeth.

"Andy Hamlin. This is going to be done properly."

The phone purred several times before the precise, resonant voice of Andrew Hamlin answered. A Superior Court judge, a Park neighbour and close friend, Hamlin had been one of the first guests to leave the party and was unaware of the thefts.

"Andy . . . Belle. I hope I haven't woken you."

"No, no. Belle, what's the matter, you sound . . ."

"Andy, since you left, the most shocking thing has happened. Four of my guests had things stolen . . . jewellery and money. But we've caught the thief. It was my new maid, the Mexican woman, Ana Patillas. We caught her red-handed, found the things in her room."

"Belle, how terrible . . ."

"Worse than terrible—one of the victims was Emily Van Doran."

Hamlin groaned.

Belle continued, her anger rising now. "I got Krantz up here to witness that the things were hidden in her closet—and I called the police. They've taken her to Miami Beach. Andy . . . I want her severely punished. You know what we agreed should anything like this happen in the Park. Well, this is the first time it has happened and it has got to be the last. Not only my servants but all our servants will be watching to see if our threats of prosecution hold good. We simply cannot afford a paltry fine or any suspended sentence rubbish. This woman has got to be put away! It's in all our interests. Can I leave you to handle it?"

"Of course, Belle, of course."

"Thank you, Andy, I appreciate it."

In the living-room of their quarters, Fidel Cesar attempted to console his grief-stricken wife. Constanza was also present.

"She's innocent!" Luisa sobbed hysterically. "Ana would never *do* such a thing!"

"Of course she's innocent!" seethed Constanza. "We all know who put those things in her closet—Elizabeth! That little bitch has been plotting this since Ana caught her stealing money from her mother's safe. Oh *God*, what a tragedy. What can we do?!"

Luisa's eyes flashed furiously. "We can tell Señora Little what we know, that's what we can do! I'll tell her what happened between Ana and Elizabeth . . . make her see Elizabeth has done this for revenge."

Constanza laughed scoffingly. "And she'll believe you? She'll take your word against her precious daughter's? Luisa . . . this could be dangerous for you, you could both lose your jobs."

Luisa frowned with surprise. "You think that matters? Do you suppose Fidel and I can go on working here now, with Ana in jail?"

Constanza shook her head contritely. "I'm sorry, I'm not thinking clearly. I'm just so . . . furious! Oh, that poor woman . . . after all she's been through . . ." She dissolved into tears of anger and frustration. "Juanita was right . . . that child *should* have drowned in the pool. Now even I could do it."

Luisa stood up, wiped away her tears and straightened her shoulders resolutely. "We're not beaten yet. Come on, Fidel, we're going to see her right now."

Belle Little turned at the peremptory knock, frowning with irritation as the drawing-room door opened and Fidel and Luisa entered unbidden.

"Yes—what is it?" she snapped, suspecting from their expressions that they had come to plead.

Luisa's jaw set defiantly, her eyes settling accusingly on Elizabeth before finally transferring to her employer. "Señora . . . there is something I have to say. My sister did not *do* this terrible thing. She is not a thief. She is an honest, hard-working woman . . ."

Belle sighed impatiently. "Yes, Luisa, no doubt you feel obliged to defend her, but . . ."

"I do not defend her out of obligation!" retorted Luisa, her unexpected vehemence shocking Belle. "It is the truth!"

"The truth as you choose to see it!" Belle retaliated, incensed by her cook's disrespect. "But your loyalty obviously blinds you to the fact that the stolen articles were found in your sister's closet! How do you explain that away?"

"Easily, señora . . . Ana didn't put them there."

Belle snorted. "Then who did?"

Luisa glared at Elizabeth. "She did."

Elizabeth's jaw dropped. "Mother!"

Belle gasped at Luisa. "How *dare* you?"

"Your own daughter did it!" shouted Luisa, hysterical now. "For revenge! Ana found Elizabeth stealing money from your safe and Elizabeth threatened to . . ."

Elizabeth seized Belle's arm, imploringly. "Mother, don't listen to her! It's all lies! Make her stop . . .!"

"It's the truth!" cried Luisa. "Elizabeth did it, don't you see . . . don't you *see*? She did it for revenge!"

"Lies, lies, lies!" screamed Elizabeth. "Mother, how can you listen to this—from the sister of a *thief*?"

Belle, white and shaking, nodded furiously at Luisa. "I can understand you trying to defend your sister . . . but I *deplore* this attempt to implicate Elizabeth."

"But it's the *truth*!" shouted Luisa.

"Luisa, stop it!"

"No, I will not stop! You must listen to the truth! You must get Ana out of jail right now . . ."

Belle flared. "*Don't* you tell me what I must do! Who in *hell* d'you think you are? Get out of this room . . . go on, get out!"

Luisa collapsed against Fidel, racked with sobs, crying hysterically.

Fidel turned to look at Belle, beseeching her, "Señora, *please* . . . search your heart for the truth. You know Ana is a good woman . . . you *know* she would not steal from your guests."

"I know nothing of the kind! I know nothing about her! Now *go*! Get out of my sight!"

Fidel nodded, his expression stone. "We *will* go . . . for good . . . tomorrow morning."

He led his sobbing wife from the room.

Belle swung away with a muttered curse.

"Mother?" Elizabeth's little-girl voice pursued her.

"What?"

"There . . . could be repercussions from this, you know. Those two could make trouble for us."

Belle turned, frowning, preoccupied. "Hmm? What trouble could they possibly cause—apart from having to find another cook and gardener this close to Christmas?"

"They could spread the story that it *was* I who put those things in Ana's room. You know how partisan these Mexicans are—and how they gossip. They could do it, you know. Their reputation is at stake. This is going to reflect on every Mexican servant in the Park. What better way of defending themselves than spreading the story that I did it out of revenge?"

Belle tutted irritably. "Oh, for heaven's sake, Elizabeth, who'd believe such a thing?"

"I know a lot of people who would *like* to believe it,"

Elizabeth insisted. "Mother ... mud *sticks*. People love to believe the worst—particularly about the Littles, you know that."

Despite her preoccupation with the problem of finding new staff, Belle showed signs of interest. She asked sardonically, "Well, what do you propose we do about them—cut their tongues out?"

"Get them out of our lives," Elizabeth answered readily. "I mean all three of them—including Ana."

Belle frowned. "Those two *are* getting out, you heard Fidel, they're leaving tomorrow. Ana's already out."

"I mean ... permanently."

Belle grimaced with growing irritation. "What d'you mean—permanently? Are you suggesting we have them dropped in the bay on a dark night?"

Elizabeth did not smile. "No, Mother ... I mean have them deported ... sent back to Mexico as undesirable aliens. They *are* undesirable, aren't they?"

Belle looked closely at her daughter. "You're really worried about this, aren't you?"

"Yes, I am. Mexicans are so damned 'family'—you hurt one, you hurt them all. They're as bad as the Mafia."

Belle winced. "Surely you're not suggesting there could be any ... physical reprisal?"

Elizabeth shrugged. "I'd rather not give them the chance to think about it. Turn Fidel and Luisa loose in the barrio, give them time to stir up resentment, and who knows what might happen? There must be fifty people from the barrio working in the Park, mother."

Belle pursed her lips pensively. "Deportation would be a drastic step ..."

"Precisely. Think how effective it would be in keeping all the other servants in line. It's the ultimate deterrent, isn't it?"

Belle nodded thoughtfully. "You may have something ... I'll speak to Andy Hamlin tomorrow."

Elizabeth smiled, moved across and kissed her mother on the cheek. "Goodnight, Mother ... sleep well."

"Goodnight, Elizabeth."

As Belle watched her daughter leave the room, a smile of pride touched her lips. Elizabeth had responded magnificently to her training . . . was all that she had hoped for. She was going to be one hell of a queen.

11

Shortly after sunrise Fidel and Luisa loaded their few possessions into the van, said goodbye to a heart-broken Constanza, and drove away from the house.

As they slowly circuited the Park, Luisa sighed despondently and shook her head. "A beautiful ... ugly ... place."

Fidel nodded. "The place *is* beautiful. It's the people who are ugly."

Luisa looked at him imploringly. "Fidel, how are we going to tell the children? What are we going to do?"

He shook his head. "God alone knows. We'll have a conference. Jose is a good man in difficult situations, I'm sure he'll come up with something. I feel numb at the moment, I can't think straight. It's unbelievable ... I just don't believe it has happened."

Luisa nodded, equally shocked.

When they reached the house they found that Jose had already left for work and the children were still asleep. Startled by the Cesars' unexpected appearance, Isabel broke down when she heard the news. Luisa made a pot of coffee, and they sat at the kitchen table to talk.

"It will be better to tell the children right away," advised Isabel. "There's no point in lying to them. Tomorrow is Christmas Eve and they'll expect their mother to be here. They'll have to know the truth sooner or later. We could wait until Jose comes home tonight, but ..."

Fidel shook his head. "No, I'll tell them as soon as they come down. The moment they see us they're bound to ask about Ana, and I don't want to lie to them now and have to break the truth to them tonight." He closed his eyes, overcome with pity. "Those poor kids ... what a terrible Christmas this is going to be for them."

Later, in the kitchen, Fidel haltingly broke the news of their mother's arrest to the children. The twins received his words in staring silence, as though unable to understand what he was telling them, or comprehend the seriousness of it.

Francisco, though, reacted violently, demanding, "We've got to get her out! We've got to do something! She can't stay in that jail . . . she . . . we've got to get her out!"

Fidel, wretched with helplessness, made a placatory gesture, touching the boy's arm. "Yes, Francisco, we will . . . we will."

"When? What can we do . . . right now . . . to get her out?"

Fidel shook his head sadly. "Francisco, it's not that easy. We need advice. It will have to be done . . . through proper channels."

Francisco snatched his arm away. "What are proper channels? What are you talking about?"

"Well . . . a lawyer . . ." Fidel felt panicked in the face of Francisco's hysteria. He wished Jose was there. Jose could calm the boy. He felt totally inadequate . . . lacking in authority. "Francisco, *please* try to understand these things take time. Your mother will have to be properly defended. We can't simply drive over to the Miami Beach police station and . . ."

Francisco swept from the table, implacable, rigid with anger. "And what good will a lawyer do? Señora Little can afford ten lawyers . . . *better* lawyers! How can we fight them? Is Elizabeth Little going to admit she put the jewellery in my mother's room? *Is* she?"

Fidel exchanged a worried, hopeless glance with Luisa and Isabel. "Francisco . . . we must leave that to a lawyer. There's nothing else we can do. There is no other way."

Francisco glared at Fidel with burning eyes, then abruptly turned and ran from the kitchen, up the stairs to his room.

The twins followed him and found him lying on his bed, staring angrily at the ceiling. As they'd done so often before in moments of danger or trouble, they sat close to him, drawing comfort from his presence. Always their strong dependable big brother, he seemed suddenly to have become even stronger, more resolute, a man. His anger frightened yet excited them, made them feel protected. With this new maturity there was nothing, they felt, that he could not accomplish or overcome.

"We can't wait for Fidel's 'proper channels,'" he proclaimed brusquely, as though addressing himself rather than them. "Proper channels could take weeks—maybe months! And in the meantime our mother is locked up in that stinking jail! We've got to try something else."

They nodded, exchanged hopeful glances and waited with pounding hearts for him to continue.

"We must go to see Señora Little," he announced decisively. "We must present ourselves at her house and plead with her to have Momma released. She is a mother herself. It's Christmas. Surely she must take pity on three children who need their momma . . ." his eyes flooded with tears, ". . . at Christmas time."

The twins nodded agreement.

"When shall we go?" Carlo asked staunchly, attempting to copy his brother's incisiveness.

"This afternoon. I have a little money, we'll take a bus. But say nothing to the adults, they're bound to stop us. We'll say we're going for a walk."

Francisco clearly saw how it would be. Although he hadn't actually seen Little Park, his mother had told them so much about the island and its beautiful homes. She had described the structure of the Park and the position of Señora Little's house in it, and in his mind's eye he saw the three of them entering the estate, crossing it and climbing the steps to her front door.

Señora Little would answer their knock. An aristocratic but benign woman, she would greet them with a smile, invite them in, maybe even give them a soda or cookies while she listened attentively—perhaps even tearfully—to what he had to say. He would tell her how wonderful their mother was, about her unhappy life and how desperately they needed her. And when he had finished, Señora Little would make a telephone call to the jail and their momma would be returned to them—perhaps that very afternoon.

90

The security booth shocked him. His mother had made no mention of it.

Ed Sloan, the senior guard on afternoon shift, saw them approaching from the causeway and with a sigh got up from his chair. "Rubber necks" on foot were far from rare. Little Park was an easy two-mile stroll from the city, and a dozen times a day pedestrians would pause and gawp at the houses, though mostly—dissuaded by the security booth and the barrier—they wouldn't venture any closer than the mouth of the service road. Then again, most rubber necks were adults, not kids, and had more sense.

Opening the booth door, Sloan stepped out and stood behind the barrier, eying the three children. Mex or Cuban, plain as day. Damned pretty girl ... only twelve or so, but already budding beautifully. He smiled to himself. When they were good they were really somethin'.

His eyes went to the older boy ... fourteen, fifteen, maybe. Tall for a Mex, and well-made. Handsome kid. Maybe he wanted work.

As they approached, Francisco offered a respectful smile and looked appropriately nervous. Ed Sloan relaxed. No trouble here.

He said easily, "Yeh, what can I do f'you guys?"

Unnerved by the presence of uniformed guards, Francisco answered falteringly, "Please ... we would like to speak to Señora Little."

Sloan grinned. "Would you now?"

"Yes. May we pass through, please?"

Sloan laughed. "No, siree, you may not."

Francisco's eyes hardened. "Why not?"

Sloan saw the challenge and bristled. "Because I damn-well say so."

Francisco swallowed, licked his lips. "Please ... it is most important ..."

"Use a phone."

"No. That won't do. We must speak to Señora Little to her face."

"What about?"

Francisco hesitated and lowered his eyes. "I cannot tell you ... it's very personal."

Sloan nodded knowingly. "Money, huh? Well, kid, I'll give you ten outta ten for gall ... now shove off."

Francisco's eyes blazed. "No! It's not money! It's very important ..."

Sloan's mouth tightened. "Now what in *hell* would the likes of you have to say to Mrs Little that could be important? Now, come on—shove off."

"No, please ..."

"Kid!" Sloan flung out his arm. "If you're not on that causeway in ten seconds, I'm callin' the cops ... be*lieve* me! Now—fuck-the-hell off!"

Carlo plucked urgently at his brother's sleeve. "Francisco, come on —"

Francisco capitulated. Despondently they trudged back to the causeway and turned towards the city. Here, out of sight of the booth which was hidden by trees, Francisco halted, leaned on the bridge rail and looked out across the bay. For a long while they were silent, the twins waiting for a decision from Francisco who was gazing with frowning intensity at the island.

From this vantage point they could see the rear gardens of several homes on the western side of the Park, their moored cabin cruisers, their swimming pools and tennis courts, and some of the houses themselves.

In the long garden of the second house two men and two women, dressed in whites, were playing tennis. The delayed *thock* of the struck ball reached the children faintly across the water. And in the fourth garden, a group of young people cavorted in the big swimming pool, while others lay around on sun-beds and played with a beach-ball on the lawn.

"*Bastados*," Francisco whispered, his eyes welling with tears. "Look at them, *niños*. What do such people care that our mother is in jail? They care more about their cats and dogs."

Racked by an aching emptiness, by helplessness, he put his arms around his brother and sister and drew them close, cursing beneath his breath.

92

"We'll never get to speak to Señora Little," Maria murmured miserably. "It's like a fortress."

"Perhaps we could wait until she comes out?" Carlo offered, adding lamely, "if we knew what she looked like."

A white cabin cruiser, a large boat with an enclosed bridge, suddenly appeared beneath them, the thrum of the powerful engines decreasing as it changed direction towards the island.

With interest, the children watched it enter the inlet wharf of the third house, its engines shutting down completely as it nudged up to the jetty. An elderly, grey-haired woman stepped ashore and secured the stern- and bow-lines to iron rings. Then an old man in whites climbed down from the bridge and joined the woman, slipping his arm through hers as they made their way across the lawn towards the house.

Francisco nodded, his expression no longer glum. "There is a way of getting to see Señora Little, *muchachos* . . . that way, by boat." He looked at the children. "We could borrow Ernesto's rowboat . . . land at her wharf after dark. Who could stop us then?"

The twins beamed, agreeing excitedly.

Francisco nibbled his lip, then gave a decisive nod. "All right, we'll do it . . . tonight!"

12

The extent of Francisco's naïvety was evident in his assumption that Belle Little's front door was reachable by means of a direct approach across an undefended lawn.

In the designing of the estate, a major concern had been security from all directions. Where there was free access to water, there was also free access from it, so to complement the guarded booth protecting the front of the houses, a system of electronic beams criss-crossed each rear lawn in an individual, irregular pattern. Any interruption of the beam set off alarm bells both in the house and in the security booth. A flashing red light on a numbered board in the booth indicated which home was endangered.

Because of noise and nuisance, no outdoor guard dogs were permitted in the Park—though many of the residents kept less vociferous pets inside their homes. The only exception was a guard dog—invariably a German Shepherd—supplied by Four Square Security and housed in a compound behind the security booth.

If an alarm was raised, a well-rehearsed defence measure went into operation. The senior guard on duty, accompanied by the dog, made for the house in question, either on foot, if close-by, or in the company station wagon.

The animals were changed at periodic intervals in order to maintain their peak efficiency, and currently the dog on duty was a German Shepherd named Khan, an animal whose particular viciousness had endeared it to none of the security guards but Carl Krantz. To Krantz, Khan was an all-time favourite, a dog whose power and lethal ferocity he'd long been impatient to put to the test.

Recently, Krantz had returned from feeding the animal to

complain to Rudy Belfar, "What a waste—keepin' a dog like that cooped up in a fuckin' pen. You know the trouble with this place, Belgar—there ain't enough crime. We oughta relax the system a bit, invite a few villains in. Man, I sure would like to see that Khan in action."

"You were born a few years late, Krantz," Belgar had murmured. "You'd have had a ball in ancient Rome."

Krantz had bared his teeth in a grin.

It was after ten when Francisco finally oar-steered the shallow rowing boat into the inlet of the Little grounds.

The crossing had been a harrowing experience for the children. The night was dark, the moon obscured by heavy cloud and the wind cold and strong—force five off the Atlantic Ocean. The boat, comfortingly large when they'd boarded it in the city basin, had appeared to diminish alarmingly as they'd nosed out into the choppy black waters of the bay, and for more than an hour they had been pitched and tossed mercilessly as Francisco had battled to make headway against wind and waves.

Now, exhausted, he clambered up on to the quay, secured the fore and aft ropes to iron rings, helped the twins out of the boat and then slumped to his knees, breathing laboriously, his thin denim jacket and jeans saturated with spray.

The twins, similarly dressed and almost as wet, stood and shivered while he regained his breath.

"Are you all right?" Maria asked anxiously, frightened by the crossing.

He nodded and panted, "Yes . . . it'll be easier going back . . . the wind will be behind us."

After a few moments he got to his feet and faced the house, a distant silhouette in which a few lights showed faintly behind closed curtains. Suddenly he was afraid. The prospect of crossing the long, dark garden appalled him. He sensed the eyes of the twins on him, waiting, hopeful and dependent upon him. Drawing a deep breath to calm his thudding heart, he gathered himself determinedly and smiled encouragingly at his brother and sister.

"Don't be afraid. Here, give me your hands."

Outwardly resolute, inwardly quaking, they set off across the expanse of lawn.

Belle Little was seated at a desk in the library writing a letter when the door from the hall suddenly burst open and a frenzied Constanza entered. "Señora! The alarm bell is ringing!"

Through the open door Belle could now hear the distant clamour from the kitchen. "Which alarm? Burglar alarm? Garden alarm?"

"The garden, señora!"

Belle came to her feet, and strode into the hall, snapping over her shoulder, "Stop shaking, woman, security will deal with it. Quickly—make sure all downstairs doors and windows are locked!"

Simultaneously, Carl Krantz slapped his sex magazine shut and shot to his feet, eyeing the flashing indicator board. "Shee-it! We got a live one! Shut that goddam bell off, Belgar."

Grabbing his cap and a dog leash from the peg, Krantz slammed out of the booth, ran to the pound and wrestled the key in the lock. The sound of his approach brought the dog hurtling from the brick-built kennel to leap excitedly at the wire gate, whining and yelping, sensing action.

"Yeh, we got one," panted Krantz. "Get back, you bastard, let me open the fucking gate!"

Krantz barely managed to clip the lead on to its collar before the dog was away, hauling him towards the car park. He yipped with laughter at the dog's desperation.

"Stay! *Stay*, you bastard, we've got him ... we've got him!"

As Krantz opened the rear door of the station wagon, the dog leapt inside and stood quivering and whining, globules of saliva dripping from its jaws. Krantz started the engine and shot out of the car park with squealing tyres.

"Yeh, me too, baby," he chuckled at the yelping dog. "We're gonna have us some fun!"

The children stood at the bottom of the steps and gaped up at the house, overwhelmed by its size and splendour. From the security barrier it had looked impressive enough, but this close its hugeness and opulence staggered them.

Francisco, old enough to reason such things, was suddenly overawed and frightened by the wealth and the social stature of the woman who owned such a palatial house, and by their own temerity. He felt cold and puny and irresolute, and began to shiver. He could no longer think clearly.. . . his mind was a blur. All the brave words he had rehearsed were gone, obliterated by fear. He wanted to turn and run, and race back across the lawn to the boat.

The twins were staring at him. He looked down into their frightened, expectant faces and despised himself—for getting them into this situation, for even thinking of letting them down and letting his mother down!

He looked up again at the forbidding front door. You are here—so do it! he chided himself.

Squeezing the twins' hands, he started up the steps.

The tall white double doors loomed before him. His heart thundering, he reached out and pressed the bell button.

Almost immediately one half of the double doors opened a few inches, restrained by a safety chain, and a woman's face appeared in the opening. *"Madre de Dios!"*

The door was closed, then instantly swung fully open to reveal a maid in uniform. Behind her, on the distant staircase, a young girl paused, her head angled enquiringly. And at that moment a stern-faced woman appeared through an archway, startled by the open door, and demanding, "Constanza! What are you doing? Who is it?"

The maid stepped back, bewildered, indicating the children. "Señora!"

The señora ... Señora Little!

Panic propelled Francisco into the hall, his eyes wild and pleading, the forgotten words tumbling from his lips in a desperate torrent. "Señora Little! I am Francisco Patillas! I have come to speak to you about my mother who is *innocent* ... she could not have done such a thing ... my brother and sister

. . . we have come to beg you . . . please listen to what we have to say . . ."

"My GOD!" Belle strode towards them, ashen with rage, her arm flung out. "Get out of my house! GET OUT!"

Terrified, the twins turned and ran out on to the verandah. Francisco also retreated but continued his pleading, his voice rising shrilly against the onslaught of Belle's shouting.

"Señora, *please* listen to me! My mother is *innocent*!"

Headlights swept the verandah. A car squealed to a halt at the foot of the steps. Doors banged. Maria cried out in terror. Francisco whirled, then froze at the sight of the security guard and the huge dog coming up the steps.

Krantz halted, jerked the slavering, whining dog to his side on a short lead.

Belle Little appeared in the doorway, hysterical with anger. "They've broken in! They're Ana Patillas's children! Get rid of them . . . get rid of them!"

Krantz grinned. "Yes, ma'am."

Belle turned and disappeared into the house. Constanza moved to the open doorway, fretful with indecision.

Krantz strode up to the verandah, grabbed the lapel of Francisco's jacket and spun him around, then kicked the boy, sending him tottering down the steps to sprawl in the driveway.

Constanza cried out, "No!"

Elizabeth slammed the door shut, then the verandah lights went out, plunging the area into near darkness.

Krantz followed Francisco down the steps. "OK—how'd you punks get in here . . . by boat?"

As he scrambled to his feet, Francisco answered with a sullen nod, which Krantz chose not to see. He threw a hard, flat-handed slap at Francisco's head, knocking the boy down. "Answer me, you bastard!"

Maria screamed, and Carlo yelled, "Leave him alone!"

The dog, triggered by the anger and violence, made a yelping lunge for the sprawled Francisco but was jerked back by Krantz with only a few inches to spare.

He grinned down at the terrorised boy. "Shall I let him go,

punk ... huh? Shall I give him six inches more lead? What d'you reckon those teeth would do to you, huh? Be interestin' to find out, wouldn't it? I'm gonna let him go on three. One ... two ..."

Maria screamed again, clutched her head, demented with terror, screeched, "No! No! Leave him alone ... please, don't do it!"

Krantz whispered hoarsely, "You hear that, boy? Your little sister's sayin' pretty please. You say it."

Francisco's lips quivered.

"I didn't hear that, boy, you'd better speak up."

"P-please," whimpered Francisco.

"Didn't hear that, neither. Did you hear that, Khan? No, he didn't. You'd better speak up, kid, before my arm gets tired."

"Please!"

"Still can't hear yuh. Say it louder!"

"*Please!*"

"Louder still!"

"PLEASE!"

"PRETTY PLEASE!" yelled Krantz.

Carlo cried out, "Mister, leave him alone!"

Krantz cracked him across the head. "Shut your mouth or you'll be down there too. You, say pretty please!"

Choking with anger, tears of impotence streaming down his cheeks, Francisco cried, "PRETTY PLEASE!"

Krantz chuckled. "Yuh hear that, Khan ... this chicken shit said pretty please. OK ... get on your feet an' get movin'—the way you came in."

The lawn stretched before them, dark and endless. Hardly had they begun to cross it when Krantz commanded, "Hey, you ... kid ... come back here."

The three children turned, but Krantz rapped, "Not you two fags ... you, girl, come here."

Francisco murmured, "Don't go," and crowded her protectively, urged her to keep moving.

"You hear me!" shouted Krantz. "You want Khan to bring you here?"

Krantz increased his stride, grabbed Maria by the arm and

pulled her away from Francisco. "You guys move on! An' keep facin' the front!"

He slowed his pace, drew Maria into his side, his hand on her shoulder, murmured gruffly. "What's your name, kid?"

"M-Maria." Her voice was a strangled whisper.

"How old are yuh?"

"Twelve."

"You guys keep facin' the front! You turn round once more I'm gonna let the dog loose, y'hear?"

Francisco walked backwards, shouted defiantly, "You leave her alone! You touch her and ..."

"KILL, BOY!"

The night echoed to Maria's scream as Krantz relaxed his arm and the dog leapt forward with an explosive yelp that in the next instant was choked off as Krantz jerked back on the lead. "Kid, you're askin' for it! Now face the goddamned front and don't look round again!"

Krantz returned his attention to Maria. "Twelve, huh. Boy, you chicks sure develop young south of the border." His hand slid from her shoulder to cup her breast.

Maria gasped and clutched at his huge hard hand, but Krantz squeezed her breast and hissed, "Make one sound and I let the dog go!"

Maria froze, rigid with fear.

"That's smart," panted Krantz, slipping his hand into the neck of her tee-shirt and grasping the small, firm breast. "Shit, that's beautiful ..." He teased the tiny nipple between finger and thumb, whispering breathlessly, "You ever give head, kid? You ever take a real man's prick in your mouth an' suck the love juice right outta him ...?"

With a tearing cry she shook his hand free and lunged forward to her brothers, pursued by Krantz's exploding laughter. "Hey, that's a real wild sister you guys got there! She just offered to blow me if I let you go!"

Francisco swept Maria into his arm, whispering frantically to her and Carlo, "Keep going ... only a few more yards to go!"

Close behind them, Krantz continued his baiting, "So you

three shitheads tried to break into Mrs Little's house, huh? Well, that's not surprisin'—considerin' your mother's a thief ..."

Francisco whirled. "Shut your dirty lying mouth!"

Krantz's face turned to stone, then, slowly, the twisted, evil grin came. "Hey, now, that's one helluva mouth you've got there, sonny ... an' didn't I tell you to keep facin' the front? Didn't I promise I'd loose the dog if you turned round once more?" He glanced down at the animal. "Looks t'me like he's just beggin' me to let you go, boy. You wanna go play with them? OK, go ahead ... KILL!"

Krantz tossed the lead away.

It took a split second for the dog to realise it was free, then with a delirious yelp it leaped forward, driving for them, instinctively selecting the weakest of its victims. Maria's piercing scream rang out as she went down under its hurtling weight. Then it was into her, straddling her, filling the night with savage snarls and bubbling growls as it ripped into the soft, yielding flesh of her face.

Frozen with horror and disbelief, the boys now came alive. Goaded by rage and terror, they threw themselves at the dog, Carlo wrenching at its collar as Francisco drove a full-blooded kick between its back legs. The animal screamed and whirled on Carlo, bit savagely at the calf of his leg, locked on and stayed with him as he crashed to the ground.

Fumbling a penknife from his pocket, Francisco fell on the dog and plunged the blade into its neck, struck bone, went for the throat, stabbed again and again. Blood spurting now, flooding from a massive hole, the jaws slackening. But still he struck, screaming insanely with each blow ... the dog's head drooping, all but severed from the body.

Krantz loomed above Francisco, smashed the knife from his hand and sent the boy hurtling sideways with a vicious blow to the head.

"Yuh killed my dog ..." He lashed a kick into the boy's back. "YUH KILLED MY FUCKIN' DOG!" Again his boot thudded into Francisco's body.

Now Carlo was on his knees, crawling for the knife. Grabbing it up, he rose up behind Krantz and drove the blade into the guard's side.

Krantz cried out, staggered a step and dropped to his knees, his fingers reaching to pluck the handle from his body.

From out of the night came Francisco, swaying before him, staring wildly. With a yell he drew back his foot and kicked Krantz mercilessly under the jaw, laying him cold.

With a whimpering cry Francisco dropped to his knees beside his sister, who lay in shock, staring up at the night sky, her hand pressed to her left cheek, the blood oozing between her fingers. Francisco held her and rocked with grief, whispering, "My God . . . my God . . ."

Carlo limped over to him, bent over, his hands clasped around his savaged leg. "Francisco, we must get to a doctor, we must get to the boat."

Francisco, dazed, battered by shock, shook his head. "No, it will take too long. We will use this . . . *pig's* . . . station wagon."

"Can you drive it?" Carlo asked with wonderment.

"I . . . have watched Fidel and Jose drive," Francisco answered uncertainly. "I must try."

"We must be quick . . . Maria is bleeding badly."

Francisco looked down at his sister and moved quickly, suddenly conscious of the appalling reality of her injuries. Laying her down, he took off his jacket, then his tee-shirt, which he ripped in two. He made a pad, saying to Maria, "Hold this against your face, it will help stop the bleeding."

The other half he tore into strips and bound around Carlo's leg.

As he helped Maria to her feet, Francisco glanced at the unconscious Krantz.

"I . . . think we killed him," Carlo whispered fearfully. "What are we going to do?"

Francisco shook his head. "I don't know. We must get home . . . Fidel and Jose will know what to do."

With his arm around Maria, he started back across the lawn. Carlo hobbled alongside, holding his leg.

When they reached the front of the house, Francisco hesitated. He was tempted to ring the bell and ask for help, but quickly abandoned the idea and opened the car door. Climbing in, he stared in bewilderment at the controls, turned the ignition key and gave a start as the engine roared.

"*Can* you drive it?" Carlo asked in an awed whisper.

Francisco nodded, worked the automatic gear shift into "drive" and grabbed the wheel as the vehicle lurched forward against the handbrake. Releasing it, he gently accelerated, moving the car round the bend in the road. Within a hundred yards he had control.

Carlo suddenly pointed. "The barrier! How do we get through?"

Francisco bit his lip. He pressed the horn, giving three imperative blasts, then triggered the headlights on to high and low beam.

The door of the booth opened and Ruby Belgar looked out, wincing against the blinding headlights.

The horn blared again.

Belgar ducked back in and worked the barrier control while his back was turned, the station wagon slid past the booth and disappeared on to the causeway to the right.

13

It was after two a.m. before the Cesars and the Leandroses finally sat down at the kitchen table to discuss this latest development in an altogether horrifying situation.

The Leandros family physician and personal friend, Doctor Paul Santino, a Cuban exile, had just left the house. He had spent more than three hours skilfully stitching Maria's cheek and the calf of Carlo's leg, then administered protective shots to the twins and anti-shock sedatives to all three children, who were now asleep.

"Thank God for such a friend," Jose said gravely. "I know of no other doctor who would so readily ignore what should be done in favour of what must be done. We're very fortunate to know such a man." He was referring to Santino's understanding of the legal danger of admitting the children to hospital.

The others murmured agreement.

Fidel gave a troubled sigh and shook his head. "My God, What is happening to us all? How can a pleasant life turn into such a dreadful nightmare in so short a time? In war I can understand it happening . . . bombs fall, enemy troops invade, the rhythm of life is destroyed. But here, in Miami, in the United States of America, in peacetime . . . how can this happen? To Ana, of all people—a woman who has never done anyone harm in her life, who came here to escape the misery of Mexico. Now she is in jail for something she didn't do." He pointed aloft, his voice rising with anger, breaking with emotion. "Her three children—molested by a brutal guard, *mutilated* because they rang someone's doorbell! And now Carlo, an innocent twelve-year-old boy, is a murderer! Two brothers in the same family murderers! How in God's name can it happen?"

In tears, Luisa reached out to take her husband's hand.

Fidel continued in a determined whisper. "We have to get the children away, Jose. As soon as Krantz's death is reported, the police will come looking for them. They must not find them."

"How will they know where to look?" Isabel asked. "Señora Little didn't know until tonight that Ana had any children, so who will give the police this address?"

Fidel shrugged uncertainly. "Perhaps Ana herself, unwittingly. The police could easily extract the information from her. All they would have to say is, 'Let us have your children's address and they can come and visit you.' We must get them away immediately."

"Where to?" asked Luisa.

Jose answered readily. "To Los Angeles. To my cousins Sal and Magda Raventos. Fidel is right. As soon as the children awaken we must move them to another address in the barrio. In a few days' time, when Maria and Carlo are well enough to travel, I will drive them in the truck to Los Angeles. It will be safer by road. Sal and Magda will be only too pleased to . . ."

The ringing of the telephone at this late hour shocked them.

"My God," murmured Jose.

"The police?" whispered Isabel.

"Who else at two in the morning?" He got up from the table, his mind working feverishly. "I'll tell them we were just about to call them because the children haven't come home—it may give us a few hours. But get ready to wake the children." Clearing his throat nervously, he picked up the receiver. "Hello?"

A woman's voice, speaking softly, asked in Spanish, "Is that Jose Leandros?"

Jose frowned, gestured to the others to remain seated. "Who is this?"

"I am Constanza Nerōn, a friend of the Cesars. Luisa gave me your number to call. Is she there? It is very important."

Jose covered the mouthpiece, asked Luisa. "Do you know a Constanza Nerōn?"

105

Luisa gasped. "Yes! She is Señora Little's maid!" She hurried to take the phone. "Constanza!"

"Luisa! Oh, Luisa, the most *terrible* thing happened here tonight . . . I've only just been able to get to the phone. It was Ana's children . . . they were *here* . . ."

"Constanza, we know all about it. They are here with us."

"Oh, thank *God*! How are they? Are they very badly hurt?"

"Yes, Maria and Carlo . . . but a doctor has seen them. They're asleep now. They . . ."

"That *evil* man! He was actually boasting that he had repaid them for killing his dog . . ."

Luisa's senses blurred and a well of hysterical relief stirred her heart. "Man? What man?"

Constanza faltered. "Krantz, the guard who . . ."

Luisa gasped, "He's alive? You've seen him?"

"Why, yes! He hammered on the door . . . he was lying on the verandah . . ."

Luisa cried, "Oh, thank God, thank God!" She turned to the others, blinded by tears. "The guard is alive! Carlo didn't kill him!"

Constanza heard her. "Luisa, you thought Carlo . . . Oh, no, no! He's badly wounded but he's all right! We called an ambulance and the police, but . . ."

Luisa stiffened. "The police? They know about the children? Dear God . . ."

"No, no!" Constanza insisted. "They don't know about them! Krantz told them a lie, said he didn't know who his attackers were. Luisa, *listen* to me . . ." Her voice became hushed, desperate. "The children, and you and Fidel, are in terrible danger. You have to get away from Miami. I overheard Krantz and the Littles talking. He was in the hall—I'd gone to the kitchen to get some bandages—and when I returned I heard him talking to them. Luisa, the man is insane! He was begging the Littles to say nothing to the police . . . telling them that he would deal with the children in his own way. Then Elizabeth said to her mother, 'I told you there'd be trouble. We have to get them all deported! *All* of them—the Cesars as well. We'll have no peace of mind until they're all back over the border.'"

Luisa groaned. "Oh, my God . . ."

"And, Luisa, Señora Little agreed! She told Elizabeth she'd speak to Judge Hamlin today. Oh, Luisa, I'm so frightened for you! They can do it . . . they can do anything!"

"Yes, yes," Luisa whispered. "We will get the children away. Constanza, thank you : . ."

"Where will you go?"

"I . . ." Luisa shook her head, glanced at the others who were sitting tense and expectant, aware of disturbing news. "I think to Los Angeles . . . Jose has family there."

"I'll be able to contact you through Jose?"

"Yes, he'll know where we are."

"All right. I'll find out what the Littles are planning and let Jose know. Oh, Luisa, what a terrible tragedy . . ." Constanza's voice broke. "*Vaya con dios*, Luisa . . ."

"Bless you, Constanza . . ."

Stunned, Luisa replaced the receiver and returned to the table, barely able to speak. "Señora Little is going to have us all deported to Mexico . . . Ana, the children and us, Fidel."

Fidel gave a start, shot an appealing glance at Jose. "But . . . she can't do that! We've committed no crime! She . . ."

"Fidel," Jose interrupted solemnly. "You know better than that. You've worked for these people and know them. They can do anything they want to do."

Fidel nodded, his face set angrily. "All right—we go. Luisa and I will get the children away immediately. We'll put matresses in the back of the truck and . . ." he closed his eyes, torn by indecision. "But what about Ana? How can we leave with her in jail?"

Jose leaned forward and gripped his friend's wrist. "What can you do for her if you stay? We will hire an attorney, get her out on bail as quickly as we can. I know a good man—Juan Perrer. I'll call him later today. Fidel, you can't afford to worry about Ana now—your responsibility is to the children. We must protect them from the Littles and that maniac Krantz. Jesus *Christ*, I only hope he comes looking for them in the barrio. He won't get out alive, I promise you."

Jose drew a breath, settling his anger. "All right . . . we had better get started. We'll prepare the truck before we waken the children. Later on I'll phone Sal Raventos in LA and tell him you're on your way ..."

Luisa interrupted worriedly. "But will the children be well enough to travel? Los Angeles is such a long way."

Fidel shook his head at her. "Luisa, we have no choice. Those children have been through too much already. We *can't* risk them being caught. Can you imagine what would happen to Francisco if he's sent back to Matamoros?"

"Yes, of course, you're right. We must go right away."

Jose said sombrely. "I'm already worried about Francisco. He'll need watching, Fidel, he's desperate. Just think of what he undertook tonight to help his mother ... I tell you, *I* wouldn't cross the bay on such a night in a rowing boat. When he returned tonight there was a look in his eyes I didn't like at all ... such hatred. I tell you frankly, unless we get him away from here, away from the people who put his mother in jail and did these terrible things to Maria and Carlo ... well, he has killed once to protect his mother. I don't think he would hesitate to do it again."

14

At six o'clock Jose entered the boy's bedroom and put out his hand to rouse Francisco. But for a moment he hesitated, moved by pity as he looked down upon the sleeping boy. So young, so innocent. A good boy. A son to be proud of. Who in Heaven had ordained that so much torment and unhappiness should befall so kind and gentle a person, could turn him into God only knew what kind of vengeful monster?

Jose's thoughts went to Ramon Patillas, a man he'd never met but about whom he'd heard so much. Was it too much to ask that instead of a brute like him, Francisco should have had a decent, hard-working father, a man to love him as he should have been loved? Jose sighed at the injustices of life. What a waste, a tragic, senseless waste. The sins of the father . . .

He reached down and ruffled the tousled, luxuriant hair. Francisco murmured in sleep, groaned and tossed his head, the grimace of remembered terror distorting the sleep-smoothed serenity of his features as he awakened and blinked up at Jose. "Hmm?"

"Sssh." Jose smiled to calm him, sat down on the edge of the bed. "I have some good news. Are you awake enough to hear it?"

Francisco nodded, still bleary from the sedative.

Jose glanced across at Carlo, a sleeping mound beneath a floral quilt, and whispered to Francisco, "Last night we had a phone call from Constanza Nerōn, a good friend of Luisa's, Señora Little's maid . . ."

Francisco nodded. His mother had often spoken about Constanza.

"You know of her. Well, she gave us good news. The guard that Carlo stabbed is not dead, he's only wounded!"

Francisco scowled. "A pity."

Jose groaned. "Francisco, what are you saying? Would you prefer your little brother to be a murderer?"

Francisco lowered his eyes, contritely. "I'm sorry, I ..."

Jose patted the boy's hand. "I know, I know. You are filled with so much hatred you're not thinking clearly. There's a prayer we say in which we ask God to grant us the strength to face the things we cannot change. Your brother over there—and Maria in the next room—they need your strength now, Francisco, and are going to need it a lot more in the future. I realise you're not yet fifteen and I know your heart is broken about your mother but you must try to be strong for the twins' sake. They're confused and frightened by what is happening and they're going to be even more frightened as the days pass. So you must be strong and cheerful ... you must put on a brave face for them, you understand?"

Francisco whispered, "Yes."

Jose was hesitant, dreading to tell the boy what he must. "Francisco ... Constanza told us ... other things ... that are not good news. She overheard Señora Little and her daughter talking. Señora Little is a vindictive woman. What your mother has supposedly done—and what you and the twins did—has made her very angry. She wants to have you all deported, sent back to Mexico."

Francisco's eyes grew large with fear. He sat up quickly, grasping Jose's arm. "No!"

"Sssh, sssh, it's all right, it's all right. We, of course, are not going to let it happen. You children are leaving here right away. We've put mattresses in the truck and Fidel and Luisa are going to drive you to Los Angeles to stay with my cousins. There you'll get a fresh start, perhaps with new names, so that the police won't ..."

"But my mother! We can't leave her here in jail!"

Jose gripped the boy's hand. "Francisco, listen to me ... think about this for a moment! Your mother's side of the story hasn't even been heard yet. This morning I'm going to speak to a lawyer—to Juan Perrer, a man of the barrio and a tough fighter. I believe he will stand a good chance of getting your mother out on bail within a day or two. Francisco—the law is for *our* protection as well as for Señora Little ... and we are going to *fight* to clear your mother's name! But your mother may have a difficult time ahead of her and think what a comfort it will be to her to know her children are out of Señora Little's reach, safe with relatives, hmm? Don't you agree?"

Francisco's nod was barely perceptible.

Jose went on, pressingly, "And another thing, I believe that once you children—and Fidel and Luisa—disappear, Señora Little will forget about this deportation thing. Ask yourself why she is doing it. She's doing it out of *fear*. She's afraid the truth will come out—that it was her daughter who stole those things and put them in your mother's room. She's afraid of the disgrace. Why do you think she reacted as she did when you appeared on her doorstep? It wasn't just because three children had the nerve to invade her island and ring her doorbell, it was because you were suddenly threatening her. You children strengthen your mother's case! Is it likely that a widow with three children would steal so stupidly and risk being put in jail? She knows very well a jury wouldn't think so. So, to protect herself, she gets rid of all the people involved in your mother's case, by deportation. But if you 'deport' *yourselves* by disappearing to Los Angeles ...?" He let the question hang, hopeful of drawing the boy's response.

Francisco nodded but with little conviction. "And what will happen to my mother?"

"Juan Perrer will do all he possibly can," Jose answered cautiously.

"Against Señora Little's lawyers? Against her and all her powerful friends?"

Jose sighed, daunted by the boy's bitterness. "Francisco, please try to remember what I've said about Carlo and Maria. They depend so much on you now. Try to be strong. For their sakes, please try." He patted Francisco's hand. "Come on, you must get dressed. Fidel wants to leave in half an hour."

They carried the twins from the house and made them comfortable on mattress beds in the back of the truck. Carlo, drowsy but cheerful, complained of pain in his leg but was less distressed than the adults had dared hope. The analgesic tablets Doctor Santino had supplied were doing their work.

Maria, though, was fretful and tearful. The left side of her face was swollen, pulling her mouth awry, and the uncovered part of her face showed a disconcerting greenish pallor against the whiteness of the dressing.

As Luisa laid her gently on the mattress, the child flung her arms around her aunt's neck and sobbed, "Tia Luisa, it hurts, it hurts! I'm going to be so ugly!"

Luisa hugged her, rocked and patted her. "Ssshh, *querida*, no, no, it's swollen. In time the swelling will go down . . . a few days. Don't worry, it will be all right."

Fidel appeared with a tablet and a flask-cup of water. "Here, take this, *angelita*, it will ease the pain and make you sleep."

The child swallowed with difficulty, then settled back.

Luisa said, "I'm going to ride in here with you. Close your eyes and try to sleep, everything is going to be all right."

Fidel turned and embraced Jose, then Isabel.

"God go with you," she whispered.

"I'll phone you along the way," he said, "let you know how things are—and for any news. Pray God Juan Perrer *can* get her out on bail. *Adios*, my friends."

Jose moved to the passenger side of the cab where Francisco stood, and hugged the boy affectionately. "Remember what I said, *muchacho*—take good care of the little ones."

"*Si.*"

Francisco climbed up into the cab and closed the door. Jose looked up at him, searching his face in the hope of finding some lessening of the awesome, blazing hatred, but finding instead a cold, impassive mask more disquieting than the anger.

Jose turned away, moved quickly around the front of the vehicle to arrest Fidel before he opened the cab door. Jose's eyes indicated Francisco. "Watch him closely," he murmured. "He's deeply hurt . . . far more than the twins."

Fidel nodded.

Jose and Isabel waved as the truck pulled away, turned a corner and disappeared from view.

112

"Pray God they'll be all right," Isabel whispered fervently. "Let us hope this terrible thing doesn't leave a permanent mark on them."

Jose shook his head gravely. "I'm afraid it may already be too late for Francisco. I fear the boy is . . ."

"Is what?" frowned Isabel.

"Deranged," he said softly.

15

Shortly after four o'clock that same afternoon, Juan Perrer entered the Miami Beach police headquarters, a black metal briefcase in one hand, the fingers of the other smoothing his bushy goucho moustache—a prop which he wore, not from vanity, but for a purpose—it added a few years to his youthful looks. Together with his heavy-framed glasses, it had a somewhat commanding effect on juries. And occasionally on policemen.

At the desk, Sergeant Alfred White looked up from his ledger at the sound of staccato marching footsteps and groaned inwardly at the approaching figure of Perrer.

"Counsellor," he nodded.

Perrer returned the nod. "Sergeant. Mrs Ana Patillas . . . I'd like to speak to her."

White reached for the phone. "We kinda wondered if you'd be along."

"I'm along," said Perrer.

Perrer entered the spartan pale-green interview room and came to a halt, arrested by the attitude of the woman who sat at the light oak table, her head bent, eyes fixed glassily on the table top. In her black dress, her raven, grey-streaked hair drawn back severely into a bun, she represented to Perrer the epitome of misery, the most forlorn creature he'd ever encountered. His pity went out to her.

He approached the table. There was no reaction from her. Not until he spoke her name did she become aware of his presence, then slowly she raised her face, her eyes dull and blank with bewilderment, searching his face myopically, like a blind woman whose sight had suddenly and miraculously been restored.

"Mrs Patillas ..." He tried a friendly, encouraging smile. "My name is Juan Perrer. I'm an attorney. May I sit down?"

He sat opposite her, placed his briefcase to one side, clasped his hands in front of him and looked intently at her, studying her as he spoke.

"I've been retained by your good friends the Leandroses to defend you. Jose came to see me today and ..." He frowned, peering closely at her. "Mrs Patillas ...?"

Her eyes did not appear to see him. "How are the children?" she whispered, her voice a spiritless croak.

Perrer was hesitant, loath to come to that too soon. "They're fine ..."

A spark of life. "You've seen them?"

"Well, no, but Jose ..."

"How are they taking this?"

"Fine, fine, they're in very good hands. Mrs Patillas ..."

"I don't want them to come here! They mustn't see me in here."

"No, of course not, don't worry, they won't be coming." He reached across to pat her hand, comforting, but also to attract her more concentrated attention. "Mrs Patillas, please listen to me. Jose has given me the facts of your arrest, and I've seen the police report, but I want to hear your side of the story. Please tell me what happened."

Ana's distant gaze appeared to be riveted on his tie, a slight pinching of her brow the only indication that she had heard him. "Happened? They arrested me. They said I'd stolen ... something." Her frown deepened perplexedly. "Jewellery? Was it jewellery ... money?"

"Did you steal it?" he asked gently.

The shake of her head was almost imperceptible. Her eyes flooded with tears of anguish, and in the shallow quickness of her breathing Perrer sensed the onslaught of acute distress.

He squeezed her hand consolingly. "Mrs Patillas, listen carefully to me. I want to tell you exactly how the situation stands. It's very important that you know what has happened and what is likely to happen ... but you must give me your complete attention. Do I have it?"

115

His directness and authority calmed her. She gave a nod.

"All right. Now I can see that you're extremely upset—and God knows it's understandable—what has happened to you is diabolical. You feel lost, abandoned, the innocent victim of a monstrous plot perpetrated by people against whom you feel utterly defenceless. Well, let me assure you such is not the case. I am here to defend you—and you have many good friends in the barrio working on your behalf. You are *not* alone—do you accept that?"

She nodded and whispered faintly, "Yes."

"Good. Now, the first thing I'm going to try to do is to get you out of here on bail *but* I'm afraid we couldn't have chosen a worse time to do it. It's Christmas Eve. The vacation period is upon us and by now ..." he glanced at his watch, a reflexive gesture since he was acutely aware of the time, " ... everyone we need has gone home. So I'm very much afraid I can do nothing until the offices re-open after the holiday."

The slump of her shoulders was slight but totally expressive.

Perrer said gently, "I know, you're thinking of Christmas and your children. But, Mrs Patillas, the children ..." He hesitated, cursing the need to tell her, drew a supportive breath and continued, gently and, he hoped, persuasively. "The Leandroses and your sister and brother-in-law have taken a certain step to protect your children, a move I personally approve of. Mrs Patillas, the children are at this moment on their way to Los Angeles by road. Fidal and Luisa are driving them there—to stay with relatives of the Leadroses."

For the first time, the light of interest entered Ana's eyes, dispelling the baleful glaze, yet quickly flared into a glare of fear and panic, which Perrer moved quickly to subdue.

"Now, it's all right, don't *worry* ..."

"Los Angeles? Why? Why is it necessary ...?"

"To protect them," Perrer answered reassuringly.

"From ... the scandal," she nodded, the panic rising.

"No! Nothing like that. Merely to ..." he contained a sigh. "Mrs Patillas ... something else has happened. There's talk of ... deportation ... of sending you and the children back to

116

Mexico. Now, I'm certain we can fight it, but rather than risk the possibility of . . ."

"Mexico?" She breathed the word incredulously.

He nodded. "Luisa received a telephone call from Constanza Nerōn, who overheard a conversation in the Little home. It appears that Mrs Little is planning to . . ."

"Mexico!" She whispered again, her fingers knotting. "She's going to send us back?"

"Not if I can help it," he said resolutely.

"But Francisco . . ."

"I know about Francisco. Jose confided what happened in Matamoros. I'm more sorry than I can say that you've had so much trouble and I shall do everything in my power to prevent . . ."

Ana fell forward on the table, her face buried in her arms, sobbing bitterly, "No, no, no."

Across the room, the policewoman escort made a move towards her distressed charge, but Perrer shook his head and she returned to her position at the door.

He reached out and touched Ana's arm. "Mrs Patillas, please try not to upset yourself. Deportation is by no means certain—and neither is a prison sentence. We haven't begun to fight yet! We have a lot going for us, numerous character witnesses who will testify to your honesty. We have . . ."

Ana was shaking her head, sobbing brokenly, "It's no good! Don't you see, we can't win! We're illegal immigrants! Soon the police will know, then we'll be sent back to Mexico whether I'm convicted or not!"

Perrer drew a subdued sigh, searched frantically for an approach that would help to console a woman whom he knew in his heart to be inconsolable. "Look, I'm not saying we haven't got problems but we're not going to give up without a fight. We have certain things in our favour . . ."

She raised her head, her eyes swollen with tears. "What things? I see nothing in my favour. How can I fight people like Señora Little?"

"*You* don't have to—that's my job. And I'm very good at it."

She nodded, profoundly unconvinced, and whispered

117

pensively, "Thank God, at least, the children are ..." Her voice tailed away.

Perrer waited, but she didn't continue. An awkward silence fell, which he interrupted with a nervous clearing of his throat. "Yes, well ..." He opened his briefcase, took out a sheet of paper and uncapped his fountain pen. "Now, Mrs Patillas, I want to know about your relationship with Mrs Little and her daughter ..."

16

By nightfall, after nine hours of turnpike driving at a relentless seventy miles per hour, the travellers in the truck were approaching the outskirts of the state capital, Tallahassee, some five hundred miles north-west of Miami.

It had been an uneventful journey. Fidel had stopped several times for food and gasoline and had been heartened each time to discover that the twins were riding comfortably, sleeping a lot under mild sedation and apparently suffering no ill effects from the journey. On the contrary, the monotonous whine of the tyres and the rhythmic rocking of the truck undoubtedly helped them to rest.

Luisa had ridden with the twins for the first three hours, then changed places with Francisco, then later had moved back with them.

During his periods in the cab with Fidel, Francisco had said very little, merely stared out of the window at a passing landscape Fidel was certain the boy did not see. And, sensing his need to be left alone with his thoughts, Fidel hadn't attempted to draw him into conversation.

Once, though, some hours after they'd got under way, Francisco asked suddenly, "What will happen to us in Los Angeles?"

Fidel, lost in his own thoughts and taken unawares, took a moment to answer. "What will happen to you? You'll be taken care of ... and loved." He smiled at the boy fondly. "Your Aunt Luisa and I love you very much, all of you, and we're going to look after you as we would our own children."

The responding smile Fidel hoped to see didn't come. Francisco, staring fixedly at the road ahead, didn't even nod. "Will we live permanently with the Raventoses?"

Fidel shook his head. "No. Certainly we will have to for the time being, until we find our feet. But later on Luisa and I will probably buy a small place of our own. And as soon as your mother is free to join us ..."

"When will that be?" Francisco asked brusquely.

"I ... really don't know. At the moment no one knows. It depends on many things."

For a long while after this exchange Francisco remained silent. From the corner of his eye Fidel watched the boy, the nature of his thoughts manifested in deep-drawn sighs, in the tight closing of his eyes and the bitter compression of his lips—the expressions of seething grief.

Eventually, Francisco again elected to express a thought in words. "Jose said we must change our names when we get to California."

Fidel nodded. "We discussed it. It seemed a sensible thing to do, the one sure way of guaranteeing our protection. I don't pretend to know how far-reaching Señora Little's influence is—but for our safety we must assume the worst. Neither do I know just how determined she is to get rid of us—but again we must assume the worst. Better to be over-cautious than over-sorry."

Francisco shook his head and murmured, bewildered, "I can't believe it's happening to us. It's like a nightmare. It was the same with my father ... when he was lying there ... I ..." Again he shook his head, as though banishing the vision. "And now this. How *can* this be happening to us? How can my mother, my *mother*, be in jail? How can people like Señora Little get away with such lies and put innocent people in jail? How can anybody be so ... *wicked*?"

Fidel answered measuredly and simply. "Because they have too much power, Francisco. Belle Little knows her daughter is a cheat and a liar, probably knows it was Elizabeth who put those stolen things in your mother's room ... but to her Elizabeth is everything, your mother means nothing. Something as insignificant as the deportation of a Mexican maid and her family will cause Belle Little no loss of sleep."

"Perhaps not," Francisco responded softly, his gaze directed through his side window. "But other things would."

120

Fidel glanced sharply at the boy. "Such as what?"

Francisco didn't answer.

"You're thinking of revenge?" Fidel shook his head. "Forget it. What could you—or any of us—possibly do to hurt Belle Little? She's far beyond our reach, quite untouchable. No, we must simply trust to Juan Perrer and the law . . . and, of course, to God. Señora Little acted in the heat of the moment—to save face. Perhaps when things have cooled down, after Christmas, she may feel more lenient towards your mother . . ."

Francisco whirled, eyes blazing. "Lenient! For something Momma didn't do? Aren't you forgetting she's *innocent*?"

"No, I am not," Fidel answered patiently. "But neither am I forgetting Señora Little's power. Francisco . . ." he shook his head and sighed, ". . . you are young and to the young everything is black and white, right or wrong. But I'm afraid life isn't like that. There are no guarantees that we will win against this injustice just because we are in the right and wish it. As much as I dread to admit it, I'm afraid your mother's fate lies more in the hands of Señora Little than in the hands of any judge or lawyer." He offered the boy a quick encouraging smile. "But let's not jump to any morbid conclusions. Perhaps a miracle *will* happen and there'll be more comforting news waiting for us when we get to Los Angeles."

"Perhaps," whispered Francisco.

Thereafter the boy drew into a long, reflective silence, staring out of the window, his forehead pressed against the glass. Fidel feared to guess what dark thoughts pervaded his tormented young mind. Pray God some good news does meet us in Los Angeles, thought Fidel, closing his mind to the consequences of the alternative.

17

Ana Patillas lay on her iron cot, staring up at the square of illuminated frosted perspex set in the cream-painted ceiling. The light was soothing, hypnotic, a white-hot branding iron that seared her brain, purged her mind of thought.

For a moment she embraced the blessed, unexpected tranquillity, the dissipation of hideous pressure, but slowly, as her pupils adjusted to the flare of light, once again the reality of her prison cell bore down upon her like a suffocating weight.

With a muted whimper she shut her eyes and turned to face the wall, away from the awful room, shutting out the sight and bathing her tortured mind with the beneficent void of blindness.

But still the visions came.

Her children ...

Heart-sickness pierced her like a plunging knife, welled up inside her and squeezed chokingly into her throat.

Her children.

Massive grief overwhelmed her, curled her into a foetus, raked her until every nerve in her body screamed with unendurable agony.

She was to blame! *She* was the cause of all their misery. *She* had married Ramon Patillas, had brought the children into a life of violence and great unhappiness. *She* had caused Francisco to kill his father. *She* had brought them to Miami, into this new hell ... she ... she ... she ...

She had failed them, failed to protect them. She had passed them into the care of Jose and Isabel, deserted them. If she had stayed with them this nightmare would not be happening, she would be at home with them at this moment, dressing the Christmas tree ...

Christmas.

A fresh wave of anguish washed through her. What a Christmas they would have, fleeing across the country like hunted animals. Her children, moving farther away from her with every passing moment. Her children, now in the care of Luisa and Fidel. What use was she to them?

No use whatever.

But that wasn't all. She was now a positive danger to them, especially to Francisco. She would be responsible for his deportation, for the terrible things that would happen to him in Matamoros, for the ruination of his life. *She*—by her very existence—was about to condemn her beloved son to God only knew what misery for the rest of his life!

By her very existence. Her useless, pathetic existence.

Her children no longer needed her. Luisa and Fidel would give them a much happier life. She alone was a threat to that happiness. Without her there would be no threat of deportation.

A sudden calm pervaded her. She opened her eyes and became aware, lucidly aware, of the wall before her face, aware of its smooth plastered texture and the shade of its cream gloss paint. She reached out and touched it, running her finger-tips over its surface, experiencing pleasure in the simple sensation of touch.

It was all so simple really. Why hadn't she thought of it before?

"My Christmas gift to you, my children," she whispered. "My gift of life to you."

She got up from the bed, pressed the call button and stood before the door, greeting her guardian's appearance with a benign smile.

"Yes?"

"I was wondering, would it be possible for me to take a bath?"

"We have no tubs, only showers."

"Then a shower?"

The policewoman's eyes softened. "You feeling better?"

"Much better."

"Good. OK, I'll check it out."

18

They stopped that first night at the Catalina Motel on the west side of Tallahassee, with the city now behind them and a clear start along the transcontinental Route 10 to look forward to in the morning.

Fidel, despite road-weariness, was in cheerful mood, well-pleased with the day's progress. As he signed the motel register at the reception desk, he paused momentarily to question his good spirits, suffering a pang of guilt that a journey prompted by such tragic circumstances could evoke such ebullience. Then he quickly salved his conscience. His satisfaction stemmed from rescuing the children.

He took two adjoining inter-communicating rooms—a triple for the children, a twin for Luisa and himself. Happily he did not envisage any emergency, since the twins had not only weathered the journey well but were showing a slight improvement.

Waking from a long sleep just before Fidel turned off the highway, Carlo had given Luisa a grin and complained of ravenous hunger, specifying a craving for "a cheeseburger with the works, french fries, and a chocolate malted".

Maria, her colour slightly better, had shaken her head in response to Luisa's quizzically arched brow and murmured stiffly, "Just some ice cream."

After they had moved into the rooms, Luisa helped undress and bath the twins while Fidel and Francisco visited the coffee shop and collected a take-away meal. Later they all ate together in the children's room in what, for Luisa and Fidel, was a gratifying happy atmosphere.

Time and youth were the great healers, Fidel reflected, covertly studying the children. Even Francisco, though still subdued, seemed to have shrugged off the black depression that had haunted him throughout most of the journey with youthful resilience.

Aware of Luisa's eyes on him, Fidel turned and caught her smile that told him she knew and agreed with his thoughts. Yes, her eyes conveyed, they're going to be all right.

At ten o'clock, the children settled down for the night, Fidel and Luisa entered their own room through the inter-communicating door. Fidel sat down heavily on his bed and massaged the weariness from his face.

Luisa moved close and stroked his hair, experiencing a surge of love and pride for her stalwart, dependable man. "You must be worn out."

"Mm," he nodded, smiling up at her, "but pleasantly so. And certainly no more than you."

"Huh," she dismissed it lightly, sat down on her bed facing him and took his strong gardener's hands in hers. "As long as the children are well and happy I don't care how tired I am. They seem to have improved a little, don't you think?"

He nodded. "Yes. In another two or three days, I'm sure we'll see a big change."

"Please God." She gave a pensive sigh. "I've been thinking about Ana all day, wondering how she must be feeling in that awful jail, and thinking about Juan Perrer. D'you suppose he was able to give her any comfort? Would he get in touch with Jose after his visit—to let him know how she is and whether he can get her out on bail?"

Fidel nodded. "He might."

"Shall we call Jose and see?" she asked eagerly.

"Of course." He bent to the low shelf of the bedside cupboard, searching for a code book.

Luisa got up. "You make the call, I must go to the bathroom."

As she entered the door at the rear of the room, Fidel began to dial the Miami number.

Jose's number rang five or six times without response. Fidel glanced at his ancient silver wrist watch. It wasn't very late,

125

only a few minutes past ten. Jose and Isabel rarely retired before eleven.

As the number continued ringing, Fidel thought at first that he was disturbing an early night. The previous night had been long and harrowing for them all; perhaps Jose and Isabel were taking advantage of an empty house to catch up on their sleep.

But almost simultaneously a grim alternative occurred to him, an intuitive apprehension that something was wrong. Irritably he shook the thought away, irked by his over-readiness to believe the worst. But was it any wonder—considering what *had* happened in the past two days? Relax, he chided himself, you were right the first time, the Cesars are fast asleep in bed.

He reached up to replace the receiver in its wall-mounted cradle.

"Hallo?" The voice reached him thinly, from a distance.

He snatched the receiver back to his ear. "Jose?"

"Fidel! Thank God . . ."

Fidel froze. There, in those few words and in the low-pitched desperation of Jose's voice, was the realisation of his fears. How few words it took to communicate so great a depth of sadness, horror, despair.

His heart thudding alarm, Fidel asked, "Jose . . . what has happened?"

There was a moment of hesitation while Jose struggled to control his voice, to assemble his words, but even so they emerged in ragged gasps. "Fidel . . . it's Ana . . . the children . . . are they there with you?"

"No, in the next room. We're in a motel in Tallahassee . . . Jose, what has *happened*?"

At that moment Luisa emerged from the bathroom, her smile of expectation draining away as she encountered Fidel's expression of blank dismay. He met her eyes, deflected the question he saw in them with an arresting gesture as Jose continued speaking.

"Fidel . . . Ana is dead."

Fidel gasped.

126

Luisa came forward hesitantly, sat down on her bed. *"What?"*

Fidel shook his head, gaped at her.

"Juan Perrer phoned not long ago," Jose was saying, his voice a desolate croak. "The police had just called him. He went to see her this afternoon . . . found her in very low spirits. He stayed two hours, tried to encourage her, cheer her up . . . but he said she was too aware of the hopelessness of her position as an illegal immigrant and was sure that, whether found guilty or not of the thefts, she and the children would be deported. Perrer was so worried about her depressed condition that he spoke to a police lieutenant about it, asked for medical attention for her. But, being Christmas Eve, the doctor wasn't immediately available. Even so, there wouldn't have been time to stop her. She must have made up her mind while she was talking to Perrer. As soon as she got back to the cell . . ." Jose was unable to go on.

"How did it happen?" whispered Fidel, his eyes communicating tragedy to his wife, his baffled mind attempting to grapple with the consequences of this shocking news.

"She . . . killed herself."

Fidel closed his eyes. "Dear Jesus . . ."

Luisa bowed her head, knowing, without hearing the words, that her sister was dead. Fidel reached for her hand and held it tightly.

"According to the policewoman in charge of Ana," Jose continued desolately, "she seemed to cheer up after Perrer had left and asked if she could take a shower. It fooled them into allowing her a few minutes of privacy."

"And?" murmured Fidel.

"She hanged herself in the shower . . . to save her children."

"Madre de Dios . . ." Tears tore at Fidel's eyes and throat.

"She's dead?" whispered Luisa.

Fidel nodded.

After a moment, Fidel asked, "What in God's name do we do now, Jose?"

Jose's reply was the ramble of a shocked and searching mind. "I . . . was upstairs when you rang . . . had to put Isabel to bed

"... we ... haven't had time to think ... there'll be the funeral to see to, of course ..."

"Yes," whispered Fidel. "We must go on ... don't you think? I mean ..."

"Oh, yes! The children mustn't come back here. Don't worry, we'll see to everything. She has many friends here ... they'll help, I'm sure."

"Yes. Dear God, Jose ..."

Luisa was sobbing now, her face buried in her hands. Fidel took her arm and drew her over to sit beside him, slipped his arm about her shaking shoulders.

"Look, Jose, I'll ring off now. We all need time to think ... to adjust. In the morning our minds will be a little clearer."

"Yes. The children ... will you tell them?"

"No. Not until we get to Los Angeles. It would be disastrous."

"I agree. All right, until tomorrow."

Jose rang off. Fidel reached up to replace the receiver, then drew his sobbing wife to him and held her tightly.

"How?" she asked.

"She hanged herself," he answered softly.

"Dear Jesus ... why? ... *why*?"

"For her children's sake, Luisa. She knew that the police would find out that she and the children were illegal immigrants and would deport them whether she was found guilty or not ..."

"But to *kill* herself! Oh, Fidel!"

A stifled cry from behind them shocked them. They turned, appalled to see the figure of Francisco standing in the doorway of his room, his face contorted with ravaging grief.

Part Three

INTERLUDE

1

On the evening of December 30th Belle Little invited Margaret Whitney, Lily Parker and Ruth Howard to her home for a "bridge night"—a euphemism for a regular get-together in which the playing of cards was invariably relegated to a matter of inconsequence.

As usual they gathered in the sitting-room, a charming, cosy room off the main hall, furnished with comfortable couches and warmed by an open fire. For an hour or so they sat at an inlaid Regency card table, desultorily going through the motions of the game.

Finally, abandoning the pretence, they adjourned to the couches arranged before the fire and got down to the infinitely more entertaining pastime of post-Christmas gossip.

For a further hour the conversation ranged vituperatively over matters of party success and failure, food, clothes and staff problems, the three guests missing no opportunity to assure Belle that from every aspect her Arabian Night party had been by far the most successful of the season.

"Poor Dolly," sighed Ruth Howard in sardonic commiseration. "You know, of course, Belle, that after she'd been to your party she dashed around like a *mad* thing trying to turn that *dreary* summerhouse of theirs into a Chinese pagoda?" Her audience laughed. "No—I mean it! I got it from Kate Dodge! Apparently Dolly even sent Charles scuttling up to Chinatown, New York, for hundreds of paper lanterns and God knows what other artifacts, and they spent the whole of Christmas Eve putting them up. And apparently the result was so absolutely hideous, they spent the whole of Christmas Day pulling them down!"

In the ensuing laughter, Lily Parker observed with a shake of her head, "I really don't know why they bother to compete, Belle. They must *know* they haven't a chance before they start."

"Not a hope," Margaret added smilingly. "Even Emily Van Doran's party was a very flat affair compared to yours. Why *does* she invite so many of those dreary art people? You ought to drop her a hint or two about balancing her guest list."

"Or, preferably, lend her yours," laughed Ruth.

Belle smiled, revelling in the compliments. She enjoyed the occasional company of these women, not only because their conversation was undemanding and soothingly obsequious, but because their presence was a poignant reminder of her own power. She owned them—or at least owned their husbands, which amounted to the same thing—and it afforded her immense satisfaction to witness, in their sycophancy, their dependence upon her.

"Ruth—your glass is empty," she smiled. "Do help yourself. Lily, Margaret, how about you two?"

Ruth made to get up. "Shall I freshen yours, Belle?"

Belle shook her head. "No, I'm going to have some tea. If I drink any more alcohol I shan't sleep. I do find tea so refreshing at night."

"What a good idea," enthused Ruth. "Mind if I join you?"

"Of course not. How about you two?"

"Perfect," agreed Lily.

Though dying for another brandy, Margaret smiled compliantly. "I'd love some tea, Belle."

Belle pointed a finger. "Call Constanza, Margaret."

Margaret got up and pressed the bell by the fireplace, then, excusing herself, crossed the room to the door. As she reached it, it opened and Constanza entered.

"Tea for us all, Constanza," Belle ordered.

"Yes, señora."

Margaret preceded the maid out into the hall and entered the washroom. Constanza continued towards the kitchen.

Emerging from the washroom a few minutes later, Margaret was arrested by a sudden peal of laughter through the partly-open door of the study. Recognising Elizabeth's voice, she changed direction, intending to pop her head through the door and say hello to the girl.

As she reached the door she paused momentarily, aware that Elizabeth was speaking on the phone.

"It's absolutely true!" exclaimed Elizabeth in a furtive, excited whisper. "God's honour! Well, it wasn't in the papers because the police naturally wanted it kept quiet and so did we. But, Jill, it *happened*. Because she deserved it, that's why . . . the way she spoke to me, threatened to tell my mother—a god-damned *maid*—and a Spic at that . . ." Elizabeth giggled ". . . It was so easy, it wasn't true . . . we had this big party, mother's annual do—a thousand people, you can imagine what it was like. I just pinched the stuff and hid it in her room, then when the things were reported missing, I sort of *casually* mentioned to my mother that I'd seen Ana nosing around her bedroom safe and suggested it might be worthwhile searching her room before stripping all the servants . . ." more laughter ". . . like she'd walked into a wall—stunned! Then the police arrived and carted her off . . . well, of course they did—her word against *ours*? . . . Well, I didn't expect her to *kill* herself . . . she must have been—you don't string yourself up in the shower unless you *are* nuts, do you?" a giggle, ". . . ooh, kinda funny—like *I'd* really done it to her . . . no—exciting . . . I guess I can say I murdered somebody . . . right—the perfect crime!"

Margaret turned away and went back to the sitting-room.

Belle turned to glance at her, expecting Constanza with the tea.

"Good lord, what's the matter with you? You look as though you've seen a ghost."

Without closing the door, Margaret advanced into the room, shocked and hesitant. "Belle, I-I've just heard something I really can't believe is true . . ."

"Heard? Heard where?"

Margaret gestured. "Elizabeth. She's on the phone in the study . . ."

Belle waited. "Yes, well?"

Margaret blinked, shook her head. "Belle, I don't know

whether I ought to . . . but I think you ought to know . . . there might be serious repercussions, if it ever got out."

Belle frowned irritably. "Margaret, what on earth . . ."

"Look, it may have been a joke. You know how children make up stories . . . but I've just overheard Elizabeth tell her friend Jill that it was *she* who stole that jewellery and hid it in Ana Patillas's room. She told her she did it because Ana threatened to tell you about something she'd done."

Belle remained motionless, her eyes fixed stonily on Margaret.

Ruth and Lily exchanged furtive glances.

Margaret shifted uncomfortably under Belle's gaze. "Belle, I'm sorry but I felt it better that you should know. I would certainly stop her telling it to anyone else . . ."

Belle snorted. "You believed her?"

Margaret nodded. "To be frank—yes. She sounded very convincing."

A taut silence descended on the room.

When Belle at last spoke she made no attempt to deny or evade, she merely stated a requirement. "You will all forget you heard this. The woman is dead and no amount of truth-searching will bring her back."

They murmured agreement.

Belle went on, "There's no telling what harm this might do if . . ." she stopped suddenly, hearing a faint click of china cups outside the door. "Is that you, Constanza?"

The door opened wider. "Yes, señora."

The maid entered and put the tray on a coffee table.

Margaret began, "Belle, you can rest assured I shall say nothing to anyone. As far as I'm concerned . . ."

Belle silenced her with a censuring frown, glancing at Constanza.

None of the women spoke again until the maid left the room.

Part Four

THE END

1

Satisfied that he had adequately terrified Margaret Whitney, the motorcycle rider reduced the speed of his Harley Davidson and continued across the causeway into the city. Stopping briefly to remove the adhesive tape from his licence plates, he turned south on Second Avenue, crossed the Miami River, and meandered through the congested streets of the barrio until he reached a backwater of decrepit frame houses, many of them derelict and abandoned, all of them due for demolition.

Here he pulled to the kerb, reached into the fold of his leather jacket for a compact walkie-talkie transceiver, pressed the button and said into it, "Rider to Hunter . . . Rider to Hunter . . . over."

He had repeated the call twice before his receiver crackled and a man's voice replied, "Hunter receiving . . . over."

"A-OK . . . open up."

"Wilco. Over and out."

Rider replaced the transceiver in his jacket, scanning the deserted street while he waited. After a while, one section of a double door in a long solid-panel fence fifty yards down the road opened up. Rider trod the machine into gear and roared off, turning through the gate and traversing the weed-infested rear yard of a large, ramshackle frame house.

As Rider ran the bike into the double garage, Hunter followed him in and pulled down the up-and-over doors. When Rider had silenced the machine, Hunter asked, "How did it go?"

Rider removed his helmet, grinning, "Perfect. Has there been any reaction?"

"Plenty. She was so scared she clipped the security boom

with the Merc. She called Security about you as soon as she got in—then phoned Belle Little and told her all about it."

"And?" Rider pulled off his boots and leather jacket, opened the rear door of a pale-blue panel truck and tossed the clothing into it, then began removing his pants.

"The call shocked Belle, but she covered up well. She didn't mention the note she got today."

"Of course." Rider quickly donned jeans, tee-shirt and sneakers, stuffed the leather clothing into a canvas hold-all and closed the truck door.

"Belle's scared," said Hunter, moving off towards an internal door. "I can hear it in her voice. She warned Margaret to say nothing about you or the note to anyone—especially not to Lily Parker and Ruth Howard. Well, you'll hear it for yourself, I'll play the tape back."

They entered a ramshackle kitchen, passed through it into a hall that had not enjoyed a lick of paint in twenty years, climbed a flight of stairs, their footsteps ringing on the bare boards, turned along a landing and entered a bedroom at the front of the house.

It was a large room, furnished with a large, ancient wooden bed, a matching wardrobe and a couple of chairs. Heavy maroon curtains hung open at the only window.

Against the left-hand wall a complex of radio and recording equipment had been installed, housed on a series of metal shelves above a desk-like control console.

While Hunter sat at the console and activated switches, Rider stood at the window and looked out over the Miami River and the distant panorama of Biscayne Bay, selecting in particular the hump of Little Park some three miles away.

"Here we go," said Hunter, drawing Rider from the window to sit close to the console.

Hunter pressed the "replay" button of a recorder. In silence they listened to Margaret Whitney's conversations with security and Belle Little, exchanging a grin at Belle's heated reaction, "Christ, Margaret, do you want to panic everyone? One *whisper* that something threatening or dangerous is lurking around here and the Miami Symphony will be playing to a congregation of *two* instead of two thousand next Thursday—that'll be Elizabeth and me!"

"Scared," nodded Rider.

"There's more later."

The tape continued. Margaret Whitney, rebuffed by Belle, put down the phone and addressed her maid. "What is it, Lucia?"

"Señora, cook would like to know if Señor Whitney will be home for dinner this evening."

A weary sigh. "No, Señor Whitney won't be home until Sunday night. Tell cook I'm not hungry—a slice of melon and some scrambled eggs will do."

"Yes, Señora. Shall I run your bath now?"

"And put out my green silk lounging pyjamas."

"Yes, señora."

"And get me another drink before you go."

Hunter switched off the tape recorder. "She's going to get drunk. I think the time is right."

Rider reacted excitedly. "Tonight?"

"I don't think there'll be a better time."

"Okay. You got the stuff?"

"In a moment. I want you to hear this first."

Hunter activated the "replay" button of a second tape recorder. The agitated voice of Belle Little demanded, "*What note? You don't have the damned note.* Now, Margaret, you listen to me . . . this wedding is the biggest . . . thing . . . of . . . my . . . life! And I will not allow anything to spoil it—not *anything!* Do you understand? You will treat this thing for what it is—a stupid practical joke. You will not say a word to anyone about it, not even to Ruth or Lily . . . *especially* not to Ruth or Lily. Do I have your solemn word on that?"

"Y-yes, of course."

"All right. Now I must go. I was about to step into the tub when you rang."

"Yes, I'm sorry. . ."

This segment of the women's conversation Rider had just heard on the Margaret Whitney tape, but Hunter had used it as a lead-in to what followed.

139

A rustle of paper was heard.

"That's the note," explained Hunter. "Belle's reading it again."

"Where's the bug?"

"In her bedroom, under her desk."

There was a soft fall of footsteps across a carpet, a small silence, the crunching of paper, accompanied by a muttered expletive.

"Now she's really mad," murmured Hunter. "Listen to this."

More footsteps, then an angry outburst, "Does he realise who he's taken on? How can he know? Who but Belle Little knows Belle Little?" A defiant chuckle. "Belle Little is the *queen*, little man, indefatigable . . . indestructible!"

Rider grimaced at Hunter, tapping his temple. "Nuts."

Hunter nodded, maintaining listening attitude.

Again the crunch of paper.

"She's reading it again," said Hunter. "It's really getting to her now."

"Who the hell *are* you?" Belle's voice demanded. "What have I done to you to deserve this? Are you out of my present . . . or my past?"

There was a long silence, disturbed only by the whisper of footsteps across the carpet.

"That bug is unbelievable," murmured Rider.

Hunter nodded. "Japanese. I can hear her peeling off her false eyelashes at night."

Belle's voice returned again, desperate now. "Harry . . . someone is threatening to take it away from me. Someone is threatening *me*! Tell him how it's going to be, Harry . . . tell the poor bastard how it's going to be!"

A door slammed.

Hunter switched off the recorder.

"Harry?" enquired Rider.

"Her dead husband—the guy who made her rich."

"She sounds loco."

Hunter nodded. "Psychotic. Too rich, too powerful, too used to having things all her own way. You should hear her rant

140

when she doesn't get her way. And she's getting worse—change of life, maybe."

He indicated a collection of tape cannisters stacked on the shelf above his head. "I've got to know Belle Little pretty well over the past few months. She is getting worse. The pressure of Miles Collier's campaign didn't help, of course. I've got a recording in here that shows how it affected her. At one point Collier dropped behind James Franklin and it began to look as though Collier wouldn't make Governor. Gus Waldron, in the State Senate, a friend of Belle's, happened to say to her, jokingly I'm sure, something like, 'Doesn't look too good, Belle. Still, it's Robert that Elizabeth is marrying, not his father. She'll just have to wait a few years until Robert makes Governor.' And, Jesus, she tore into him, yelled, 'Miles is going to make it! He's *got* to make it!'"

"And he did—thanks largely to her."

"Yeh—half a million dollars largely. She's bought herself a governor and it's done something to her. I reckon she sees herself as another Rose Kennedy—on the way to founding a political dynasty. Which is good. The higher she climbs, the farther she'll fall. But now . . ." he got up and crossed the room to a battered dresser, "let's deal with Margaret Whitney."

Opening a drawer, he took from it a bottle of blue capsules, a small bottle of clear liquid and a flat, oblong tin box.

Shaking two of the capsules into an envelope, he sealed it and gave it to Rider. "Tell Lucia to open the capsules and put the contents in Margaret's brandy—only *one* dose if Margaret is very drunk, two if she's so-so."

"Right." Rider folded the envelope and put it in his shirt pocket.

From the tin box, Hunter took a plastic hypodermic syringe, filled it with the contents of the bottle, replaced it in the box and handed it to Rider. "Shoot the works."

"OK."

Hunter moved back to the console. "I'm going to lift Margaret's conversation with Belle on to a cassette. I want you to use it."

. . . . . .

A little after seven that evening, Rider turned the truck off the causeway into the approach road of the Park, bringing Sam Webb out of the booth, grinning. "Hi, young fella."

"How's it goin', Sam?"

Webb nodded at the swim trunks dangling from the truck's radio aerial. "Bin to the beach?"

"You bet. More dames than sand there today, yuh shoulda seen them."

"You are not wrong."

"Hey—somebody clip your boom?"

Webb made a face. "Mrs Whitney. Came roarin' in here like Steve McQueen. Claims some punk on a motorbike chased her all the way from Bal Harbor." He winked. "Wishful thinkin' maybe."

Rider grinned. "I hear her old man's away a lot. Why don't you do somethin' about that?"

Webb nodded. "Well, now, maybe with her I could. There ain't many in here I'd fancy without a sack over their heads, but her . . ."

"I'll put in a word for you," laughed Rider, driving through.

Reaching number sixteen, he turned into the driveway and ran down the side of the house, parked the truck under a lean-to at the rear, collected the canvas hold-all from the passenger seat and entered the staff bungalow. In his room, he threw the hold-all into a closet, sat down on the bed and dialled a number.

She answered immediately. "Lucia speaking."

"Hi . . . it's me."

"Hi."

"It's tonight." He heard her indrawn breath. "OK?"

"Yes."

"Meet me at nine—behind the garage."

2

At nine-thirty that evening Margaret Whitney roused herself from her brandy stupor, got up from the armchair and switched off the television set at which she had been staring, unaware of what had been showing, for the past hour.

Earlier, having bathed and changed into the green silk lounging suit, she had come downstairs determined not to succumb to the dejection brought on by her telephone conversation with Belle Little, not to capitulate to the temptation of drowning her ennui in alcohol, of flopping spiritlessly into an armchair and passing the lonely evening in an oblivion of brandy and televised distraction.

Surprising her maid, she had even insisted on dining formally, taking her simple meal not, as usual, on a tray in the den, but seated in the dining-room with ludicrous, lonesome pomp at the head of the long walnut table designed to accommodate twenty guests in spacious comfort.

It hadn't worked.

Before her slice of melon was half eaten, the futility of the gesture, the splendour and silence of the beautiful room—of the entire goddamned house—overwhelmed her, and with a whimper of defeat she rushed into the den, demanding that Lucia pour her another, large, brandy.

Now, sickened by her own weakness, she was making another effort. A sudden thought had stirred her with mild excitement. She moved quickly into the hall, climbed the curving white staircase and entered her bedroom—a large, sumptuously appointed room in pink and white, with one entire wall, a thirty-foot run, of mirrored closets.

Taking a swallow of brandy, she set the glass on her dressing table, opened several closet doors and began taking out her entire wedding and Christmas wardrobe, hanging each garment on a rail that ran the length of the closets.

The exquisite clothes excited her, restored her spirits and obliterated thoughts of the faceless madman, Belle Little, and her own ineptitude. Smiling, she caressed the delicate fabrics with her finger tips and pressed them to her cheek, closing her eyes ecstatically.

Stirred by a sudden impulse, she kicked off her shoes and undressed completely. Naked, she stood before a mirror and studied herself, her head inclined, liking what she saw. Her body, never having been distended by childbirth, had changed little since early womanhood. Her flesh was still gratifyingly firm, her breasts the same generous mounds Arthur had jokingly swooned over during their first sexual encounter.

She frowned, the thought of Arthur denting her ebullience, but she shook him away and turned her attention to the gown she had collected from Neiman's that afternoon, its opulence thrilling her yet again. Removing it from its hanger, she stepped into it and drew its gossamer silkiness up over her thighs, gasping at the sensuousness of its caress.

Facing the mirror, she turned this way and that, grinning with pleasure at her image. "Margaret Whitney, you're a knockout. That old bitch is going to collapse with envy when you take the dance floor. Terr-ummm ... ter-umm ... terr-umm ... tum tum ..."

Arms held in dancing pose, she whirled away across the room, humming *Tales from the Vienna Woods*.

Laughing, she returned to the mirror for one final pose, then slipped out of the gown and replaced it on the hanger.

Item by item she tried on all the clothes—evening gowns, day dresses, suits, hats, gloves and shoes. Thirty-seven thousand dollars-worth in all.

And worth every goddamned cent, she thought challengingly. Arthur, having set a limit of fifteen thousand, would explode when the bills started rolling in. Well, to hell with Arthur—what else was he good for?

In any case, he would pick up many times thirty-seven thousand dollars in business during the festivities—Belle Little

144

would see to that. She was going to make sure her new gubernatorial connections paid off handsomely—and wherever she went, Arthur, Sam Parker and Bernard Howard were bound to follow.

Re-locking the clothes in the closets, away from servants' prying eyes, she slipped into a blue satin peignoir, drained her brandy glass and left the room.

As she reached the foot of the stairs, Lucia appeared from the passageway leading to the kitchen.

"Señora, I was wondering . . . it is ten o'clock."

Margaret nodded. "Are all the alarms on?"

"Yes, señora."

She proffered her empty glass. "Pour me another brandy, I'll have it in the den. Then you may go."

The hall clock, an exquisite nineteenth-century French boulle mounted on an ornate pedestal, delicately chimed eleven.

In the den, Margaret looked up from the historical romance she was reading and snatched her reading glasses from her face, suddenly alarmed by an attack of dizziness—almost of nausea.

She breathed deeply and shook her head, panicked by the giddiness and loss of visual focus. What was happening to her? She wasn't drunk. She'd come downstairs quite sober and nursed her final drink for almost an hour. What on earth . . . was happening . . . to her . . .

A sound, a loud click—like the closing of a door—reached her from the hall. Her glance swept to the closed door, her heart pounding unmercifully. The click came again. There was someone out there! But who? A servant? Lucia was the only servant on duty that night and she'd retired an hour ago.

Margaret struggled to get up and swayed, overwhelmed by dizziness. She staggered forward. Good God, what *was* the matter with her? Clutching her forehead, she moved falteringly to the door, fell against it, opened it and peered out.

"Lucia . . .?" Her voice was a croak, strangled by fear.

But for the ticking of the clock the hall, the entire house was heavy with silence.

"Lucia . . ." she tried again, a whimper, her heart pounding within her.

Dizziness again swept through her, causing her to cry out, to clutch at the door for support. Icy sweat bathed her body. She *was* ill. She was having an attack of some kind and yet she didn't *feel* ill . . .

A sudden noise came from the passage on her left, kitchen noise . . . the whir of appliance motors. A shiver ripped through her. Who could be in the kitchen at this time of night, using appliances?

"LUCIA!"

Releasing the door, she tottered across the hall and into the passage, fell against its wall, lunged for the kitchen door and opened it.

She gaped.

The lights were on—and the dish-washer, food mixer, electric carving knife and vacuum cleaner were working . . . but there was no one in the room!

"Lu . . . CIA!" she yelled, stunned, dizzy, terrified.

She whirled as a new sound reached her. From the den she had just left came the blaring of the television!

With a stifled cry she stumbled back along the passage and into the hall, clutching at the balastrade of the staircase, and stared incredulously at the den's open door.

Someone was moving around the room!

With a keening cry she threw herself at the stairs, started up them, stumbled, went on, tripped over the hem of her peignoir and ripped the garment away. Now scrambling up on hands and knees, whimpering with terror, casting terrified glances down towards the open den door, she reached the landing, and tottered into her bedroom and slammed the door, her fingers fumbling to turn the key.

Dear *God*, what was happening? A burglar . . . she was alone with a burglar!

No, not alone. Security! Call Security!

Throwing herself at the bed, she snatched up the receiver, her finger freezing over the buttons as the sound of breathing filled her ear.

146

"Wh-who's there?"

The breathing became a chuckle—male, mocking, sexual. "Hello, Mrs Whitney."

A cry grated in her throat. "Who *are* you?"

"You know who I am. I followed you home. I've come to get you."

Her vision blurred, the thunderous beat of her heart shook her body. She was going to die!

He said quietly, "Right now you're thinking—this can't be happening to me. Not to Margaret Whitney, not here in the Park. But it is. I'm really here, Mrs Whitney, downstairs in your den. And in a moment I'm coming upstairs to get you."

She cried out. "Why? WHY ME?"

"Because you're guilty."

"Of *what*?"

"Of concealing a murder."

"That's ridiculous." A tidal wave of dizziness struck her now. She swayed, almost toppling from the bed, and groaned.

"What's the matter, Mrs Whitney—don't you feel well? Bit dizzy, are you? You'd better lie down and rest. And while you're resting, try to remember whose murder you concealed. If you can't, don't worry—I'll be up there soon to remind you, before I murder *you*".

The connection was severed.

She stared, horrified, at the phone and dropped it slowly back in its cradle. This was a nightmare, a shocking hallucination. And yet she knew she was wide awake. This was her bedroom—physical, real. This was her hand—touchable, responsive. She . . .

Security! Call Security!

She snatched up the receiver, then dropped it with a whimpering cry. The line was dead.

A fresh onslaught of dizziness buffeted her. The room began to blur . . . she was going to pass out!

The moment of her waking brought horror beyond belief. A scream exploded in her throat but died in silence, muted by the gag that filled her mouth.

She hurled herself away from the hideous black faceless thing that sat beside her, its head encased, robot-like, in a gleaming helmet ... but found she could not move. She was manacled, her wrists and ankles secured by steel handcuffs to the rails of her bed, spread star-like, legs apart, the folds of her peignoir laid aside. And she was *naked*!

"Helpless."

The word came down to her, muffled by the visor of his helmet.

He leaned close to her, his leather clothing squeaking, smelling faintly of oil—enormous, inhuman, terrifying.

"Helpless, vulnerable. No one to turn to for help. Can there be anything more frightening than dying alone?"

He sat upright again. "Perhaps so. Perhaps having to leave behind someone you love, children, for instance, is worse. You're very fortunate, Mrs Whitney. You have no children, nobody you love at all. Oh, there's Arthur—but you don't love him. And he certainly doesn't love you."

He laughed softly. "You bore him, did you know that? Everything about you bores him—your conversation, the mindless existence you lead here in the Park, your lovemaking ... especially your lovemaking. He's planning to get rid of you, did you know that? He's going to divorce you and marry his secretary, Judith Harmer ..."

Margaret jerked her head away, whimpering her protest.

"Oh, surely you knew that—or at least guessed. Why do you think he spends so much time away from you ... and with her? Not that anyone could blame him, she's a beautiful girl. Much younger than you, of course. Much sexier, too. They spend an awful lot of time in bed together, she and Arthur. Like right now, for instance. Right at this moment they're tucked up nice 'n' cosy in the Berkley Hotel in Galverston." He chuckled. "Boy, I'll bet she does things to him you never dreamed of doing ... and vice versa. Do you know what you are, Mrs Whitney? You're a has-been. You're washed up and wiped out. Did you know that nobody gives a damn whether you live or die?

"Ah, I see by your eyes that you don't believe that. Your

friends would care, you're thinking. Lily Parker, Ruth Howard and Belle Little would care." He sighed regretfully. "Well, I hate to break it to you, but you're wrong. They don't give a damn about you. Heck, no one in the Park gives a damn about anybody but themselves—especially Belle Little, you know that. All she cares about is marrying off her daughter to the Governor's son—right? That's the *only* thing that matters to her."

He put a gloved hand into the fold of his jacket and brought out a miniature tape recorder, activating the "replay" button.

Margaret's eyes widened with shock as she heard her own voice plead, "Then you don't think I ought to tell the police?"

"No! I most certainly do not! Christ, Margaret, do you want to panic everyone? One *whisper* that something threatening or dangerous is lurking around here and the Miami Symphony will be playing to a congregation of *two* instead of two thousand next Thursday—that'll be Elizabeth and me! Now—*please*—not a word to anyone about this. Besides, what could you tell the police? That a man in black followed you home and kept staring and nodding at you?"

"But, Belle, the *note* . . ."

"*What* note? You don't *have* the damned note. Now, Margaret, you listen to me . . . This wedding is the biggest . . . thing . . . of . . . my . . . life! And I won't allow anything to spoil it—not *anything*! Do you understand? You will treat this thing . . ."

He switched off the tape recorder and tucked it back into his jacket. "'Not anything.' Sounds pretty final, doesn't it, Mrs Whitney? But I wonder if she really does mean *anything*? Even, say, the threatened torture . . . mutilation . . . *death* . . . of a friend?"

The direction of his gaze shifted deliberately to the junction of her legs, and with taunting slowness he stretched out his hand and brought it to rest on her exposed pudenda, his thumb insinuatingly caressing the crevice of her vagina.

Margaret arched violently, straining against the handcuffs, groaning out a muted cry of terror.

"That's quite pointless, Mrs Whitney. Why not relax and enjoy it? Because this will be the very last time a man touches you there. Or anywhere else. Tell me, do you know what the Nazis did to women prisoners in the Second World War?"

She stared at a distant wall, her eyes bulging.

"They did terrible things to them ... tortured them with electricity ... and acid ... and soldering irons ... and lighted cigarettes ... to find out how much pain they could endure before they died. Can you imagine the pain, the *agony* of a lighted cigarette on a woman's nipple?"

His hand went into his jacket pocket to produce a packet of Lucky Strike.

Margaret's head jerked around, her eyes flaring with terror as he shook out a cigarette and brought it close to the nipple of her right breast. He held it there for a tormenting moment, then, with a symbolic "Tsssssss!" lightly touched its unlit end to the nipple.

She screamed.

He laughed and trailed the cigarette down her body, over the flat plane of her belly and drew indolent circles around her triangle of auburn pubic hair.

"Or, can you imagine a red-hot soldering iron inserted into her vagina? Can you *feel* the excruciating agony of that, Mrs Whitney? Sure, you can. All women can. Even Belle Little.

"*But* I wonder if she could be persuaded—by the threat of such torture to a friend—to give up her political ambitions? Do you think she would call off the wedding to save a friend from torture and death? I doubt it. But there's really only one way to find out, isn't there?"

Again he reached into his pocket, this time producing the flat, oblong tin box. From it he took the hypodermic syringe.

At the sight of it, Margaret flung her head away, her face crimson with terror and strain as she wrenched against her manacles.

Deliberately he brought the needle into her view.

"Nasty things, aren't they? This one even frightens me—and

150

I'm on the safe end of it. You know why it frightens me? Because it contains the cells of a disease for which there is no known cure, a disease that destroys tissue at incredible speed. You have a good body, Mrs Whitney, not a blemish anywhere. But if—or when—I inject this bacteria, your lovely body will become a mass of superating sores within two days, a rotting skeleton within a week. Just by doing that."

She screamed as he lightly traced the needle along the inside of her thigh.

He laughed. "No, no, that's not the truth at all, Mrs Whitney. It was a little joke, a practical joke. Why aren't you laughing? You like practical jokes—at least you go along with them. Elizabeth Little's practical jokes, for instance—you certainly go along with hers, hmm?"

He paused for her reaction, her frown of bewilderment, before continuing.

"No," he said confidentially, "let me tell you what is *really* in this syringe. It's a virulent culture that causes terrible vomiting."

Margaret shut her eyes and whimpered in distress.

"You just vomit and vomit, and when you can't vomit any more, you begin to bleed internally. Then your body begins to swell up and up like an inflated balloon, and after several days it bursts! Bang! I'm told it's not very pleasant."

He gave a cheerful laugh. "Hey, Mrs Whitney, you should see your face! You look really scared! Not surprising, though. It's the uncertainty that does it, isn't it? Not knowing what is going to happen to you. That's always the worst part. D'you know something—prisoners on death row hardly ever go off their heads, because they *know* what's going to happen to them. It's the torment of not knowing that drives you crazy."

He leaned closer, the needle only inches from her face. "Imagine the torment of—say—a mother of three young children who is suddenly arrested and slung into jail for a crime she didn't commit. And while she's sitting in that prison cell, shocked, lonely, desperate, helpless, she's told that she and her children are going to be deported back to the country they've

151

just escaped from. Can you imagine that woman's torment, Mrs Whitney, her fear of the unknown? Sure you can—because you're feeling it right now. You don't know what is in this syringe—or even if I'm going to inject it into you. You don't know what is going to happen to you."

He sat upright. "OK, I'm going to put you out of your misery. This is a drug that will put you to sleep in ten seconds and keep you asleep for eight hours. The question is, where will you wake up? Well, I'll tell you that, too. When you open your eyes you'll see nothing. Everything will be so black you won't even be sure your eyes *are* open. Then you'll notice the air is hot and stuffy around you, that your own breath is reflecting back into your face from a close surface. You'll put out your hand and realise you're in a box, a coffin. You'll panic. You will shout and scream and kick, trying to break out, hoping you'll be heard. And you will be heard—but only by a few passing bonefish and maybe a tarpon or two—because you'll be lying at the bottom of the Atlantic Ocean under two hundred feet of water." He laughed suddenly. "Hey, don't take it so badly, you won't die immediately. If you keep absolutely quiet and still, you could last maybe five or six hours."

He leaned right into her, thrust his visored face close to hers. "Fact is, Mrs Whitney, you don't know *now* whether I'm telling the truth or not. Don't you wish I would tell the truth and put you out of your misery? Sure you do—just like that mother of three I was telling you about. She was praying somebody would tell the truth and get her released—right up to the moment she hanged herself in the jail washroom to save her kids."

Margaret's eyes widened with sudden understanding.

He nodded with satisfaction. "Ah, I see the nickel's finally dropped. Yes, that's right, Mrs Whitney—Ana Patillas. She is what this is all about. OK, I know she was already dead when you learned that Elizabeth was responsible for those thefts, but Ana Patillas died known as a thief—something you and Lily Parker and Ruth Howard could have corrected but didn't. You and they are guilty of concealing a crime. And now you and they are going to help me expose it. You are going to force Belle and Elizabeth Little to tell the truth!"

152

He got up, caught her wrist, squeezed it, and slid the hypodermic into a corded vein.

"Enjoy your nap, Mrs Whitney, and while you're sleeping dream of Ana Patillas hanging in that jail washroom. Because if Belle Little doesn't publicly confess to her daughter's crime, that is how *you* are going to die."

3

The guards on duty that night were Carl Krantz, and a handsome, swarthy young man whose name was Lawrence West.

Krantz disliked the kid. He was too quiet, too studious, too fucking know-all—one of the new breed of security cop he detested. They were all pushers these days, too smart to be satisfied with old-style security duty. They couldn't be satisfied to just sit there and guard the goddamned place any more, they had to study, take part-time courses in police science, electronic surveillance, penal psy-fucking-chology, and drive, drive, drive up that ladder.

This one, West, who'd been his night-shift partner for four months, was worse than most—taking courses at Miami University and Four Square headquarters during the day, a stack of smart-ass books in the booth at night. No women talk, no dirty jokes—just books. A real shit-head.

Krantz, his feet propped on the corner of the desk, a hardcore porn magazine open in his lap, interrupted his study of a naked black girl from whose vagina protruded the head of a live, spitting snake, and directed his own venom at the kid whose nose was buried in an electronics text book.

"How 'bout some cawfee, West?"

West looked up. "Yes, sure, Mr Krantz."

Always fucking polite, too. Never an "Aw, shit, Mr Krantz, how about you making it for a change." Never anything that he, Krantz, could justifiably take exception to or pick a quarrel over. The kid really pissed him off. Yet, for all that, he was better company than the string of dumb jerks he'd had to share the death-watch with over the years, the big-cock jocks whose only conversation was how many times they got it up in a week.

He checked his watch and inwardly groaned. It was only a bit before two. Four hours to go. The night shift was getting longer and longer, it seemed. Maybe he was gettin' old or something.

He got up and opened the door. He took a deep breath of the cool December air, wincing as a lance of pain pricked his side.

"What's the trouble?" West asked from across the room. "You got a pain? I've seen you do that a couple of times."

"Yeh."

"Lumbago?"

Krantz's head whipped round, suspecting mockery, but West's expression was bland, sincere. "Shit, no, that's an old man's complaint. Knife wound."

"No kidding? You get it on the force?"

Krantz scowled, as though the subject, as well as the wound, pained him. "No, right here in the goddamned Park."

"A knife wound *here*? Geez, how did it happen?"

"It was six years ago . . . three Spic kids got into Belle Little's garden from the bay and tripped the alarm. I went up there with the dog we had at the time, Khan—a real mean bastard, beautiful animal, tear the head off a fucking tiger." His thin mouth twisted in a sour grin. "The nerve of them young fuckers . . . marched right up to Belle's front door, claimin' they wanted to speak to her. She'd just put their mother in the slammer for stealing—she was a maid there—and the kids came pleadin' for her release. Well, you know what Belle's like. She screamed bloody murder, yelled at me to get 'em outta the Park and make sure they stayed out. Well, I sure as hell did. I took them half-ways back to their boat, then let Khan take them the rest of the way."

West frowned ruefully. "You let the dog go?"

Krantz grinned. "Sure."

"Jesus."

"Yeh—Jesus. Man, you shoulda seen it . . . he went straight for the chick, tore away a piece of her face. Shit, it was flappin' around like a pound of raw sirloin. One of the brothers kicked Khan in the balls and he damned near tore the kid's leg off. Then, by Christ, the older brother whipped out a shiv and slit the dog's throat ear to ear. I belted him away and started kickin' crap outta the punk, when the other brother, who shoulda bin lyin' there bleeding to death, crept up behind me and stuck the shiv in me. When I came round they'd got away in my station wagon."

West brought a mug of coffee over. "Any follow-up?"

Krantz sipped the coffee and shook his head. "No. A coupla days later their old lady strung herself up in jail and the Beach cops closed the book on it kinda fast, figured the kids had left town and liked it that way. Never heard no more about them."

West smiled. "But you'd like to, hmm?"

Krantz's pale eyes fastened on him. "What do you think? If I ever get a hand on that Spic scum, I'll stick 'em in the compound with Rebel there and count the pieces as they fly off. After I break their backs, that is."

West frowned. "Be a bit risky, wouldn't it, Mr Krantz? The company rules say . . ."

Krantz flared. "Shit, I know what the rules say, West—don't you book-talk me. I wus a cop before you were crappin' your diapers. It's gone two—do your tour."

"Yes, sir."

Collecting his cap and a four-cell flashlight, West left the booth and headed across the unlit parking area at the rear of the booth towards the company Chevrolet station wagon, parked between Krantz's green Plymouth and West's own sand-coloured Dodge.

Reaching the Chevrolet, he glanced back at the booth, seeing that Krantz had now resumed his seat, his back to the parking area and his head bent to his magazine.

Ignoring the Chevrolet, West opened the door of his Dodge and got in, started the engine and turned into the Park, cruising slowly.

The estate lay in somnolent silence. Lights showed in most houses, but they were hall and landing lights, left on for additional security. Being either elderly or business people, the residents invariably retired before midnight during the week.

West cruised the circuit road in a clockwise direction, slowing as he encountered the driveway of Number Seventeen. Although no lights showed in the house, Margaret Whitney's Mercedes was parked in an attitude of abandonment at the front steps, and the garage doors, to the right of the house, stood open.

West turned the Dodge into the driveway and drew up alongside the Mercedes.

Switching off the engine, he collected the flashlight and got out, climbed the half-dozen stone steps to the verandah and pushed at the front door. It opened. He swept the hall with his flashlight, stepped inside, closed the door and stood listening. The house was silent. On his toes he crossed the hall to the stairs and began to climb. Reaching the landing, he turned to the left. Suddenly a bedroom door on his right jerked open. West brought the flashlight up, illuminating a grotesque figure dressed in black leather, the torchlight reflecting blindingly off the black plastic visor of the motorcycle helmet.

"You're late," said Rider. "I was beginning to get worried."

West smiled. "Krantz was gabbing, telling me about his old knife wound and what he was going to do to those three Spic kids if he ever caught up with them."

"Oh yeh?" Rider laughed.

West nodded into the room. "Everything go OK?"

"Like a dream—no pun intended. Maria . . . Lucia, I mean, helped me. Margaret's dressed and ready to go."

"Good—let's move."

They carried Margaret Whitney, dressed in slacks and sweater, downstairs and folded her into the specially prepared trunk of the Dodge, then pushed the Mercedes into the garage and closed the doors.

"You'd better get some sleep," said West, "or you'll be dropping off in the azaleas tomorrow."

"Yeh. Hey . . . it's going to work, hmm?"

"Damn right it is. Kiss Maria for me, tell her to be brave."

"You don't have to worry about her, she's stronger than both of us." Rider embraced his brother. "*Vaya con Dios*, Francisco."

"*Dios le guarde*, Carlo."

As Carlo melted into the darkness, returning to the staff bungalow next door, Francisco climbed into the Dodge and drove back to the booth.

"All quiet?" murmured Krantz without raising his eyes from the centrefold.

"As the grave," answered Francisco. "I reckon they're all storing up sleep for next Thursday. That wedding is really going to be something, hmm?"

"Yeh—one big pain in the ass for us. Christ, did yuh ever see a cunt like this one? I'd sure rather be inside that than San Quentin."

Francisco leaned in the open doorway and looked out across the Park at the distant silhouette of Belle Little's house. "Yep ... that wedding is certainly going to be an occasion to remember."

4

He had arrived back in Miami in September the previous year and taken a room in a modest hotel in the barrio. While he waited for her to arrive, he read yet again the letter she had sent to Los Angeles so long ago, the letter, now considerably worn, that he had carried with him constantly since that day.

"My Dear Luisa and Fidel,

How sad that this news must come too late. This evening Señora Little held one of her bridge nights and as usual Señoras Howard, Parker and Whitney were here. Late on, I was taking tea into the sitting-room and chanced to overhear Señora Whitney tell the others she had just overheard Elizabeth talking on the telephone to a friend, telling her it was she who had put the stolen jewellery in Ana's room in an act of revenge!

As you might imagine, Señora Little did nothing —except to warn the three women to keep silent about it.

The moment I heard I went to my room and telephoned Jose, who in turn called Juan Perrer, Ana's lawyer. Alas, Perrer says no such hearsay evidence could possibly be used against the Littles and he advises me to say nothing to anyone about the incident for fear of trouble from the Littles.

If it would do any good, if it would bring dear Ana back, I wouldn't hesitate to stand up against them. But at least the children may now rest assured that Ana's friends in the barrio know the truth—that she died innocent of any wrongdoing.

I think of you all constantly and can still not believe the

terrible thing that has happened to you. I pray to God that in time the children will get over their loss and learn to live a happy life with you both.

If there is any way in which I can help, don't hesitate to write. I despise these people for what they have done and continue to do. It seems so unjust that we now know the truth of Elizabeth's crime and are helpless to do anything about it.

Perhaps in God's good time they will pay for all their wickedness.

Your loving friend,
Constanza

Believing the letter might help assuage his grief, Luisa and Fidel had shown it to him. Its effect had been to consolidate his hatred, and, later, to form the foundation of his determination to avenge his mother's death and publicly clear her name.

With no clear plan of retribution, yet sensing that Constanza, with her position in the Park, might well provide the mainstay of any future plan, he had maintained a regular correspondence with her.

Now, a quiet knock sounded at his door.

As he opened it, the memory of that night in the Park came flooding back. Constanza had aged a little in five years, had put on a little weight, yet the image he had retained of her had been substantially accurate.

It was not so in her case. She frowned enquiringly at him, her smile registering agreeable surprise. "Francisco?"

He returned her smile. "It's really me. Come on in."

She entered, a stout little figure in a floral summer dress, her dark hair caught neatly in a bun. She smiled maternally. "Can this be the skinny young man who stood there at the front door five years ago?"

"The same—though I guess I've put a little meat on since then."

"A little," she nodded approvingly.

He took her arm, led her to one of the armchairs by the open window. "Would you like a drink ... an orange or a Coke, perhaps?"

"No, thank you, I'm fine."

He sat facing her, sat forward, elbows on knees. "Constanza, thank you for coming. I apologise for stealing your afternoon off."

"And what better things would an old spinster be doing on her afternoon off—lying on the beach in her bikini?"

He smiled, the smile quickly dying as he said earnestly, "And thank you so much for writing. It has meant so much to me."

She shook her head. "At first your letters made me very sad, Francisco. When you first began writing about trying to clear your mother's name, I could feel your anguish, your frustration, and I felt so helpless. I didn't know what to write, how to comfort you."

"You did help, though. You wrote what I wanted to hear. The fact that you were still working for the Littles helped enormously. I kept expecting to hear that you'd left or been fired. If that had happened I'm sure I couldn't have gone on with the plan. Right now you're the most important part of it."

She sighed, an expression of deep concern. "Francisco, are you sure you know what you're trying to do ... who you're going up against? These people are so powerful. They have such powerful friends. They can do whatever they put a mind to. I know because I hear them ... plotting and scheming and arranging things to suit themselves. You wouldn't believe the things that go on in that house."

He smiled at her. "I think I would. What kind of things are you talking about?"

She shrugged, gave it thought. "Only last week I heard Señora Little on the phone. I don't know who she was talking to or quite what it was about—but it obviously had something to do with an important building contract. I heard her shouting to whoever it was that unless Arthur Whitney's company got the contract, and both Señor Parker and Señor Howard handled the business, she'd see to it that whoever it was didn't get so much as his big toe inside City Hall." She laughed humourlessly. "Needless to say, she got her way."

161

Francisco was nodding, his eyes bright with excitement. "Political and business chicanery. Constanza, that's exactly the kind of thing I'm looking for."

She frowned. "Oh?"

"Look, I do know what I'm up against and I do realise how powerful the Littles are—but I also know how crooked and greedy they are, and that the only way of getting to them is to get to know their secrets, their crooked dealings, and to use them against them. That is the only way I can hope to do it."

She shook her head, with sympathy but incredulity. "Francisco, what if you did learn something—how could you possibly use it? Who would listen to you? For instance, we *know* it was Elizabeth who put the stolen jewellery in your mother's room—I actually overheard them talking about it—but you know what Juan Perrer said about hearsay evidence. It can't be used! And the same would apply to anything else you learned about them."

Francisco smiled, undeterred. "But what if their conversations were not only overheard but tape recorded? What if we had something tangible like a cassette recording to send to the newspapers or the TV stations—or the Justice Department. What then?"

She frowned thoughtfully. "Well, I don't know. I suppose it could make a difference."

"It could make an enormous difference. You know what the papers are like—anything for a story—and they'd really go to town on a scandal involving people from the Park. Belle Little is *news*. The media would jump at a chance to expose her if we could prove corruption."

Constanza was silent for a moment, then with a censorious smile, asked, "But what has this got to do with clearing your mother's name? It sounds like you're out for revenge."

"No, not merely revenge, Constanza. But there's no reason why the two things shouldn't be accomplished at the same time. If I could get some hard evidence against Belle Little, maybe I could use it to get a confession about the stolen jewellery from her or Elizabeth."

Constanza frowned. "Blackmail?"

He met her eyes, replied with determination that was close to anger. "I don't care what label is put on it. When you're fighting overwhelming odds you use every trick in the book and a few that aren't. We tried the decent approach—remember? Three innocent kids knocked on her door to ask for pity and pardon, and you know what it got them. Well, now I'm prepared to match dirty pool with even dirtier pool. I'm ready to try anything—providing there's a reasonable chance of getting away with it."

She nodded, shaken by his vehemence, not realising until this moment how truly determined he was. His boyish charm had misled her. When he chose to set it aside, he revealed a ruthlessness that frightened her.

"When you say that you're ready to try anything," she asked hesitantly, "... what exactly do you mean? Surely you don't mean ... violence?"

He shook his head. "I intend using brains, not brawn. Violence would bring the police down on us—and would probably antagonise the friends we do have in the Park. We can't afford to let either happen. I need to be able to come out of this in such a way that Carlo, Maria and I can live a normal life afterwards."

She grimaced, overtly sceptical. "How on earth are you going to do that? You hope to take on the Littles, force a confession out of them, cause a scandal that will ruin them—and then walk away and live a normal life! Francisco, I really don't see how—"

"Constanza, I don't profess to know how myself yet. We'll have to see what kind of breaks we get as we go along. It really depends on what we pick up on tape."

She smiled crookedly. "And how in heavens name are you going to pick up *anything* on tape? You can't hide tape recorders all over the Little house ..."

He got up, crossed the room to a grey Samsonite case, opened it and took out a small cardboard box. Returning to his seat, he removed a small metallic object from the box and held it out to her in the palm of his hand.

"What is it?" she frowned.

"It's a tape recorder."

She gaped at him in astonishment.

He grinned. "Well, as good as. Have you ever heard of a 'bug'—not the insect kind, the kind they put in rooms and telephones to ..."

Her eyes widened excitedly. "Oh, yes! On television ... the Rockford Files and ..."

"Right. This is a bug."

She stared at it, fascinated. "I was never sure whether they were real things or just made up for TV."

"Oh, they're real, all right. You'd be amazed how many are in operation all over the world at this moment, hidden in embassies and board rooms—even bedrooms—picking up all kinds of secrets."

"And ... how do they work?"

"This tiny grille, here, is a highly sensitive microphone. The bug transmits sound on a certain frequency which is picked up by a radio receiver up to thirty-five miles away—farther over open water."

She gaped. "Thirty-five miles! You mean ... you could sit in this room and hear everything that goes on in the Littles' house?"

"As clearly as though I were sitting with them. This is the basis of my plan, Constanza."

She nodded, impressed by his expertise, his degree of preparedness. Suddenly she was no longer so afraid for him.

He was looking at her intently. "This is where I badly need your help. It's up to you whether the plan goes ahead or stops right here."

"What do you want me to do?" she asked quietly.

"Nothing just yet. I'll need some time to get ready. I'm going to rent a house here in the barrio and set up some equipment. It'll take a month or two. But when the time comes, I'll want you to hide these bugs in certain places, I'll tell you where. It's really quite easy."

She whispered, "Yes ... all right."

"And there's something else. This may not be so easy, but we have time on our side. I need to get Carlo and Maria into the Park ... working for either Mrs Whitney, Mrs Parker or Mrs Howard.''

She frowned, taken aback. "Doing what? Domestic work? Have they had any experience? I don't think it would be possible if they ..."

Again his confident smile made her feel a little foolish for doubting. "They're doing it right now—in Los Angeles. Maria is working as a maid in Beverly Hills, Carlo is gardening in Bel Air.''

With a rueful grin she shook her head at him. "You've really got it all planned out, haven't you?"

"Not all, Constanza, but as much as we can. Do you think it will be possible to get them into the Park?"

She shrugged. "Anything is possible."

"I was thinking that perhaps we could appeal to a maid and a gardener already employed there, pay them to take a job elsewhere ... and have Carlo and Maria available to fill the vacancies—as my mother did when ... what was her name?"

Constanza smiled sadly. "Juanita."

"Yes—when Juanita left to get married. It worked once, it could work again.''

She nodded. "It's possible. There is a lot of sympathy among our people in the Park for your mother and you children. I'm sure it could be done."

He smiled his gratitude. "Well, I think that's as far as we can go at this moment. I must now find a suitable house and bring Carlo and Maria from LA. After that we'll take one step at a time, adapt as we go along.''

He saw her to the door, took her hand and kissed her cheek. "Thank you ... for everything."

She patted his hand. "I'll do anything I can to help clear your mother's name. What they did to her was evil and unforgivable. I only hope and pray that what you're about to do doesn't bring any more unhappiness to you and the twins. You've already had more than enough trouble in your lives.''

"We'll be very careful." He opened the door. "I'll be in

165

touch, Constanza. I'll write, rather than phone." He grinned. "You never know who's listening in to a telephone conversation."

As she moved into the hallway, he asked, "Carl Krantz . . . he still works in the Park, I trust?"

She turned and met his eyes, saw in them the hate that lay behind the question. "Yes, he's still there. But, Francisco, he's not a man to fool with. He's a brutal, sadistic . . ."

He smiled gently. "I know exactly what Krantz is. We have a very special plan for him."

She made to reply but decided against it, checked by the hardness of his eyes. With a faint nod of acceptance, she turned away and walked towards the stairs.

It took him almost a year to infiltrate the Park, and yet at no time was he plagued by any sense of impatience or frustration. With the calm deliberation of a skilled chess-player he advanced each piece of his plan with unhurried precision, allowing time for each move according to its degree of difficulty and experiencing immense satisfaction from each successful coup.

When, in the following August, the final vital segment of his endeavours—his appointment to the Park as night security guard—was accomplished, he called his brother and sister to the house for a celebration.

He raised his beer in a toast. "Phase One completed, *muchachos*."

Carlo nodded. "Now we've got everything set up, what do we do with it?"

"We wait and we listen."

"For what, exactly?" asked Maria.

"I don't know—exactly," answered Francisco. "But one of these days we're going to pick something up on the tapes that we can use against the Littles, pressure them to make a public confession. Then we'll not only rock their smug boat, we'll blow them out of the water. It's coming, *muchachos*, it's coming."

But when at last it did come, it arrived not in a spectacular

166

way, not the sudden, startling revelation of secret wrong-doing he'd envisaged. Indeed, on hearing it for the first time, the information was so mundane it almost passed him by.

It was only later, as the news was repeated and repeated, as excitement about it grew, expanding it into a matter of huge importance, that he realised that this was the lever he'd been waiting for.

Again he summoned Maria and Carlo to the house.

"The wedding!" he exclaimed.

Maria groaned. "Please—don't mention that subject. It's all I hear from morning till night ... the wedding, the wedding, the wedding. You'd think Elizabeth Little was the first woman in the world to get married."

Francisco smiled. "Would we have it any other way?"

Carlo looked puzzled. "Sorry, I don't follow."

"Working in the garden you obviously haven't heard as much about it as we have," said Francisco. "Since Belle and Elizabeth Little got back from Europe I've picked up *seventeen hours* of phone conversation about it. It's the only thing in Belle's mind right now—the most important event of her life."

"A wedding?" frowned Carlo.

"Not just *a* wedding, Carlo—*the* wedding. *The* wedding of the year. Belle's made her mind up about that."

"It's true," nodded Maria. "Everyone in the Park is going crazy about it."

Carlo shrugged. "So—what's so special about Elizabeth getting married?"

"The *groom* is what's so special," answered Francisco. "He's Robert Collier—the only son of Miles Collier who is ..."

Carlo grinned, suddenly enlightened. "The Governor of Florida."

"The same," nodded Francisco. "And also the man tipped to get the Republican nomination in the next presidential election. So is it any wonder Belle is going ga-ga over the wedding?"

"No," said Carlo. "But how is it going to be of use to us?"

"OK, let's run through it," said Francisco. "The wedding is planned for December 23rd. I've heard Belle's plans for it and they're stupendous—more like a production of Aida than a mere wedding. She's having a circus big top erected in the rear garden of the house—big enough to accommodate two thousand guests ..."

The twins murmured, "Wow."

"Inside the tent she's having a wooden floor put down and a stage built. The ceremony will take place on the stage, accompanied—get this—by the Miami Symphony Orchestra ... and the Miami Tabernacle choir ... *and* with the Bishop of Miami doing the honours."

He paused for their expressions of surprise.

"But that's only the beginning," he grinned. "She's hired none other than Tyrone Gambretti, the New York stage director, to direct the whole operation. He's having canvas flats designed which will turn the tent into a church, and when the ceremony is over, these flats will be turned around to transform the church into a Viennese ballroom!"

The twins whooped.

"She's really going to town on this," Francisco went on. "She's making damn sure everybody in Florida knows her daughter is marrying the Governor's son. There'll be dozens of media people covering it—TV, radio, press. She's even having a special stage erected for the media—to make sure they get a good view of the proceedings. After the ceremony there'll be a party like you wouldn't believe—steers spit-roasted on the terrace, dancing to the Symphony Orchestra, a trad jazz band and a rock group till dawn—at which time Robert and Elizabeth Collier will depart by helicopter to Miami Airport, where the Littles' private jet will be waiting to fly them to the Littles' villa in Hawaii for their honeymoon."

Maria rolled her eyes. "Oh, wow ..."

"Two hundred thousand dollars—that's what it's going to cost," Francisco continued. "And in return, Belle Little will pull ten million dollars' worth of publicity—and so will Miles Collier ... OK?"

Carlo nodded, frowningly. "But I still don't see how we can use it ..."

"OK, picture the scene. It's three o'clock on December 23rd. Two thousand guests—big money, big business, the cream of

168

Florida society—are sitting in that big top, watching it all happen. Up on the stage the orchestra, choir, the Bishop, the Governor and his wife, the bride and groom and, of course, Belle Little.

"To one side of the tent, on their own stage, are dozens of media people. The TV cameras are transmitting, tape recorders are turning, cameras flashing, pencils scribbling and live radio commentaries going out. The Bishop begins the service . . . the eyes and ears of the state are on the bride and groom.

"Suddenly, Belle Little jumps up from her seat, grabs a microphone, and stuns everyone by announcing, 'I have a confession to make! Six years ago my daughter stole some jewellery and put the blame on Ana Patillas, my maid at that time, who was arrested and hanged herself in jail. I now admit to concealing this crime and, with Elizabeth, accept responsibility for Ana Patillas's death.'"

Maria shrieked and clutched her cheeks. "Oh, wow!"

Carlo roared with laughter. "Oh, man!"

Francisco smiled with them, allowed their exuberance to run its course, then said quietly, with an earnestness that ended their humour abruptly, "It could be done."

They frowned at him, overtly sceptical.

"Aw, come on . . ." said Carlo, hesitantly.

"How could we possibly get her to do that?" asked Maria.

"By giving her an even more terrifying alternative," Francisco answered. "Carlo—would you voluntarily cut off one of your fingers?"

Carlo grimaced. "Of course not."

"But say it was poisoned, had just been bitten by a rattler and by cutting it off you could save your life? Would you then?"

Carlo nodded pensively. "I guess I would."

"Sure you would—because it would be the lesser of two evils. And that's the kind of choice we're going to give Belle Little. We've got to get her into a situation in which a public confession is more acceptable to her than the alternative."

"And what on earth would that alternative be?" frowned Maria.

Francisco looked at them in turn and answered softly. "The death of three friends."

No one spoke for what seemed a very long time. Carlo finally broke the silence with a release of stifled breath. "Phew . . ."

Maria bit at her lip, frowning worriedly. "We . . . we're going to *kill* three women?"

"That's the alternative we're going to give Belle Little," Francisco answered solemnly. "Either she publicly clears Momma's name at three o'clock on the day of the wedding—just as the Bishop begins the ceremony—or her three friends, Margaret Whitney, Lily Parker and Ruth Howard, will be hanged at the very moment Elizabeth becomes Robert Collier's wife."

"But . . . how are we . . ." Carlo glanced incredulously at his sister, back to Francisco, ". . . going to be able to do that?"

"We're going to kidnap them," answered Francisco.

5

Saturday, December 18th.

At six a.m., his shift ended, Francisco returned to the barrio house, drove the Dodge into the garage, closed the doors and unlocked the trunk.

Margaret Whitney was sleeping soundly. From the tapes he'd learned she slept badly, even with pills. This had probably been one of her better nights.

With difficulty he pulled her out of the trunk, draped her over his shoulder in a fireman's lift and carried her into the house and up to the control bedroom, where he laid her on the bed and secured her wrists and ankles to its wooden rails.

After she had succumbed to the drug, Carlo removed her gag to prevent choking. For the time being Francisco decided not to replace it; she wouldn't waken for another hour.

From the wardrobe he took a black leather outfit, identical to the one worn by Carlo, went down the hall to the bathroom, washed, shaved and changed into the leather clothing, then returned to the bedroom and donned a hood of black cloth in which eye and mouth holes had been cut.

Seating himself at the console, he rewound Belle Little's tape recorder and activated the "replay" button.

A man's voice, pretentiously droll, announced, "The Little residence."

The voice of another man, breathy, nervous, said, "Storey . . . this is Wendell Selby. Is Mrs Little there?"

"One moment, sir, I shall enquire."

A receiver was put down. Footsteps crossed the marble hall floor and a door was tapped on and opened. Distantly Storey could be heard to announce, "Excuse me, madam, Mr Wendell Selby is calling."

An extension receiver rattled. "Selby?" answered Belle Little.

Selby gushed, "Mrs Little, I've just got back from . . ."

Belle hissed, "Ssssh! For God's sake wait till Storey hangs up!" The clack of approaching footsteps was heard, then the clatter of a receiver being replaced. "All right—how did it go?"

Selby swallowed. "Not well, I'm afraid. I've just this moment got back from the lake. The stubborn old fool refuses to budge."

"Damn! You offered him the extra ten thousand?"

"Of course. He didn't even pause to consider it—just kept shaking his head. Money doesn't mean a thing to him, Mrs Little."

"Maybe," Belle replied pensively. "It does to the son, though. Did you tell him about the extra ten?"

"Yes. I drove over to Pierson right away and met him in a bar there."

"Was he lucid?"

"Just. A mess, though. He needs a hundred a day for heroin now."

"Good. How did he react to the offer?"

Selby grunted a laugh. "His eyes popped out. He needs that ninety grand worse than air."

"All right. Keep him alive, but keep him short. Let *him* pressure the old man. You don't suppose Franks could have got wind of the development, do you?"

"Not a chance. He's a recluse, no one speaks to him. He's so senile he doesn't know what year it is. All he cares about is fishing the lake. Fishing's the only thing he'll talk about."

There was silence for ten seconds. When Belle spoke again her voice had changed, was lower-pitched, cunning. "How does he fish the lake, Selby?"

"Hmm? Oh, by boat. He uses one of those inflatable dinghies with a small outboard."

"Inflatable . . . that's interesting." She allowed the word to hang, poised like a Damoclean sword. "Don't you find that interesting, Selby?"

Selby's mouth clicked tackily. "Yes, ma'am, very."

Belle's voice descended to a virulent whisper. "Selby, I *want* that land. *Get* it for me."

"Yes, ma'am."

Selby replaced his receiver, though Belle did not replace hers and the line remained open.

"The fool," she murmured.

A younger female voice asked off-handedly, "What's wrong?"

"Nothing—yet. An old idiot named Frank Franks—can you believe that name?—is sitting on fifty acres of scrub up at Lake George that I want for the new leisure development. I've offered him ninety thousand but he won't budge. *But* he has a junky son who is bleeding for the money . . ."

"Whom Selby is using as a gentle persuader?"

"Maybe not so gentle if Franks doesn't agree to sell. The kid hasn't got a monkey on his back—it's a full-grown gorilla."

"A habit we are drip-feeding, I take it."

"Business is business, Elizabeth."

"Of course." Elizabeth's voice drew closer. "Well, I'm off to bed. Sleep well, Mother."

Belle gave a dry, chesty laugh. "Don't I always?"

"True—though God alone knows how," Elizabeth smiled. "Are you coming up now?"

"Not just yet, I've another call to make. Selby needs help."

"All right. Goodnight, Mother."

Faintly, the drawing-room door closed.

A phone call was made, and after several rings a gruff male voice answered. "Yeh?"

"Bannerman?"

"Who's speakin'?"

"Mrs Little. I have an underwater job for you. Get in touch with Wendell Selby, he'll give you the details. There's ten thousand in it—five up front, five when successfully completed. All right?"

"What's the job?"

"Nothing difficult . . . a little boat-rocking, that's all."

The line closed down, stopping the tape recorder.

. . . . . .

173

Margaret Whitney groaned and attempted to turn on to her side. The restraining tug of the handcuffs brought her awake quickly, aroused by alarm as the nightmare returned ... intensified now by the squalid strangeness of her surroundings.

She gaped, horrified, around the room. Recalling her former state of nakedness, she stared down at her body, confused by the jeans and sweater ... now cringed with fear as her tormentor got up from the console chair and came to stand over her, his dark eyes peering down at her through the eye-slits in the hood.

He spoke coldly and authoritatively. "You are in an old house on the edge of the Everglades, miles from anywhere and anybody. The house is entirely sound-proofed, so it would be useless to scream. If you keep quiet and do exactly as you're told, I shall release you and allow you to go to the bathroom. If you try anything, I shall handcuff you again and leave you to lie in your own filth. Understood?"

She nodded.

Taking a key from his jacket, he unlocked her handcuffs.

She swung her legs over the edge of the bed and sat there, hunched and trembling. "M-may I use the bathroom now?"

He took her arm, led her out of the room and along the landing. The window of the bathroom was boarded over and there was no lock on the door.

"You have three minutes," he told her.

When she was finished, he took her back to the bedroom and sat her in a chair, then seated himself at the console, facing her. "All right, you want to know why this is happening to you."

She nodded, croakingly whispered, "You want money, I suppose."

"No, Mrs Whitney, I do not want money. I want justice. You people in the Park are a law unto yourselves, aren't you? Anything you want done, you just snap your fingers. There's nothing you can't arrange or buy ... even murder."

She frowned, protestingly.

"You refute that? You don't believe Belle Little is capable of arranging a murder to get what she wants?"

He swivelled to face the console, punched the "replay" button on the tape recorder, then sat back, arms folded, watching Margaret's reaction to Belle Little's conversations with Selby, Elizabeth and Bannerman.

Francisco stopped the machine and turned to Margaret. "Nice people, hmm? Are you telling me you didn't know such things went on in the Park? Are you telling me you don't know your husband is tied in with Belle Little in all kinds of crooked deals—like bribing city council officials, quotation rigging and using money, muscle and blackmail to land those big fat building contracts?"

She stared at him, shaking her head. "I . . . didn't know . . . he never . . . confides in me."

He laughed sardonically. "I know he doesn't—because he can't trust you to keep your mouth shut. He confides in Judith Harmer, though." He saw the pain etch her face. "Hurts, doesn't it, Mrs Whitney? You've been replaced by a younger, smarter, more beautiful woman. Arthur *is* planning to get rid of you, you know. I've heard him discussing it with Judith. You're going to wind up a lonely old drunk in a Coral Gables condominium . . ."

"Stop it!" she cried, hunched over, her hands squeezing into fists.

"Not talking about it won't change it, Mrs Whitney. You've got to face reality, quit playing ostrich. You're all washed up."

She asked in a hoarse whisper. "What are you going to do to me?"

"You're going to help me."

"To do what?"

"Bring down Belle and Elizabeth Little."

Her face came up, eyes swollen and red. "You're crazy . . . they . . ."

"Don't bother telling me what they are—I know as much about those two bitches as they know themselves."

She averted her eyes from his, afraid of him.

He looked at his watch, swung back to the console, activated the tape recorder, reached for the phone and dialled a number.

Puzzlement smoothed out the grimace of anguish from Margaret's face as the sound of the purring phone, then Storey's voice, emerged from the loudspeaker mounted on the shelf above the console.

"The Little residence."

Francisco whispered breathily into the phone, "Storey ... this is Wendell Selby again. I have to speak to Mrs Little—urgently!"

"One moment, Mr Selby."

Francisco busied himself with the console controls, altered the frequency of a radio receiver to that of a particular listening device in the Little household.

Margaret Whitney's face registered blank amazement as the voice of Belle Little, in conversation, came from the speaker.

". . . begin the Wedding March a few seconds earlier. That would give you and Andy Hamlin a chance to make an absolutely stunning entrance from the terrace steps into the marquee, rather than have you standing there like a couple of mannequins waiting for the orchestra to strike up . . . Yes, what is it, Storey?"

"Mr Selby is on the telephone, madam."

"Oh ... all right, I'll take it in here. Bring me a phone."

"Certainly, madam."

"Don't you agree, Elizabeth?"

"Of course I agree. I have no desire to stand around anywhere like a window dummy, least of all at my own wedding."

Francisco turned to Margaret, ancitipating the bewilderment he encountered on her face. "Their breakfast room is bugged. So is every major room in the house. So is your phone and the phones of Lily Parker and Ruth Howard."

She gasped. "Who *are* you?"

The sound of the closing phone extension drew him back to the console.

"Yes, Selby," said Belle.

Francisco spoke with a gruff, distorted voice. "This is not Selby, Belle Little. Now listen *carefully*. Your friend Margaret Whitney has been kidnapped. Unless you make a public confession to unjustly accusing Ana Patillas—your maid of six years ago—of the jewellery theft ..."

Belle's shocked gasp exploded from the loudspeaker. "Who *is* this?"

"Shut up and listen! Until you make a public confession to the press and television that it was your evil daughter who planted the stolen jewellery in Ana Patillas's room and caused her to commit suicide in jail, Margaret Whitney will be tortured every day. And, if you don't, she will be *hanged* at three o'clock on Thursday—the time of Elizabeth's wedding. Do you understand?"

There was an appalled silence, a period of shock and indecision.

Behind Francisco, Margaret was sobbing piteously.

"Who *are* you?" demanded Belle Little, her voice desperate, tremulous.

"Here is Margaret to speak to you." He turned and thrust the phone at her.

"Belle ..." she whimpered. "Belle, he's really got me! You've got to do it. H-he'll kill me, I know ..."

"Margaret—where are you?"

Margaret shook her head, lips quivering, tears wetting her cheeks. "I don't know ... he ... broke into the house ... the man on the motorcycle! Belle, he's got me ... he'll do what he says unless you tell the press ..."

"For God's sake, Margaret, how can I? Don't you appreciate the implications? Elizabeth is marrying the Governor's *son* ..."

"Belle, I know! But he's going to torture me and kill me if you don't! Surely my life is more important than ..."

The burr of a disconnected line came loudly from the speaker.

Margaret stared at the receiver and cried into it, "BELLE!"

Francisco took the instrument from her and replaced it in the cradle, simultaneously gesturing towards the loudspeaker, advising her to listen.

"My ... GOD!" thundered the voice of Belle.

A chair scraped back. "Mother, what is it?"

177

"Oh, my GOD!"

"Mother, for heaven's sake . . . you've gone deathly white. Come and sit down. Now, what was that all about?"

"Dear God, it has happened . . ." Belle whispered incredulously, ". . . what you said would happen . . ."

"Mother, *what*?"

"Ana Patillas . . ."

"Hmm?"

"Ana Patillas! That was the man on the motorcycle . . . the one who frightened Margaret yesterday! Elizabeth, he's kidnapped her! He wants me to confess to the press that it was you who stole that jewellery . . . or he'll . . . oh, dear God, where did this come from?"

"Or he'll what?"

"Torture Margaret every day I don't make the confession . . . and then . . . hang her at three o'clock on Thursday."

There was a long silence.

"What are we going to do?" asked Elizabeth.

Another silence.

"Mother, what . . ."

"Nothing!" rapped Belle. "Not a damn thing. He's out to stop the wedding, to ruin you . . . ruin both of us. It's got to be that, Elizabeth. Well, no *way* is he going to stop you marrying Robert . . ."

"Mother . . ." Elizabeth's voice was tinged with hysteria, wild disbelief, ". . . who can he *be*?"

Belle said breathlessly, "I don't know . . . someone from the barrio. You were right, you said they'd make trouble. We should have deported them—that cook and her husband, all of them. Oh, my God, Elizabeth . . ."

"Mother, we've got to do something!"

"No! The wedding goes ahead exactly as planned."

"And Margaret Whitney?"

"To hell with Margaret Whitney! What does she matter compared to our future? Margaret is stupid, worthless, expendable."

Margaret blinked her dismay at her hooded captor.

"But we won't be able to keep this quiet!" argued Elizabeth.

"Everyone's going to know she's missing—her maid, Arthur, for heaven's sake! He's bound to call in the police . . ."

"No, he won't," Belle retorted desperately. "We'll cook up a story, tell him she has found out about him and Judith Harmer and has gone away for a while . . . Palm Beach . . . Europe . . . anywhere! Just so long as we get through that wedding."

"And if he *should* find out she's been kidnapped?"

"He'll still keep his mouth shut! God in heaven, I've got enough on Arthur Whitney to put him away for several lifetimes. We'll tell the maid that Margaret had to go away unexpectedly for a few days, that'll keep her quiet."

"And what happens if that maniac carries out his threat and *does* hang her on Thursday?"

There was a pensive silence. "To us—nothing. We shall simply deny all knowledge of the kidnapping and the death threat. We shall say it was our belief that Margaret *had* found out about Arthur and gone away for a while. Who will disbelieve us?"

On Elizabeth's response of congratulatory laughter, Francisco cut the sound and turned to find Margaret clutching her stomach, her face contorted with abject misery.

"Now you know how Ana Patillas felt in that jail cell, Mrs Whitney, knowing that the Littles could have told the truth and saved her."

"What are you going to do to me?" she asked in a cracked whisper.

"That depends on the Littles, doesn't it?"

Her face was paste white, eyes alive with fear. "But you *know* she'll never make that confession!"

"Of course she won't. I'm counting on it."

He took her downstairs to the ground floor, opened a door to the cellar stairs and switched on a light.

Margaret gave a start, a muted cry of fright.

At the foot of the stairs stood a large black German Shepherd dog, its bronzed-metal eyes the manifestation of primeval violence.

"Your guardian," explained Francisco.

He led her down the dusty wooden stairs, along a passage that reeked of ancient damp and into a large, dismal room furnished with three iron cots and a table.

"Toilet in there," he pointed. "Drinking water, too. The dog will be outside this door at all times. Incidentally, he never barks . . . only bites. He's a killer."

He closed and locked the door and returned upstairs.

6

At ten o'clock that night Francisco reported for duty at the booth, signed in and said goodnight to the departing guards.

Carl Krantz, in brittle mood, sat hunched over the desk, studying a company memorandum. "Fuckin' wedding."

"What's up?" asked Francisco.

Krantz slapped the memo. "This! Extra duty for all shifts next Thursday. You an' me finish at six in the morning, then we're back on at noon, right through till six Friday morning! Eighteen hours straight."

Francisco shrugged. "Golden hours, though, Mr Krantz. What are they paying—double time?"

"Yeh, who needs it? Christ, she doesn't need me here until six Friday morning. This place is gonna be swarmin' with cops and Secret Service guys ..."

"Who—Belle Little?"

"Who else? I called Buller at HQ, he said she ordered it ... says she's as jumpy as a cat with piles suddenly."

"Well, I guess it's understandable. Big responsibility—playing hostess to the Governor. She doesn't want anything to go wrong."

"What the hell could go wrong with a zillion cops an' plainclothes dicks in the Park? A guy'd have to be a nut to try anythin' in here Thursday."

"Maybe that's what she's got in mind." Francisco picked up a stapled sheaf of Xeroxed papers bearing the company heading. "This the run-down for Thursday?"

"Yeh."

Francisco glanced through it.

Under separate headings, the memo instructed in detail the procedure to be followed regarding the checking of invitation cards against a guests' list; the direction of traffic along the causeway and into the Park; the parking of guest and press vehicles; specific areas of duty for Four Square personnel; liaison with local police and the Secret Service in (a) uneventful circumstances and (b) cases of emergency.

Francisco dropped the directive on to the desk. "I see I've drawn patrol duty in the Littles' garden. Too bad . . . I'd like to have seen the wedding, it'll be quite a sight."

"No reason you can't take a look in," muttered Krantz. "Christ, there'll be fifty cops out there with yuh, all wantin' a look-see. Get one of them to cover for you for a minute."

"Sure. Too bad you'll be stuck on the gate, Mr Krantz."

Krantz scowled. "You'd better check out the Littles' garden on your rounds from now on, West. They put the big top up today."

Francisco's heart missed a beat. "Already? Yeh, I guess they'll need five days to get it ready."

"They've put a night watchman down there—old coot named Prescott. He's keepin' an eye on the equipment, but it won't harm any to double check on your rounds."

"Will do." Francisco picked up the directive again and settled into his chair to study it in detail. "Boy, they've really gone to town on this. Not even an ant could get in here Thursday without being stamped on."

"God help the guy who fouls up, is all," muttered Krantz, snapping the afternoon shift report into a box file. "Belle Little will hand him his balls in a paper bag . . . if I don't get to him first."

A few minutes after eleven, Francisco stopped the company station wagon on the road in front of the Little house and cut the engine. Collecting his flashlight, he got out and walked up a narrow flagged path leading to the rear gardens.

The house was lit up, and several cars were parked in the circular driveway, some of which he recognised as belonging to Park residents. Others, including two Rolls-Royces, had been admitted to the Park during the afternoon shift. The Security record sheet indicated that the midnight-blue Silver Shadow belonged to Charles Ingman, the conductor of the Miami Symphony Orchestra, and the beige Corniche to Tyrone Gambretti, the stage director.

Continuing down the side of the house, Francisco reached the rear garden and was confronted by the big top, an immense pale-green structure towering half as high again as the house, its canopied entrance abutting the bottom steps of the terrace.

Ducking under guy-ropes, he pulled aside the entrance flap and entered the tent. Two huge naked bulbs, working lights, palely illuminated the vast interior. Never having been to a circus, or inside a tent of any kind before, Francisco was overwhelmed by its size.

Slowly he walked across the grass floor, pausing to slap one of the massive king-poles, craning his neck as he followed its soaring height up into the dark reaches of the canvas roof, smiling to himself as he imagined a trapeze troupe up there, performing the death-defying leaps he'd seen on television, drawing gasps from the crowd.

"A dollar yuh don't make it!" a voice called from the far end of the tent.

Francisco peered into the gloom at the advancing figure, stooped with late middle-age, wearing crumpled grey pants and a thick navy sweater.

Francisco waved his flashlight. "Hi . . . Security."

"Yessir."

The old man came on, limping, grinning amiably as he pointed aloft. "Time was I could scale a tree that height in twenty seconds."

"Oh? Lumberjack?"

"Yessir. Worked the Oregon forests for twenty years." He slapped his left thigh, making a chunky, wooden sound. "Left a leg there somewheres. Brown bear. Name's Bob Prescott . . . night watchman."

"They told me. Larry West. I do the ten to six shift."

"Nice t'meet yuh. Can't say the same f'yuh pardner, though. Didn't like his eyes . . . remind me of a timber wolf." He spat into the lawn, dismissing Krantz, and pointed to a stack of planked squares, one of a score of stacks piled at intervals, around the tent floor. "That's the floorin'—to protect the lawn and for dancin'. Down along the bottom is where the big stage is gonna be—built up high so's everybody can see. I seen the plans. Rows of foldin' chairs across here—two sections, one thousand chairs apiece, aisle down the centre and down each side. Over there, the press stage."

He pointed aloft, traversing the roof. "Chandeliers, Viennese-style. First off, this here's gonna be a church, kinda ..." his out-swept arm covered the walls. "They're puttin' up canvas flats, painted like a church, get th'idea? Then, soon as the weddin's over, they turn the flats around and they've got a Viennese ballroom. The flats are bein' delivered Monday an' they'll be rehearsin' the whole show Wednesday. You oughta git t'see it, should be quite an eyeful."

"I'll try and do that."

Prescott shook his grizzled head. "'magine, the Governor sittin' right up there on that stage. Yuh wouldn't have a cigarette on yuh, would yuh, young fella?"

"Sure." Francisco took out a packet, removed several cigarettes from it and handed them to Prescott. "There yuh go, pop."

"Well, that's mighty nice of yuh. Would yuh have a light, too?"

Francisco gave him the book. "How about loudspeakers? There'll be quite a few, I guess."

"Oh, sure. All th'equipment's here right now—out back. They'll be doin' the speakers first thing Monday ... gotta lay the cables before the floorin' goes down, otherwise there'd be wires snakin' all over the place, trippin' folks up."

Francisco nodded. "My boss told me to take a look around. Mind showing me the equipment store, Bob?"

Prescott's faded blue eyes twinkled mischievously. "What's the matter—don't he trust me?"

Francisco smiled. "No, it's not that ... just a double check, that's all. You're responsible to the equipment people, he's responsible to Four Square."

"Sure, I know. Come on, I'll show yuh."

They crossed the tent and made their exit through a flap on

184

the north side, farthest from the house, emerging on to lawns lit, for security, by a series of caged working lights strung on wires that ran between the marquee and five portable offices mounted on low brick supports.

Prescott pointed at the nearest portable. "Gambretti's office—where all the plannin' and co-ordinatin' will be done. The second one's the equipment store. The third's gonna be a mobile cop shop. The other two are toilets—ladies' and gents'."

"You got keys to them all, Bob?"

"Yessir—in case of fire. You wanna take a look inside?"

"Just this once—then Krantz won't be able to chew me out."

Prescott pulled a bunch of keys from his pants pocket, unlocked the door of Gambretti's office and went in, switching on a light. Francisco followed.

A deep inclined shelf serving as a desk top ran the length of one wall. On it were strewn plans and sketches showing seating arrangements, stage lay-outs and details of painted flats.

Francisco approached a huge artist's impression pinned across an end wall that illustrated how the marquee would look both during the ceremony and after the transformation. He whistled, "Hey, just look at this. Clever, huh?"

"Yessir. An' I wouldn't mind one tenth of what it's all costin', neither. I heard two hundred thou, could that be right?"

Francisco nodded. "I heard that, too."

Prescott chuckled as he turned for the door. "Kinda reminds me of my own weddin' back in '45. I wus so pie-eyed I spent a three-day honeymoon with three wrong women, swear t'God."

"Three!" laughed Francisco.

Prescott hobbled down the steps, leaving Francisco to put out the light and pull the door to. At the equipment store the old man opened the door and put on the light, continuing his story.

"Yessir . . . married a Chinese girl up in Klamath Falls. Trouble was there were 'bout fifty of 'em in camp, cookin' an' washin', an' they all looked so danged alike yuh couldn't hardly tell them apart sober, never mind drunk. Well, my buddies played a trick on me . . . got me drunker 'n a skunk, then packed me off to th' honeymoon cabin with my bride ... 'ceptin' it *weren't* my bride, it wus her sister or cousin or somesuch. Next night they pulled her out an' put in anuther one ... then anuther on the third night." He cackled a laugh. "Never did git t'sleep with my missus that trip. Not that it mattered any ... I wus too goldarned footless ta git it up anyways!"

Francisco laughed with him, his eyes ranging over the neatly-stacked equipment—the big tannoy speakers, the coils of cable, the stand microphones, a tape recorder, an amplifier and a sound mixer.

"Where are they setting up, Bob?" he asked casually. "Where's the control point going to be?"

"The annex tent—where I'm livin'."

Francisco's hand dropped casually on to the big amplifier, his eyes searching out its make and model number. "Nice equipment. The folks should hear every word through these speakers."

"Yessir."

They left the equipment store, quickly inspected the other portables, then made their way to the annex tent, a twenty-foot-square accommodation attached to the big top, which could be entered from the annex through a flap-covered opening.

In the annex, a wooden floor had been put down, and a small table, canvas chair, electric heater, kettle and cooking ring had been provided for Prescott. On the table was a supply of groceries.

"Fancy a cawfee?" he asked. "I got a pot made."

"No, thanks, Bob, I'd better be getting back. Next time round, maybe."

"Drop by any time, I'll be glad of th' company."

Francisco pulled the entrance flap aside and looked into the vast, deserted big top. From this position on Thursday he would be looking through the superstructure of the main stage towards the press gallery to his right.

He visualised the scene ... dozens of journalists and TV people, their eyes riveted on the stage above him ... and up there on the stage ... the orchestra, choir, Bishop, Governor,

186

Belle Little and Elizabeth Little, about to become Mrs Robert Collier.

And out there ... two thousand people, hushed, expectant ...

The Wedding March ends ... the Bishop begins to speak, his voice booming through the marquee from those big loud-speakers ... "Dearly beloved ... we are gathered together here in the sight of God, and in the face of this Congregation, to join together this Man ... and this Woman ... in holy Matrimony ..."

"Anythin' wrong, young fella?"

Francisco turned. "Hmm?"

Prescott was peering closely at him. "You wus starin'. You see somethin' out there?"

Francisco smiled, shook his head. "No ... I was just think-ing ... wondering how it'll go on Thursday."

"Oh, smooth as butter, shouldn't wonder. These bigwigs don't *allow* their weddin's ta go wrong."

"No. Well, see you later, Bob."

Francisco moved through the flap into the big top, walked slowly down the centre aisle, smiling agreeably at the unsus-pecting congregation.

7

Francisco arrived home at 6.15 Sunday morning, checked Margaret Whitney and found her sleeping, then went up to the bedroom and spot-checked the tapes.

Belle Little had made two phone calls after ten o'clock the previous night but they concerned only matters pertaining to the wedding. So far, since he had told her of Margaret's kidnapping the previous morning, Belle (as far as he could ascertain from the tapes) had made no reference to it, either in telephone or direct conversation, and was obviously resolved to ignore his threat completely and do nothing whatever about Margaret's dilemma.

It was time to increase the pressure.

He dialled her number. Her phone rang several times before a voice he recognised as Constanza's answered quietly, "The Little residence."

Smiling to himself, he cleared his throat authoritatively. "This is Judge Hamlin. I must speak with Mrs Little at once . . . it's most urgent."

Torn between obedience and loyalty, Constanza pleaded hesitantly, "Sir, I'm afraid Mrs Little is still asleep. She . . ."

"I realise that, but this is of the utmost importance. Tell her it concerns Mrs Whitney."

A further hesitation, then a whispered, "Yes, sir."

Francisco hated putting Constanza in such a dilemma but it couldn't be helped.

As she put the receiver down, he tuned the radio receiver to the frequency of Belle's bedroom, picking up a faint fluttery snore. Moments later a tentative knock sounded at the door, then a louder knock.

Belle stirred, grumbled, "Who is it?"

Constanza entered. "Señora . . . I'm sorry to waken you, but Judge Hamlin is on the telephone. He says it's very urgent, it's about Señora Whitney."

A murmur of surprise. "Judge Hamlin? All right . . . go down and hang up the extension."

The bedroom door was closed. There was a rustling of bed-clothes, the rattle of the receiver being replaced.

"Andy—?" Belle's voice was urgent, thick with sleep.

"You have wasted one day," Francisco whispered. "Margaret Whitney was tortured at midnight last night."

Her rage erupted. "You . . . BASTARD! You . . ." She became incoherent with choking anger.

"That behaviour is going to do Margaret no good, Belle Little. Only a confession can save her. At ten o'clock this morning you will phone the *Miami Herald* and Channel Six's *Eyewitness News* and tell them . . ."

Anticipating her reaction, he snatched the receiver from his ear to avoid her deafening bellow and the slamming down of the receiver.

Replacing his own receiver, he continued to listen to her tirade on the radio pick-up. There were unintelligible mutterings, a furious gasp, the crash of ceramic shattering.

An urgent knocking sounded at the door, then the door opened and Elizabeth demanded, "Mother, what in heaven's name . . . I could hear you down the hall! You woke me up!"

"It was HIM! He just called, told Constanza he was Andy Hamlin! *Jesus!*"

Elizabeth came closer. "What did he say?"

Belle's reply was anguished, furious. "He said he'd tortured Margaret, that I had to call the *Herald* and Channel Six at ten this morning . . ."

"Oh, my God, Mother, we've got to *do* something about him! We can't just let this go on . . ."

"Like *what*? Tell me how I can stop him and I'll do it!"

"Get a private investigator on to him . . . that man Connolly who got you the information on the Clerk of Works . . ."

"NO! This must not go beyond us two, Elizabeth! What could any investigator accomplish in three days? Nothing! We

189

don't even know who this kidnapper is or where he is. You tell me—where is Margaret at this moment? Miami? Miami Beach? Dade County? *Florida?* Is she even in this *country*, for God's sake? Is *he*? What chance would an investigator have of finding him before Thursday? Oh *Christ*, Elizabeth, if only you . . ." Her voice tailed away.

"If only I what?" snapped Elizabeth.

Belle sighed, then came back resolutely. "If only you hadn't been so goddamned spiteful six years ago!"

"What do you mean?"

"You know very well."

"Mother, I haven't the faintest idea what you're . . ."

"Oh, come *on*, Elizabeth, this is *me* you're talking to! You don't believe for one moment I thought Ana Patillas really stole that jewellery, do you? As dumb as she was, she would never have been that stupid. Where are you going? Elizabeth, where . . ."

"I'm certainly not going to stand here and listen to this."

"Elizabeth, don't! I'm sorry, please don't go."

Silence.

Then from Elizabeth, "He's getting to you, Mother. You'd better take a tranquilliser."

"I don't want one."

"Take it!"

Water was poured.

"You've got to relax," Elizabeth said firmly. "You've got three days of tremendous pressure ahead of you without this trouble. If you don't calm down, we'll be holding your funeral on Thursday instead of my wedding. Look at your hands, they're shaking . . ."

"I'm all right."

"Obviously you're not."

"It was the shock . . . being woken up like that and finding him on the phone!"

"It won't happen again. In future I'll take all calls, he won't fool me. Come on, get back to bed and get some sleep."

"Elizabeth . . ."

"Mm?"

"Oh, God, child . . . we're so *close* to it! He *can't* spoil it for us!"

"He's not going to. He's tried and he's failed. Think it through. His only weapon is the threat of Margaret's death. By Wednesday night, when he realises you're not going to make the confession, what can he do? What's the point of killing her then? Really, Mother, there's nothing to worry about."

Belle sighed heavily. "No, I must be getting old. Ten years ago I wouldn't have given this a moment's thought."

"You still don't have to—because you've got me here to deal with it. You know something? I hope he does call again. I'll fix that bastard like I fixed . . ." She stopped abruptly.

"Like you fixed whom, Elizabeth?" Belle pursued, a smile in her voice.

"Never mind."

"Ana Patillas?"

"Yes, dammit! And everyone else who ever got in my way! Now try and get some sleep, we'll have breakfast together later."

The bedroom door closed.

Francisco switched off the tape recorder, remained absolutely still, his heart pounding, bursting with elation. He had it!

He had Elizabeth's confession!

Sunday was his free day, so Carlo came to the house mid-morning. Francisco greeted him with the exciting news, took him upstairs to hear the taped confession.

Carlo gasped, "We've got them!"

"Yes, we've got them. But we've got to be very careful how we use this tape. It's dynamite—and like the real stuff, it's got to be placed accurately for maximum destruction. Belle has friends in a lot of high places. If we hand this over to the wrong person it could disappear without trace—and by the time we realised it had disappeared, the wedding would be over."

Carlo nodded agreement. "Got any ideas?"

"Yes. But for the moment, let's put aside the confession and think about the rest of that tape. I believe we've got Belle on the run."

191

"She sounds scared stiff. It's understandable—she's being shot at and doesn't know where the bullets are coming from or who's firing them. She's pretty shaky."

"I want her shaking a lot more yet. I want her shaking so bad by Thursday they'll have to carry her to the wedding on a stretcher."

"How are we going to do that? If Elizabeth is going to take all calls from now on, you won't be able to pressure Belle by phone."

Francisco shook his head. "I don't intend to. I'm going to use somebody else to pressure her."

"Who?"

"Her friends. Arthur Whitney is due back from Galverston at six this afternoon. He phoned from there this morning and spoke to Maria. She told him what Belle Little has told her to tell anyone who calls—that Margaret is in Palm Beach, staying with friends. I'll call him around six-thirty and tell him different—that'll stir something up."

Carlo smiled. "How is Margaret enjoying her stay?"

"Funny you should ask that. She seems lonely down there. I think she could use some company. Do you think we could persuade a friend to drop by for a visit?"

Carlo grinned. "Lily Parker, maybe?"

"Lily Parker precisely. Sam Parker is going up to Fort Lauderdale tonight—an all-night Christmas stag-thrash with the real-estate fraternity. Lily does not, however, intend staying at home alone with her knitting. She's got a new boyfriend—a muscle-freak named Bo Sangster, pool attendant at the Flamingo Hotel. He runs a speedboat and that's how he'll be coming in from the Beach, not through the gate. They've arranged to meet at ten o'clock in the summerhouse at the bottom of the garden."

Carlo nodded. "OK. How do I handle it? Wait until he leaves?"

Francisco grinned. "Why not? Let Lily enjoy life while she may."

192

8

From an approach altitude of two thousand feet, Arthur Whitney gazed down abstractedly at the Miami skyline, pre-occupied with the matter of his marriage.

A plump man of medium height, dressed formally in a dark blue suit, white shirt and red tie, his brown eyes framed by heavy spectacles, he looked anything but a builder of multi-million-dollar projects. A bank manager, maybe.

That people invariably took him to be something less success-ful than a millionaire builder did not surprise him. He was only too aware of his overgrown-schoolboy appearance—and of the tentative, often irresolute, nature it harboured.

He hadn't set out to be a millionaire builder—nor a builder of any calibre. He had wanted to be an architect. College, how-ever, had soon revealed an absence of the imagination and artistic flair essential for that profession, and so he had reluc-tantly lowered his sights to the allied profession of draughts-manship—the technical interpretation of the architect's dreams.

After college, he began work for his father, a builder of low-cost houses in the West Palm Beach area. During the post-World War Two boom, the company had prospered and expanded, and in 1948 his father had died, leaving Arthur sole ownership.

Reluctant to sell, to dispose immediately of a business his father had worked so hard to build up, Arthur continued to run it on a limited-time basis, promising himself that after a suitable period of mourning he would get out of building and into something that better suited his aesthetic leanings.

That moment never came. The continuing property boom picked Arthur up and swept him along from one project to another, as helpless as a weak swimmer in a swift current.

He met Sam Parker, an ambitious real estate agent who was handling the purchase of a tract of land in Carol City, north Miami. His client was planning to build a low-cost housing development and looking for a right-price builder.

Her name was Belle Little.

Arthur expressed interest and a meeting was arranged at Mrs Little's home in Little Park. Present at the meeting were Belle, Arthur, Sam, and a lawyer named Bernard Howard—a quiet, watchful little man whom Arthur instinctively distrusted.

Forceful, ruthlessly direct, Belle conducted the meeting and laid down her requirements with an icy incisiveness that left Arthur breathless. Towards the end of the discussion—more a Belle Little soliloquy—she fixed Arthur with her reptilian gaze and informed him, "These men know me. You don't. They will tell you that if you work for Belle Little there is only one way that work will be done—Belle Little's way. There is money in this project for us all. If your work is satisfactory, there will be other projects and more money—a lot more. That's a promise. But you will do *precisely* what you're told with no argument—is that clear?"

He had mumbled assent.

A deal was formulated, and Arthur rushed back to West Palm Beach to give his wife, Margaret, the news.

"We're in the big money, I can smell it," he told her excitedly, yet with such obvious reservation that she remarked on it.

"But there's something about it you don't like."

He shook his head, uncertainly. "I don't know. I don't like *her*, that's for sure . . . she's as hard as granite. Don't care much for the other two, either. Bernard Howard looks a shyster lawyer . . . and Sam Parker would look more at home on a used-car lot. They're up to something not quite kosher, I can smell it."

"Then drop it, Arthur—don't get involved."

"No . . . we'll go with this one, Margaret, see what happens. Maybe I'm wrong. Maybe they're just damned hard business people. Anyway, the money's too good to turn down. A few projects like this and I'll be able to get out. We'll see what happens."

What did happen was that he got very rich—another housing project, a light industrial complex, a shopping centre followed.

Later, Belle offered him a home in the Park at a bargain price; Sam Parker and Bernard Howard were already residents.

He gladly accepted.

It was not long after their removal into the Park that the breach began to develop between Margaret and himself. The pace Belle Little set for him was a furious one. With projects to build all over Florida, he was frequently away from home for weeks at a time, and during these long absences there were other women.

He enjoyed the freedom and the flattering attention. He was wealthy and virile, and in return for money, gifts, favours, they flocked to his bed, their expertise serving not only to satisfy his needs but to remind him of how unadventurous and insipid was his wife's lovemaking.

The breach had gradually widened to become an unbridgeable chasm.

And now Judith Harmer had come into his life. Young, beautiful, intelligent, vivacious, unbelievably exciting in bed, she was everything he could possibly wish for in a wife. The time had come to part from Margaret. Though fifty-five, he was still healthy and energetic, with many good years to enjoy. The prospect of wasting those years with Margaret . . . of returning home time after time to her vapid conversation about coffee mornings and charity drives and the clothes she'd bought, and to her lukewarm body, sickened him. And he wouldn't do it.

He'd talked it over with Judith in Galverston. Margaret could have half of whatever he was worth and welcome to it, just so long as she got out of his life immediately and stayed out.

He'd rehearsed his approach to her during the night, as Judith lay asleep at his side, and stealed himself for what he knew would be a vituperative, hysterical encounter. During the morning, from the hotel, he had called Margaret to advise her of his precise time of arrival and had been annoyed to learn that she was in Palm Beach. Ordinarily, her absence would

195

have pleased him; but now, geared for the confrontation, it angered him.

How like her, he thought peevishly, to irritate him even in this matter.

The jet landed and seemed to take an age to reach its parking bay. Disembarking, Arthur caught a cab. He was so immersed in thoughts of Judith and their future that he took in nothing of the journey until the taxi was turning into the Park.

As he entered the house, Lucia came from the kitchen to greet him. He smiled warmly, his eyes appreciative of her body. He'd often wondered how she would react to an advance, but had always refrained from taking it beyond speculation. "Never on your own doorstep" was his creed. He had enough complications in his life.

"Lucia," he nodded, handing her his overcoat and briefcase. "So Mrs Whitney is in Palm Beach. When did she leave?"

"I don't know, señor."

Arthur frowned. "You don't know?" He moved towards the drawing-room. Lucia disposed of the coat in a closet and followed him in.

"No, señor. When I came on duty yesterday morning, she'd already gone. May I get you a drink, señor?"

"Yes, please—scotch over ice. Then how do you know she's gone to Palm Beach?"

"Señora Little phoned yesterday and told me," she said, making for the cocktail cabinet.

Arthur frowned. "Mrs Little? How did she know?"

"I've no idea, señor."

"How did my wife go—by car?"

"I'm sorry, I don't even know that. The last time I saw Señora Whitney was ten o'clock Friday night."

"And she said nothing then about going to Palm Beach?"

"No, señor."

"How very strange. What time did you come on duty yesterday morning?"

"The usual time for Saturday—eight o'clock. I took Señora Whitney's breakfast tray up to her room—and was surprised to find she wasn't there."

"How very odd."

Taking the drink from her, he sat down on the settee and reached for the phone.

Elizabeth Little answered. "The Little residence."

"Is that . . . Elizabeth?" he said with surprise. The Littles never answered the phone.

"Yes. Who is this?"

"Arthur Whitney . . . I've just got back from Galverston . . ."

"Oh, hello, Arthur."

"Is your mother there? I'd like to speak to her."

"Er, no . . . she's sleeping right now. She's . . . feeling a bit exhausted. Anything I can do?"

"Well . . ." he gave a small laugh, ". . . it's about Margaret. Lucia tells me Belle phoned yesterday to tell her Margaret had gone to Palm Beach. I'm just a bit puzzled as to why she left so early without telling Lucia . . . and yet presumably told your mother. Do you know why?"

Elizabeth hesitated, then said, as though with regret, "Yes, Arthur, I do know. Mother told me. I'm afraid Margaret has left you."

It took a moment for Arthur to respond. "Left me?"

"Yes. She telephoned Mother late Friday night, obviously distressed. She said she knew about you and . . . Judith Harmer . . . and had to get away . . . said she couldn't face you today and that you'd be hearing from her lawyers."

Arthur expelled a sigh. "I see. Tell me—had she been drinking?"

"Apparently."

"Of course. So—she won't be attending your wedding?"

"It seems that way."

"Yes . . . well . . . thank you, Elizabeth."

He put the receiver down, picked up his drink, heart pounding, mind racing. Well, well, Margaret had done it for him. He felt elated.

Lucia was hovering near the door, awaiting instructions.

He grimaced at her. "Looks as though Señora Whitney won't be home for a while."

"No, señor. Will you be dining at home tonight, señor?"

"Hmm? No, I ate on the plane. That'll be all, Lucia, I'll ring if I need anything."

He was sipping his second scotch, attempting to adjust to his new position, when the phone at his side purred.

Margaret?

He picked it up, heart racing. "Hello?"

"Your wife has been kidnapped."

Arthur blinked. "Hmm?"

"Belle Little knows all about it . . . ask her."

Arthur roused himself, frowning with bewilderment. "Who is this? Is this some kinda sick joke?"

"No joke, Mr Whitney—unless you consider the kidnapping of your wife a humorous matter. Margaret has been kidnapped. She was taken from the house by boat on Friday night. Ask Belle Little—she knows all about it."

"Look! Whoever you are . . . my wife happens to be in Palm Beach!"

"How do you know?"

"Because I've just been told!"

"By whom? Belle Little?"

"By her daughter."

"Elizabeth is as big a liar as her mother. Your wife is not in Palm Beach. I have her."

Arthur's mind was blurred. "Why? What do you want . . . money?"

"I want justice. Ask Belle Little."

Francisco rang off.

Arthur murmured, "Jesus!" and prodded the Littles' number. Elizabeth answered.

"Elizabeth . . . it's Arthur again. Look . . . I've just had the weirdest phone call . . . from a man . . . who claims that Margaret has been *kidnapped*, for God's sake! And he said your mother knows all about it!" He heard her intake of breath. "Elizabeth? Do you know anything about this?"

"No!" she rapped, curt, defensive.

Arthur's eyes narrowed. "Let me speak to your mother."

"*No* . . . she's sleeping . . . she's . . ."

"Elizabeth! For Chrissake, this is *serious*!"

"It . . . was a crank call."

"I don't think so. Elizabeth, please . . ."

"Mother can't be disturbed. She's going through a terrible strain . . . the wedding. She's sleeping badly . . ."

"Elizabeth! He says he has Margaret and that Belle knows all about it! Now, are you going to put your mother on or am I coming over there? Either way I mean to speak to her!"

Elizabeth tutted furiously. "Hold on."

Belle came on the line almost instantly, very much awake. "Arthur . . . he was right, she has been kidnapped."

Arthur gaped. "*What?*"

"Listen to me," she commanded, her voice fluttery with emotion. "This is a plot . . . against Elizabeth and me. He's a crank who is trying to prevent her marrying Robert Collier. Don't ask me why—it might be politically motivated, revenge of some kind, or just plain sick. I favour the latter. But whatever the reason, I'm sure you can see that under *no* circumstances can we give in to him."

Arthur's face was screwed up with bewilderment. "Belle . . . let me get this straight . . . firstly—how do you know all this?"

"Because he has called me—several times."

"And told you what?"

"That . . . the wedding must be called off."

"Or what?"

"Or . . . Margaret will be killed. Arthur, *listen* . . . it's nonsense . . . an empty threat. He won't do it."

"How d'you *know* he won't? Have you called the police?"

"No."

"No! Belle . . . Jesus Christ, I can't believe what I'm hearing! All right, I'll call them myself . . ."

"NO!" Her bellow deafened him. "Arthur, don't you dare call them! My God, Elizabeth is not marrying a *plumber* . . . she's marrying the Governor's son! Think of what is involved! Think of her future!"

"And what about Margaret's future?"

"What in hell do *you* care about her future or about

Margaret's anything? It would suit your plans perfectly if he did kill her!"

Silence.

"Nothing to say, Arthur?"

"I . . . couldn't let it happen!" he protested, unconvincingly.

"No? Arthur . . . the wedding is in four days' time. Just four days! We are that close to . . . well, I don't have to tell you what this marriage can mean to all of us . . . government contracts, political clout. Arthur, we are just four days away from a fortune! Do you want to throw it all away by calling the police? Four days . . . the difference between disaster and unimaginable reward. Which do you want, Arthur?"

"You . . . really think he's bluffing?"

"Of course he is. What can he possibly gain by killing Margaret if the wedding goes ahead?"

"I don't know. I don't know anything about anything! Why Margaret, for God's sake?"

"Because she's a close friend of mine, that's all. A means of pressure."

Arthur permitted himself a bleak smile. Some friend.

"Arthur . . ." her voice was different now, no longer hysterical, but controlled and deadly, ". . . I don't *want* to lean on you to keep quiet, but I will if I have to. You know how, don't you?"

"Yes," he answered quickly. "I know what you've done for me."

"Good. Keep it in mind. And keep the future in mind. It could be very good for you and Judith."

"Yes . . . I . . ."

She rang off.

For a long time after he'd replaced the receiver Arthur sat staring, stunned. Margaret kidnapped. By whom? And for what *real* reason? He couldn't buy Belle's explanation, there had to be more to it than that.

He got up and went to the cocktail cabinet, poured a large scotch and downed half of it.

Why had he reacted so . . . so loyally to Margaret's kidnapping? He'd done it instinctively . . . as one would to alarming news concerning a friend . . . acquaintance, even.

200

Forget it.

Think of the future . . . the bright, bright future. Belle Little was poised to become super-rich—and would take him right along with her. And all he had to do was . . . nothing. Just do and say nothing at all.

He drained his scotch and poured another.

Four days, that was all.

All?

He paused, the glass at his lips, struck by the sudden presentiment that an awful lot was going to happen during those four days.

And none of it good.

9

At nine-thirty that same evening, Lily Parker sat before her dressing-table mirror, carefully applying her make-up.

She was naked. She enjoyed being naked. The sight of her naked flesh thrilled her. Often she would play naked games, flitting along the landing from one bedroom to another, or dashing quickly downstairs to retrieve a book from the library, titillated by the risk of observation by her domestic staff, and occasionally thrilling to the astonished expression of her maid or cook when they caught sight of her disappearing buttocks.

Lilly Parker was an ardently sensuous woman. She adored sex, had done so since early puberty.

In Senior High, her dark attractive looks and big breasts had drawn the boys like wasps to honey. Losing her virginity to Allan Rossiter, the tall blond football captain, in her family's beachhouse at the age of fifteen, she so enjoyed the experience that there and then she decided to forsake academic endeavour in favour of sexual conquest—and succeeded brilliantly.

Later, in college, she majored—she was prone to quip—in the Four Fs, achieving an astonishing number of sexual encounters with members of the student body and faculty.

After college, she joined an insurance company as private secretary to the manager. On her first day, she seduced him on the floor of his office. Three months later, having enjoyed most of the attractive men in the five-storey building, she moved on to fresh pastures.

Marriage to a Daytona Beach motel-owner, a man thirty years her senior, ended after three weeks when he discovered her in bed with his brother.

Then into her life came Sam Parker, a real estate agent whose ruthless ambition excited her, whose needs precisely complemented her own.

For his part, he required a decorative, vivacious woman of independent mind and means, a partner who would contribute her share of money, sex, companionship whenever he required it, but who would allow him to pursue his private interests—business, gambling, other women—whenever the inclination arose. In return, he offered her the prospect of great future wealth, social advancement and equal sexual freedom.

From the beginning, the partnership had succeeded. His association with Belle Little quickly brought the wealth and social stature he had promised. Lily responded with her contribution of beauty, glamour, sex and unrestricted freedom.

Though her own freedom to philander had been part of the deal, she chose to keep her affairs covert, deriving poignant satisfaction from the secret planning, meeting and execution.

On this Sunday evening Sam was in Lauderdale enjoying his stag-night of porn films and private strip show (or whatever). She could as easily, and perhaps more comfortably, have invited her latest amour—the exquisite Bo Sangster—to spend the evening with her in the house, in her bedroom with its huge bed and mirrored ceiling, rather than in the relatively spartan summerhouse by the water's edge.

But where would be the fun, the intrigue, in that arrangement?

What she required was a furtive assignation—a run through the dark gardens in time to witness his arrival by speedboat from across the moonlit bay . . . two hearts, two bodies, coming together in secret tryst, an evening of wild abandon before an open fire.

She giggled at her mirror image. How ludicrously romantic.

There was, however, nothing ludicrous about the body with which she was about to tryst. She'd spotted it the moment she and Carol Ann Downey had entered the Flamingo pool area. Carol Ann was a Miami friend of long-standing, now living in New York but visiting Miami alone for a winter break and staying at the Flamingo.

The tall, muscular blond youth had immediately registered their arrival and come over, white teeth flashing, his experienced eyes drifting impertinently over their bikinied bodies, preferring Lily's and returning for a second, more leisurely appraisal.

Lily had also been doing her own appraising. He was wearing white cotton swim trunks, one size too small, the thin material clearly revealing a penial bulge of such extraordinary size she literally blinked with astonishment. Then the excitement came, squeezing her throat and causing her heart to pound so hard she believed she might faint.

He stood close to her, overwhelming her with his outrageous masculinity, his smile only for her.

"Ladies . . . what is your pleasure? Sun, shade, under the trees, by the pool?"

They chose the sun by the pool, settled on to loungers and oiled their bodies. He hovered all afternoon, transmitting signals of rapport to Lily, showing off a little for her on the high board.

Later, while Carol Ann was visiting the washroom, he sauntered over, ostensibly to collect a towel from an abandoned bed.

"Enjoying your vacation?" he asked.

"I'm not on vacation, I live here," she murmured drowsily, her eyes devouring his tan, athletic body from behind dark glasses.

"Oh? Where?"

"Little Park."

He made a face, impressed. "Very nice. I ride over there now and then . . . to catch a glimpse of how the other half live."

"How?"

"How do you live? You ought to know."

"How do you ride over there?"

"Oh . . . speedboat. Beautiful homes. Which one's yours?"

"Number sixteen."

He grinned boyishly. "I don't know from numbers. What colour are your sun-blinds . . . cabin cruiser?"

"Brown-and-yellow stripes . . . the blinds, not the cruiser.

That's white with a blue trim and a blue dinghy. It's called *Lily*."

He nodded. "Got it. This side of the big house ... Belle Little's, isn't it?"

"That's hers."

"Yeh—you've got a Swedish-style summerhouse down by the dock."

She nodded, her heart beating wildly at the closeness of his huge penis, wanting to reach out and release it from the restriction of his trunks, watch it grow in her hand, kiss it, lick it, suck it ...

"Maybe ... I'll see you in the garden ... sometime."

His voice was ragged, constricted with excitement, sensing hers. "OK if I give you a wave?"

"Why not?" she murmured, distrusting her voice.

He smiled. "A jealous husband, maybe. I wouldn't want to embarrass you."

"I don't embarrass—but thanks for the thought."

He grinned flutteringly. "Bo Sangster is nothing if not discreet."

"Bo?"

"Short for Bob ... Robert. And you must be ... Lily?"

She nodded. "Parker."

"Mrs Lily Parker, of course," he said, his eyes shifting to her wedding ring.

"Now and then."

He cleared his throat. "And the other times?"

"Business-widow Parker."

"That's too bad. Often?"

"Too often."

"That is too bad. I was ... thinking of taking a run out to the island tonight, as a matter of fact. It's going to be a fine, clear night ... big moon. If you should happen to be at the bottom of your garden, on the summerhouse verandah, maybe, sometime around eight o'clock ..."

"Sunday would be better."

He licked his lips. "Sunday would be terrific." His eyes went to a point beyond her. "Your friend is coming back."

"I'll call you. What's your room number?"

"Seven-ten."

"Goodbye, Bo Sangster."

"Au revoir, Business-widow Parker."

Lily got up from her dressing table and stood before her closet mirror, stretched sensuously, cupped her breasts and teased her nipples, ran her hands down her body and brought them up between her thighs, shuddering at the vision of her new lover and his incredible body. Trembling with excited anticipation, she turned her attention to her wardrobe. Everything had to be perfect—the setting, the clothes she wore, everything.

Opening the closet doors, she went along her collection of evening gowns, finally selecting a simple, sexy sheath of coral satin with splits up the sides to mid-thigh.

Throwing it across the bed, she opened a drawer of underwear, but paused, grinning, shut the drawer and stepped into the gown. She smoothed it around her slender thighs and posterior inspecting the result in the mirror.

She was still practically naked.

Stepping into a pair of delicate gold pumps, she added a little gold jewellery, squirted perfume at her throat and wrists, and was ready.

No, not quite.

The thought came to her with a ripple of excitement. He would almost certainly be casually dressed—slacks, sports shirt, jacket—so she would provide a direct contrast, shock him with ostentatious formality.

Opening another closet door, she took out a full-length Black Diamond mink coat and slipped it on. She tugged its deep collar around her ears and hugged the sumptuous fur delightedly.

Laughing, trembling with anticipation, she turned out the lights and left the room.

From his position of concealment in a bed of shrubs behind the summerhouse, Carlo, dressed in black leather, saw her leave the house and head towards him across the lawn, a phantom figure in the pale grey moonlight.

She came silently and quickly, the rustle of her clothing a whisper as she passed close to where he crouched, trailing a faint wake of heady, fragrant perfume as she rounded the side of the wooden building and disappeared from view.

Now he left the cover of the shrubs and took up a position beneath a rear, partly-open window, settling there as a light came on inside the room.

The summerhouse was, of course, familiar to him since he tended its flower beds and potted plants daily.

It consisted of one large multi-purpose room, with a bathroom. To Carlo's left was a bar area with pine bar and yellow-cushioned stools. The centre of the room consisted of a square of polished oak floor for dancing. To the right was the den area, furnished with colourful, chunky sofas and armchairs arranged before a wall-sized stone fireplace. The bathroom door was in the right-hand corner.

Though it looked authentic, the fire was a convenient gas fake—its logs, set in a stainless steel basket, made of ceramic which glowed red hot but never burned away.

Lily moved directly to the fireplace, crouched and lit the fire, then circuited the room, turning on table lamps, arranging furniture, plumping cushions until she was satisfied with the setting.

From the bar fridge she took a bottle of champagne, filled a silver bucket with ice and placed them, with drinking glasses, on a low table in front of a settee by the fire.

She glanced at her wrist-watch, prompting Carlo to do the same. It was almost ten o'clock. She looked excited, nervous. She crossed to the door and walked out on to the verandah. Carlo could see her looking out across the moon-struck waters of the bay towards Miami Beach.

Suddenly she gave a start, seeing or hearing something, and re-entered the room, leaving the door slightly ajar. She crossed to the fireplace and settled into a provocative pose, her arm resting on the mantelpiece, one foot on the stone hearth.

Now Carlo heard the distant buzz of a powerful marine

engine. It quickly drew closer, shutting down abruptly as it neared the jetty, puttered quietly while the boat was tied, then ceased all noise.

Moments passed. Lily looked towards the door with smiling anticipation. Confident footsteps approached along the flagged path, rang hollowly across the wooden verandah. The door began to open and a handsome, boyish face peered in, grinning with relief as he discovered Lily.

"Hi."

"Hi."

Closing the door, he moved towards her, dressed with casual elegance in a deep blue blazer, pale blue open-necked shirt, white slacks and moccasins.

"Everything all right?" he asked.

She smiled warmly. "Everything's just dandy. You look delicious."

"So do you. Hey, you didn't say formal."

She moved into him, slipped her arms around his neck and kissed him deeply. His strong arms enfolded her, drawing her close, his hands burrowing into the fur of her coat. She moaned softly, clutched his head and kissed him voraciously. His hands disappeared inside the coat. She surged against him, suddenly broke away, panting, caught his hand and led him to the settee.

"Open the champagne," she said flutteringly, her hands shaking as she took a cigarette from a carved-wood box.

The cork exploded across the room. He poured two glasses, gave her one which she raised in a silent toast.

"I wasn't sure you'd come," she said, drawing nervously on her cigarette.

He frowned, smilingly. "You're kidding. Why shouldn't I?"

"Oh . . . all those pretty young girls around the pool. I'm sure you're always over-booked."

He made a dismissive gesture. "Young isn't everything. Quite often it's nothing . . . no sense, no style, no experience."

She smiled. "And you reckon I have those qualities?"

"You invented them."

She laughed delightedly. "Go and put some music on."

He got up, went to the stereo unit and leafed through a file of

208

LPs, selected one and put it on. The easy strains of a romantic Latin beat seeped into the room.

"Nice," she said. "Just right."

He stood before her, hands extended. "Dance?"

She stood up, shrugged off her coat, reached out and eased the jacket from his broad shoulders and discarded it on top of the mink.

Holding her at arms' length, he whistled approvingly. "Oh, boy . . ."

Smiling, she melted against him.

The pretence at dancing lasted no time at all. With a murmured groan she surged against him, finding his mouth. He caressed her, held her tightly against his groin. With a small cry she went down on her knees, opened his zipper and released his penis from the confines of his shorts.

She gasped, "My God . . ." pressed him to her cheek, covered him with fleeting kisses, then slowly took him into her mouth.

He clutched at her head, sucked in his breath as she began working on him.

Suddenly she came to her feet, slipped the straps from her shoulders and shrugged the satin sheath to the floor. He gaped at her nakedness.

"Quickly," she whispered, attacking the buttons of his shirt.

They came together, ferociously. Lily urged him down on to the rich warm pile of the Indian rug, brought him over her to lie between her legs, cried out in ecstasy as he entered her.

She climaxed almost instantly, her bellow filling the room, but continued on, driving into him, urging him deeply into her, coming again as he exploded with a shout, shuddered, for a moment hung suspended above her, then with a great gasp collapsed upon her.

When their breathing had calmed, she got up and went into the bathroom, returned to throw him a towel, then disappeared again.

He dressed and sat on the settee, swallowed the glass of champagne and poured another. She emerged from the bathroom, still naked, and curled up beside him, sipped his champagne and asked, "Why did you get dressed?"

He said hesitantly, "Well . . . I thought . . ."

Smiling, she shook her head, her fingers working at the buckle of his belt. "I didn't invite you here to think."

Outside the window, Carlo heaved a sigh and settled down for a lengthy wait.

10

Bo Sangster did not leave until four-thirty on Monday morning.

Another half an hour and Carlo would have been forced to abandon the kidnap. Francisco toured the Park every hour on the hour—five o'clock was his final tour of the shift. After five it would have been too late.

Cold, stiff and hungry, Carlo had been sitting behind the summerhouse for six and a half hours, listening to the drone of their conversation, to occasional peals of laughter and the sounds of renewed lovemaking, disbelieving that Sangster could perform yet again, when suddenly the thump of a closing door roused him from a shallow doze. Heart banging, he sprang to his feet, mortified that after waiting all night he might have missed his chance.

Peering through the window, however, he saw Lily moving from the door towards the settee, hugging her fur coat around her, her hair dishevelled, body slack, yet smiling the smile of the cat who had just swallowed all the cream.

She lay down on the settee and closed her eyes, the smile still moulded on her attractive mouth. He waited until she appeared to be dozing, then moved.

Silently he crossed the verandah, eased the door open, and slipped into the room, buffeted by its warmth, the aroma of polished wood, champagne, perfume and sex.

Closing the door, he stood at it for a moment, allowing his visor-protected eyes to adjust to the meagre light, then he advanced towards her.

Perhaps instinct rather than any sound roused her. She opened her eyes uncertainly, then saw him, her eyes growing huge with terror. She shot up into a sitting position, gathered for the scream, but he leapt at her, his gloved hand smothering the sound. "Sshhh! Don't scream and I won't hurt you!"

Her eyes blazed at him, filled with dread.

"Quiet now!" he commanded. "Make a sound and I'll kill you!"

Cautiously he eased the glove from her mouth.

She cringed from him and whispered croakingly, "What do you want? I have no money. Please . . . don't hurt me . . ."

"I don't want money, Mrs Parker."

She blinked at him. "You know who I am? Who are you? What do you want?"

He pointed. "Your coat."

She gulped, shook her head. "I . . . haven't anything on under it."

"I know. That's why I want it."

She gasped, "Oh, my God . . ."

He laughed. "You're afraid I'm going to rape you? After what Bo Sangster's been doing to you for the past six hours, you're afraid of being *raped*?"

Her face contorted. "You've been *watching*?"

"Only the first time. After that it got pretty boring. Stand up and take your coat off."

With dire reluctance she got off the settee, slipped off the coat and crouched over to conceal her nakedness. He looked down on her, and kept on looking until at last she could stand the tension no longer and crumbled to the floor. "Do it if you're going to! Do it and go!"

He kicked the dress towards her. "Put it on."

She looked up at him, confused.

"Go on—put it on. You look a mess."

She got up, turning her back to him as she slipped the dress on. "What do you want? What are you here for?"

"Certainly not to rape you, you're too old."

She flashed anger at him.

He threw the coat at her. "Put it on." She did so. "OK—now lie face down on the settee, your arms above your head."

Awkwardly, she got into the position.

212

Carlo moved in front of her, taking the flat metal tin from his pocket and extracting the hypodermic syringe.

"What are you going to do?" Her anxious protest came muffled from the cushion.

Grabbing her wrist, he located the vein and slid the needle in.

She jumped, but he held tightly to the wrist. "What the hell are you doing?"

"I'm putting you to sleep." He replaced the syringe in the box and moved into a crouch in front of her. "You've just made love for the very last time. You're going to die."

She moved to scream but he stifled it with his hand. "When you wake up you will be lying on a narrow parapet, one hundred feet above the pavement. Your arms and legs will be tied. There will be a noose around your neck, attached to a ninety-foot rope. Ponder on those figures, Mrs Parker . . . a ninety-foot rope and a one-hundred-foot drop. For a few moments after you wake I shall allow you to enjoy the unimaginable terror of your situation . . . then I shall push you over the edge."

She writhed against his grasp.

He chuckled. "Imagine how you will feel while you're falling . . . knowing the rope is getting shorter and shorter. Then suddenly . . ." he slapped his hands together sharply, ". . . bingo! I think your head would come clean off your shoulders."

She slumped, her eyes rolling up into their sockets.

Carlo got up and turned off the fire, put out the lights and hoisted Lily over his shoulder.

A little after five she was sleeping soundly in the trunk of Francisco's Dodge.

11

Lily Parker opened her eyes and saw above her a confusion of cob-webbed rafters and a naked glowing light bulb. She shut her eyes tightly, overwhelmed by terror. Him . . . the needle . . . his threat! But he'd said a roof parapet.

There was a soft scuffle close by. Her heart erupted. Rats? She would die.

Dreading to look yet compelled to, she slowly turned her head and peered through slitted eyes.

She'd gone mad. Margaret Whitney was sitting there on the edge of an iron bed staring at the floor. The drug! He'd injected her with LSD. This was a hideous hallucination! But then where, in reality, was she? Up on that roof? Was that horror yet to come?

Her whimper brought Margaret's head snapping around. With a muted cry she leapt up from the bed and came to crouch at Lily's side, her face etched with her own anxiety, her eyes searching Lily's face with concern. "Are you all right?"

Lily gaped at her and reached out to touch her arm, astounded to find it real. "Margaret?"

Margaret patted her hand. "Sshh . . . it's all right . . . you're in shock, I know, but it really is me."

Blinking, Lily slowly sat up, swung her legs off the bed and gaped about her with growing awareness, repulsed by the squalor of her surroundings. "Where in God's name . . . ?"

"We're in a cellar in an old house in the Everglades," Margaret whispered. "You've been kidnapped—did you know that? What happened to you, Lily?"

"I . . . was in the summerhouse . . . and suddenly he was there . . . told me . . . he was going to hang me . . . oh, my God!"

214

Margaret quickly sat beside her, put her arm around her shaking shoulders. "Sshh . . ."

"Margaret, what is *happening*? What are *you* doing here? Why *me*?"

"Didn't he tell you?"

Lily shook her head. "He didn't say anything except that . . . he was going to hang me . . ."

"Do you remember Ana Patillas, Belle's Mexican maid who hanged herself in jail six years ago?"

Lily looked hard at her, bewildered. "Yes . . ."

"She is what this is all about. This man, whoever he is, wants Belle to confess in public that it was Elizabeth who stole that jewellery and put the blame on Ana. He's trying to bring the Littles down."

Lily stared. "My God . . . but . . . where do we come into it?"

"He's using us to enforce a confession from Belle. He's using our lives, the threat of our deaths to . . ." Margaret shook her head, fighting tears. "He's given her an ultimatum. Unless she confesses to the press and TV by three o'clock on Thursday . . . the time Elizabeth gets married . . . he's . . . going to hang us."

Lily's mouth dropped open. "Who *is* he, Margaret?"

"I don't know."

Lily got slowly to her feet, shocked, bemused. "Why has he waited so long . . . six *years*?"

"Perhaps he's been waiting for something like this to happen to the Littles—the wedding. He couldn't have chosen a better time."

Lily whirled. "But Belle will never confess! It would ruin her!"

Margaret nodded despairingly. "He knows that."

"He *knows* it? Then what's the point?"

"I don't *know*, Lily . . . but he's got something planned. I was with him when he phoned her . . . He's got tape recorders and things . . . he can hear every word the Littles say. He's bugged their house! And my telephone! Yours, too, and Ruth's. He's known every move we've made!"

Lily clutched her face. "Good God, Margaret, this is *crazy* . . ."

"I know—but he's doing it! He must have been planning this for months, years."

"And . . . when did he kidnap you?"

Margaret sighed tremulously. "On Friday night."

Lily gaped. "*Friday?* And no one in the Park knows you're *missing?*" Margaret bowed her head. "Belle and Elizabeth know," she whispered. "I was with him when he phoned and told them, and I heard their conversation after they'd rung off. Lily, they don't care whether I live or die! I heard them say it! They called me . . . expendable."

Lily shut her eyes. "This gets more hideous by the minute! You mean to say the Littles are just going to stand by and let this maniac . . ." Her eyes flared open. "Arthur! What about Arthur? If you've been missing since Friday, he must be crazy with worry by now . . ."

Margaret was shaking her head, abjectly miserable. "No. Arthur was in Galverston when it happened, he only got back last night. But . . ." She bit her lip, choked back tears.

"What?"

"Belle and Elizabeth lied to him to keep him quiet. They told him I'd found out about his affair with his secretary, Judith Harmer, and had gone away to Palm Beach . . ."

"Jesus Christ. Is it true—about him and Judith?"

Margaret nodded.

Lily groaned. "Oh, Margaret . . ."

"The point I'm making, Lily, is that our kidnapper heard the conversation, then phoned Arthur to tell him the truth—that I'd been kidnapped and Belle was lying. Arthur got straight back on to her and demanded an explanation, and she . . ." Tears welled in her eyes.

"She what?"

"She told him . . . that she'd ruin him if he went to the police before the wedding . . . but that she'd make him rich if he kept his mouth shut."

Lily grimaced with disbelief. "And what was his reaction?"

"He agreed to say nothing," Margaret whispered.

Lily stared at her. "Margaret, tell me this can't be happening. Tell me that people can't behave this way towards people—least of all to their friends ... and a *wife*, for Chrissake? For money! I don't believe it!"

"It's true," Margaret said in a small, vanquished voice. "And now that it is happening, it doesn't really surprise me. Belle Little ... why should my life matter to her? And Arthur ..." she shrugged. "It has been over between us for a long while. He's been working towards a divorce for ..."

"A divorce—yes!" Lily protested. "But to stand by and see you *die*!" She turned away across the awful room, stopped suddenly and frowned at her wrist watch. "Margaret, how long have I been here?"

"A few hours, I don't know exactly. With no windows, I've lost track of time."

"My watch says eleven o'clock. He kidnapped me at about four-thirty Monday morning, so I presume it's now eleven Monday morning. That means Sam should be home from Lauderdale ..." She shivered. "Margaret, I'm frightened! She's going to make the same proposition to Sam, isn't she? Belle is going to give him the same ultimatum she gave Arthur!"

Upstairs in the control bedroom, Francisco, who had been listening to their conversation, reached for the phone and dialled the Littles' number.

12

When Elizabeth answered, Francisco switched on the pocket
tape recorder and held it to the mouthpiece of the phone.

The voice of Judge Hamlin said, "Elizabeth, Andy. Is your
mother there?"

"Yes, just a moment, Andy."

Francisco switched off the recorder. He had spent a couple of
hours lifting the opening greetings of several regular callers to
the Little house on to a cassette tape. It was a device he couldn't
hope to use more than once or twice—Elizabeth was bound to
counter with defensive questioning—but it would serve to
throw confusion into the enemy camp.

Belle answered cheerfully. "Andy, I was just this moment
talking to Gareth Owen about you . . ."

"This isn't Andy," whispered Francisco.

Belle's outcry brought Elizabeth on to the extension.
"Mother! What is it?"

"It's HIM!"

"Mother, get off the phone!"

"NO!" shouted Francisco. "I have some news for you, Belle
Little! Stay on the line! It's about your friend Lily Parker . . ."

He could hear her laboured breathing.

"Well?" she demanded.

"She's been kidnapped."

Elizabeth gasped.

From Belle came a spiralling groan, culminating in an explosive bellow. "You . . . BASTARD!"

Elizabeth cried, "Mother, don't listen to him! Get off the
line! Now, listen to me, *you* . . ."

Francisco shouted her down. "ARE YOU STILL THERE,

218

BELLE LITTLE? Unless you publicly confess by three o'clock Thursday ... both Margaret *and* Lily will be hanged. Their lives are in your hands!"

He slammed down the receiver.

Elizabeth ran from the library into the drawing room, where her mother was in the grip of some kind of seizure, her eyes staring apoplectically, her breathing shallow and rasping.

"Mother!" Elizabeth caught her by the arm and urged her towards the settee. "Sit down, sit down."

"Who is he?" gasped Belle. "How can he just ... *kidnap* people out of the Park?"

"We don't know that she has been kidnapped!" retorted Elizabeth, shocked by her mother's reaction to this man. Belle was losing something. In all her life Elizabeth had never known her mother to be frightened of anything or anybody. But this fiend was getting to her. It was the wedding, of course—its importance and imminence. Had she the time to deal with this properly, Belle wouldn't have tolerated the situation for a moment. The telephone number would have been changed, a small army of police and/or private investigators would have been hired to deal with it, and it would have been all over in no time.

"Call her and find out!" demanded Belle.

Elizabeth hesitated.

"Call her!"

Elizabeth snatched up the phone.

A heavily-accented female voice answered. "The Parker residence." "Is that you, Delores? This is Miss Elizabeth. Is Mrs Parker in?"

The maid seemed puzzled. "No, señorita ... an' I don't know where she is."

Elizabeth's heart stumbled. "Is Mr Parker there?"

"Yes, señorita, but he's asleep."

"*Asleep?*"

"He didn't get in till late, señorita."

"Oh. Well, wake him up, I need to speak to him."

It was a while before Sam's sleepy growl responded. "'Lizabeth?"

"Sam, where is Lily?"

"Lily? I don't know ... I haven't long got in."

"Don't you sleep with her?"

He reacted with surprise, affronted by her forthrightness. "Not always, if you must know, not when I know I'm going to be in late. I guess she's in her room."

"She's not. Delores doesn't know where she is. Sam, later on you *may* get a call concerning Lily. If you do—for God's sake don't panic and call the police. Call me first. Do you understand?"

"Er ... a call from whom? What about Lily?"

"Never mind—it may not happen. Just don't call the police or anyone else—call *me*."

She put down the receiver.

During the call, Belle had got up and now stood looking out across the Park through the front window, her features grey and set. "He's got her," she whispered fearfully.

Elizabeth joined her. "Probably," she reluctantly conceded.

"How in God's name can he just walk in the Park and kidnap two women! I'm frightened, Elizabeth ..."

"Oh, Mother, come on ..."

Belle's head flew around. "No, I mean it! I sense terrible danger! This man is *dangerous*! You know something? I don't think he wants that confession ... I think he wants just the opposite. He wants me *not* to confess—so that he can kill Margaret and Lily, then I shall be blamed for their deaths!"

Elizabeth's eyes danced with anger. "You're not thinking of *making* that confession, by any chance?"

Belle returned her gaze to the window and murmured in a tight frightened voice. "Either way, he's got us, hasn't he? If I make the confession, you lose Robert and I ... lose everything. If I don't make it, he will kill them and ..."

"Mother!" Elizabeth caught her mother's arm and spun her around. "What's the matter with you? Are you sick? You're talking defeat! My God, I've never seen you like this before. Now, *please* get your mind back on the wedding and keep it there. It's the only thing that matters to us. Three

220

more days—that's all. Ignore him. Forget him! Think wedding!"

Belle nodded, murmured, "You're right ... I'm sorry. Just keep him away from me. I don't want to hear his voice again."

"You won't, I promise. He fooled me this time, but he won't again. Now, come on, cheer up ... let's go down to the tent and see how things are coming along."

Astounded by Elizabeth's phone call, Sam Parker was about to step into the shower when his bedroom phone rang. Naked, he went into the bedroom, believing it would be a call from his office. Though normally at his desk in Miami by eight-thirty, he'd taken the morning off.

"Hello?"

"Mr Parker?"

"Yes, who is this?"

"Never mind. I'm calling about your wife, Lily. She's been kidnapped. I have her."

Sam stared at the yellow flock wallpaper.

"Does your silence indicate shock or indifference?" asked Francisco.

Sam's face crumpled. "Who the fuck *is* this?"

"You've already asked that."

"OK—how much?"

"Belle Little knows the price."

"What has she got to do with this?"

"Everything. She is the cause of Lily's kidnapping. She could also be the cause of her—and Margaret Whitney's—release this afternoon if she wanted to."

Sam croaked, "Margaret Whitney! You got her, too? Look, man ... what's going on? Let me have it straight."

"All right. Six years ago, the Littles conspired to have a Mexican woman unjustly arrested. She died in prison. Lily and Margaret knew about it but kept their mouths shut. All I want is a public confession from Belle Little—before the wedding on Thursday—and Lily and Margaret will be set free."

221

"And if . . . Belle doesn't confess?" stammered Sam.

"Your wife and Margaret will be hanged at three o'clock on Thursday."

"You're mad!"

"No, I'm not. It's Belle who is mad—power mad. She's willing to sacrifice Lily and Margaret provided Elizabeth gets to marry Robert Collier."

"Sweet Jesus," Sam gasped. "Does Arthur Whitney know his wife's been kidnapped?"

"Yes. He heard last night. But Belle has ordered him not to call the police or talk to anyone. She's going to tell you the same thing."

Sam's mind darted, searching for a solution that wasn't there. "Look, be reasonable . . . you can't kill Lily just because she kept quiet about the Mex woman. I mean, Christ, how could she *not* keep quiet? I do business with Belle Little, so does Arthur. Our wives couldn't blab about the Littles . . . they'd ruin us!"

"I appreciate your problem. Next time choose your business partners with greater care."

"Aw, *shit*. Look, let's get down to it . . . one hundred thousand dollars in small bills and no questions, what d'you say?"

"I say no, Mr Parker."

"*Two* hundred thousand! OK—you name it, give me a figure and I guarantee there'll be no . . ."

"Parker! I don't want your money. I want that confession. Now, if you and Arthur Whitney want to see your wives alive again, make sure Belle Little publicly confesses before Thursday. You have three days left—so get moving."

The phone hummed in Sam's ear.

He slumped down on to the bed. This wasn't real. Lily and Margaret *kidnapped*? These things happened in fiction or to other people.

Arthur! He'd check with him. He depressed the cradle buttons and punched out Arthur's office number.

The secretary put him through. Arthur said, "Sam, hi, what can I do for you?"

"Arthur, I just heard about Margaret. Lily's been kidnapped, too."

There was a silence, then a groan. "Oh, my God . . ."

"Art, we've got to *do* something!"

"What? Tell me what the hell we *can* do."

"Belle . . . we've got to talk to her, see if there isn't some kind of compromise she'd agree to."

"Waste of time, Sam, I've already tried. She refuses to utter a word—publicly or privately—in case it kills the marriage. She's got her claws out on this one, prepared to fight to the death."

"Whose death—Lily's and Margaret's?"

"Or *ours*, Sam—that's the choice."

"Then we can't lose anything by trying. Meet me here in half an hour."

Arthur sighed heavily. "OK." And rang off.

They assembled in the Littles' drawing room. Belle looked pale and distraught.

Elizabeth opened up, defensively, as soon as the doors were closed. "As you can see, Mother is not feeling well, so I'd be glad if you'd keep this short. You've no idea what we're having to cope with. This place is a madhouse eighteen hours a day, people wanting decisions, the phone never stops ringing, press, police security, business . . . Mother, sit down, you look terrible."

Sam cleared his throat nervously. "We . . . appreciate the pressure you're under, Elizabeth . . . but you've got to appreciate our position too. Damn it, our wives have been kidnapped!" He glanced at Arthur for support. "Belle, Arthur and I were wondering if there isn't some kind of compromise you could . . ."

Belle's eyes flashed. "Is that what you've come for—to talk me into making a confession?"

"No! Not a confession. But we thought maybe a statement of some kind . . . something that would satisfy him . . . that you could withdraw after Lily and Margaret were released."

"Like what?" snapped Belle.

223

Sam shuffled and licked his lips. "Well, how about telling the press the truth . . . that you're being blackmailed with your friends' lives into making a confession and rather than risk . . ."

Belle came to her feet. "NO!"

"But, Belle, you could come out of this covered in glory . . ."

"You fool, I'd come out of it covered in . . . Good God, can't you get it into your heads that Elizabeth is about to marry the son of the Governor! Miles Collier is tipped for the White House! He's sitting on a political powder keg. The slightest hint of a scandal and, well, the consequences don't bear thinking about. Look . . . all I'm asking from you both is three days' silence. By three-fifteen on Thursday it will be all over. Once Elizabeth is married, there'll be no point in this man harming Lily and Margaret. We'll have called his bluff . . ."

Elizabeth interrupted. "Mother, don't beg them—tell them! Tell them how much they owe you. Tell them how they got rich. And tell them how you're going to put them away for a thousand years if they screw up this wedding!"

Sam swallowed. "Now, Elizabeth . . . nobody's talking about jeopardising your wedding . . ."

"Oh, get out, Sam, you're upsetting Mother."

With an exchange of hopeless glances the two men left the room.

Elizabeth snorted. "Well, you'll have no more trouble from them."

Belle responded with the faintest of nods.

Elizabeth peered closely at her. "What's the matter now?"

"I just wish," Belle whispered, "that I could believe what I told them . . . that we'll have called his bluff."

Elizabeth snorted again and left the room.

13

At four-thirty that afternoon, Francisco drove into the city and visited two stores—the first specialising in hi-fi equipment, the second in books.

In the hi-fi store he purchased a specific model of jack-plug and fifty feet of cable; from the bookshop he bought a copy of the Anglican Book of Common Prayer.

Returning to the house, he spent several hours in the control bedroom, sifting through his transcribed notes, selecting certain segments of recordings he had made since beginning the project and transferring those passages on to a separate reel, introducing each passage with his own recorded comments and explanation. When the master-tape was completed, he made four copies of it.

Finally, from a written script, he recorded an explanatory message on to a cassette tape, then made four copies.

At ten o'clock he reported for duty, finding Carl Krantz poring over the day's reports compiled by the earlier shifts, the vehicle registrations running to eight full sheets.

"One hundred and thirty-seven vehicles came in today," he commented. "One hundred and fourteen for Belle Little. The canvas flats arrived. So did all the stage iron, the lighting, chairs, trestle-tables . . ."

At eleven o'clock Francisco made his first round. Parking the station wagon, he went up the path to the rear of the Little house and entered the big top, whistling with surprise at how much had been accomplished during the day.

The flooring had been laid, two thousand chairs set out in two sections, a small elevated stage constructed over on the left side for the media, and a huge stage, extending from one side of the tent to the other, built at the far end.

His eyes went aloft to the loudspeakers mounted on the king-poles and subsidiary poles. Gazing about, he made his way down the centre aisle, his footsteps ringing echoingly on the wooden flooring.

The figure of Bob Prescott appeared from beneath the web of steel scaffolding supporting the main stage. "Howdy."

"Hi, Bob. I see you've been busy."

Prescott cackled. "Use a cawfee?"

"Yes, sir. Here ... brought you some cigarettes."

"Well, that's mighty nice of yuh ... 'preciate it."

They ducked beneath the stage and went through the flap into the annex tent, Francisco's eyes following the trail of cables that emerged from beneath the floorboards and came together as they entered the annex.

Immediately inside the small tent, a trestle-table had been set up and on it stood the amplifier and sound-mixer into which all the loudspeaker and microphone cables fed. Above the table a small monitor speaker was attached to a support pole.

"See they've got the sound in," he observed.

Prescott poured the coffee. "Yep, they've bin testin' it this afternoon."

Francisco hung in the entrance to the big top, ostensibly looking into it but in fact studying the sound equipment on the table and the grouping of the cables that fed into it, and calculating distances.

"Wonder when the Governor will arrive?" he asked with apparent interest.

"Not till noon Thursday," answered Prescott. "They say he'll be arrivin' by helicopter 'bout noon. The dicks wus in today ... snoopin' around, sniffin' this an' that. They seemed satisfied with the security set-up. I reckon Collier can rest easy while he's here. No great drama's gonna interfere with *this* weddin'."

"You bet," winked Francisco.

14

Ruth Howard awoke in an irascible mood, her normal pre-breakfast condition. Today it was aggravated by the remnants of a head cold that had kept her confined to bed for two days.

Pressing a bell to summon her maid, she got out of bed and entered the bathroom, performed her ablutions, then returned to bed as a quiet knock sounded at the door.

A Cuban woman in her mid-thirties entered carrying a silver tray.

"Good morning, señora. How are you feeling today?"

"Terrible ... hardly slept at all. This ghastly cold ..."

"It sounds much better today, though."

"Well, it isn't."

The maid settled the tray in Ruth's lap and crossed the room to draw back the drapes.

"No, leave them," Ruth winced. "That sun's too bright."

"Yes, señora."

Ruth released an irritable sigh. "Marta, this tomato juice is *warm*, for heaven's sake. How many times have I told you not to put it next to the coffee? *Why* is it necessary for me to repeat everything four hundred times before it sinks in?"

"I'm sorry, señora ..."

Ruth repeated the sigh. "And the toast is cold. Marta, take this back and get it right. I want cold juice and hot toast, not the reverse."

"Yes, señora."

Nervously, the maid collected the tray and made for the door, turning to say, "Señora, your hair appointment ..."

"I *know* about my hair appointment."

"You asked me to remind you."

"Thank you. Please hurry with the juice and toast, I would prefer it before lunch time."

As the maid left the room, the telephone rang. Ruth answered it. The lifting of the receiver and her spoken "Hello" activated the tape recorder in Francisco's control bedroom.

"Ruth? Wendy Rayner. How are you feeling?"

"Frightful ... absolutely ghastly, Wendy, and I've got *the* most hectic day to face. Two days to the wedding and I haven't done half the things I intended doing. This cold has thrown my schedule completely out. I shall have to spend most of the morning on the telephone, then I've got a hair-do at eleven, lunch with Marion at twelve-thirty—God *knows* I need Marion and War On Cancer today ... and umpteen other things to do this afternoon."

"You poor dear. I obviously called at a bad time, so I'll leave you to your telephone. See you at the wedding. Bye for now."

Ruth pressed down the cradle buttons and immediately dialled a number to make the first of several afternoon appointments.

At four o'clock, smartly dressed in a tailored two-piece suit of fawn gaberdine over a brown silk blouse, her short brown hair newly set, Ruth Howard left the house, got into her sage-green Continental and drove towards the city.

Stopping briefly at a flower shop to collect the wreath she had ordered by phone that morning, she continued towards Coral Gables.

At four-twenty-five she returned through an arched gateway, reducing her speed, as instructed by the road sign, to a circumspect twenty miles per hour. She followed the macadamed avenue through acres of rolling lawns and finally stopped the car beneath a willow tree.

Pleased that the cemetery was deserted, she switched off the engine, collected the wreath from the passenger seat and made her way across the velvet grass to the tiny grave.

As she crouched over the grave, the sound of an approaching vehicle caused her to glance around. She frowned with vague annoyance at the sand-coloured car that drew up behind her Continental.

Two young men got out, dressed alike in denim jackets and jeans, their hair shoulder-length and umkempt, their faces hidden behind mirrored sun-glasses.

Ruth suffered a stir of apprehension until she noticed one of them was carrying a small bunch of flowers. Fellow mourners.

She relaxed, dismissed them from her mind, turned her attention to the grave and began clearing away a light scattering of leaves and twigs.

The youths approached, passed behind her and knelt beside a grave close to hers. For a moment they busied themselves clearing the site of debris and setting the flowers in a vase, then stood and moved away as though returning to their car. But as they reached her, they stopped suddenly, one of them tutting sympathetically as he read the epitaph on the marker stone.

"Seven years old. How did he die, lady?"

Ruth primped her lips, annoyed by their intrusion and their hippy appearance. "A car accident," she answered stiffly.

"Too bad. I see today's the fifth anniversary. You bin coming here every year for five years?"

"He was very dear to me."

"I'll bet. You care more about a dead spaniel than you do about a dead human, don't you, Mrs Howard?"

It took a beat for his words to penetrate. She whirled to face him. They were standing close behind her, faceless behind their frightening mirrored glasses.

Terrified, she struggled to get up but they were on her, each grabbing an arm, forcing her back down into a crouch. She stared vacantly at the hypodermic syringe and opened her mouth to scream but a gloved hand stifled the sound. The needle went in. Paralysed with terror, she watched the colourless liquid empty into her vein. This couldn't be happening to her, not to *her* . . .

She slumped against Francisco.

He tutted. "Poor woman . . . quite overcome with grief."

"'To My Beloved Spaniel—Sasha'," Carlo read. "'A True Friend and Good Companion Sadly Missed.'"

"I wonder if anyone will miss her?" Francisco glanced around the cemetery. "OK, let's go."

Supporting her between them, they carried her to the cars and placed her in the Dodge trunk.

"Lose it in a long-term car park," said Francisco, tossing Carlo the Continental keys. "I shall go home and break the tragic news to Bernard."

15

There had been a time when Bernard Howard was very much in love with his wife, but that had been in the beginning. Later on, after their two children were born, love had cooled to fondness, and that warmth had persisted up until Ruth's first encounter with Belle Little.

The change that then quickly overtook Ruth had annoyed, even disgusted him.

When they lived in Coral Gables on the substantial though unspectacular income he derived as a partner in the law firm his father had started back in the 'thirties, Ruth had seemed more than satisfied with their unpretentious suburban life, happy enough simply to look after their home and him and raise the children.

Then, through Sam Parker, an estate agent he'd known for some time, he and Ruth had been invited to a cocktail party at the Little home in the Park—a realty get-together to celebrate, with press coverage, the opening of a Hialeah shopping centre.

During the party he'd discussed the real estate scene briefly with Belle—a token conversation between guest and busy hostess—but a few days later Sam Parker had phoned to tell him Belle wished him to handle the legal aspects of a property purchase for her. More work followed. Within a year his income had quadrupled. Within two years the Howards had moved into the Park.

But Ruth had fallen under Belle Little's spell long before the move. With stirrings of irritation, even distaste, he noted his wife's attempt to emulate the woman whose personality, power and socal status Ruth regarded with awe, envy and a respect that fell little short of idolatry.

Listening to Ruth's conversations, Bernard would wince at

the outpouring of snobbery and pretentiousness, the hardness and hauteur, hearing in her pronunciation and inflexion the echo of Belle's imperious tone.

Often he would be induced to mutter disgustedly, "Silly bitch", but would immediately regret it, appreciating how easy it was for a woman—or man, for that matter—to abandon her own personality under the influence of the omnipotent Belle.

Hadn't *he* sacrificed more than a few principles on the altar of expediency during his association with her? Decidedly. And yet his case was different, he convinced himself. He had *had* to toe the Little line for the sake of business; Ruth had done it by choice.

At times, as he covertly studied his wife, the thought crossed his mind that this behaviour was the emergence of her true nature, not a Belle-induced metamorphosis. Perhaps at heart she had always been this tough, this pretentious, this ambitious, but had been held in check by their modest circumstances?

Lately, to his surprise, he found himself not caring either way. Perhaps, he reasoned, it was middle-age that was prompting the indifference. Being wholly honest with himself, he had to admit that only his work really mattered to him these days. His children were no longer his children but married, independent adults, and Ruth ... well, she was a woman he was accustomed to having around.

So he believed—until the telephone call that Tuesday evening.

It came a little after seven, as he was entering the house from the garage. Hearing the phone, he hastened into the hall, put down his hat and briefcase and lifted the receiver.

"Howard," he announced, reflexively checking his appearance in a wall mirror and finger-combing his sparse grey hair into place.

"Your wife has been kidnapped."

Bernard's concentration momentarily remained riveted on a smudge of dirt above his right brow. Obviously he had not heard what he imagined he'd heard. "I beg your pardon?"

"I said ... your wife ... Ruth ... has been kidnapped."

Bernard grimaced, his heart reacting now with heavy beating. "Who is this?"

"They all asked that ... Belle Little, Sam Parker, Arthur Whitney. A reflex question, of course, but redundant. Ruth is not alone. Margaret Whitney and Lily Parker have also been kidnapped. The reason, Mr Howard, is this ..."

Bernard slowly crumpled, slumped down on to the telephone bench and listened in awed silence until Francisco had completed the explanation. Then, as though all but the opening statement had passed through him unheard, he asked falteringly, "You mean to say ... that Margaret has been kidnapped since last Friday ... and Lily since Sunday ... and nobody told us?"

"That is correct."

"But ... their husbands!"

"Know about it and have kept quiet—have *been* kept quiet. Belle Little has silenced them."

Bernard passed a trembling hand over his damp forehead. "I can't believe they'd *do* nothing ..."

"Are you saying that you will do something, Mr Howard? Are you telling me you can persuade Belle Little to make that confession?"

Bernard shut his eyes. "My God, I don't believe this. You're asking the impossible, don't you know that? How can I possibly persuade her to commit social suicide?"

"That's your problem—and Sam Parker's and Arthur Whitney's. Talk to them. Go to see Belle Little, all three of you. Tell her you're not willing to sacrifice the lives of your wives merely to support her political ambitions. Do it *now*. You only have one day left. Unless she makes a public confession by three o'clock Thursday ... your wife *hangs*!"

Bernard phoned the Whitney home. Arthur answered, sounding drunk.

Bernard asked shakingly, "Art ... is it true ... about Margaret?"

There was a silence, then, "Who told you?"

233

"The goddamn kidnapper? He's got Ruth, too!"

Arthur groaned. "Oh, bloody Christ . . ."

"Art . . . I can't believe you are doing nothing about it! We've got to do *something*! We've got to persuade Belle . . ."

"Sam and I have already tried that . . ."

"Well, we've got to try again! Let's discuss it—the three of us. Is Sam at home now?"

"He's right here. Bernie, there's nothing we can do . . ."

"I don't believe that."

"*Believe* it, Bernie."

"Art, let's at least talk!"

Arthur sighed. "OK . . . we'll be there in five minutes."

Bernard watched for them from the drawing room window and hurried to open the door.

Arthur, as Bernard had suspected, was quite a bit drunk. Sam Parker looked fatigued, though whether from worry over Lily or a long day at the office Bernard could not be sure.

He ushered them into the drawing room and made for the drinks cabinet. "What'll it be?"

"Scotch . . . straight . . . very large," muttered Arthur.

"Same for me," said Sam.

Bernard poured three and handed them round. Nobody felt inclined to sit. They drank deeply and in awkward silence, then Bernard said, "For God's sake, somebody tell me this isn't happening. Tell me it's a sick joke. Tell me I'm having a nervous breakdown! Tell me anything . . . but f'Chrissake, don't tell me our wives have all been kidnapped!"

Arthur blinked myopically into his whisky.

Sam turned to the window and looked out across the Park towards his home, saying quietly, "I remember thinking exactly the same thing the day Kennedy was assassinated. Bobby, too. And King. It hits you that way. These things don't happen in real life, you tell yourself, only in fiction. How can the President of the United States be assassinated? It's preposterous." He turned and looked earnestly at Bernard. "Our wives have been kidnapped, Bernie, they really have."

Bernard blinked disconcertedly, unable wholly to accept the horrific reality. "Who is he? What in hell is this *really* about?"

234

"Didn't he tell you?" asked Sam.

"He told me what he wanted—a public confession. But to what end? To clear Ana Patillas's name? To frustrate the wedding? To ruin the Littles?"

"Why not all three?"

Bernard frowned bewilderedly. "What are we going to do?"

"Nothing," grunted Arthur.

Bernard's eyes hardened. "Art, it is common knowledge that you are no longer in love with your wife . . ."

"Cut that out, Bernie," Arthur muttered, draining his scotch.

"No! It has a bearing! It's also common knowledge that you're sleeping with Judith Harmer! So maybe this is precisely what you want—an easy out!"

Arthur erupted. "I said cut that out! Jesus, that's a shit thing to say, Howard . . ."

"Fellas, fellas!" Sam cut in. "For Chrissake, this we don't need . . ."

Bernard rounded on him. "You, too, Sam, you and Lily . . ."

Sam speared a finger at him. "Stop right there, Bernie! Now, knock it off! I realise you're shocked and upset, but there's no call for that. OK—things may not be so great at home for Art and me, but, fucking *hell*, there's one stink of a difference between not loving your wife and not caring if some psycho hangs her! Art's just giving it to you straight—there *is* nothing we can do!"

"We can go and see her!" Bernard insisted angrily. "We can talk it through, see if there isn't some way . . ."

"A compromise?" retorted Sam. "We've already thought of that—*and* been to see her about it . . ."

"Well, I haven't! And I've got to try! I just can't sit here and do nothing . . . and you two ought to come with me."

Sam sighed, looked at Arthur who shrugged.

Bernard put down his glass. "Come on—let's go."

Elizabeth was coming down the stairs when the door chimes sounded. Crossing to the door, she glanced through a side

235

window and swore beneath her breath as she saw who the callers were, suspecting the purpose of their visit.

Opening the door, she confronted them with a defiant stance, determined they wouldn't get in.

Bernard cleared his throat. "Elizabeth, we must speak to your mother."

"What about?"

He met her aggressive gaze with equal determination. "Ruth has been kidnapped."

She gaped, then murmured a groan.

"We must speak to Belle," he insisted.

She recovered and shook her head. "No. She's lying down. She's not well. I can't allow it . . ."

A tic twitched in Bernard's cheek. "You can't allow it? *You* can't allow your mother's business partners to speak to her?"

"About business—yes. But not about this. She's under tremendous pressure, it's hitting her from all sides . . ."

Bernard stepped forward, demanding, "Elizabeth, she's got to *do* something!"

Elizabeth made to shut the door. "No! Leave her alone . . ."

His hand slammed against the door, then he was in the hall. "Where is she?"

"Get out!" She grabbed at his arm. "How dare you! Get out of this house! Get OUT!"

He swept her aside and walked stiff-legged towards the drawing room doors. Elizabeth ran after him. Sam and Arthur stepped into the hall and closed the door.

Elizabeth grabbed again at Bernard's arm. "How DARE you burst in like this!"

"Elizabeth, for God's *sake*!" He pushed her away, opened the double doors and walked into the drawing room.

Belle, in a housecoat, her hair in disarray, was getting up from the settee on which she'd obviously been sleeping. She blinked at the intrusion, her eyes heavy with sleep. "Wha . . .?"

Suddenly unsure of himself, Bernard faltered, glancing around at the other men for support.

Elizabeth ran in front of him, her fists clenched in fury.

236

"How *dare* you break in like this! I told you," she flung out her arm, "... look at her! She's not well! She was asleep!"

Bernard stammered, "Belle ... I'm sorry ... but I have to see you. Ruth has been kidnapped! He phoned half an hour ago ... he's got her! He's got all our *wives*!"

As though she had not heard him, Belle drew herself up, her face stiff with anger, and gasped, "This is unforgivable! Are you out of your minds? This is my home! I will not tolerate you bursting in like this!"

Bernard, astounded, shouted, "Belle! For God's sake ... Ruth has been kidnapped! Don't you understand?"

She turned away, livid, took a faltering step or two across the room. "I understand perfectly. What do you expect me to do about it?"

Bernard mouthed perplexedly and shot a futile glance at Arthur and Sam for support. "Belle, you've got to do *something* to appease him. By ignoring him you'll make him angry and in that condition he's more likely to do something drastic than if he thinks he's winning! Can't you ... issue some kind of ..."

Belle whirled on him, savage, desperate. "NO! I can issue NOTHING!" She raised both hands, balled into fists, above her head, a gesture of demented helplessness. "My God, don't you understand what's at stake here? In less than forty-eight hours Elizabeth will be married to the son of our Governor! *I* am largely responsible for Miles Collier *being* Governor! Don't you realise what that means ... for *all* of us? The POWER ... the CONTROL ... And you want me to throw it all away just to save your miserable WIVES?"

Bernard's jaw dropped.

A charged silence gripped the room.

Belle looked away, daunted by the eyes of the three men. Only Elizabeth appeared unmoved by her mother's outrageous outburst.

"I see," said Bernard in a hushed whisper, face ashen, body trembling. "So that's what you think of us." He turned abruptly, pushed between Sam and Arthur and made for the door.

Belle came alive, bellowed after him, "Bernard! I warn you!

Don't do anything stupid. I can ruin you . . . all of you! If I go down, you *all* go down! All I'm asking is forty-eight hours—so little in return for so much. I've made you rich, Bernard, you OWE me! Do you hear? YOU OWE ME?"

Bernard slammed out of the house.

Sam and Arthur shifted uncomfortably, Sam muttering, "It wasn't our idea, Belle. We're willing to go along . . ."

Elizabeth jumped in. "Then get hold of Bernard and sort him out! If he goes to the police, we'll hold you two responsible. Stay with him, sit on him, get him drunk, drug him, hit him over the head, if you have to—but keep him quiet!"

They nodded, quickly left the room and hurried after Bernard, finding him in tears of anger, shame, confusion.

They escorted him into his home, where Arthur poured fresh drinks.

Bernard slumped into an armchair, his head in his hands. "She doesn't care, d'you know that? She doesn't give a goddamn if our wives live or die!"

"Why should it surprise you?" Sam asked quietly. "You know her. You knew what she was like when you started working for her."

Bernard shook his head. "No, she wasn't like this . . . not this cold-blooded. Jesus, she's inhuman!"

Sam patted his shoulder. "Look, take it easy. There's no sense getting screwed up about somethin' you've got no control over. As she said—there are less than forty-eight hours left. If you phoned the cops right now, there isn't a goddamned thing they could do in so short a time . . . all you'd succeed in doing is fucking us all up. Belle's only hope is to bluff this guy out—so you may as well sit here and get drunk . . . and stay drunk till the wedding's over."

Bernard stared into his glass. "No matter how this turns out . . . I'm getting out."

"Out?"

"Out of here. Out of the Park. Out of Belle Little. She owns us . . . owns our businesses, our lives, our future. Everything! She's too powerful . . . and after the wedding she'll be even more powerful. That's too rich for me. But it's not even that

238

that worries me—it's her. You saw her. She's sick, Sam, she's going crazy. And I don't care for the idea of having my business, my life and my future controlled by a woman who is going mad. Or her daughter."

Sam frowned. "No, certainly not Elizabeth." He drew a heavy sigh. "Jesus, how did it get to this? All I ever wanted to do was make a buck."

16

Wednesday began badly in the Little household.

At seven o'clock Elizabeth was awakened by angry shouting on the landing. Slipping into a housecoat, she opened her bedroom door and found Constanza hurrying down the stairs in tears.

She approached her mother's bedroom, knocked and opened the door. Belle was on the edge of her bed, doubled over, rocking as though in pain.

"Mother! What's the matter?"

Belle's face came up, enraged. "That stupid bitch!" She turned, indicating a brown stain on the bedsheets. "She spilled boiling tea over me!"

Elizabeth started. "You're scalded?"

"The bed! She's ruined the sheets! God, *why* am I surrounded by such idiots!" She came to her feet, clutching her head. "Get rid of her! I can't stand her near me!"

"Mother, are you *hurt*?"

"The bed! Can't you see she's ruined the sheets!"

Elizabeth tutted with exasperation, turned to the bedside cupboard, uncapped a bottle of Valium capsules and poured a glass of water. "Here, take these. You've got a long, hard day ahead of you ..."

Belle struck out, swiping the glass and capsules from her hand. "Don't treat me like a child, Elizabeth! I don't need Valium and I *do* need my wits about me to keep watch on all the fools around me. If you want to do something useful—order me some more tea!"

Elizabeth left the room and went downstairs to the kitchen, interrupting a tearful exchange in Spanish between Constanza and the Cuban cook.

"What happened?" demanded Elizabeth.

Constanza shook her head. "Señorita, it wasn't my fault. I leaned over to waken the señora and she . . . she must have been having a bad dream. She screamed . . . struck out at me . . . knocked the tray from my hand!"

"All right, calm yourself. Make some more tea and I'll take it up. My mother is tired, that's all. It's a very worrying time for her. I'll come back for the tea."

Elizabeth left the kitchen and went into the library and called the home number of Doctor Harold Tyson, the Littles' physician.

Tyson answered drowsily after four rings. "Hm?"

"Harry, it's Elizabeth. I'd like you to drop over some time this morning and take a look at mother."

"Oh? What's wrong?"

"Pre-wedding nerves, I guess."

He smiled. "Is it surprising?"

"Harry . . . I'm worried."

"Oh?"

"There's more to it than the wedding—which, God knows, is enough. There are other pressures . . . business. She doesn't look good. She has blown up once already this morning. I tried to give her Valium and she knocked the glass out of my hand. See what you can do."

"I'll do my best, of course—but even doctors tend to have limited powers of persuasion against runaway trains. Belle is wound up tight for the wedding and won't run down until it's over. You should know better than anyone."

"What worries me is how *far* she'll run down. Come over, Harry."

At breakfast in the conservatory, Elizabeth covertly studied her mother as Belle opened her personal mail. These past few days, there had been an excessive amount.

To ease her mother's burden, Elizabeth had suggested bringing in one of the many secretaries employed by the numerous Little enterprises in Miami, but Belle had declined on the grounds that she didn't want outsiders nosing into her private affairs.

Among the morning's mail was the usual quota of junk, which went unopened into a waste basket at Belle's feet. There was a heavier-than-usual quota of begging letters—requests from private individuals and associations for donations, gifts, for her sponsorship of their cause—a variety of requests which Belle normally dismissed without comment and put into the basket barely scanned. Today, however, she tutted and fretted over each one—a further manifestation, in Elizabeth's eyes, of her worsening nervous condition.

Slitting open a pink envelope, Belle extracted a short note, glanced over it and with a disgusted, "Damn!" tossed it to Elizabeth. "Dolly Gale can't make the wedding . . . that fool George has come down with mumps. How *like* him to do it now."

Elizabeth picked up the note and was reading it when Belle suddenly let out a strangled cry. Elizabeth looked up with a start. Her mother was staring in horror at the sheet of paper in her hands.

"What . . ." Elizabeth began.

Belle threw down the paper, broke from the table and hurried into the house.

Elizabeth snatched up the note. On it was a pen drawing of three women hanging naked from a gallows. In place of their drawn faces were the photographs of Margaret Whitney, Lily Parker and Ruth Howard.

Typed beneath the drawing was the message: "A public confession . . . or this at 3 o'clock tomorrow! The choice is yours."

"Damn!" Crumpling the note, Elizabeth ran after her mother, cursing herself for not having anticipated this avenue of attack.

In the hall she found the butler, Storey, standing in a perplexed pose, his gaze directed towards the head of the stairs.

"What?" she asked.

"Er . . . most regrettable, miss. Constanza has just walked out . . . and in telling your mother, I'm afraid I rather upset her. She ran upstairs . . ."

242

"Christ, what else is going to happen today?" She took the stairs two at a time and entered Belle's room, finding her at the window overlooking the Park.

Elizabeth went to her. "You mustn't let it upset you, we'll get a temporary maid ..."

"He's going to do it," Belle said distantly. "He's going to hang them."

"Nonsense. That's precisely what he wants you to believe!"

Belle whirled. "How can you be so damn sure? Do you know him? Do you know what he's capable of? He has kidnapped three women out of this park, Elizabeth—do you fully appreciate what that means ... what it says about this man? It means he's clever, daring—and desperate! It means he has already taken enormous risks. Do you imagine he's going to back down at three o'clock tomorrow, simply release those women and disappear from our lives? Don't you see—he's got to hang them!"

Elizabeth met her mother's gaze and flung out an arm. "Look out there ... all you've worked for all these years. Do you want to trade all that for three empty-headed women?"

"Damn it, you know I don't!"

"Then stop worrying about this! Forget him!"

"It's not only him I'm worried about."

"Well, what then?"

"The *unknown* terrifies me ... what could happen tomorrow. We don't know who he is. We know *nothing* about him except that he's doing this to avenge Ana Patillas—but do we even know that? He might be just using her as an excuse to bring me down. He might be a business competitor. He may be doing this out of jealousy, for gain, or from plain insanity. He may not be 'him' at all—but a gang, an organisation, a corporation! This may not have anything at all to do with Ana Patillas! The frightening fact is we know *nothing* about him, Elizabeth—and it worries the hell out of me. I'm afraid for tomorrow ... because I've got the most awful premonition something dreadful is going to happen before the wedding ..."

The bedside telephone purred. Elizabeth went to answer it.

243

"Storey, miss ... Mr Gambretti is waiting for madam and yourself in the marquee. He wishes to begin rehearsal."

"All right, Storey, tell him we'll be right down."

She returned to Belle. "It's Gambretti, he wants us in the tent. Mother, this is going to be a difficult day—I've asked Harry Tyson to drop by this morning and take a look at you."

Belle's face set determinedly. "Then call him again and tell him to stay away!" She turned for the door. "I don't wish to be pumped full of Valium. I want to know what's going on!"

Tension built up throughout the morning, precipitated by the overcrowding in the marquee, the noise, the heat, the manifold problems—and not least by the close-quartering of so many wilful, opinionated personalities.

By mid-morning, Ruby Gillespie, the obese, dynamic leader of the hundred-voice Miami Tabernacle Choir, had rowed volubly with Charles Ingman, the conductor of the Miami Symphony Orchestra; Ben Klein, union spokesman for the small army of scene-shifters employed for the transformation scene, had threatened to walk out unless his men were permitted to rehearse while the orchestra and choir were rehearsing; Belle Little had argued with Tyrone Gambretti, the director, on matters concerning the canvas flats, the lighting, the quality of sound and the positioning of the principal guests on the stage; Elizabeth had argued with her mother about her mother's constant arguing; and one of the workmen had tripped over a microphone cable, fallen off the stage and fractured a collarbone and two ribs.

Tyrone Gambretti, a diminutive, flamboyant personality of infamous temper, finally blew the whistle for a fifteen-minute cooling down period and coffee break, then erupted with fury to learn there was no coffee available because the catering van had collided with an oil tanker on its way to the Park.

At this news, Belle threw up her hands and strode towards the exit, ignoring Gambretti's re-blown whistle and megaphoned directive that the rehearsal would continue until the coffee *did* arrive.

Incensed that he was being ignored, he ran after Belle and fatally demanded that she return, whereupon she rounded on him and in a voice that reached all corners of the marquee demanded, "Who in *hell* d'you think you're talking to, you . . . pipsqueak!"

Puce with rage, he turned and stalked out of the tent to his mobile office, while Belle stormed off in the direction of the house.

Amused and calmed by the exchange, the remainder of the company, under the relatively mild direction of Tony Amboyne, Gambretti's young assistant, returned to work in good spirits and accomplished more in the following hour than in the previous three.

Elizabeth followed her mother into the house and encountered Doctor Tyson, who had that moment arrived.

"Trouble?" he asked, reading her expression.

"It's hell on wheels out there. Mother's just had a tiff with Gambretti. You didn't see her?"

He shook his head.

Elizabeth looked up the stairs. "She'll be in her room, let's go up."

Elizabeth tried Belle's door and found it locked. "Mother, open up, Harry's here . . . Mother, come on, let him take a look at you."

There was no response.

Elizabeth frowned at Tyson and knocked more insistently. "Mother, for heaven's sake, let us in . . ."

"Go away! Leave me alone!"

Elizabeth sighed exasperatedly. "Stop being childish! Let Harry give you a tranquilliser . . . you must go on with the rehearsal."

"Go away. I'll be down later."

Elizabeth slapped her forehead, said to Tyson as she turned for the stairs, "What I wouldn't give for it to be four o'clock tomorrow and all over."

He smiled. "It'll soon come."

"Not soon enough."

As she opened the front door, Tyson said, "Call me if you need me."

She smiled sardonically. "I just did."

The afternoon proved even more harrowing than the morning.

Belle appeared in the marquee at two o'clock after the lunch break looking drawn and grey and suddenly old.

Shocked by her appearance, Elizabeth went to her, frowning. "Are you sure you're all right?"

Belle nodded and answered brusquely, "Let's get on with it."

As they moved farther into the marquee, Tyrone Gambretti, still smarting from Belle's insult, detached himself from a group of technicians and came to meet them, his expression peeved and his manner stiff.

"Madam, I wish to conduct a full rehearsal for the television cameras. This man . . ." he gestured to a middle-aged man in a grey suit who stood nearby talking to another man dressed in a blue suit, ". . . Elliott, will act as stand-in for your escort. The other man, Bryant, will stand-in for the Governor. Tomorrow, at precisely two-forty-five, you will all appear in the entrance. The Governor and Mrs Collier . . ." he looked about him with quick, bird-like movements of his head. "Where is Mrs Collier's stand-in? May Middleton? Where is May Middleton? For Chrissake, she's supposed to be *here*! Somebody find her!"

A score of people dashed off in various directions. Gambretti walked off, muttering darkly, striving to keep his temper.

Belle sighed, "Jesus Christ . . ." and sat down heavily on a wooden chair.

It was ten long minutes before the ageing actress was located, by which time Gambretti had worked himself into a purple rage and tension had once again spread throughout the marquee.

When at last she did appear, flushed and frightened, an apology forming on her lips, Gambretti leapt from his chair and berated her volubly, reducing her to tears. "Where in *hell* have you been! Do you realise you've kept us all waiting for fifteen minutes! Get over there! Everybody, get back to the entrance!"

His anger now fully aroused, he could not hold it in check. He shouted and bullied; charged back and forth between the entrance, the stage and the press stage, bellowing instructions and vilifications through a loud-hailer, over-reacting to any error of timing or movement, his noise and bluster unnerving the assembly and causing more errors than there might well otherwise have been.

A TV network director was the first to object to Gambretti's behaviour. An argument ensued. Other members of the media rushed to the director's support. Gambretti, faced by this wall of fraternal solidarity, threw down his loud-hailer and stormed from the marquee.

Once again Tony Amboyne took over and a period of relative calm prevailed. But suddenly Gambretti was back, delivering a tirade about the enormity of his responsibility for producing a theatrical spectacle in minimal rehearsal time, and demanding that everyone show him respect and professional discipline.

The TV director countered that Gambretti was the only one among them not behaving professionally and the insult sparking off another spate of Gambretti fury which came close to provoking blows.

Belle Little intervened, reminding the warring parties why they were there and who was paying their salaries and managed to restore a semblance of order.

The rehearsal continued in a charged atmosphere.

As the afternoon wore on, things began to go unbelievably wrong. Outside the marquee, a truck inadvertently ran over a box of cable couplings and put four TV cameras out of action for an hour until replacement cables were rushed from the city.

The tympanist, positioned at the rear of the orchestra, noticed a sagging of the stage in one corner. Inspection revealed part of the superstructure sinking into a subterranean hole beneath the lawn, and the entire orchestra was obliged to leave the stage while steel sheets were laid down.

Then a mobile generator burned out, putting out all the television lights.

Tyrone Gambretti, by now past shouting, sat locked in seeth-ing fury, ignoring anyone who approached him, emerging from his trancelike state every now and then to bellow through his loud-hailer, "FOR CHRISSAKE ... HOW MUCH LONGER?"

Belle Little sat on a chair near the entrance staring distantly, her eyes muddy with fatigue, her features slack and ugly.

Elizabeth, seated on the opposite side of the aisle, suddenly ground out her cigarette and stood up, saying to her mother, "Come on, you've had enough of this fiasco, I'm taking you in."

Belle looked up. "Hmm?"

"You look ill, I'm taking you in ..."

Gambretti's whistle screamed shrilly. "All right, everybody, the lights are working—first positions!" He came towards the entrance at a run. "First positions here ... outside the tent everybody ... come on, come on!"

Elizabeth met him with a withering glare. "You bellow at me through that thing, I'll ram it down your throat! Get a stand-in for my mother, I'm taking her into the house."

"You can't! We're ready to go!"

Elizabeth flared. "*What* did you say?"

Belle interceded. "Elizabeth, it's all right, we must get it right. It has to be perfect tomorrow ... nothing must go wrong."

Elizabeth nodded.

The afternoon dragged on into early evening.

Gambretti, dissatisfied on a score of points, called for an hour's overtime and got it. At seven o'clock he called for another hour and met with refusal from the unions. He begged, pleaded, cajoled to no avail.

Suddenly Belle Little grabbed the loud-hailer from Gambretti's hand, climbed the steps to the stage and addressed the assembly, urging them to remain, to rehearse until it was perfect, promising them double money, becoming hysterically vociferous in her pleading.

A voice behind Elizabeth asked incredulously, "What on earth's going on?"

She turned to find Judge Hamlin there, the man who would escort her down the aisle and give her away to Robert Collier. She was relieved to see him and put a hand on his arm. "Andy..."

He grimaced at the scene. "What's happening?"

"Everything. You name it—today it has happened. We're under-rehearsed—one delay after another. The unions have worked one hour overtime but have just refused another. Mother, as you can hear, is trying to persuade them otherwise."

Hamlin's face, directed at Belle, showed concern.

Elizabeth, following his gaze, nodded. "I know . . . she looks ready to crack. I brought Harry Tyson over this morning but she refused to see him. She . . . oh my God, look what she's doing! She's going to screw everything up!"

Leaving Hamlin's side, she hurried across to where Belle was now locked in nose-to-nose confrontation with Ben Klein, the union spokesman, haranguing him and prodding him in the chest.

"You'll do as you're damn-well told! You don't leave the Park until everything is perfect! I'm paying you to work *my* hours—not *yours*!"

Klein swiped away her poking finger. "Don't touch me, lady. Who the hell d'you think you are? If you hadn't stuck your nose in everything today, we'd have finished by now."

Apoplectic, Belle whirled on Gambretti. "This man is fired! Get him off my property!"

Gambretti hid his face in his hands and groaned.

Elizabeth broke through the ring of spectators and caught hold of her mother's arm. "Mother, come along and let Gambretti handle this."

Belle snatched her arm away. "Gambretti isn't *capable* of handling it! *I'll* handle it! Everybody back to your places!"

Klein shook his head. "We're finished for today, lady." He raised his arm in a signal to his members. "Home!"

Belle seized his arm and pulled it down. "No! You leave when I say you leave!"

Elizabeth broke her mother's hold, pulled her away, seething, "For Chrissake climb *down*! You're going to ruin everything!" She urged Belle through the crowd, kept her moving towards the exit. "What's the matter with you? My God, if Miles Collier sees you like this tomorrow, Robert will be on the jet for Hawaii *before* the wedding and *without* me!"

Belle whirled. "Who *cares*?"

Elizabeth faltered in her stride. "*What* did you say?"

Belle strode on up the terrace steps.

With a cry, "Mother!" Elizabeth ran after her, caught her by the arm. "What did you say?"

Belle erupted, flung out her arms in frenzy. "Self . . . self . . . SELF! That's all you think about! Don't you realise what is happening to *me*? Don't you realise I could lose everything tomorrow . . . *everything*!"

"Don't be ridiculous . . ."

"I'm not *being* ridiculous! Can't you see it could happen . . . can't you *see*!"

Judge Hamlin came hurrying up the steps, his eyes communicating grave concern to Elizabeth, his arm going around Belle's shoulder. "Come now, Belle, this won't do at all. Let's go inside and calm down. I insist that you let Harry Tyson take a look at you . . ."

Belle angrily shook his arm away. "For God's sake, will everyone stop treating me like an excitable child! Leave me *alone*!" She strode into the house.

Judge Hamlin turned, his expression challenging. "What is it, Elizabeth? What's happening to your mother? And don't tell me it's just wedding nerves, because I won't believe it. Belle Little could handle that with ease. What did she mean when she said she could lose everything tomorrow?"

Elizabeth shook her head and moved towards the french windows.

"And what does that mean?" pursued Hamlin. "No—you don't know, or no—you won't tell me?"

The evasiveness of Elizabeth's eyes was answer enough.

He grunted. "Funny—I thought I could be trusted around here. Obviously I've been deluding myself."

"Oh Andy, stop."

They entered the drawing room.

250

"Why can't you tell me?" he pressed.

"Because . . ." Again she shook her head. She reached into a box for a cigarette. "I'm sorry, Andy."

"It must be serious."

"It's bloody unbelievably serious."

"Elizabeth, I've got to know! Dammit, I'm your mother's oldest and closest friend. If she's in trouble, I want to help. Why can't you tell me? Is it too personal?"

She met his eyes. "It's too dangerous. Andy . . . you know what we've got riding on tomorrow—everything! I don't have to draw you pictures."

He nodded.

"Somebody is trying their damnedest to stop it happening."

He frowned. "How?"

"That's what I can't tell you."

"Blackmail?"

"Sort of. But Mother is bluffing. She's ignoring his demand because it's impossible to pay and because she believes he won't carry out his threat after Robert and I are married."

"What threat?"

"I can't tell you."

"Is it *very* serious?"

"Deadly."

He grimaced. "My God. But Belle obviously thinks there's a chance that he will carry out his threat?"

She nodded. "That's why she's behaving like this. If he does carry it out, it will happen at precisely the same time as the wedding. The prospect is driving her crazy."

"And if he should do what he threatens to do?"

She shut her eyes. "Then God help us both."

17

At eleven that night, Francisco entered the marquee, paused to admire its ecclesiastical transformation, then continued down the centre aisle, his heart beating strongly as he imagined how it would be in only—what—sixteen hours' time . . . the crowd, the press, the orchestra playing.

Only sixteen hours more. After so many years, it was now reduced to a handful of hours.

Memory of his mother warmed him, bolstering his resolve. He smiled at her vision and murmured, "Not long now, Momma."

He found Bob Prescott in the annex tent, about to pour coffee into a mug. "You musta smelled it," he said, and filled two. "Ho, did you miss the circus today!"

"Oh? What happened?"

"What didn't, s'more like. Wish I'd had a movie camera—the Keystone Cops were never this funny. It was full rehearsal—orchestra, choir, TV cameras—the lot. You never seen a cock-up like it in all yuh born days. That Tyrone Gambretti fella wus flyin' around like a fart in a storm, bellerin' through his bull-horn an' tearin' his hair every time somethin' displeasured him—which was about three times a minute. A truck ran over some cables and screwed 'em up good . . . the stage damn-near collapsed . . . a gennie burned out an' killed the TV lights for an hour or more. Then the unions got snotty over double-overtime and Belle Little stepped in and damn-near caused a strike. Fun, fun, fun. Still, as we show-biz folks are prone t'say, I guess it'll be all right on the night." Chuckling, he looked at his silver pocket watch. "Time fer rounds, you comin'?"

Francisco stifled a yawn. "No, I'm going to sit right here and finish my coffee."

"Suit yourself . . . back in ten minutes."

Prescott left the tent, whistling tunelessly.

Francisco followed him to the external flap and peered out to make sure Prescott was clear, then moved quickly across to the amplifier and mixer units, taking from his pocket a miniature tape recorder and a short length of cable to which jacks were attached.

Crouching behind the units, he inserted one jack into an appropriate outlet, tucked the cable out of sight among the proliferation of loudspeaker and microphone leads, inserted the other end of the cable into the tape recorder, removed the protective greasepaper from the adhesive pad on the back of the tape recorder and pressed the tiny machine to the underside of the trestle table.

From his shirt pocket he now took a small, flat remote-control unit, and activated the "start" button. The reels of the tape recorder began to turn. Satisfied, he stopped the machine, wiped it and the cable free of finger prints and returned to finish his coffee.

He looked at his watch . . . fifteen hours and forty minutes to go.

His heart thumped wildly.

18

At five o'clock on the morning of the wedding day, Belle Little stood at her bedroom window, watching her Park gradually emerge in the first grey light of day. *The* day. The day whose creeping dawn should be igniting her heart with excitement, the thrill of success. For thirty years she had known success, had soared like an indomitable eagle from peak to peak, often challenged but never vanquished, up and up towards this highest summit, this pinnacle of desire, hope, ambition, need. This day.

The irony of the threat and its timing agonised her, squeezed her heart bitterly and rendered her so impotent, so furious that she wanted to cry out, shout, hurt, maim . . . kill! How *dare* he! How dare he do this to *her*! And *now* . . . at the very threshold of success.

Who in God's name was he? Who would have the nerve to challenge Belle Little? His temerity astounded her. Her fury walled up, choking her so that she could scarcely breathe. She shook and trembled, and turned from the window, searching for a victim on which to vent her seething anger.

An exquisite Benjamin Lunds vase, filled with flowers, fell under her wide-eyed gaze. Seizing it, she hurled it against the wall, the tumult of its disintegration piercing her like a knife blade. Riven with disgust and ecstasy, she searched wildly for her next victim. The twin bedside lamps, fashioned from ancient Chinese porcelain, became a sudden obsenity to her.

A weapon! She needed a weapon, a club, an avenging sword . . . the poker! She snatched it up, swung it high and shattered the first lamp with a vicious scything blow. She battered the silk shade to ruin and kept on striking, pounding the inlaid walnut cupboard until it erupted into jagged splinters.

254

Crying hysterically, she ran around the bed and swung at the second lamp. She struck out at the Degas oil painting above the bed, blasting its precious canvas, then whirled on her Queen Anne bureau and drove the iron poker-head into its priceless surface again and again. She ran across to the mirror-fronted closets and shattered their faces with successive blows, brought the Louis wall mirror crashing down into the fireplace . . . then, with a keening cry, buckled to the floor and hugged herself, rocking with despair as Elizabeth hammered at the door.

She burst in and stood gaping at the devastation. "My . . . GOD!" She ran to kneel at her mother's side. "Why? . . . WHY? Come on, get up, get out of here."

Leading the sobbing Belle to another bedroom, she returned for the Valium and phoned Doctor Tyson. He arrived within half an hour and tended Belle, then joined Elizabeth in the kitchen, accepting a cup of coffee from her and adding brandy to it.

"She ought to be in hospital," he told her.

"Impossible."

"I know. I've sedated her as much as I dare in the circumstances. She'll make the wedding—just."

"What is it, Harry?"

He shrugged. "Excess. She's pushed herself too hard for too long." He frowned uncertainly. "But something else, too. If I didn't know your mother so well, I'd say she was frightened. Am I mistaken?"

Elizabeth avoided his eyes. "I don't know of anything."

"The destruction of her bedroom, that was deep-seated frustration . . . frightened anger. She has the look of a cornered woman. Is she being threatened, Elizabeth?"

"Only by events. You know what a perfectionist she is, how everything must go perfectly today. We had a lousy rehearsal yesterday. She's terrified of a disaster."

Though Tyson said nothing, his expression conveyed disbelief.

"There won't *be* a disaster, of course," Elizabeth continued. "Everything will go just beautifully. I'm sure we'll see a very different Belle as soon as the ceremony is over."

255

"Probably." He put down his cup. "I'll look in on her later—around one o'clock." He smiled encouragingly. "And how are you feeling?"

She returned the smile, determinedly confident. "Terrific."

He nodded. "Of course . . . you are your mother's daughter. That's what worries me—she should be feeling the same."

Belle drifted into a sleep induced as much by exhaustion as by drugs, a shallow, nervous sleep, barely venturing beyond the boundary of consciousness, touching but lightly on the region of therapeutic oblivion, yet descending deeply enough to tap the well of dreams. Bad dreams. Anguished, prophetic visions . . . the crowded tent . . . Elizabeth joined to Robert . . . and at the very moment of their union—three corpses hurtling down from the roof, jerking to an abrupt stop on the end of long ropes, necks snapping hideously, the crowd in uproar . . . terrorised . . . fighting to escape . . .

She awoke, drenched in perspiration, to the sound of traffic in the Park. Throwing back the covers, she weaved unsteadily to the window. The Park was alive with traffic—trucks, cars, police vehicles. Panicked, she turned to read the mantel clock, relieved to find its hands at nine o'clock.

Despairingly now, she recalled the devastation of her lovely room. How could she have done such a dreadful thing? Engulfed by black depression, she returned to sit on her bed and pressed the button for her maid.

Moments passed. A tap on the door and Elizabeth entered, accompanied by a young dark-skinned girl in maid's uniform.

Belle frowned at Elizabeth bewilderedly. "Who is this? Where's Constanza . . ."

Elizabeth sighed. "Mother, you know very *well* Constanza walked out yesterday. This is Lucia . . . Margaret Whitney's maid. I thought rather than get someone new at such short notice . . ."

Belle stared. "Are you *mad*? *Margaret's* maid . . .?"

"Mother, stop it! For God's sake remember what day this is! The Colliers will be here in three hours! You need help to get ready. *I've* got to get ready. The hairdressers are waiting for us

256

now in the guest wing. Here, put your robe on. Lucia, take Mrs Little to the guest wing."

Lucia put out her hand, but Belle shrugged it off, rose and walked towards the door, imperiously but unsteadily. "Go home, Lucia, I shan't need you."

As they went out of the door, Elizabeth swore beneath her breath. Six hours to go. Six hours and the worst would be over.

How fervently she *prayed* that the mantel clock was now showing ten past three.

19

Wearing a crisply-laundered uniform, Francisco reported for duty on the rear lawn of the Little home in time to witness the arrival of the Governor and his family.

Joining the group of welcoming politicians, civic dignitaries, uniformed and plain-clothes police and news media people, he watched the dot in the western sky become the recognisable form of a large helicopter. He smiled with excitement as the machine came clattering in low across the bay to land as gently as a settling leaf.

The engine ceased its clamour, the rotors slowed and drooped. The door was opened and the steps run out. Aides disembarked. The welcoming committee surged forward. Miles Collier appeared in the doorway, brown-suited, big and handsome, waving, grinning his honest politician's smile for the cameras, turning now to take the hand of his wife, Amy, wholesome-looking in a floral suit and little grey hat.

Robert appeared behind them, a blond replica of his father, tall, broad-shouldered, grinning boyishly.

The press crowded in, requesting a statement. With patent delight, Miles Collier obliged. He stressed the informality of the occasion and declared his delight at Robert's choice of partner.

"I'd like to say . . . in all sincerity . . ." he continued, slipping his arm about his wife's shoulder, drawing her into the picture, ". . . that if Robert and Elizabeth enjoy one half of the love . . . companionship . . . and happiness that Amy and I have shared during the past twenty-three years . . . then they may count themselves blessed indeed."

To warm applause the family moved off towards the house, where they would rest, take luncheon and change into formal attire for the three o'clock ceremony.

.   .   .   .   .

By one o'clock the flow of traffic into the Park had become a flood as one thousand vehicles converged on the island from both ends of the causeway and squeezed single-file through the bottleneck at the security booth.

Although the boom was permanently raised, each vehicle was obliged to stop while its occupants and their invitation cards were checked against a guest list. When cleared, the vehicle passed through and was guided by a succession of baton-waving police into a predetermined parking slot, either on the road or in the driveway of a home. Minimum clearance was allowed since it was assumed that few, if any, of the guests would wish to leave the Park before the end of the festivities.

The arrival of the Governor had signalled the start of state-wide radio and TV transmission of the ceremony, so the media now seized upon the traffic congestion on the causeway as a newsworthy filler. The commentators milked every aspect of the influx—from aerial commentaries by helicopter on the two-mile bumper-to-bumper tie-up, to roving ground-level interviews with the guests in their cars—as a means of maintaining audience interest during the two-hour hiatus until the ceremony.

Well-primed in its subject—and with an abundance of time to fill—the media offered its public a wealth of information concerning the bride, the groom, their respective families, other residents of the Park and the Park itself.

Across the state, viewers and listeners were regaled with such fascinating minutiae as the total tonnage of concrete in the foundations of the thirty-million-dollar homes, the total number of bathrooms in the Park and even the brand of pet food preferred by Judge Andy Hamlin's pedigree Persian cat.

Special emphasis was, of course, given to the bride and to her locally famous foster-mother.

Gleaning their information from a specially-prepared brief, the commentators revealed that Elizabeth was the daughter of close friends of Belle Little tragically killed in a car accident in Europe soon after Elizabeth's birth. They described her as a beautiful, talented, warm-hearted girl with dedicated interests

259

in the welfare of the aged, the orphaned and mentally-handicapped children. Belle was extolled as a generous, hard-working pillar of the community, a tireless supporter and benefactress of numerous charitable causes and a determined champion of social justice for the under-privileged.

These blandishments were greeted by more than a few sardonic guffaws throughout Florida.

At two o'clock the members of the Miami Symphony Orchestra and Tabernacle Choir arrived at the Park by coach under police escort.

By two-fifteen both orchestra and choir had taken up their positions on the stage, and by two-thirty the orchestra had tuned its instruments and, together with the choir, was ready to begin the overture.

As the opening strains of the anthem *Jesu, Joy of Man's Desiring* filled the great marquee, Francisco ventured into the annex tent and peered through the flap into the big top, his heart bursting at the spectacle before him and at the stirring sound of full orchestra and choir.

To his right, a man whose ID badge identified him as Cyril Kovak peered intently at level-indicators and made adjustments to the slide controls which balanced instrument and voice and evenly distributed the harmonious whole throughout the marquee.

Francisco nodded and smiled. "Sounds mighty good to me."

Kovak winked. "Betcha."

Francisco's eyes drifted to the jack he had inserted, relieved to discover it was still in position. Eagerly he touched the remote-control in his pants pocket and checked the time on his wrist-watch.

Two-forty. Only twenty minutes to go.

His thoughts went out to his brother and sister, who would be watching the ceremony on TV in their rooms. And he thought also of his mother.

"Are you watching, too, Momma?" he whispered silently.

He knew she was.

260

20

In their basement prison, the three women, acutely conscious of the time, fell to distracted silence. Margaret Whitney and Lily Parker were seated on their beds, Ruth Howard on the wooden chair at the table.

With Ruth's arrival on Tuesday evening had come momentary hope of encouraging news from the outside world, news perhaps that either the Littles or Sam and Arthur were taking action to alleviate the nightmare situation. But that spark of hope had quickly faded with Ruth's revelation that she had known nothing of Margaret's or Lily's kidnapping.

Since that time, all three women had experienced moods encompassing almost every human emotion from fury to despair. And now, with so little time left before the wedding ceremony and the moment of their promised execution, they had withdrawn into petrified silence, not daring to bring to conscious thought the likelihood of their fate as the hands of their watches touched three o'clock.

"It's cold," said Margaret in a small, whispered voice, hugging herself.

Lily got up and draped a blanket around her shoulders.

"I can't believe it of Bernard," Ruth said suddenly, her tone ringing with hysteria. "He wouldn't do . . . *nothing*. I won't accept that." She glanced savagely at the other women. "Your husbands may be different. I *know* they're different! But Bernard loves *me*. He would force her to make the confession, or go to the police. He wouldn't sit cowardly by and let this happen."

Lily looked hard at her. "So—why haven't we been released? Why aren't the police breaking down the door?"

"We will be . . . there's still time," Ruth replied in desperate,

261

staccato bursts. "Naturally . . . Belle will maintain the bluff till the last possible moment . . . but she won't . . . I mean, she simply *can't* . . ." She released her breath in a fluttery exhalation, suddenly burst into tears and cried out dementedly. "For God's sake . . . what's going to happen to us! He can't hang us . . . HE CAN'T!"

She sprang up and fell against the door, beat on it with her fists, then fell away from it, terrified, as the guard dog outside filled the cellar with deafening, savage barking.

"Oh God . . . oh God . . .!" She fell across her bed and wept uncontrollably.

Lily went to her, sat beside her and patted her shoulder. "Sssh, Ruth . . . you musn't give up hope . . . someone must be doing something for us!"

"He was right . . ." intoned Margaret, rocking as she hugged herself, staring at the stone floor, ". . . it's the uncertainty that terrifies, the not knowing. That poor woman . . . Ana Patillas . . . she must have . . ." She shook her head. "I had no idea."

They fell to silence again, an ominous, hopeless silence disturbed only by Ruth's racking, muffled sobs.

A similar silence pervaded the library of the Parker home.

The three men sat or stood in statuesque poses, as though paralysed or hypnotised to immobility by the sombre ticking of the ancient grandfather clock.

Bernard was seated on the edge of a leather armchair, his elbows on his knees, his head lowered between his shoulder blades, staring at the carpet. Sam sat opposite, gazing with similar vacuity at the bronzed face of the clock. Arthur was standing at the window, a drink in his hand, looking out unconsciously across the Park.

He hiccupped, an obscene self-indulgence which wrought a scowl of disgust on Bernard's twisted countenance.

"Ten minutes . . ." Sam Parker uttered the words in a croaking growl and followed them with a frantic exhalation. "Holy . . . shit!" He suddenly came to his feet, moved swiftly across the room and snapped on the television.

Bernard came alive. "What the hell are you doing?"

"I've got to see it! I can't sit here in fucking silence ... wondering ... I've got to know if she's going through with it!"

"Of course she's going through with it! Turn that thing off! I don't want to know ..."

Sam rounded on him. "Bernie ... ignorance is not bliss, man, not in this case! Ignorance is goin' out of my mind sittin' here watching that goddamn clock go round. I've gotta know!"

"And then what? So you see that bitch married—and then what?"

"I don't know!" yelled Sam. "Maybe something will happen ... maybe there'll be a newsflash ... maybe he'll release the girls and they'll walk into the goddamned tent ... shit, I don't *know*, but I gotta watch it! And if you don't want to—go sit in another ..."

He stopped, arrested by the cessation of music from the television set. "It's starting," he murmured, slowly reseating himself, eyes glued to screen.

Arthur turned from the window and came to stand behind him, his face frozen with apprehension.

Bernard, despite himself, was drawn to the screen. He sat hunched forward, his hands white with tension, gripping the arms of the chair. "Dear God ..." he whispered.

The cameras cut from a wide-angled view of the orchestra to a close shot of the entrance of the marquee, and as orchestra and chorus began the opening strains of the processional hymn *All Creatures That On Earth Do Dwell*, Governor Miles Collier and his wife made their entrance from the terrace.

21

Behind the Colliers, escorted by her friend Doctor Frank Soper, came Belle, dressed in dark-green velvet under black mink, emeralds and diamonds adorning her throat, ears and fingers. In trancelike state, looking neither to left nor right, she followed the Colliers down the long aisle and mounted the stairs to the stage.

The Bishop and his attendants appeared, and with due solemnity proceeded to the stage, timing their arrival to coincide with the final verse of the hymn.

As the hymnal echoes died, Charles Ingman, conducting the orchestra, turned to glance towards the entrance, received the signal that all was ready and brought down his baton for the commencement of the wedding march.

Two thousand heads turned and a whisper of exclamation filled the marquee as Elizabeth appeared, a vision in white satin and lace, her gloved hand resting on the arm of Judge Andrew Hamlin.

Smiling, acknowledging the presence of friends, she moved slowly down the aisle, carefully mounted the stairs to the stage and took up her position beside her groom.

The wedding march ended.

The congregation noisily took their seats.

The Bishop opened his prayer book, cleared his throat and regarded the congregation over his spectacles, willing them to silence, then in rich, resonant tones began his address.

"Dearly beloved ... we are gathered together here in the sight of God, and in the face of this congregation, to join together this Man and this Woman in holy Matrimony; which is an honourable estate, instituted of God in the time of man's innocency, signifying unto us the mystical union that is betwixt Christ and his Church, which holy estate Christ adorned . . ."

His words washed over Belle Little as a meaningless drone. Seated between Miles Collier and his wife, she gazed out over the sea of faces, her heart thudding with dire apprehension, her mind a vortex of confusion and horrific expectation.

Where was he at this very moment? Where were Margaret and Lily and Ruth? Was he right now slipping nooses around their necks?

Panic welled within her, urging her to believe he would not, could not do it. No one could cold-bloodedly hang three innocent women for the sake of revenge. She felt it now with sweeping certainty. He was no murderer. There had been something in his voice, a gentleness. Why hadn't she detected it before? His had been the voice of a gentle man trying to sound tough. Angry—yes. Frustrated—yes. But not the voice of a cold-blooded killer. He had fought hard, taken risks, shown courage. She admired that. But it had all been a bluff. And she had called it. She'd won. She . . . had . . . won!

Elation reconciled her to the present, to the glorious reality of the occasion. Her daughter standing before her, so beautiful, soon to become Robert Collier's wife. Only moments now . . . just a few . . . short . . . seconds . . .

From his position at the flap of the annex tent, Francisco watched Belle Little, saw her expression change from glazed abstraction to ebullient awareness and from it read her thoughts.

He smiled. How fitting that she should be brought down in a moment of believed triumph.

He returned his attention to the ceremony and to the Bishop's words, registering the precise stage reached in the Solemnisation of Matrimony he had learned by heart.

It was close now, very close.

Easing back into the annex tent, he moved behind the sound-mixer, Cyril Kovak, and took up a position near the outer exit of the tent, palming the ultra-sonic remote control from his pocket.

The Bishop's voice, becoming declamatory now as he drew to the close of his opening preamble, resounded richly throughout the marquee.

"Thirdly ... for the mutual society, help and comfort, that the one ought to have of the other, both in prosperity and adversity. Into which holy estate these two Persons present come now to be joined."

A half-turn towards the congregation, his voice soaring majestically, "Therefore ... if any man can show any just cause ... why they may not lawfully be joined together ... let him now speak ... or else hereafter for ever hold his peace."

The big top rang with silence.

Having observed the obligatory pause, the Bishop returned his attention to the bridegroom.

And simultaneously, Francisco directed the remote control towards the hidden tape recorder and pressed the "start" button.

"I CAN SHOW JUST CAUSE!"

His voice, bold and challenging, boomed from twenty loud-speakers.

The silence that followed was absolute.

The Bishop froze, lips parted.

The vast assembly were paralysed, stunned with disbelief.

The voice continued. "IN THE NAME OF JUSTICE ... ROBERT COLLIER AND HIS PARENTS SHOULD KNOW THAT HE WILL BE MARRYING INTO A FAMILY OF LIARS ... CRIMINALS ... AND MURDER-ERS!"

The congregation erupted in confusion.

Belle Little swayed in her chair.

Miles Collier gaped at his wife.

Two aides moved to his side, hovering uncertainly.

Robert Collier stared dumbfoundedly at Elizabeth, Elizabeth at her mother.

On the press stage, TV directors, radio commentators, photographers and journalists, momentarily petrified, now

266

came alive to the reality of this incredible development and to its overwhelming news value. A swarm of photographers leapt down from their positions and gathered together, a jostling rabble before the main stage, lighting the marquee with a barrage of stark white flashlight.

Miles Collier came to his feet, ashen, rooted with indecision, peering this way and that as though searching for rescue from this nightmare situation.

The voice continued. "SIX YEARS AGO ..."

A wave of hissing, a demand for silence, issued from the crowd, most of whom were now on their feet, agog, searching for the source of this monstrous ... unbelievable ... exhilarating intrusion.

"... A MEXICAN WOMAN, ANA PATILLAS, A MAID IN BELLE LITTLE'S EMPLOY, WAS FALSELY ACCUSED BY MRS LITTLE OF STEALING MONEY AND JEWELLERY BELONGING TO CERTAIN HOUSE GUESTS ... PEOPLE WHO ARE PRESENT HERE TODAY AND ABLE TO CORROBORATE THIS STATEMENT.

"NOT ONLY DID MRS LITTLE HAVE ANA ARRESTED, BUT SHE ALSO PLANNED TO HAVE HER AND HER THREE CHILDREN DEPORTED TO MEXICO. AS A RESULT OF THIS THREAT, THE BALANCE OF HER MIND BEING DISTURBED BY THE FALSE ACCUSATION OF THEFT, BY THE SHAME OF IMPRISONMENT AND TO SAVE HER CHILDREN FROM DEPORTATION, ANA PATILLAS TOOK HER OWN LIFE IN MIAMI BEACH JAIL ..."

Once again the congregation erupted in uproar but quickly silenced itself as the voice went on.

"SHORTLY AFTER ANA'S SUICIDE, BELLE LITTLE DISCOVERED THAT IT WAS HER DAUGHTER, ELIZABETH, THE FUTURE MRS ROBERT COLLIER, WHO HAD COMMITTED THE THEFT AND HAD HIDDEN THE JEWELLERY IN ANA'S ROOM IN AN ACT OF REVENGE ..."

Bedlam!

267

Anticipating the furore, Francisco's recorded voice rose in volume.

"THERE ARE THREE WITNESSES TO ELIZABETH'S CONFESSION OF THIS CRIME ... MARGARET WHITNEY, LILY PARKER AND RUTH HOWARD! THREE CLOSE FRIENDS OF BELLE LITTLE WHO, FOR THE PAST FEW DAYS AND WITH BELLE LITTLE'S KNOWLEDGE HAVE BEEN HELD BY ME IN PRIVATE CUSTODY UNDER THE THREAT OF DEATH SHOULD BELLE LITTLE FAIL TO PUBLICLY ADMIT HER DAUGHTER'S CRIME AND HER OWN CONCEAL-MENT OF IT ..."

The voice was all but drowned by the vociferous reaction of the crowd but resolutely Francisco continued.

"... BUT SUCH IS THE *ARROGANCE* OF THIS WOMAN ... SUCH IS THE ENORMITY OF HER *AMBITION* ... THAT SHE HAS IGNORED THE THREAT AND HAS BLATANTLY RISKED THE LIVES OF HER FRIENDS IN ORDER TO ACHIEVE THIS POLITICALLY AND FINANCIALLY ADVANTAGEOUS MARRIAGE OF HER DAUGHTER TO ROBERT COL-LIER! AND SUCH IS THE EXTENT OF HER *POWER* AND HER *EVIL* THAT SHE HAS SUCCESSFULLY BLACKMAILED THE HUSBANDS OF THE THREE WITNESSES INTO REMAINING SILENT!

"I DO HERE PUBLICLY CHARGE BELLE LITTLE, ELIZABETH LITTLE AND THE THREE WITNESSES WITH CONSPIRACY TO CONCEAL A CRIME ... WITH WITHHOLDING EVIDENCE ... AND WITH INVOLUNTARY MANSLAUGHTER ..."

The remainder of the charge was lost in a storm of reaction, a holocaust of uproar as two thousand people broke, milled and surged towards the exit, led by a phalanx of journalists frantic to reach their automobile telephones.

Belle Little, clutching her head, staggered across the stage and collapsed against Elizabeth, who went down under her mother's weight and stayed there, her face buried in Belle's shoulder.

268

Miles Collier, galvanised by imperative advice from his aides and by his own foreboding of political disaster, grabbed his wife's arm with one hand, his son's with the other and rushed them down the steps of the stage and out towards the waiting helicopter.

The stage, emptying rapidly of choristers and musicians, swarmed with journalists and photographers, desperate for a picture or a statement. "Mrs Little! Miss Little! What's your answer to these allegations? Elizabeth . . . this way!"

Judge Hamlin, exhorting Belle and Elizabeth to get up and make for the house, struck out at the crushing press. "Get away! Leave them alone! Clear the way there!"

Elsewhere in the marquee a frantic search was being made for the source—either mechanical or live—of the mystery voice.

At first, Cyril Kovak, the sound technician, assumed the broadcast was a live transmission, delivered through one of the dozen or so microphones on the stage, and in consequence he spent half the duration of the broadcast at the flap entrance, craning to check each mircophone visually. Baffled, his next assumption was that the voice was using an amplified loud-hailer, and that the microphones on stage were picking up the delivery and relaying it through the marquee speakers.

Not until the message ended and his annex was suddenly invaded by police and Secret Service personnel did the possibility occur to him that his own equipment had been used. And even then, he reacted with open-mouthed incredulity as a burly plain-clothes detective emerged from beneath the trestle table with the miniature tape recorder captured in a handkerchief.

"How did that get there!" gaped Kovak.

Detective Sergeant Valdosta of the Miami Police Department lifted a lugubrious brow. "You don't know?"

"Swear to God! *I* sure as hell didn't put it there!"

"OK . . . stick around, Kovak." Valdosta turned to his black assistant. "Get on the air to Lieutenant Spielman. Tell him to get over here fast."

22

The departure of the helicopter carrying the Governor and his family precipitated an exodus of Florida's wealthy and important from the Park that was, according to one TV commentator, "... reminiscent of the panicked flight of the populus in a 'monster' movie."

Desperate to avoid contamination—through the exposure of their presence by TV camera or press photographer—from this highly virulent situation, they feverishly sought the antisepsis of the open road, creating nightmare chaos in the Park as they fought to remove their automobiles from close-parked and even inextricable positions.

Horns blared, glass tinkled, tempers flared. Bewildered police and security men, ignorant of the cause of this sudden tidal-wave of panic, ran from one crisis to another, yelling unheeded commands and futilely blowing whistles, and finally threw their hands in the air and let the crazy bastards get on with it.

Lieutenant Harry Spielman of the Miami Police, summoned from the city by Detective Sergeant Valdosta, arrived with whooping but ineffectual siren. He was forced to abandon his vehicle on the choked causeway and walk two hundred yards to the Park entrance, where he met Valdosta.

Spielman gaped. "What the fuck hit this place?"

Valdosta took the handkerchief-wrapped tape recorder from his pocket. "This did. You shoulda *seen* what happened in that tent!"

"OK, let's go sit in the car."

By four o'clock the Park had quietened down. Those guests—and they were few—who had not voluntarily departed had been urged to do so by the police.

The media, though, were there in far greater numbers than had attended the wedding. Alerted to the furore and the possibility of gubernatorial scandal, many editors from upstate newspapers and radio and TV stations, previously content to pick up mere wedding reportage from indirect sources, had hurriedly sent off personnel for first-hand coverage. Some had already arrived and now clustered outside the Little home and the homes of the three kidnapped witnesses, urgently seeking a statement, any kind of statement, from virtually anybody connected with the four houses.

But no statement was forthcoming.

Judge Hamlin, applying a calm judicial mind to a situation he regarded as potentially lethal for the five protagonists—Belle, Elizabeth and the three witnesses—had issued a caution to the three husbands and to their domestic staff to avoid all comment to the press until he personally advised otherwise.

Seated in the back of the patrol car parked a short distance from the Little house, Lieutenant Spielman listened to Francisco's recording three times, then blew out a troubled sigh and shook his head.

"What d'you think?" asked Valdosta.

Spielman curled his lip in a sardonic grin. "What do I think? I think this guy—whoever he is—has opened up a b-i-g can of maggots. My guess is they're already sniffing this stink in Washington."

"Where in hell do we start, Mike?"

Spielman lifted his shoulders in a shrug. "With Ana Patillas's relatives?"

"And where do we find them?"

"Start with Florida," sighed Spielman.

By early evening the news of the sensational development in the Park had spread with sonic speed throughout the state.

A story combining gubernatorial involvement, acute human interest and social scandal par excellence, it captured voracious interest at every social level—in Hispanic barrios, corridors of political power and exclusive strongholds of the rich in every major centre.

271

The name "Little" was seized upon as a heaven-sent gift by journalists and news compositors, who wielded it pithily in evening paper banner headlines. "GOVERNOR COLLIER IN BIG LITTLE WEDDING FIASCO!", "LITTLE WEDDING OFF—BIG ROW ON!", "LITTLE SCANDAL?—BIG SCANDAL!" were typical.

So numerous were the vital, fascinating and newsworthy facets of the story—big society wedding, the chaos that had ensued, the Miles Collier walk-out, the criminal charges levelled against two high-ranking socialites, the jail suicide of a mother of three and, not least, the kidnapping and threatened death of three Park residents—that news editors were overwhelmed by the cornucopia of riches.

Sharing Lieutenant Spielman's problem, they didn't know where to start.

The police departments of Miami and Miami Beach were in uproar, their switchboards besieged by callers protesting at the silence that had accompanied the Ana Patillas suicide, demanding that Belle and Elizabeth Little be formally charged and forced to tell the truth, demanding immediate action be taken to apprehend "that crazy kidnapper".

Having returned to his desk from the Park, Lieutenant Spielman threw down his pen and said angrily to a Detective Ansell, "You know what's so sick about all this? Nobody knows if those three hostages died today at three o'clock—and nobody seems to give a fuck!"

Francisco, assuming the role of confused security guard, hung around the annex tent for an hour after the exodus, joining in discussions with groups of police and Secret Service personnel who, like him, were awaiting orders from higher authority.

Eventually, receiving no such directive from Four Square, he wandered through the Park to the security booth and encountered Carl Krantz in a mood of brooding fury.

"Shoulda killed the fuckers when I had the chance."

Francisco frowned. "Who?"

"Those Patillas kids! They've got something to do with this, betcha ass. Who else would it be? Six years, they've been sittin' on this for six years. They've likely got a gang workin' for them ... three kidnappings outta the Park, f'Chrissake! This is organised!"

"Jesus, they must hate the Littles something awful. Do you think they'll come after you, Mr Krantz?"

Krantz's eyes flared maniacally. "Shit, I hope so ... 'cause now I could do a real number on those flakes an' the cops would shake my hand." He caressed the butt of his holstered .38. "You ever see anyone gut-shot and knee-capped, West? That's what I'm gonna do to those finks if they come within range."

Francisco nodded soberly. "You might well get your chance. They're obviously out to settle all old scores. If it is them, of course."

A tic fluttered in Krantz's cheek. "It's them. I can smell them. And they're close."

Francisco noted with jubilation the sheen of perspiration on Krantz's face, the sweat of a frightened man.

23

At five o'clock Judge Hamlin sat in the drawing-room of the Little home with Elizabeth. The lights were on and the curtains drawn against the probing long-range lenses of the press cameras outside.

Doctor Harold Tyson had just left the house. Two nurses now attended Belle, asleep upstairs under sedation.

Elizabeth had changed from her wedding dress into jeans and sweater. She ranged in simmering fury about the room smoking a cigarette, appearing to Hamlin, apart from her anger, to be inhumanly well-collected.

He had always regarded her as a strong, determined girl. Nevertheless he observed with astonishment her apparent dismissal of the romantic aspect of the disaster—the loss of Robert Collier as a husband—and her seemingly total preoccupation with the criminal aspect of the case, essentially as it might affect her personally.

"I was only fifteen, for Chrissake!" she blurted. "Surely that has a bearing?"

Hamlin frowned, taken aback—disgusted, even—by her display of ruthless self-interest. "Elizabeth, there's so much *more* to this fiasco than your initial participation. My God, we've only glimpsed the merest tip of the iceburg so far. The repercussions could well be profound!"

"How profound?"

He raised his hands in a gesture of helplessness. "I don't know! Nobody can possibly know until this thing has been fully investigated."

"And it will *be* investigated?"

Again he frowned. "You're suggesting a cover-up? With that pack of voracious news-hounds out there, you're hoping to sweep this under the mat? Elizabeth, this is already state-wide news . . . maybe already national news! There have been three kidnappings—which means the FBI are already in on it. The Governor is involved—which means the State Capitol and Washington are in on it. There have been criminal charges made—which means the police are in on it. Think about Miles Collier's involvement alone! Our Governor and likely Presidential candidate caught up in a criminal case and three kidnappings! My God, don't you appreciate the terrible predicament he has been subjected to?

"Who *knows* what pressures are going to be applied to him because of this? It's no secret that your mother contributed magnanimously to his election fund. Can you imagine the field-day the press and his political opponents are going to have with that? Jesus!"

Hamlin got up and paced across the room, his hand to his forehead. "He may be forced to resign, you know. At very least, to save political face, to prove he had absolutely nothing to do with this Ana Patillas affair, he's going to move for a grand jury investigation."

He stopped by the fireplace, leaned on the mantel and ran a hand through his silky grey hair. "Dear God in heaven, how did this happen?"

Elizabeth crushed out her cigarette in an ashtray and immediately lit another, her hands trembling. "We've had it, haven't we, Mother and I?"

Hamlin barely nodded. "You are rich, powerful and now very famous, Elizabeth—prime meat for the media sharks. You're going to be tried, hung, drawn and quartered long before any official investigation gets under way. Belle has many enemies and they'll join in the hunt with glee. I believe you're going to be hard-pressed to find many supportive friends."

Elizabeth snorted. "Yes, I observed the rats leaving the sinking ship this afternoon."

He shook his head. "You can't blame them, Elizabeth. This thing has shocked everyone. It's big and it's dirty. And the instinct for self-protection is particularly sensitive among the rich."

275

"And how is *your* instinct for self-protection, Andy?"

He looked up into her arrogant young face, suddenly dislik-ing Elizabeth Little intensely. He stood erect, meeting her aggressive sneer with judicial dignity. "You and your mother will need legal representation. I shall make certain you get the very best."

She smiled. "But you personally are bowing out, I take it?"

His eyes grew cold. "I shall do what I must to protect my office, Elizabeth."

"Of course . . . your office." She made a mocking gesture towards the door. "Dry land is that way, judge."

He turned from her and quickly left the room.

As the front door closed behind him, Elizabeth deliberately dropped her cigarette on to the white carpet and ground it with her heel. Leaving the room, she climbed the stairs and entered her mother's bedroom. Ignoring the nurses, who rose from chairs to greet her, she approached the bed and looked down on her mother.

Even in drugged repose Belle's features maintained the dis-tortion of her conscious anguish and displayed a sudden and shocking advance of age, years that were no longer held at bay by an ebullient, confident spirit.

This metamorphosis, this precocious decaying of her mother's flesh, reached up to taunt Elizabeth, to evoke in her, more poignantly than had any other threat, a sudden awareness of imminent disaster. Under its invisible caress, she shuddered. Death was coming . . . social death . . . imprisoned death . . . a public hanging no less lethal for being metaphorical. Their end was near.

Her lips compressed with bitter determination. Well, maybe for you, old Queen, but not for your protégée. This is one grand entrance you're welcome to make alone.

What could they possibly charge her with? A teenage prank? Cruel—yes. Irresponsible—by all means. But she had never intended the practical joke to go so far. Her mother had over-reacted, had Ana Patillas arrested and imprisoned, and plotted her deportation. The blame for Ana's suicide lay firmly on her mother's shoulders, no one else's.

276

Gazing down upon the unconscious woman, Elizabeth's lips fashioned the faintest smile. It's you they want, Mother dear, and it's you they're going to get.

Leaving the room, she entered her bedroom, plucked a novel from the bookcase and lay down on her bed to wait.

24

Early next morning a bombshell, in the form of a package containing three reels of tape—each of six hours' playing duration—a ninety-minute cassette, and a short explanatory note typewritten on plain white paper, arrived in the first mail on the desks of the Head of News of all five Miami commercial TV stations, the Mayor and the Chief of Police.

Beth Robespierre, thirty-year-old personal secretary to Rory Callaghan, head of Channel Six's *Eyewitness News* programme, opened the package, glanced at the covering note and let out a whoop that startled her boss, seated at his desk across the office.

"Your divorce come through?" he asked laconically.

She waved the note, proffered the reels. "We gotta scoop!"

He smiled. "You dear old-fashioned thing."

"I mean it!" She crossed to him. "All this is from the Park Avenger! The *kidnapper*! The Belle Little thing!"

"Eh? Hey, watch your finger prints. Put it down here."

He smoothed out the note with two pencils. It said, "On these tapes you will find the truth about Belle Little and Elizabeth Little. Play the cassette first." It was signed: "The Park Avenger."

"Jesus," muttered Callaghan, quickly taking from his drawer a battery-operated tape recorder and carefully slipping in the cassette. He pressed the start button.

A young male voice began: "I am the man the press refer to as "The Park Avenger". By now you will know of my accusation against Belle and Elizabeth Little, Margaret Whitney, Lily Parker and Ruth Howard. Every word of that accusation is true. Elizabeth did steal money and jewellery from her mother's house guests and plant them in Ana Patillas's room. It was done for revenge—because Ana caught Elizabeth stealing money

278

from Belle Little's wall-safe and thereafter Elizabeth wanted to get rid of Ana.

"Elizabeth's confession of the crime during a telephone conversation with a schoolfriend was overheard by Margaret Whitney, who then told Belle Little in the company of Lily Parker and Ruth Howard. This fact will be corroborated by the three women towards the end of this recording.

"Realising there was no other way of securing a public admission by Belle Little of this crime and its concealment, I resorted to the kidnapping of Belle's three closest friends —not so much as a direct means of inducement, because I doubted that even the kidnapping and threatened death of these women would persuade Belle to jeopardise her social position and her daughter's marriage to Robert Collier, but as a means of attracting attention to the crime, and of revealing to Margaret, Lily and Ruth the contempt for their lives held by Belle and Elizabeth Little, the women their silence is protecting.

"As you will hear later in the tape, the kidnapped women no longer wish to remain silent. The statements they will make are quite voluntary and have been obtained without threat or coercion. The women are unharmed. They have been well looked after during their incarceration. They have seen the aborted wedding ceremony on TV and now, no longer feeling threatened or obliged to remain silent, wish to admit freely their part in the conspiracy to conceal a crime.

"For my part, I no longer hold a grudge against these women. The law may require their punishment, but I plead clemency, believing that they have been punished enough.

"Not so Belle and Elizabeth Little. They are ruthless women who are guilty of criminal conspiracy and various acts of criminal business manipulation—the facts of which are contained in the enclosed eighteen hours of tape-recorded telephone conversations. I draw particular attention to the conversation between Belle Little and a Wendell Selby concerning the acquisition of land owned by a Mr Frank Franks of Lake George—a clear case of conspiracy to murder, the knowledge of which, as you will hear, is shared by Elizabeth Little."

279

Rory Callaghan grimaced with astonishment and delight at his secretary. "*Jesus!*"

Francisco's voice continued: "The next voice you will hear will be that of Margaret Whitney."

Margaret came on, her voice reedy, nervous. "This is . . . Margaret Whitney. I confirm that I am speaking freely . . . without coercion . . . and that I have been treated well and am completely unharmed. I admit and very much regret my silence in the matter of Elizabeth Little's guilt. My only defence is that I did it to protect my husband's business interests. This man . . . I don't know who he is . . . has promised to release us in the near future . . . unharmed. If he does this . . . no charge of kidnapping will be pursued by me."

After a short pause, Lily Parker identified herself and said substantially the same thing. Then Ruth Howard spoke.

Finally, Francisco returned to make an announcement which, within the hour, was to enflame the city and the county, and bring about a condition of unprecedented, horrific civil disorder.

He said: "This is The Park Avenger. The three hostages will be released today, Friday, December 24th. At noon *precisely* they will be set free in the Park. People of Dade County . . . be there to greet them! And learn the TRUTH!"

25

The people of Dade County responded. Overwhelmingly.

As the televised newscasts began transmitting in detail the contents of the Park Avenger's taped message, the migration began. The Miami police, forewarned by their own copy of the cassette recording, moved swiftly into action, drafting men from a score of peripheral communities to control the building traffic congestion.

The MacArthur Causeway was closed to all but emergency vehicles, but this in no way deterred the converging battalions of spectators, who abandoned their cars in the streets of the city and Miami Beach and crossed the causeway on foot.

Television cameras arrived in force, setting up at points along the causeway and inside the Park, and taking to the air in helicopters.

At eleven o'clock, Frank Roselli, roving correspondent for Channel Six's *Eyewitness News*, hovering above the causeway at four hundred feet, excitedly declared, "I've never seen anything like it! Suddenly there's no concrete down there—only people! They are arriving in their thousands ... tens of thousands ... streaming across the MacArthur Causeway to converge on the entrance to Little Park.

"To my recollection, not since V-J Day, that momentous day on which Japan surrendered and brought the Second World War to an end, has the City of Miami witnessed a public gathering of such magnitude.

"Although it's impossible for me to identify specific attendance at this altitude, my colleague, Nick Sheldon, reporting from the Park entrance, tells us a high proportion of the huge crowd are people of Hispanic origin—Mexican and Cuban residents from the Miami barrio. Considering the nationality of

Ana Patillas—the tragic victim in what has become known as the Little Affair—Ana was, of course, Mexican, this ethnic attendance is not surprising.

"Official statistics indicate that more than half a million Spanish-speaking people now live in the Miami area ..." Roselli smiled, ". . . and by my reckoning every one of them is down there right now. There, you have a closer picture from our causeway camera.

"The Park Avenger story is, of course, a phenomenon. Just once in a while a story breaks and sweeps the nation, excites the attention and captures the hearts of people of all ages. The Avenger—or perhaps we ought to call it the Ana Patillas Story—has certainly done that.

"While intending neither to pre-judge the Little Affair nor condone the kidnappings, I believe it is true to say that the Park Avenger—whoever he is—is attracting massive public attention and simultaneously exciting great public sympathy. His seems a classic case of little David taking on the mighty Goliath, a case with which many people—and perhaps in particular Ana Patillas's own people, an underprivileged ethnic minority, can and do identify.

"And they are down there now in their tens ... possibly hundreds ... of thousands to cheer their champion.

"The intriguing questions which must be foremost in everyone's mind are—who *is* the mysterious Park Avenger? By what method does he intend releasing his hostages into the Park at noon? Does he intend accompanying them and revealing his identity? From which direction will they arrive? How will they get through this great mass of people into the Park?

"The time is now eleven-fifteen. We have but forty-five minutes to wait for the answers to those questions. In the meantime, I'm going to hand you over to my colleague, Nick Sheldon, down there at the Park entrance, who is putting those and other questions to members of this mighty crowd. Let's hear what kind of opinions he's getting. Over to you, Nick Sheldon."

Sheldon, a tall, handsome, dynamic member of the *Eyewit-*

ness team, spoke from a protected position just inside the Park security barrier and acknowledged the hand-over with a smile at camera.

"Thank you, Frank. Those questions are, as you rightly guessed, on everyone's lips. I've already spoken to a dozen or so members of this incredible crowd—which incidentally . . ." he grinned, ". . . from down here seems closer to ten million than five hundred thousand—and everyone I've interviewed does sympathise with the Park Avenger.

"Being largely—though by no means solely—residents of the Hispanic barrio, they regard him as a hero, a champion of their fight against social injustice and prejudice. They admire him for single-handedly taking on the rich and powerful residents of the Park, for the astuteness of his campaign, for the cleverness of his timing and for the dogged patience he has shown in the preparation of his battle against injustice.

"I have learned from these good people that six years ago the arrest of Ana Patillas, the threat of deportation for her and her children, and Ana's eventual suicide created a furore in the barrio at that time. For six long years the barrio has nursed the memory of that injustice and it is that memory that has prompted this incredible show of support today.

"The Park Avenger's campaign against the Little family, his dramatic disruption of Elizabeth's wedding and the way in which he has drawn national attention to this six-year-old injustice, is about to heal that long-festering ethnic wound. And these, his people, have come to cheer their hero home. You, sir . . ." Sheldon proffered the microphone to a swarthy middle-aged man in a well-cut business suit. "How do you suppose the Avenger intends returning his three hostages to the Park, considering the obstacle presented by this gigantic crowd?"

The man smiled. "Assuming he anticipated this kind of response, I'd guess he has something pretty dramatic in mind—a helicopter arrival, maybe. I really wouldn't know. He appears to have thought every other move out very carefully. No doubt he has this one under control, too."

"One guess for a helicopter arrival," said Sheldon. "Any other guesses . . . you madam?"

An obese brown-skinned woman answered in a pronounced Spanish accent. "In an ambulance, maybe, with its siren going?"

"Sounds good. Any other guesses? Come on—shout them out!"

He received a deluge of responses, some serious, others frivolous.

"By boat!"

"Submarine!"

"Parachutes!"

"Hang gliders!"

Sheldon laughed. "OK, OK, well, how about this question? Do you think he'll accompany the hostages and reveal his identity?"

"Why should he?" asked a tall, bearded youth. "Why should he risk being arrested by the dumb cops when he has done nothing to be arrested for?"

"He *has* kidnapped three women, sir," Sheldon challenged.

The youth shook his head. "Borrowed them," he said, drawing laughter. "Tell you somethin'—if the cops did arrest him, they'd have a riot on their hands."

The crowd in his immediate vicinity responded volubly, "YEHHHH!"

"You all feel that way about the Avenger?" shouted Sheldon.

"YEHHHHHHHHH!!"

"Anybody disagree?"

There was silence.

Standing a short distance behind the bearded youth, Francisco was moved to tears by the crowd's response. "We're going to win, Momma," he whispered silently.

As the time drew close to twelve noon, an expectant stillness settled upon the multitude. A sea of heads turned in this direction and that and peered out across the bay and up into the sky, searching for a boat, a plane, a sign.

"The spectacle before me is awesome," Nick Sheldon reported in a hushed, astounded tone. "This vast, vast crowd . . . standing perfectly still . . . waiting. There are now only five minutes left till noon. How *is* the Park Avenger going to realise his promise?"

26

In the main cabin of the sixty-foot cabin cruiser *Seraphim*, moored to the Whitneys' jetty, Carlo Patillas, in black rubber wet-suit, checked the time by his waterproof watch. It showed two minutes to noon.

Settling the diving mask on to his face, he crossed the cabin to where Margaret Whitney lay handcuffed and blindfolded.

All three hostages had awakened from their drugged sleep more than an hour before. Carlo had spoken to them then, allaying their fears, promising them release within the hour.

Now, as he unlocked Margaret's handcuffs, he said, "It's over. I will now tell you where you are. Early this morning you were brought to the Park by boat and transferred aboard the *Seraphim*. You are now on Mrs Whitney's cabin cruiser."

Margaret uttered a cry and attempted to sit up.

"No!" Carlo ordered. "Lie still for a moment longer and don't touch your blindfold." He moved across to Lily Parker and removed her handcuffs, then released Ruth Howard. "Mrs Parker and Mrs Howard—you will go straight to your homes. Your husbands are waiting there for you.

"One final thing ... the statements you made on tape were this morning made known to the press and to the police. You may, of course, retract them now and claim you made them under threat. But I'd advise you not to because it wouldn't be the truth. And I believe that the only way in which you're going to be able to live with yourselves is by telling the truth and staying with the truth. Do that and you'll hear no more from the Park Avenger. All right, count to sixty ... then you may remove your blindfolds."

There was a scuffle of movement, a door was opened, the boat rocked a little, then came the sound of a quiet splash.

The women dragged the blindfolds from their eyes and blinked in the bright sunlight streaming in through the open cabin door.

"He's gone!" whispered Margaret, tears of relief welling in her eyes. "And we *are* on the *Seraphim!*"

They tore from the cabin, jumped ashore and ran up across the lawns, stumbling in their haste, crying with relief.

They burst into the house, startling Lucia, who cried out and clutched her cheeks as though she was seeing ghosts. "Señora!"

Margaret, half-laughing, half-crying, caught her maid's arm. "It's all right, we're all right!"

Lily and Ruth ran through the house, out of the front door, down the steps and across the lawn, out into the Park.

A cry went up from the media. "They're here! He's done it! They're in the Park!"

The news went out, spreading back through the crowd, provoking a roar of wild cheering. The human mass surged forward, threatening to crush those in front against the security barrier. As the first cries of alarm rang out, a guard activated the switch and the barrier began to rise. A cheer went up. The crowd pressed forward, its front ranks breaking into the Park.

The dam wall burst, releasing a deluge of humanity into the estate, a seething tidal-wave of destruction that ploughed across perfect lawns, trampled down beds of lovingly-tended flowers, smashed shrubs and bushes and desecrated all form of beauty in a frenzy of vengeful destruction.

The Park—the Avenger's enemy—was now their enemy. He had shown them the way, had begun its destruction . . . they would complete it.

They swarmed on to the central oasis, toppled its statuary into the flamingo pool, unearthed its plants and flowering shrubs and scattered its flamingos to the safety of private gardens. In moments the oasis was destroyed.

Now they turned their venom on the homes, on their immaculate gardens, trampling, smashing, uprooting every living, beautiful thing in their path, scything their way across the Park until at last they faced the most opulent home of all.

A chant began and in an instant became a full-throated roar.

"BELLE LITTLE ... OUT! ... ELIZABETH LITTLE ... OUT!"

Elizabeth gaped down in terror from the window of her mother's room, disbelieving the ocean of people that choked the Park, aghast at the vehemence and direction of their fury.

Behind her, awakened by the uproar, Belle stirred from sedated sleep. "Elizabeth ... what's happening out there?"

Elizabeth could only stare.

Belle struggled from her bed, shrugging away the nurses who moved to intervene, tottered across the room to Elizabeth's side.

"My Park ..." she gasped, cried out, "MY PARK!" and threw the window wide, leaned out and shook her fist, screaming, "GET OUT OF MY PARK ...! GET OUT! ... GET OUT!"

Elizabeth grabbed at her, fought to pull her back inside. "MOTHER ...!"

A voice rose from the crowd. "THE MURDERERS! KILL THE MURDERERS!"

The chant roared up. "KILL! ... KILL! ... KILL! ... KILL!"

A heavy arrow-head of stone flew up, smashing into Elizabeth's face and driving her backwards into the room.

Another stone, a third, now a fusillade striking the head and the body of the raging Belle. With a demented scream she fell forward and hung out of the window, arms dangling.

Seized by blood-lust, the crowd scoured the ground for pebbles, stones, sticks and rocks and hurled them in frenzy at the ragged body, cheering as a heavy rock opened the skull and blood and brains began to pour out.

The nurses dragged Elizabeth from the window and turned her over. She was dead, her forehead penetrated by the pointed stone, one eye shattered in its socket.

The window exploded into the room, devastated by a barrage of missiles. The nurses screamed and ran out of the room and down the stairs, out through the kitchen to the rear gardens as the frenzied mob burst in through the front door and set about the destruction of the grandest house in the Park.

27

One debt remained unpaid.

At nine o'clock that night, Carl Krantz sat in the living room of his one-bedroom apartment on the ground floor of a small modern block in south Miami Beach, watching for the fourth time a replay of the noon riot in the Park.

He had returned to the apartment at six o'clock that morning after the excessively long wedding duty and gone straight to bed and slept until the ringing of his phone had wakened him at three in the afternoon.

The call had been from Four Square Security, informing him of the riot, of the deaths of Belle and Elizabeth Little, of the pillage and almost total destruction of their home, and of the extensive damage to every home in the Park.

"Don't report for duty tonight," his superior had concluded. "The Park is out of our hands now, the cops have taken over. Besides—there's damn-all left to guard."

After the call, he had gone into the living room, opened a can of beer and watched a replay of most of the event. Later, he had watched a re-run of the entire event—from the gathering of the crowd on the causeway through to the arrival of the National Guard, the disbursement of the crowd and the dramatically silent camera tour of the devastated Park.

Riveted by the destruction of something which, only moments before, had been so perfect and beautiful, Krantz excitedly switched channels, opened another beer and luxuriated in yet another replay and in the commentary and discussion that attended it.

At five o'clock, eager to see the desolation first-hand, he had put on his uniform and driven to the Park, only to be refused admission at the security booth that he himself had so recently commanded, now manned by an armed National Guardsman.

In deference to his uniform, though, the guardsman had allowed Krantz to linger at the barrier and wallow in the outrageous spectacle.

"Where are all the residents?" Krantz asked.

"All moved out. There isn't a single window left in any house."

"Jee-zus ... looks like a howitzer barrage hit the Little place."

The guard shook his head. "Man, you wouldn't believe it. There's nothing left inside, it's a shell. It'd break yuh goddamned heart."

"Yeh," grinned Krantz.

Returning to the apartment, he settled in front of the television set with a fresh beer, and was watching it all again when his door buzzer sounded.

He frowned, for visitors were rare, got up from his chair and went down the narrow hall to open the door.

A figure in black leather stood there, its face obscured by a black-visored motorcycle helmet, a silenced .38 revolver in its right hand. Its left hand held the lead of the huge black German Shepherd that stood immobile by its side.

"Back up," Francisco commanded.

Wild-eyed with shock and fear, Krantz shuffled backwards. "What is this ... a heist?"

"Keep going."

Francisco kicked the front door shut, followed Krantz into the living room, motioned him to sit in the armchair he had just vacated.

Krantz was sweating freely, his eyes, bright with fear, riveted on the dog. "What d'you want? I've only gotta few bucks ..."

"I don't want your money, Krantz."

The ice-blue eyes flared. "You know me? Who are you?"

"Can't you guess? It's been a long time, Krantz ... almost six years to the day ..."

Krantz's mouth dropped open. "Jesus Christ ..."

"I've thought a lot about you in those years, what I was going to do to you when I finally caught up with you. I've got something for you." Francisco's hand dipped into the fold of his jacket for the photograph nestling there. "I heard you like pictures of girls. Here, I've brought one for you." He tossed the photograph into Krantz's lap. "Take a look at it."

Krantz turned it over, shutting his eyes to blot out the portrait of a young, once-beautiful girl whose cheek was hideously disfigured by a stitched, jagged scar.

"Bring back old memories, Krantz? Of course, you remember Maria ... thirteen years old ... a really beautiful little kid. And you remember that night ... how you took those three youngsters across that dark lawn ... and terrified them with your dog ... and put your filthy hands on Maria ..."

Krantz swallowed down the cloy of fear. "Look ... f'fucksake ... it was six years ago! Things got outta hand! I'm sorry ... I didn't mean to ... the dog got away from me! F'Chrissake, don't shoot ..."

Francisco smiled, addressing himself to the dog. "He's begging, boy, the big tough Krantz is begging. OK, Krantz, say please."

Krantz's lips quivered.

Francisco's finger tightened on the trigger. "Say please, Krantz."

"Please." The murmur was scarcely audible.

"I didn't hear that. Did you hear that, boy? Louder, Krantz."

"Please."

"Louder!"

"Fuck you, please!"

"Say pretty please, Krantz."

"You ... bastard ..."

"Remember, Krantz, how you made that kid grovel and say pretty please? Say it, you heap of shit, SAY IT!"

"Pretty please."

"Louder!"

"Pretty please!"

"SHOUT IT OUT, KRANTZ!"

"PRETTY ... PLEASE!"

The noise, the excitement, triggered a deep, rumbling growl in the dog's throat. It surged forward against the lead, its wild amber eyes fixed satanically on the seated Krantz.

Krantz stared at it terrorised, knowing dogs, knowing its terrible strength and killing potential.

"You like my dog, Krantz?" Francisco murmured savagely. "Does he remind you of another dog? The dog you set on those three innocent kids? What was his name, Krantz?"

"K-khan."

The dog's ears twitched.

Francisco laughed softly. "What a coincidence—my dog's name is Khan, too. And d'you want to hear another coincidence? This one is a trained security dog, also ... a killer, Krantz, a deadly, silent killer. Krantz ... reach out and turn up the sound on your television set."

"What ... are you going to do?"

"DO IT!"

Krantz leaned forward, fingers fumbling for the control. "Don't ..."

"KILL!" Francisco yelled.

The dog flew, struck Krantz in the chest, its weight and power bowling the man backwards out of the chair, its glistening fangs snapping into the unyielding flesh of his face and tearing it from the bone.

"KHAN! HEEL!"

The dog stilled, hung above the cowering man, blood dripping from its jaws down into the gaping wound.

"HEEL, KHAN!"

The dog responded, loped to Francisco's side and there stood guard.

Slowly Francisco raised the revolver and took sight on Krantz's forehead.

Krantz whimpered.

Francisco advanced and stood above the giant. "No, I'm not going to kill you, Krantz—not now. You're going to wait ... and sweat ... a bit longer. How much longer? Maybe a week ... maybe another six years. *Adios*, pig." He brought the butt of the revolver down hard on Krantz's head.

292

28

Three young people, two men and a girl, entered the flower shop in the concourse of Miami International Airport.

The female assistant approached them. "May I help you?"

Francisco proffered a slip of paper. "We'd like a wreath of red roses delivered to this plot number in Miami Cemetery."

"Certainly, sir. Do you wish to write a card?"

"I've already written one." From his pocket he took a small white envelope, drew out the card and read it again. It said: "Sleep in Peace now, Momma. From your loving children."

He replaced the card, sealed the envelope and gave it to her.

When she had completed writing the order, he said, "We'd also like to send a wreath of white lilies to Carl Krantz at this hospital address." He gave her the note.

"You have a card for him also?"

"Yes."

Francisco produced it, read its message. "*Hasta mañana*, Krantz ... but which tomorrow? Happy New Year from Francisco, Carlo and Maria Patillas."

He gave the card to the girl.

"Will there be anything else, sir?"

"No, thank you. I believe that takes care of everything."

He followed his brother and sister out of the shop, and arm-in-arm they made their way along the concourse to their waiting plane.

FICTION

CRIME/ADVENTURE/SUSPENSE

☐ The Killing In The Market	John Ball with Bevan Smith	£1.00
☐ In the Heat of the Night	John Ball	£1.00
☐ Johnny Get Your Gun	John Ball	£1.00
☐ The Cool Cottontail	John Ball	£1.00
☐ The Megawind Cancellation	Bernard Boucher	£1.25
☐ Slow Burn	Peter Cave	£1.50
☐ Tunnel	Hal Friedman	£1.35
☐ Barracuda	Irving A. Greenfield	£1.25
☐ Tagget	Irving A. Greenfield	£1.25
☐ Don't be no Hero	Leonard Harris	£1.25
☐ The Blunderer	Patricia Highsmith	£1.25
☐ A Game for the Living	Patricia Highsmith	£1.25
☐ Those who Walk Away	Patricia Highsmith	£1.25
☐ The Tremor of Forgery	Patricia Highsmith	£1.25
☐ The Two Faces of January	Patricia Highsmith	£1.25
☐ Labyrinth	Eric Mackenzie-Lamb	£1.25
☐ The Hunted	Elmore Leonard	£1.25
☐ Confess, Fletch	Gregory Mcdonald	90p
☐ Fletch	Gregory Mcdonald	90p
☐ Fletch's Fortune	Gregory Mcdonald	£1.25
☐ Flynn	Gregory Mcdonald	95p
☐ All the Queen's Men	Guiy de Montfort	£1.25
☐ Pandora Man	Kerry Newcomb and Frank Schaefer	£1.25
☐ Sigmet Active	Thomas Page	£1.10
☐ Crash Landing	Mark Regan	£1.25
☐ The Last Prisoner	James Robson	£1.50
☐ The Croesus Conspiracy	Ben Stein	£1.25
☐ Deadline in Jakarta	Ian Stewart	£1.25
☐ An H-Bomb for Alice	Ian Stewart	£1.50
☐ The Peking Payoff	Ian Stewart	90p
☐ The Seizing of Singapore	Ian Stewart	£1.00
☐ Winter Stalk	James L. Stowe	£1.25
☐ Rough Deal	Walter Winward	£1.10

HISTORICAL ROMANCE/ROMANCE/SAGA

☐ Hawksmoor	Aileen Armitage	£1.75
☐ Blaze of Passion	Stephanie Blake	£1.25
☐ Daughter of Destiny	Stephanie Blake	£1.25
☐ Flowers of Fire	Stephanie Blake	£1.50
☐ So Wicked My Desire	Stephanie Blake	£1.50
☐ Wicked is My Flesh	Stephanie Blake	£1.50
☐ Lovers and Dancers	Michael Feeney Callan	£1.50
☐ The Lofty Banners	Brenda Clarke	£1.75
☐ The Enchanted Land	Jude Deveraux	£1.50
☐ My Love, My Land	Judy Gardiner	£1.25
☐ Walburga's Eve	Elizabeth Hann	£1.35
☐ Lily of the Sun	Sandra Heath	95p
☐ Strangers' Forest	Pamela Hill	£1.00
☐ Royal Mistress	Patricia Campbell Horton	£1.50
☐ The Rebel Heart	Anna James	£1.25
☐ Gentlemen Callers	Nancy Lamb	£1.50
☐ Fires of Winter	Johanna Lindsey	£1.50
☐ A Pirate's Love	Johanna Lindsey	£1.25
☐ Trade Imperial	Alan Lloyd	£1.35
☐ Dance Barefoot	Margaret Maddocks	95p
☐ The Open Door	Margaret Maddocks	£1.25
☐ All We Know of Heaven	Dore Mullen	£1.25
☐ The Far Side of Destiny	Dore Mullen	£1.50
☐ New Year's Eve	Jeannie Sakol	£1.50
☐ The Pride	Judith Saxton	£1.50
☐ Heir to Trevayan	Juliet Sefton	£1.25
☐ Never Trust a Handsome Man	Marlene Fanta Shyer	£1.25
☐ Shadow of an Unknown Woman	Daoma Winston	£1.00
☐ Call the Darkness Light	Nancy Zaroulis	£1.95

FICTION
HORROR/OCCULT/NASTY

☐ Death Walkers	Gary Brandner	£1.00
☐ The Howling	Gary Brandner	£1.00
☐ Return of the Howling	Gary Brandner	95p
☐ The Sanctuary	Glenn Chandler	£1.00
☐ The Tribe	Glenn Chandler	£1.10
☐ Crown of Horn	Louise Cooper	£1.25
☐ Curse	Daniel Farson	95p
☐ Transplant	Daniel Farson	£1.00
☐ Trance	Joy Fielding	90p
☐ The Quick and the Dead	Judy Gardiner	£1.00
☐ The Janissary	Alan Lloyd Gelb	£1.25
☐ Rattlers	Joseph L. Gilmore	95p
☐ Slither	John Halkin	95p
☐ The Wicker Man	Robin Hardy & Anthony Shaffer	£1.25
☐ Devil's Coach-Horse	Richard Lewis	85p
☐ Parasite	Richard Lewis	£1.00
☐ Spiders	Richard Lewis	£1.00
☐ Gate of Fear	Lewis Mallory	£1.00
☐ The Nursery	Lewis Mallory	£1.10
☐ The Summoning	John Pintoro	95p
☐ Bloodthirst	Mark Ronson	£1.00
☐ Ghoul	Mark Ronson	95p
☐ Ogre	Mark Ronson	95p
☐ Return of the Living Dead	John Russo	£1.10
☐ Childmare	Nick Sharman	£1.00
☐ The Scourge	Nick Sharman	£1.00
☐ Deathbell	Guy N. Smith	£1.00
☐ Doomflight	Guy N. Smith	£1.10
☐ Locusts	Guy N. Smith	95p
☐ Manitou Doll	Guy N. Smith	£1.10
☐ Satan's Snowdrop	Guy N. Smith	£1.00
☐ The Specialist	Jasper Smith	£1.00
☐ The Scar	Gerald Suster	£1.25
☐ The Worm Stone	Derek Tyson	£1.10

HAMLYN WHODUNNITS

☐ Some Die Eloquent	Catherine Aird	£1.25
☐ The Case of the Abominable Snowman	Nicholas Blake	£1.10
☐ The Worm of Death	Nicholas Blake	95p
☐ Thou Shell of Death	Nicholas Blake	£1.25
☐ Tour de Force	Christianna Brand	£1.10
☐ A Lonely Place to Die	Wessel Ebersohn	£1.10
☐ Gold from Gemini	Jonathan Gash	£1.10
☐ The Judas Pair	Jonathan Gash	95p
☐ Blood and Judgment	Michael Gilbert	£1.10
☐ Close Quarters	Michael Gilbert	£1.10
☐ Hare Sitting Up	Michael Innes	£1.10
☐ The Weight of the Evidence	Michael Innes	£1.10
☐ There Came Both Mist and Snow	Michael Innes	95p
☐ The Howard Hughes Affair	Stuart Kaminsky	£1.10
☐ Inspector Ghote Draws a Line	H. R. F. Keating	£1.10
☐ Inspector Ghote Plays a Joker	H. R. F. Keating	£1.25
☐ The Perfect Murder	H. R. F. Keating	£1.10
☐ The French Powder Mystery	Ellery Queen	£1.25
☐ The Siamese Twin Mystery	Ellery Queen	95p
☐ The Spanish Cape Mystery	Ellery Queen	£1.10

NON-FICTION

GENERAL
☐ **Truly Murderous** — John Dunning — 95p
☐ **Shocktrauma** — Jon Franklin & Alan Doelp — £1.25
☐ **The War Machine** — James Avery Joyce — £1.50
☐ **The Fugu Plan** — Tokayer & Swartz — £1.75

BIOGRAPHY/AUTOBIOGRAPHY
☐ **Go-Boy** — Roger Caron — £1.25
☐ **The Queen Mother Herself** — Helen Cathcart — £1.25
☐ **Clues to the Unknown** — Robert Cracknell — £1.50
☐ **George Stephenson** — Hunter Davies — £1.50
☐ **The Borgias** — Harry Edgington — £1.50
☐ **The Admiral's Daughter** — Victoria Fyodorova — £1.50
☐ **Rachman** — Shirley Green — £1.50
☐ **50 Years with Mountbatten** — Charles Smith — £1.25
☐ **Kiss** — John Swenson — 95p

HEALTH/SELF-HELP
☐ **The Hamlyn Family First Aid Book** — Dr Robert Andrew — £1.50
☐ **Girl!** — Brandenburger & Curry — £1.25
☐ **The Good Health Guide for Women** — Cooke & Dworkin — £2.95
☐ **The Babysitter Book** — Curry & Cunningham — £1.25
☐ **Pulling Your Own Strings** — Dr Wayne W. Dyer — 95p
☐ **The Pick of Woman's Own Diets** — Jo Foley — 95p
☐ **Woman X Two** — Mary Kenny — £1.10
☐ **Cystitis: A Complete Self-help Guide** — Angela Kilmartin — £1.00
☐ **Fit for Life** — Donald Norfolk — £1.35
☐ **The Stress Factor** — Donald Norfolk — £1.25
☐ **Fat is a Feminist Issue** — Susie Orbach — 95p
☐ **Living With Your New Baby** — Rakowitz & Rubin — £1.50
☐ **Related to Sex** — Claire Rayner — £1.25
☐ **The Working Woman's Body Book** — Rowen with Winkler — 95p
☐ **Natural Sex** — Mary Shivanandan — £1.25
☐ **Woman's Own Birth Control** — Dr Michael Smith — £1.25
☐ **Overcoming Depression** — Dr Andrew Stanway — £1.50

POCKET HEALTH GUIDES
☐ **Migraine** — Dr Finlay Campbell — 65p
☐ **Pre-menstrual Tension** — June Clark — 65p
☐ **Back Pain** — Dr Paul Dudley — 65p
☐ **Allergies** — Robert Eagle — 65p
☐ **Arthritis & Rheumatism** — Dr Luke Fernandes — 65p
☐ **Skin Troubles** — Deanna Wilson — 65p